MacCallister
STRANGLEHOLD

MacCallister
STRANGLEHOLD

William W. Johnstone
with J. A. Johnstone

PINNACLE BOOKS
Kensington Publishing Corp.
www.kensingtonbooks.com

PINNACLE BOOKS are published by

Kensington Publishing Corp.
119 West 40th Street
New York, NY 10018

PUBLISHER'S NOTE
Following the death of William W. Johnstone, the Johnstone family is working with a carefully selected writer to organize and complete Mr. Johnstone's outlines and many unfinished manuscripts to create additional novels in all of his series like The Last Gunfighter, Mountain Man, and Eagles, among others. This novel was inspired by Mr. Johnstone's superb storytelling.

All Kensington titles, imprints, and distributed lines are available at special quantity discounts for bulk purchases for sales promotions, premiums, fund-raising, educational, or institutional use. Special book excerpts or customized printings can also be created to fit specific needs. For details, write or phone the office of the Kensington sales manager: Kensington Publishing Corp., 119 West 40th Street, New York, NY 10018, attn: Sales Department; phone 1-800-221-2647.

PINNACLE BOOKS, the Pinnacle logo, and the WWJ steer head logo are Reg. U.S. Pat. & TM Off.

ISBN-13: 978-0-7860-4358-3
ISBN-10: 0-7860-4358-X

First printing: March 2019

10 9 8 7 6 5 4 3 2 1

Printed in the United States of America

Electronic edition: March 2019

ISBN-13: 978-0-7860-4359-0
ISBN-10: 0-7860-4359-8

Chapter One

Ebenezer R. Schofield and Ulysses S. Grant had been classmates at West Point, and Schofield had risen to the rank of major general during the Civil War. After the war, though not a member of the president's cabinet, nor even a government official, he had been given an influential position of personal trust by his old classmate, President Grant.

Schofield used that position to enrich himself, first as a participant in the Whiskey Ring, then in receiving bribes from railroad construction companies who were looking for government approval of their projects, particularly those that cut through Indian lands.

Schofield was caught up with the other corrupt officials in Grant's administration, and sentenced to prison. After serving five years in prison (his sentence ameliorated by his connection to the president), Schofield was discharged, along with a decree barring him from ever again working for the government.

Part of his sentence was the government decree that Schofield forfeit all ill-gotten gains. They recovered over ten thousand dollars in cash, and were satisfied that he had made full restitution.

What the government did not know was that they had recovered less than twenty percent of Schofield's money. Before going to prison Schofield had hidden a little over forty thousand dollars and he was ready to make up for lost time.

Schofield intended to institute the plan he had come up with while he was still in prison. Studying some of the maps that he found in the prison library, he saw something about New Mexico Territory that was particularly intriguing. Part of it was shaped like a bootheel that protruded from the extreme southwest corner of the territory in such a way that it was bordered on three sides by Mexico. It was, he saw, the most isolated and detached part of the United States.

One of the men Schofield had met while in the federal prison was Julian Peterson, also a graduate of West Point. After the war he'd absconded with an army payroll, but was caught and imprisoned. By coincidence, his prison sentence ended less than one month after Schofield was released. They had agreed to meet in Lordsburg, New Mexico Territory, after Schofield had provided Peterson with enough money to buy a train ticket.

Well aware that Peterson might just keep the money, Schofield was pretty sure he would show up. He had tempted his fellow prisoner with promises of wealth and power and knew Peterson didn't have any other viable options.

Schofield's trust was justified when he'd received a telegram from Peterson telling him the date and train on which he would arrive.

* * *

Schofield was standing on the depot platform in Lordsburg as the train rolled into the station. He saw Peterson, the third person to step down from the train, peruse the depot platform looking for him.

"General Peterson, I'm over here," Schofield called.

Peterson walked toward him with a broad smile. "Hello, Schofield. What's with the *general*? I never got higher than captain."

"It's Prime Director Schofield," he corrected. "And I have just appointed you to the rank of general, assuming you accept the offer to join Schofield's Legion."

Peterson got a confused look on his face. "Schofield's Legion? What is that?"

"I'll tell you over dinner," Schofield said.

Later, Schofield showed Peterson a map of the Territory of New Mexico. He pointed specifically to the Bootheel section. "This is the part that will concern us. I intend to sever it from the Territory of New Mexico, indeed from the United States, and establish a new nation."

Peterson laughed. "Uh, you may recall that has already been tried, and the Confederacy didn't work out so well."

"That's because eleven states seceded, and had they been successful, the nation would have been split in half. Believe me when I say that what I have planned is of no threat to the United States. The most we'll have to deal with will be local law, and with our army, they can be easily overwhelmed."

"You have an army already?" Peterson asked.

Schofield smiled. "At the moment, I have only a

general and enough money to outfit an army, complete with weapons and uniforms. Your first job, General Peterson, will be to help me raise the soldiers. That is, if you are interested in the idea."

"This starting your own country business, is there money in it?" Peterson asked.

"Indeed. As an independent country, we can assess taxes. Every working copper, gold, and silver mine will be taxed. Every rancher and merchant will be taxed. Oh yes, my friend, there is a great deal of money in the future of *Tierra de Desierto.*"

"*Terra* what?"

Schofield repeated the name. "It means Desert Land," he explained. "And it is the name of our new nation. As Prime Director, I will be the unelected, but absolute, ruler, and as my general, you will be second in charge. Are you interested?"

"Damn right I'm interested," Peterson replied.

"Very good, General," Schofield said in response. "Our first job is to raise an army. I will provide weapons, uniforms, and a bonus for fifty men."

"May I make a suggestion as to the organization?" Peterson asked.

"Of course. After all, you will be the general in charge."

"I would suggest a captain, two lieutenants, and four sergeants. The remaining forty-two men will be privates."

"Excellent suggestion, General. I'll leave the business of recruitment to you."

Cheyenne, Wyoming Territory

Duff MacCallister stood to one side and watched as his prime Angus cattle were being loaded into the freight cars after a cattle drive of eight hundred beeves from his ranch to the Cheyenne rail head. Unlike the long drives of a few years earlier, it had been an easy, two-day journey of only forty miles. From there the cattle would go by train to market in Kansas City, where he had contracted them for forty-five dollars per head.

When the last cow was loaded, Arnold Dupree, who was the buying agent, walked over to see him. "Here's the bank draft. Thirty-six thousand dollars is a lot of money."

"Aye, but there was a lot of work in getting the creatures to market, and a lot of expenses, too. Still, 'tis a good payday," Duff agreed.

"I'm told that you're the man to thank for getting so many to switch to Angus," Dupree said.

"Aye, some have listened to my suggestion. 'Twas in Scotland where I first began to raise the creatures, and when I came to America, I decided this would be a good place for them."

"It's been good for us. We get a better price for Angus beef than we do for any other breed, even Herefords."

The locomotive whistle blew.

"I must go," Dupree said. "I'll be accompanying the cattle to market. It's been good doing business with you." He extended his hand and Duff took it.

It had taken six men to drive the cows down from Duff's ranch, Sky Meadow, but the six men, including Elmer Gleason and Wang Chow, had returned to the ranch as soon at the herd had been delivered. Only Duff remained in Cheyenne to receive payment, and because it was too late to start back, he waited until the next morning.

* * *

The next morning three men were waiting at Bristol Ridge, watching the road north from Cheyenne.

"Thirty-six thousand dollars?" Foley said. "You sure that's how much money he's carryin'?"

"Yeah, I was workin' at the loading chutes when I heard MacCallister 'n another man talkin'," Otis said. "He was a cattle buyer 'n he had just bought all the cows MacCallister had brung in, 'n he paid 'im thirty-six thousand dollars for 'em."

"Which one of you is the best at cipherin'? How much money will that be for each one of us?" Clemmons asked.

"Ten thousand for each of you, 'n sixteen thousand for me," Otis said.

"Wait a minute. How come it is that you'll be gettin' most of the money?" Foley asked.

"On account of I'm the one that found out that MacCallister had all that money 'n he would be comin' by here on his way back home, 'n that he would be all alone," Otis explained. "'N I'm the one that let you two in on it."

"He's right, Foley," Clemmons said. "Hell, we wouldn'ta knowed nothin' 'bout the money if Otis didn't tell us nothin' about it. Besides, ten thousand dollars sounds good to me. I prob'ly ain't had me ten thousand dollars all tolled up in my whole life."

"Yeah," Foley agreed. "I'm fine with ten thousand dollars."

"It's good that you are because—"

"Here comes someone, 'n he's all by hisself. You reckon this is him?" Clemmons asked.

Otis looked around the edge of the butte. "Yeah! That's him! Get ready boys, we uns is about to be rich!"

Duff was sitting easy in the saddle, letting his horse, Sky, proceed at his own speed. He was seriously considering running a few hundred head of sheep, though he knew he'd have to sell that idea to Elmer Gleason and Meagan Parker, both of whom were partners in the ranch. Elmer would be the most difficult to sell the idea to. He had an inherent prejudice against sheep, believing that sheep and cattle could not be raised together. Duff knew better. He'd seen such operations in Scotland. And unlike cattle, sheep could bring in money without being sacrificed.

He wasn't concerned about Meagan. Her partnership wasn't a hands-on arrangement and she would acquiesce to anything he wanted to do. The real question was, is this something he really wanted to do? Or is it just an idea that he found intriguing and—

"Hold it right there, mister!" someone shouted as three men jumped out from behind a butte and pointed pistols at him.

Sky was well enough trained that the sudden appearance of the men didn't arouse a startled reaction.

"Well now. Ye would be Mr. Otis," Duff said, nodding toward the man in the middle.

"What the hell, Otis? He knows you?" one of the men asked.

Duff chuckled. "Well, I wouldn't say we were old friends, but I do remember seeing him at the loading docks."

"Yeah, I'm Otis."

"And, let me guess. 'Tis thinking I am that ye would be for wanting the thirty-six thousand dollars I was paid for the cattle. Am I right?"

"You're just real smart, ain't you?" Otis said.

"Oh, smart enough to keep ye from getting the money."

"How you goin' to do that?" Otis asked, lifting his pistol to make a point. "'Cause the truth is, you're either goin' to give us that money, real peaceable like, or we'll shoot you 'n take it offen your dead body."

"Oh, well, I wouldn't be wanting ye to take the money from my dead body, so I suppose I should give it to ye now. Then we can both be on our way."

Otis nodded. "Yeah, that's what you should do all right. Where is it? In them saddlebags?"

Duff shook his head. "Nae, I've got the money right here in m' shirt pocket." He raised his hand to his shirt pocket.

"Your shirt pocket? What kinda fool do you take us for, mister? There ain't no way you can put thirty-six thousand dollars in that shirt pocket."

"Sure you can." Duff pulled out a small slip of paper. "Here it is, right here."

"What? What are you talkin' about? What is that thing?"

"'Tis a bank draft. 'N the only way to get money from it, is to take it to the bank," Duff explained.

"So, what you're a-sayin' is iffen we take this here piece o' paper to the bank, they'll give us the money?" Foley asked.

"Ah, nae, I'm afraid not," Duff said, shaking his head. "Ye see, they'll only give the money to the people whose names are on the draft. That would be me, 'n two others."

"Let me see that!" Otis demanded.

"Sure, if ye care to take a look," Duff said, holding the draft out for Otis to take.

As soon as Otis took the draft, he, Foley, and Clemmons began to study it, diverting their attention away from Duff. Foley and Clemmons were holding their pistols down by their sides. Duff took advantage of their distraction, pulled his pistol, and fired twice. Immediately, both men let out shouts of pain and dropped their guns.

Otis looked up in surprise and saw that the odds had changed. He was the only one of the three would-be robbers who still had a gun in his hand, and he wasn't pointing it at Duff.

On the other hand, Duff was pointing his gun at Otis.

"I'll be for taking my bank draft back now, if ye don't mind." Duff smiled. "After all, it wouldn't do ye any good, for nae bank would cash it for you."

Otis held up the bank draft and Duff retrieved it. "And I'll be taking the pistols as well."

"Mister, this pistol cost me twenty-five dollars," Otis complained.

"Aye, 'n it nearly cost ye your life," Duff said. "Hand it over. You," he said to Foley. "If ye would be so kind, dismount and pick up the other two pistols and hand them to me as well."

Reluctantly, the man did as requested.

Duff stuck their three pistols down into one of his saddlebags. "And your long gun as well," he said to Otis, who was the only one of the three who had a rifle in his saddle sheath.

Reluctantly, Otis handed over the long gun.

"Thank ye kindly," Duff said with a friendly smile. "I'll be taking my leave of ye now." With a nod of his head, he rode away, leaving three dispirited and weaponless men behind him.

Chapter Two

"What do we do now?" Foley asked after Duff rode off.

"We follow him, 'n when we get the chance, we'll take the money from him," Otis said.

"That's what we was goin' to do this time, only there ain't no money," Clemmons said. "All he's got is that bank draft, 'n even if he had given it to us, it wouldn't be no good."

"Yeah, well, that paper is worth thirty-six thousand dollars. And soon as he shows it to the bank, why they'll count out the money 'n give to 'im," Otis said. "'N this time when we stand 'im up, we'll know that he actual has the money," Otis insisted.

"Yeah, well, there's another problem that maybe you ain't thought nothin' about," Foley said.

"What's that?"

"Maybe you ain't noticed or maybe you done forgot, but we ain't got no guns."

"I got one," Otis said. Reaching down into his saddlebag, he pulled out a Colt .44.

"That's good," Clemmons said. "But that's only one

gun 'n they's three of us. What are we sposed to do whilst you're holdin' a gun on 'im?"

"If we've got one gun, we can get two more," Otis said. "I been this way before, 'n I know where they's a store that's real close by. There ain't nothin' else around the store, 'n it sells guns."

"We ain't got the money to pay for no more guns," Foley pointed out.

"Who said we were goin' to pay for 'em?"

Welcome to
CHUGWATER, WYOMING TERRITORY
POPULATION 285
The jewel of Chugwater Valley

Duff rode by the sign, happy to be back home, or at least what had been his home since having left Scotland some years earlier. At first he had thought it might be difficult to adjust to America, but he had made many friends in Chugwater and he no longer felt like a displaced Scotsman. He considered himself a true resident of Chugwater Valley, secure on his ranch and comfortable with the little settlement that had become his new hometown.

There were two saloons in Chugwater. One was the Wild Hog, and while the owner of the Wild Hog was a law-abiding citizen, he had no pretensions about his place of business. It existed for the sole purpose of providing inexpensive drinks to a clientele who didn't care if the wide plank floor was unpainted or stained with spilled liquor and expectorated tobacco juice. The biggest thing that set the Wild Hog apart from

Fiddler's Green, the other saloon in town, was its women. Whereas the girls who worked the bar at Fiddler's Green provided pleasant conversation and flirtatious company only, the women who worked at the Wild Hog were soiled doves who, for a price, would extend their hospitality to the brothel that was maintained on the second floor of the saloon.

Just as Duff rode by the Wild Hog, he heard a woman scream, but the laughter that followed immediately afterward gave evidence that the scream had been in fun. An out-of-tune piano ground out loud and discordant chords that may have been part of a song, though it certainly wasn't anything Duff had ever heard before.

The laughter and music fell behind him as he continued to ride down Bowie Avenue. Although he occasionally had a drink in the Wild Hog, it was just to maintain a cordial relationship with the owner. Duff's personal choice of saloon was Fiddler's Green. Everyone agreed that it was an establishment equal to anything you could find between St. Louis and San Francisco. It was owned by Biff Johnson, a retired army sergeant who, while he was with the Seventh Cavalry, had served with Custer, Reno, and Benteen.

Fiddler's Green was practically a museum to the Seventh Cavalry. The walls were decorated with regimental flags and troop pennants, with arrows, lances, pistols, and carbines picked up from more than a dozen engagements. Biff even had one of Custer's hats. It had been personally given to him by Libbie Custer when he escorted her back to Monroe, Michigan, after George A. Custer was killed.

Even the name *Fiddler's Green* was indicative of Biff's

service in the cavalry. Cavalry legend had it that anyone who ever served as a cavalryman will, after they die, stop by a shady glen where there is good grass and a nearby stream of cool water for the horses. There, cavalrymen from all wars and generations will drink beer, chew tobacco, smoke their pipes, and visit. They will regale one another with tales of derring-do until that last syllable of recorded time, at which moment they will bid each other a last good-bye before departing for their final and eternal destination.

When Duff stepped into the Fiddler's Green Saloon he was greeted warmly by at least a dozen customers, as well as receiving a personal greeting from the proprietor.

"Duff, my boy, Elmer and Wang were here earlier and they told me that you got your cows delivered with no problem," Biff said.

"Nae problem at all." Duff didn't mention the incident that happened on the return trip. "And I'll be for havin' a wee drop of scotch if ye would be so kind."

Biff, one of Duff's first friends in Chugwater after leaving his native Scotland, took a bottle of Dewar's Scotch from under the bar, one he kept personally for Duff. In addition, Biff was married to a Scotswoman, which helped cement the bond between them.

Duff lifted his glass and gave his toast. "Here's to the heath, the hill and the heather, the bonnet, the plaid, the kilt and the feather!"

"And while goin' up the hill of fortune, may we never meet a friend comin' down," Biff replied.

"Aye, m' lad. Well spoken." Duff took a sip of the drink and held it on his tongue for a moment to enjoy the flavor before swallowing. "I'll be going now," he said as he set the empty glass on the bar. "I've some business to conduct."

The business Duff spoke of was the deposit of the thirty-six-thousand-dollar draft into the local bank. And since the draft was made out to Duff, Meagan Parker, and Elmer Gleason, he had to round the two of them up.

That wasn't a difficult task, as Elmer was the foreman of Sky Meadow and was there when Duff rode up.

"See there, Wang, I told you Duff would come back," Elmer said. "'N here, heathen that you are, you were so sure that he would run away with all the money."

"I said no such thing," Wang Chow said with no sense of umbrage in his denial of the specious charge. He knew that Elmer was teasing.

Upon arriving in Chugwater, Otis, Foley, and Clemmons had gone straight to the Wild Hog.

At the moment, Otis was holding a mug of beer in his hand as he stood at the front of the saloon, looking out over the swinging batwing doors. He saw Duff MacCallister and an older man come riding into town. "Foley, Clemmons," he called to his partners.

When neither of the two answered him, he looked around to see that they were sharing a table and drinks with two of the Wild Hog women. Not only had they acquired two more pistols and some ammunition from the store called Grant City, they had also taken all the money—$112—from the cashbox, part of which paid for the drinks. When they left the store Emile Grant was lying dead on the floor behind them.

"Foley, Clemmons," Otis called again, much more forcefully this time. "Get over here!"

Duff and Elmer stopped by Meagan's Dress Emporium.

"Lass, can ye leave the store for a bit?" Duff asked. "We'll be for needing your signature." He showed the draft to Meagan.

"For this, I'll be happy to close the store," she said.

A moment later with a sign that read CLOSED on the door, she accompanied Duff and Elmer to the Bank of Chugwater to make the deposit. The proceeds of the bank draft were divided three ways in accordance with the percentage each of them were to receive. Elmer was junior partner in the ranch itself, while Meagan owned some of the cattle that had been sold. The entire operation was a cashless transaction, as the bank credited the three accounts with the proper amount.

"Elmer, go on back to the ranch without me," Duff said. "I'll come along a little later."

"All right." Elmer smiled at Duff and Meagan. "Now don't y'all go gettin' into no trouble now."

"We'll try not to," Duff said, returning the smile.

"Oh, come now, Duff, that wouldn't be any fun," Meagan said with a little laugh.

Pistols in hand, Otis, Foley, and Clemmons were waiting across from the bank on Swan Avenue.

"Whenever we stopped him the first time that piece of paper he had warn't no good for us," Otis said. "But now that he's gone to the bank, why, he more 'n likely has all that money on 'im."

"We goin' to just shoot 'im, right here in town?" Foley asked.

"No, but we're goin' to keep a eye on 'im,'n soon's we see him by hisself, we'll shoot 'im 'n take his money."

"Here he comes out o' the bank," Clemmons said excitedly. "That old man and the woman are still with him."

"Does that mean we'll be killin' all three of'em?" Foley asked.

"If we have to," Otis said.

"Looks like him 'n the woman's goin' into the saloon," Foley said.

"Good. I could use another drink," Clemmons said. "Come on. Let's go."

"Don't be an idiot, Clemmons," Otis scolded. "Soon's we stepped in through the door, he'd recognize us. How far do you think we could get with him seein' us?"

Biff Johnson prided himself on keeping an establishment well enough regarded that women could visit the place without fear of a stain on their reputation, so it was not unusual to see Meagan coming in with Duff.

"Well, did you get your business taken care of?" Biff asked.

"Aye."

"When are we going to Scotland?" Meagan asked after one of the young women delivered the drinks to their table.

"Scotland is it? 'N would ye be for telling me why ye want me to go to Scotland? Is it tired of my company, you are?"

"No," Meagan replied with a smile. "But you did say that you would like to take me on a trip once we got the cattle sold. Well, they are sold, the money is in the bank, and I'm ready for that trip you promised me."

"Aye, lass, sure 'n 'twas a promise I gave for taking ye on a trip, but 'twas no mention made o' goin' to Scotland."

"Wouldn't you like to go back for a visit?"

Duff paused for a moment, then he nodded and gave her his answer. "Aye, 'twould be good to hear people talkin' with the brogue o' m' own tongue."

"Och, Duff, 'n would ye be for telling me now, is it not the Scottish tongue ye are hearing from this wee lass?" Meagan replied, teasing him with an almost perfect mimicry of his brogue.

"Would ye really like to visit Scotland?"

"Yes, I would love to see the land of your birth."

"But I could nae leave Sky Meadow for that long."

"Duff, don't you think Elmer and Wang could run Sky Meadow while we're gone?"

"Aye, perhaps they can," he replied with a broad smile. "Returning to Scotland, is it? 'Tis something I will consider."

"There they are," Otis said, pointing out the fact that Duff and Meagan were leaving Fiddler's Green. The outlaws watched as Duff walked Meagan back to her dress shop, told her good-bye, then started toward his horse which had been tied up in front of the shop.

"When are we going to do it?" Foley asked.

"We'll follow him out of town. Only this time, we ain't goin' to stop 'im 'n talk to 'im, 'cause we've already seen how slick the son of a bitch can be. This time soon as he's out of town good, we'll just shoot 'im down, 'n take the money offen his body."

* * *

As Duff began to untie his horse, Sky, he saw three men across the street standing in the gap between Vi's Pies and Guthrie's Building Supply. After a closer look, he recognized them as the men who had accosted him during his ride back from Cheyenne. He stopped untying his horse, wrapped the reins back around the hitching rail, and started across the street to investigate.

"Damn, Otis, the son of a bitch has seen us! He's comin' right toward us!" Foley shouted in alarm.

"Pull your guns, boys," Otis ordered. "We ain't got no choice now but to shoot 'im!"

Duff heard Otis give the order. He pulled his own gun and shouted, "Hold it right there!"

"The hell you say!" Otis yelled back at him as all three men raised their pistols.

For the next ten seconds the citizens of Chugwater were surprised and alarmed to hear the sound of battle being conducted right in the middle of town. Several shots were fired, many on top of each other. Then it fell silent, the only remaining mark of the gunfight being the acrid-smelling gun smoke that rolled down Swan Avenue.

Once it was quiet, customers and proprietors of the businesses emerged for a cautious and curious look at what had just happened. They saw Duff, a smoking pistol in his hand, examining the bodies of the three men who lay on the boardwalk, halfway out into the street.

Chapter Three

After raising his army and giving each of the men an advance against their salary based upon their assigned rank, Schofield was ready to conduct his first military operation. He chose the town of Hachita, which was the northernmost town in the Bootheel. And though it would have been a natural target because of its location, there was also a bonus in attacking the town, because it had a producing silver mine that would more than triple his available resources.

Schofield was mounted at the head of his troops, waiting just on the outside of Hachita. Earlier he had sent a couple of his men—Captain Greg Bond and First Sergeant Dan Cobb—in to reconnoiter the town. They hadn't been in uniform, so as to not arouse any undue suspicion. Their ranks had been assigned to them by Schofield.

"What have you found?" he asked, as the men returned.

Bond had a big smile on his face. "Right now there are seventy-six men working the mine. I don't know how many men are still in town, but there aren't that many and most of them are store clerks and such. None of them are currently armed, and I doubt that half of them even have a gun."

"The sheriff?"

"He's an old man who probably hasn't even drawn his pistol in the last year."

"All right, get in uniform. General Peterson?"

"Yes, Prime Director?"

"Form the regiment into operational battalions."

"Yes, sir."

Half an hour later the mine supervisor and the operators of the stamping mill looked up in surprise as more than fifty mounted and uniformed men came galloping up to the mine.

The supervisor stepped out of the headquarters shack to greet them. "Who are you men? What kind of uniform is that you folks are wearing?"

Schofield nodded and several of his men began shooting. The supervisor, and every other mine worker who was on the surface at the moment, went down under a hail of gunfire.

Schofield's next move was to have his men take several sticks of dynamite from the supply shack and put them in key positions around the mouth of the mine. The resultant explosion collapsed the mine, trapping every miner inside.

The people of the town heard the explosion, and though it was not unusual to hear dynamite blasts, the explosion was much louder than any time previous. Many feared the worst, and they were out in the street when Schofield and his army swept in.

There was absolutely no resistance to Schofield's demand that the town surrender to him.

Shortly after the town came under his control, he

visited the local newspaper, where he ordered one thousand copies of a document to be printed.

DECLARATION OF AUTONOMY

I, Ebenezer R. Schofield, by assumption of authority over all towns, villages, settlements, individual ranches, farms, estates, and homes, do by these presence make the following declaration:

That the portion of land in the current Territory of New Mexico known as the Bootheel, which is bordered on the north by the 32nd Parallel, and on the east, south, and west by the country of Mexico, is herein separated from the United States to be established as the new, and independent nation that is now and forever known as Tierra de Desierto.

The type government by which this new nation is to be administered will be an autarchy, with all authority resting in the Prime Director, that position being occupied by the author of this document.

The decrees of this document, as well as lex non scripta with regard to the dominion of the Prime Director, are to take immediate effect.

Schofield had several of the documents posted around town. Then he wrote a letter to the Secretary of State of the United States and included a copy of the Declaration of Autonomy.

To the Honorable James G. Blaine
Secretary of State, United States of America
I have the honor, Sir, of informing you that with immediate effect, the nation of Tierra De Desierto has been formed by the declaration herein enclosed. It is

*my desire that the severing of all laws, regulations,
and military responsibilities of the United States be
accomplished peacefully, and that a fruitful alliance
may be quickly established between our two nations.*

> Ebenezer R. Schofield
> Prime Director,
> Nation of Tierra De Desierto

At first he addressed the envelope specifically to
Secretary Blaine, then he thought better of it, and
readdressed the letter only to *State Department, Government of the United States, Washington, DC.*

He smiled at his ploy. The letter would go to the
lowest level of the State Department, perhaps to be mis-
filed so that it might never reach Blaine, but, legally,
the letter will have been sent.

Antelope Wells, New Mexico Territory

The town of Antelope Wells, the southernmost town
in the territory, sat on the border with Mexico. It was
also the biggest and most important town in the entire
Bootheel region.

The mayor of the town, Charles McGregor, was reading one of the copies of the Declaration of Autonomy
that Schofield had caused to be circulated. The town
sheriff, Duncan Campbell, was also reading a copy.

"This can nae help but have an adverse effect upon
us, Sergeant Major."

"Aye," Campbell replied. "'Tis for sure 'n certain
that the bloke has in mind taking over every town 'n
wee village, 'n he'll nae stop before he has Antelope
Wells."

"'Tis said that he has an army," McGregor said.

"Fifty men or more. Schofield's Legion, they are calling themselves."

"Leftenant Colonel, I am without a deputy. I can nae stand up to an army of fifty men."

"Nor would I be for expecting such a thing," McGregor said. Smiling, he put down the copy of Schofield's Declaration. "That's why I'll be sending for help."

"Who would that be?"

"'Tis someone we both know, 'n hold in the highest regard," McGregor said without being any more specific.

Chugwater

Because Duff could remember having seen Otis at the loading pens in Cheyenne, they were able to establish by telegraph that his name was John Otis. The same telegram said there was good reason to believe that the two men with him were Martin Foley and Edgar Clemmons. They were wanted by the Laramie County sheriff for questioning in the murder of Emile Grant, a store proprietor.

That information had come from a customer who had arrived just as the shooting took place and had hidden outside the store as the three men were leaving. He was positive as to Otis's identification because he had once worked with him. He had seen the other two, but didn't know them by name. He did, however, identify them by photos he was shown in the sheriff's office.

The three outlaws were buried in the Chugwater cemetery, the expenses of their burial borne by the county.

Judge Marshal Craig conducted the hearing related

to the shooting that had taken place a week earlier. Because there was neither courthouse nor government building of any kind, the hearing was held in Fiddler's Green.

Abner Kilmer, a cowboy from an adjacent ranch, was the first witness. "I was in the Wild Hog, 'n seen them three fellers come in. I hadn't never seen none of 'em before, so bein' as I was some curious, I kinda kept an eye on 'em. Two of 'em got to talkin' and carryin' on with Jill 'n Cassie, but the other 'n didn't do nothin' but stand in front 'n look outside. Then he seen somethin', 'n he called out for the other two, 'n all three of 'em left."

"Mr. Kilmer, are you able to tell the court what the man saw?" Lee Hicks was from the Laramie County prosecutor's office.

"Yeah, I know what it is he seen, 'cause I looked out the winder to see what it was. It was Mr. MacCallister 'n Mr. Gleason, the two of 'em ridin' into town at the time."

"Did he make any comment that might be germane to this hearing?" Hicks asked.

"Did he do what?"

"Did Otis or either of the others make any comment that you can remember?"

"Oh, yeah." Kilmer smiled, showing two missing teeth in front. "He said, 'We ain't goin' to let the son of a bitch get away from us this time.' That's what Otis said."

"He didn't call him by name?"

"No, sir, he called him a son of a bitch." Kilmer glanced quickly toward Duff. "Mr. MacCallister, I don't mean nothin' by that, exceptin' that's what Otis called you. I don't think you're a son of a bitch at all. I think you're a good man."

Those present for the hearing laughed.

Duff did as well. "I appreciate that, Mr. Kilmer."

"You may step down, Mr. Kilmer," Judge Craig said.

All four eyewitnesses to the shooting testified that when the three men confronted Duff they already had pistols in their hands.

Duff was the last to testify, and he told how he had been accosted by the three men as he was coming back from Cheyenne. "I disarmed them, and thought that would be the end of it. I must say that 'twas quite a surprise to me when I saw them again."

The result of the hearing, to no one's surprise, was that the shooting was ruled justifiable homicide by reason of self-defense.

Three days after the hearing, Duff MacCallister was standing out in the backyard of his house, drinking coffee and looking at the work being done on one of his wagons. The rear of the wagon was up on stands with the back axle and both wheels removed.

Elmer Gleason was sitting on the ground with one of the wheels on his lap. "The boys did a good job with them. I've inspected every spoke 'n they're all good 'n tight."

"Then you're sayin' that we'll not be having a breakdown with this wagon as we did with the other one?" Duff asked.

"Duff, you could drive this wagon from here to St. Louis without the slightest bit of worry."

"'N would you be for tellin' me Elmer, my good man, why I would be wanting to go to St. Louis?"

"Why go to St. Louis? Why, there's a brewery in just about every block in town, and each one makes a better beer than the other one," Elmer replied.

Duff laughed. "I don't think 'tis possible for each brewery to make a better beer than the other one."

"Then you ain't never been to St. Louis 'n tasted any of the beer, on account of ever' beer you drink is better than the other beer, 'n that don't matter none whichever beer it is that you drink," Elmer said, failing to catch the meaning of Duff's comment.

"Perhaps not," Duff replied with a little laugh.

"Here comes Wang Chow," Elmer said, looking up as Wang passed through the gate. "You have to wonder just what kind of trouble that heathen Chinaman has got hisself into, him bein' gone so long today. More 'n likely he's been down at Lee Fong's Chinese Restaurant makin' eyes at Mai Lin, instead of pickin' up the new bearings." Elmer was speaking in fun, as he and Wang Chow were actually very good friends.

Wang dismounted, then handed two sacks to Elmer, one of paper and one of cloth.

"I figure the bearings are in the cloth bag, but what's in the paper bag?" Elmer asked.

"Mai Lin asked that I bring you some spring rolls. I don't know why she did this, unless she finds it pleasing to look upon the face of an ugly old man."

Elmer laughed. "I'll be. You are jealous ain't you? Here, you spend all your time with that pretty little China girl, 'n it's me she thinks is the good-lookin' one."

Wang removed an envelope from his saddlebag and held it out toward Duff. "I stopped at the post office as you asked, and there is a letter for you."

"Thank you, Wang." Duff took the envelope and

examined the return address. "Well, I'll be," he said in surprise.

"What is it?" Elmer asked.

"'Tis a letter from m' past, it is."

"Trouble, are you thinkin'?" Elmer asked.

"I'll nae be knowin' till I read it," Duff said as he opened the envelope and removed the letter.

My dear Captain MacCallister,

Learning that you, like I, had migrated to this magnificent country of the United States, I began to follow your exploits with the great pride of one in whose command you once served.

An unfortunate set of circumstances leads me to step out of the position of admiring observer and again interject myself into your life. As I once depended upon you in battle, I find that I am again in need of your help. I would not ask this of you were circumstances not so dire.

Should you be ready to render such service to an old friend and colleague in arms, you'll find me in the wee township of Antelope Wells, New Mexico. This borough 'tis in the extreme southwest part of the territory of New Mexico, a part that, like the heel of a boot, projects south into Mexico. And 'tis that, and the machinations of an evil rogue by the name of Ebenezer Schofield, which has brought great trouble upon every citizen of the town.

You'll nae have difficulty in locating me, for 'tis the mayor of the village I am.

> *Yours, once in service to the Queen*
> *Charles McGregor*

"Lads, would either of ye be knowin' anything about New Mexico?" Duff asked.

"I spent some time in New Mexico," Elmer said.

Duff laughed. "'N would ye be for telling me, Elmer, if there be any place ye haven't been?"

"I ain't never been to New York," Elmer said. "But I have been to New Mexico."

"'N would ye have spent any o' that time down in the southwest part o' the territory?"

Elmer shook his head. "I'm afraid not. My time was mostly in the central part, in Lincoln County. I got caught up in a little fracas there. Tell me, Duff, why are you interested in New Mexico? There ain't hardly nothin' there but sand 'n cactus, coyotes 'n mountains, 'n damn little water."

"I have a friend who is in a wee bit o' trouble down there, and 'tis my help he's asking for."

"Is it somebody I know?" Elmer asked.

"Nae, 'tis a man I was in the army with, my old commander, Leftenant Colonel Charles McGregor. No finer soldier ever served the Queen."

"And he's askin' you to come near a thousand miles to help him?"

"Aye."

"Is he a man of honor?" Wang Chow asked.

"Aye, he is one of the most honorable men I've ever known."

"Then you must do what honor demands," Wang Chow answered.

"'Tis my thinking as well."

"I see no reason why we can't leave on tomorrow's train," Elmer said.

"'Tis my obligation to an old friend 'n commander," Duff said. "I cannae in good conscience ask the two of ye to come with me, for who knows what may lie ahead?"

"That's a hell of thing for you to say to us, Duff," Elmer said. "Most especially seein' as we was just talkin' 'bout honor 'n all. If you're goin' down to New Mexico, me 'n Wang is goin' with you. Besides, like I said, I been down there before, 'n the last time there was near 'bout as much shootin' goin' on, as I seen durin' the war.

"The onliest way me 'n Wang won't be a-goin' is if you're just so selfish that you don't want nothin' to do with us."

Duff laughed. "Well now, Elmer, since ye've made such an elegant and tender supplication to be included, I would nae be a friend if I turned you down, would I? It will be an honor to have the two of ye make the journey with me."

The three men worked hard to get the wagon ready and put everything in shape so that Sky Meadow could be left in the care of the ranch hands without worry.

Chapter Four

George Gilmore was the only lawyer in the town, and C. D. Matthews owned the Bank of Antelope Wells. Because of the positions they held, they were two of the leading citizens of the town. At the moment, the two men were in Mayor McGregor's office.

"Sixty-four men! Sixty-four killed in Hachita. Fifty-one of them buried alive!" Matthews said.

"Aye, 'twas indeed a tragedy," McGregor agreed.

"What are we going to do about this? You don't really think Schofield is going to stop with Hachita, do you?" Gilmore asked, holding up one of the Declarations of Autonomy. "If he has no intention of going any further why would he issue such a document as this?"

"I admit that 'tis a thing of some concern," McGregor said. "But unlike Hachita, we have no silver mine. There is little here, I think, that would entice such a man."

"We are the biggest town in all the Bootheel, and we are right on the Mexican border," Matthews said. "If this person really does have the grandiose idea of forming a new country, it would be of paramount importance to him to control the gateway city to another country."

"Aye, there may be something to what ye say," McGregor said. "But I dinnae see this as an immediate worry."

"And so you plan to do nothing?" Gilmore asked.

"Oh, now, I dinnae say that. As a matter of fact I've already sent a letter to someone I trust to come take a hand in our situation. He is a man of proven and rather remarkable abilities."

"One man?" Matthews asked. "From what we have learned, this man Schofield has a veritable army, and you are putting the faith of our entire town in the hands of one man?"

"He is a man in whom I have absolute confidence," McGregor said.

"Do you think he will respond to your request?" Gilmore asked.

"Aye, I've nae doubt but that he will."

"All right. Let's hope that he does, and let's hope that he is all that you say he is," Gilmore said. "But C.D. and I have discussed this situation and we've come up with an idea that might be the solution to our problem. That is, if you are amenable to a suggestion."

"Of course, I'm open to any suggestion," McGregor said.

"We think you should ask the army to send troops down here to help us," Gilmore said.

"If the army comes, we won't be needing this man you have sent for," Matthews said.

"Perhaps that is so, but ye've nae objections to him coming, do ye?"

"No, none at all," Matthews replied. "To be honest

with you, Mayor, I think we might soon find ourselves in a situation where we would welcome any help we can get, whether it's the army or your friend. By the way, what's your friend's name?"

"MacCallister. Duff MacCallister."

"MacCallister? Would this be the man who broke up the Kingdom Come Gang in Texas?" Gilmore asked.

McGregor smiled. "Aye, 'tis the same man."

Gilmore nodded. "Well, if it's the same MacCallister, I agree that it would be good to have him here."

"The Kingdom Come Gang? I've never heard of them," Matthews said.

"It was a group of murdering outlaws led by a man named Jaco," Gilmore said. "I was a lawyer in the small Texas town of Runnels when Jaco and his gang came through, murdering people and burning buildings. This man, Duff MacCallister, broke up the gang. He would be a good man to have with us, that's for sure."

Matthews sighed. "Well, if we're going to be putting all our hope in him, I'm glad he's as good as you say."

Chugwater

On the evening before Duff, Elmer, and Wang were to leave for New Mexico, they crossed the creek Chugwater was named for and rode into the town on which it was built to say good-bye to people who were particularly important to them.

In Duff's case, that was Meagan Parker. She owned Meagan's Dress Emporium, and because she was not only an excellent seamstress but a good businesswoman, her business was one of the most successful commercial establishments in town.

In the early days of building his ranch, when Duff

needed a loan, Meagan had talked him into letting her buy an interest in the herd. As a result, she continued her position and since that time, continued to own some of the cattle on Sky Meadow.

In addition to their business connection, Duff and Meagan were, as the wags of the town liked to say, "keeping company," and were so often diners at the City Café that the proprietor, Kathy Nelson, had a table on permanent reserve for them. Over dinner that evening Duff showed Meagan the letter he had received from Charles McGregor.

"Charles McGregor," Meagan said. "I don't believe I've ever heard you speak of him."

"Leftenant Colonel Sir Charles McGregor, Baron by Writ of Summons from Her Majesty Queen Victoria, and, during the Battle of Amoaful, my battalion commander."

"You're going to help him," Meagan said. It wasn't a question. It was a declarative statement.

"Aye, for I cannae refuse such a request from an old friend, and a brother in arms. 'Twas Wang who pointed out the need to be true to honor, though I needed no reminder from him. By the way, as it turns out, Leftenant Colonel Charles McGregor is also a writer."

"A writer? What kind of writer?" Meagan asked, perking up at the announcement.

"He is a novelist, and quite good, I'm told. At least Charles Dickens seemed to think so."

"Oh, how interesting."

"I have two of his books if ye would like to read them."

"Oh, yes, I would very much like to. What is this battle you mentioned, that you and you friend fought? The battle of . . . ?"

"Amoaful," Duff answered. "'Tis a wee village in West Africa."

Meagan reached across the table and put her hand on Duff's arm. "Tell me about the battle. I know that you fought battles in places that I never heard of, but you very rarely ever talk about them. Perhaps if you would speak of this particular battle I would have a better understanding of why you feel such an obligation to go to the aid of this man who was once your commanding officer."

"All right." Though Duff had become an avid coffee drinker since arriving in America, he still enjoyed tea, and he finished his cup before he began the story.

"The battle happened in January of 1874, and with the music of the pipes playing, the 42nd Foot of the Black Watch led the way into the village. We were under fire for the whole way from the Ashanti defenders."

As Duff told the story, he told it with such intensity and imagery that Meagan could almost believe that she was there, witnessing the battle, rather than just hearing about it.

It was many years ago, but Duff remembered it like it was yesterday.

Reaching the village, the battalion commanded by Leftenant Colonel Sir Charles McGregor formed a square.

"Captain MacCallister!" McGregor called.

"Aye, sir?"

McGregor pointed to a group of small huts built of bamboo and straw. "We cannae advance farther until the heathens are driven from their stronghold there, 'n musketry alone will nae do the trick. Have ye' any ideas?"

"Perhaps a bayonet charge will dislodge them," Duff MacCallister offered.

"Aye, lad, that's an excellent recommendation, 'n 'twas hoping I was, that ye would have a suggestion as to how we might deal with this wee problem," McGregor replied.

"I'll form the company."

"Ye are nae going to lead the charge yourself, are ye?"

"Aye, 'tis my company, and who would lead it but me?"

"Captain MacCallister, as ye be the second in command, the loss, should ye be killed, would be a severe blow. Perhaps First Leftenant Robertson could be put in charge."

"Colonel, I'll nae be sending my company into battle without being at the head."

Colonel McGregor nodded. "Aye, 'tis the honorable thing to do. But I ask ye, lad, to take Sergeant Major Campbell with you."

"There's nae need for the battalion sergeant major to be put in danger, sir. M' own first sergeant will be enough."

"The sergeant major has seen more battle than anyone else in the regiment, 'n 'tis thinkin', I am, that he would be a good, steadying influence for your younger lads."

"Aye, perhaps you're right. Very good, sir. I'll be happy to have the sergeant major join me," Duff replied.

Five minutes later, advancing in a battle front formation and with fixed bayonets, Duff MacCallister led his company through the village square right into the heart of the resistance.

The enemy fire was intense, and when Sergeant Major Duncan Campbell went down just as they reached the defensive perimeter, three of the Ashanti warriors rushed toward him, hoping to use him to their advantage.

Duff hurried to Campbell's side, killed all three Ashanti with pistol fire, then helped the wounded soldier to his feet. "Can ye stand on your own, Sergeant Major?"

"Not without a wee bit o' help," Campbell replied in a voice strained with pain from the wound.

"Put your arm around my shoulder, and we'll continue the advance," Duff invited.

With Duff's support, Sergeant Major Campbell resumed the advance, holding the pistol in his free arm and firing at targets of opportunity.

With one final, bayonet-slashing rush, the Ashanti retreated, and with a triumphant shout of victory the first battalion of the 42nd Regiment of Foot, better known as the Black Watch, carried the day.

As they made their bivouac that night, Colonel McGregor was extremely complimentary of Duff. *"Captain, 'twas your bayonet charge that carried the day for us and, believe me lad, 'tis just such a thing I'll be writing in my report."*

"How is Sergeant Major Campbell?" Duff asked.

"He's fine, thanks to you."

"He is a good man, going to the front as he did."

"You were very brave," Meagan said, her eyes shining with the pride she felt in him.

"I dinnae mean for the story to be as self-aggrandizing as it turned out," Duff said. "For it was nae a major battle when compared against so many other battles of history, but it was the last battle I fought with Colonel McGregor. Ye can see then, lass, why I cannae refuse his call for help."

"Of course we must go to his aid," Meagan said.

"*We?* Lass, I have nae asked you to go. There may be danger, and I've nae wish to subject you to same."

"Oh, don't be silly, Duff. The letter says your colonel is the mayor of Antelope Wells. That means there is a town there, and I'll be quite content to stay behind in the town while you, Elmer, and Wang save the day," Meagan said with a bright smile. "Besides, you have promised me a trip, and since it is unlikely that we will be going to Scotland anytime soon, this one will have to do."

"Would ye be for promising me that you'll nae clutch a knife between your teeth and go charging against whatever nefarious forces are holding the town at bay?"

Meagan laughed. "I promise. By the way, did Elmer and Wang come into town tonight?"

"Aye. The three of us are to meet at Fiddler's Green at nine tonight."

"They would be with Vi and Mai Lin?"

"Aye."

"Good for them."

Chapter Five

While Duff and Wang had ridden farther into town, Elmer had peeled away from the others and headed directly for Vi's Pies. Owned by Vi Winslow—an attractive widow in her early forties—Vi's Pies was a small business, but one of the more successful in Chugwater.

Like Duff and Wang, Elmer had a background of experiences that far predated his arrival at Chugwater, Wyoming. It could be said that he had the most diverse background of any of the three because he was, more than most men, the sum total of all his experiences.

During the Civil War, Elmer had ridden with Quantrill's irregulars, and had taken part in the raid at Lawrence, Kansas.

Quantrill's men had ridden through the town, killing every male of military age, finishing off the wounded and those men they found hiding. Though Elmer was as ferocious as any of the others in battle, he was surprised by the mass killing and, not only did he not participate in the wanton slaughter, he saved as many as he could.

As he rode toward Vi's his thoughts turned to memories.

Elmer approached one of the wounded men in the arms of a grieving woman.

She put herself in front of her wounded husband. "If you are going to shoot him, you'll have to shoot me as well," she said defiantly. "I don't want to live without him."

"I ain't a-goin' to shoot you, ma'am. I ain't a-goin' to shoot him neither." Elmer looked directly at the man who had been shot in the shoulder and one leg. "Mister, when I shoot, put some o' that blood on your face 'n pretend you're dead." Elmer shot in the ground beside him.

"Bless you," the woman said.

"You'd best commence a-cryin' 'n, makin' out like I kilt your man," Elmer said.

The woman began weeping loudly as he left.

In that way, Elmer spared the lives of fifteen men but even so, when Quantrill's Raiders left Lawrence, 155 men and boys lay dead or dying behind them.

After the war was over some of the men who had ridden with Quantrill and who had nothing to come back to continued just as they had before. Jesse and Frank James were just such men, and for a short while Elmer had been a member of the James Gang. He'd been with them when they robbed the bank in Liberty, Missouri.

The memories stayed with him a little longer.

* * *

It was cold and it was snowing when a group of men calling themselves the James Gang rode into town. Elmer walked into the bank with Frank James, while Jesse and most of the others stayed outside. There were no customers in the bank, and only two employees. Elmer stood by the fire, warming his hands, while Frank stepped up to the counter.

"How can I help you on this cold, dreary day?" the bank clerk asked with a practiced smile.

Frank and Elmer pulled their pistols.

"We'll take all your money," Frank said.

When they walked out of the bank a minute later, they had over $60,000 in cash. As the group of men made off with their loot, they fired several shots to create a diversion. During the escape one of the men purposely shot and killed an unarmed boy who couldn't have been over sixteen.

That night, after having successfully escaped from the posse, Jesse and Frank divided the money, taking forty percent and dividing the remaining sixty percent with the other members of the gang.

"I'm leaving," Elmer told the James brothers.

"Why? You're a good man to have around," Jesse said.

"There was no reason for Jarrett to shoot that kid like he done."

"What the hell, Elmer? We just came through a war, where there was a lot of killing."

"We were in a war then. We ain't now, 'n the boy that Jarrett shot didn't even have a gun."

The Jarrett that Elmer was talking about was Jesse and Frank's first cousin, John Jarrett.

"Don't be so damn delicate, Elmer. Robbin' banks ain't

like plantin' corn. From time to time folks are goin' to be shot," Jesse said.

"Yeah, well, I don't plan to be robbin' no more banks, 'n I don't plan on shootin' no more people lessen they need to be shot. Like I said, I'm leavin'."

"If you leave now, you don't get your cut from the job we just pulled," Jesse warned.

"Fine," Elmer said. "I don't get my cut."

Leaving the James Gang meant leaving behind six thousand dollars, but Elmer had no wish to be a part of that life anymore. He'd gone West, where he'd lived with the Indians for a while, then when the Indian woman he had married died, he'd gone to sea.

For five years Elmer had sailed the seas, visiting exotic ports of call from the South Sea Islands, to India, the Philippines, Japan, and China, rising in rating from an able-bodied seaman to boson's mate. After leaving the sea he'd wound up in New Mexico long enough to take part in the Lincoln County War. From New Mexico he'd drifted up to Wyoming, and that's where he and Duff had met.

Living in an old, abandoned mine, Elmer had located a new vein of gold. Unable to capitalize on it because the property wasn't his, he was living a hand-to-mouth existence in the mine, unshaved and dressed only in skins.

Duff had just filed upon the property that included the mine, which meant everything Elmer had taken from the mine actually belonged to Duff. While he had every right to drive Elmer off, he didn't.

Instead, he'd offered Elmer a one-half partnership in the mine.

That partnership had paid off handsomely for both of them. Elmer became Duff's foreman and closest friend, and Duff's half of the proceeds from the mine had built Sky Meadow into one of the most productive ranches in Wyoming.

Eventually, Elmer had earned a vested interest in the ranch as well as the mine.

Arriving at Vi's Pies, he hung the reins over the hitch rail and entered the shop.

"Hello, Elmer," Vi said, obviously pleased that he had come to call on her. "I don't know how it is that every time I make a new batch of cherry pies, you seem to know about it."

Elmer smiled and lay his finger aside his nose. "I can smell a cherry pie cookin' from a hunnert miles away."

Vi laughed. "All right. Have a seat. I'll cut you a piece."

"You got any coffee made?"

"Of course I do. How can you eat pie without coffee?" Because it was after business hours, she cut a piece for herself and joined Elmer.

"I'm goin' to be gone for a while," Elmer said.

"I sort of thought as much."

"What give you the thought?"

"I don't know. There was just something about the way you looked when you came in here. Is it dangerous?"

"Life is dangerous, Vi. You know that."

"I'm not even going to ask you to be careful. You've made it this far in life, so I figure you've learned when to duck."

Elmer leaned over and gave her a quick kiss.

"What are you doing?" Vi asked in protest. The fact that the protest was feeble was advertised by her laughter.

"I couldn't have kissed you like that, if *you* had ever learned to duck," he teased.

"You're an old fool," Vi said, though she tempered her response with a broad smile. "Are Duff and Wang in town?"

"Of course they are. You think I'm the only one who came in to visit his girlfriend?"

"Girlfriend?"

"Well, ain't you my girlfriend?"

"I'm forty-four years old, Elmer. I'm long beyond the stage of being anyone's girlfriend."

"Forty-four is a little young for me, but you'll do," he said with a grin.

At the far end of the street, Wang Chow was sitting across the table from Mai Lin. She was an exquisitely beautiful young woman who dressed to accent her beauty by wearing a formfitting dress split up the side. With her elbows on the table and her chin resting on her folded hands, she was staring at him through dark and sparkling sloe eyes.

"There is something about him, Mai Lin," her father had told her, the first time Wang had come into the restaurant. "He is not like the men who worked on the railroad. He is *tebie*."

"In what way is he special, Father?"

"I don't know, Daughter. I look with my eyes, but I cannot see. I listen with my ears, but I cannot hear, for who he is cannot be perceived in such a way. I know, because I know."

Mai Lin's father had correctly discerned that Wang Chow was considerably more than the average man, for he'd been a priest of the Shaolin temple of Changlin, having entered the temple as a boy of nine. He didn't leave until he was twenty-eight years old, by which time he was a master of the Chinese martial art of *wushu.*

As Mai Lin stared at him, Wang remembered his life in China and reflected on how he'd ended up in Chugwater, Wyoming.

After leaving the temple, Wang returned home to the simple life of providing fish for his father's fish market. One day as he was casting his nets into the river, the Taiyang came to the market and killed Wang's father. The Yuequi went to the house and murdered Wang's mother and sister. In both incidents they left their mark—a red card representing Taiyang and a black stone for Yuequi.

After Wang buried his family, he cut the topknot to his hair, which was his spiritual connection to Changlin, and donned a changshan. Arming himself with a sword, he took revenge, killing fifteen men in his personal vendetta.

Upon hearing about the carnage caused by Wang, the Changlin Temple expelled him from their order, and the Empress Dowager Ci'an issued a decree for his death. Disguised, Wang left China with a group of laborers who were going to America to work on the railroad.

When the railroad was completed, he supported himself in a number of menial tasks, never disclosing to anyone that he was a Shaolin priest.

At some point, men with a penchant for evil decided to

lynch a Chinaman. They chose Wang, but Duff happened by just before they were able to carry out their plan. Duff asked the men to release their would-be victim, informing them that he wished to hire the Chinaman. When they resisted, Duff made his pitch even more convincing by killing two of them.

Wang was happy working for the man who had saved his life, and he'd made a personal vow to be ever loyal to his employer. If required, he would give his life in defense of *Shifu* MacCallister.

He was also happy to spend time with Mai Lin.

Duff, Elmer, and Wang gathered in Fiddler's Green for drinks before they returned to Sky Meadow. Biff Johnson joined them.

"New Mexico is a long way from here," Biff said in response to being told about the upcoming trip.

"Aye, but there's not a one of us who hasn't been farther," Duff said.

"That's true," Biff agreed.

"We'll be leaving by train, tomorrow. I've already got the tickets and made arrangements for our horses."

Biff lifted his beer, then held it out over the table. "Here's to you, boys. May the next Fiddler's Green I see you in be this one, and not the one in the hereafter." He recited a poem.

Halfway down the trail to Hell in a shady meadow green,
Are the Souls of all dead troopers camped near a good old-fashioned canteen,

*And this eternal resting place is known as Fiddler's
   Green.*
*Marching past, straight through to Hell, the Infantry
   are seen, accompanied by the Engineers, Artillery
   and Marine,*
*For none but the shades of Cavalrymen dismount at
   Fiddler's Green.*

"'Tis quite a good idea, this Fiddler's Green," Duff
said. "And 'tis wondering I am if any o' the lads there
would accept a wee visit from men o' the Black Watch."

"I'll vouch for you 'n all your mates," Biff said.
"There be many o' my friends there now—General
Custer 'n his brothers Tom 'n Boston, their nephew
Autie, 'n their brother-in-law, James Calhoun. Myles
Keogh is there, and many an NCO I shared a beer
with. First Sergeant Ed Bobo, Corporal John Brody,
Trumpeter Andy Bucknell. Ah, that lad could blow a
sweet tune and "Taps," when he played it, would
bring a tear to your eye. Bucknell was with Reno when
he was killed. The trumpeter that stayed with Custer
most of time called himself John Martin, but his real
name was Giovani Martini. He was an Italian who
could barely speak English."

"Ye have said that ye would vouch for me 'n my
mates," Duff said. "Would you be for tellin' me if there
would be a piper there as well, to pipe a welcome to
the lads who have served with the Black Watch?"

"Damn right, there will be," Biff said, and again, all
hoisted their beer mugs for the toast.

Chapter Six

The Bootheel of New Mexico Territory

The next target for Schofield's military operations was the town of Cottonwood Springs—a town more centrally located within the Bootheel. The centralized location meant that Cottonwood Springs was better positioned than Hachita for Schofield's temporary headquarters.

Ever the tactician, Schofield had conducted a thorough reconnoiter of Cottonwood Springs. He learned that the town had a population of 169. Of that number, 83 were men and boys, but 20 of them were either too old or too young to take part in any sort of defense effort. That would leave 63 men who could be counted on to defend the town, and though the number 63 was more than the number of attackers, Schofield knew that he would have the greater advantage of surprise.

"Also," Schofield said, speaking with a degree of arrogant pride, "it is as the great Greek Tragedian, Euripides once said. 'Ten men, wisely led, are worth a hundred without a head.' I think all will agree that with me in command, our attacking force will be wisely led."

"Indeed, we will be," General Peterson said.

"General, you will take half the force around to the south end of town. When you are in position let me know by messenger. The signal to attack will be transmitted by the firing of three shots, thusly. *Bang*, a short pause, then, *bang, bang*, the last two shots to be fired in rapid succession.

"As soon as you hear that signal, count to ten. I will do the same, then we will have a simultaneous attack from each end of the town.

"I do believe that the resultant surprise and rapidity of our attack, as well as the fact that they will be without effective leadership, while I will be in command of our forces, will result in a veritable slaughter of their men, followed by an unconditional surrender."

At that very moment, the citizens of Cottonwood Springs, unaware of the fate that awaited them, were going about their normal routine. At the stage depot one of the hostlers was putting a six-horse team into harness for the trip to Lordsburg. Inside the depot the ticketing agent, driver, and four passengers waited. As there was no money being transferred, there would be no shotgun guard making the trip.

In an empty lot between Walker's Grocery Store and Waggy's Café, four young boys were playing marbles. Nearby, three little girls were skipping rope to the rhythm of a nursery rhyme they were chanting. *"Peas porridge hot, Peas porridge cold, Peas porridge in the pot nine days old."*

Just down the street from the rope-jumping little girls, close enough to hear them, Mayor Rodney Gilbert was sitting in a rocking chair on the front porch of the Cottonwood Springs Hotel. He was holding council with City Marshal Asa Powell.

"What do you think about this feller who has put out some flyers saying as how we ain't a part of the United States no more?" Marshal Powell asked.

Mayor Gilbert chuckled. "It didn't work for Jeff Davis, 'n he had almost a million men with 'im. I don't see it working for this man Schofield, either."

"I reckon not," Powell said. "You got to give the man credit for havin' some gumption, though."

A few men and women were strolling along the boardwalks on either side of Malone Street, bound on personal errands. Not one person in the town was aware of Schofield's Legion, a veritable army camped on either side of the town, poised to attack.

It had been almost forty–five minutes since Schofield repositioned General Peterson to the other side of town, when Private Lemon came riding up. "Sir, General Peterson says he's ready whenever you are."

"Very good, Lemon, take your position with the troops," Schofield ordered. Drawing his pistol, he pointed it straight up, then pulled the trigger, hesitated for a couple of seconds, then pulled it two more times. After that he counted down aloud, from ten and immediately shouted, "By company front, charge!"

With pistols in hand, the men of Schofield's Legion rode at a gallop toward the peaceful little town that lay before them. The fact that there were groups of armed men approaching at a gallop from both ends of town so shocked the citizens of the town that many stood immobile, unable to react in any way.

Marshal Powell, who was the only one armed as the two armies swept into town, stepped out onto the edge of the hotel porch and fired. One of the attackers was hit and tumbled from his horse, but the courageous marshal went down under a hail of gunfire. Mayor Gilbert picked up the marshal's pistol with the intention of returning fire, but he was cut down before he could even pull the trigger.

By the time the two armies merged, the street and boardwalks were littered with bodies. In the empty lot where the children had been playing, one of the little girls and two of the young boys lay dead. A man came running out of a business, waving a white towel over his head.

"Cease fire, cease fire!" Schofield shouted and the town grew quiet. A rather significant cloud of gun smoke drifted down the street, partially obscuring the view and burning everyone's nostrils.

"Please, no more killing! We surrender!" The call for mercy came from the man who was holding the towel.

"Are you the mayor?" Schofield asked.

"No."

"I will accept the surrender of the town only from the mayor."

"He can't surrender because he's dead. You killed 'im," The townsman holding the white flag pointed to the bodies of the mayor and the city marshal.

"Very well. I will accept the surrender from you,"

Schofield agreed. "You are now free to gather the bodies and arrange for their burials."

An unexpected gunshot interrupted the dialogue. On the opposite side of the street someone lay face-down with a pistol in his hand.

"Who shot that man?" Schofield demanded.

"I did, Prime Director," First Sergeant Cobb replied. "He was pointin' a gun at you."

"Good job, First Sergeant." Schofield turned his attention back to the man holding the white flag. "What is your name, sir?"

"Toomey. George Toomey."

"Mr. Toomey, I am Prime Director Ebenezer Schofield. Perhaps you have seen some of the flyers I recently caused to be published."

"Yes, I saw them."

"Then, as you know who I am, you also must know that I have absolute power over everyone in the sovereign state of Tierra de Desierto. And because I have that authority, I hereby appoint you as acting mayor of the town of Cottonwood Springs. Your first duty is to make certain nobody else attempts to shoot us." Schofield held up a finger to make a point. "From this point forward, if we see anyone with a gun, we will kill him and five more of your citizens, who we will select at random. Included in the five that we kill will be at least one woman and one child."

"What?" Toomey asked with a gasp. "Why would you kill the innocent?"

"It is called incentive," Schofield replied. "Having such a specter hanging over your heads will give you incentive to see to it that nobody else tries anything so foolish. Have I made myself clear?"

"Yes," Toomey said.

"When you speak with me, you will call me Prime Director," Schofield demanded.

"Yes, Prime Director," Toomey corrected.

As the men of Schofield's Legion watched the citizens recover their dead, Schofield looked around town until he found the most substantial-looking house.

"This," he said, taking in the house with a wave of his hand, "will be my headquarters. First Sergeant Cobb?"

"Yes, sir?"

"Take two men with you, go into the house, and turn out anyone that you find."

A few minutes later two women, one of whom was a Mexican, and two young children were herded out of the house.

"Who is your husband?" he asked.

"Rodney Gilbert. He is the mayor," the older of the two women said defiantly.

"You have my condolences, ma'am," Schofield said.

"Condolences?"

"Your husband was a brave man. He died attempting to defend his town."

"Dead? Rodney is dead?"

"I'm afraid he is. Now, I will be taking your house. Have you anywhere else to go? Do you have any other relatives in town?"

Mrs. Gilbert was crying so that she couldn't answer.

"Her mother lives here," the Mexican woman said.

"What is your name?" Schofield asked.

"I am Frederica Arino, maid to the mayor and Mrs. Gilbert."

"Well, Frederica, I want you to get Mrs. Gilbert and the children safely moved, then come back here." Schofield smiled, almost leeringly, at the exceptionally attractive young woman. "From now on, you will be working for me."

Chapter Seven

Schofield and his army had moved through the New Mexico Bootheel in an unstoppable juggernaut. After capturing and occupying Hachita and Cottonwood Springs, the next target was La Tenja.

Sitting astride a large white horse, Schofield, like the others, was wearing a uniform. However, his was the most glorious of them all.

Beside him sat General Julian Peterson, nearly as splendidly dressed. Behind them were fifty more uniformed men, including a captain, two lieutenants, and four sergeants.

"What are your instructions, Prime Director?" General Peterson asked.

"Be ruthless in the attack," Schofield ordered. "There must be none left behind who are capable of leading a revolt against us."

The sleepy little town was totally unaware that on a slight rise but one mile from town, a small army of men, mounted and well-armed, were about to attack. The townspeople went about their business as they did every day. Ike Rafferty was sweeping off his porch prior to opening his general store, and down at Fred Miller's Freight Company, a wagon was being loaded. Carpenters were getting ready to resume work on a house for the newlyweds, Ted and Emma Morris, and water was being heated behind the Mighty-Clean Laundry. Ed Hanover was moving bags of feed from inside the store to the outside so that they would be more visible to the customers, and Sid Goren was repairing the sign for the La Tenja Hotel. One end was hanging lower than the other.

On the night before, some impertinent boys had thrown mud clods onto the sign in front of the St. Francis Catholic Church, which was the very first building at the extreme north end of the town. Father Hernandez, armed with a bucket of soapy water and a cloth, was cleaning it, when he heard a sound like a low, rumbling thunder. Turning toward the sound he was shocked to see a large number of uniformed men galloping toward the town. Riding abreast of each other, as soon as they hit Tanner Street, they spread all the way across the road from one side to the other.

"Here, you men!" Father Hernandez called, stepping out with his arms raised. "You can't come galloping into a town like this!"

His dark garb and collar notwithstanding, at least three of the riders fired at the priest. He went down with a blood-soaked cassock, dead before the last rider passed him by.

As Schofield's Legion swept into the town, the thunder of the hoofbeats awakened everyone, some from their slumber and others from their inattention. To the sound of the galloping horses was added the throaty shouts of the soldiers, then the sound of gunfire as all began firing indiscriminately.

Ike Rafferty was killed first, then Vernon Jones and Ben Carter, who were loading the freight wagon. Ed Hanover ducked down behind the sacks of feed, and Sid Goren ran back into the hotel.

New sounds were added to the cacophony as the men of the town shouted in alarm, and the women of the town screamed in terror.

Schofield's men began to ransack homes, shoot civilians, loot stores, and set fire to buildings. Some of the townspeople had managed to grab guns, but they were too few and too late, as most were killed before they could even get a shot off.

As the day went on, terror spread throughout the town, with panicked citizens fleeing into nearby ravines, hiding in cellars or cornfields, and attempting to escape. By noon almost fifty percent of the male population had been killed, and half the buildings, private homes and businesses, had been burned. Schofield took over the lone hotel of the town, establishing his temporary headquarters in the hotel dining room.

"Captain Bond," Schofield called as he cleaned off a table then turned it lengthwise and sat behind it so that it became more of a desk than a dining table.

"Yes, Sir?"

"Take some men with you and locate the mayor of this town. If he has been killed, find the vice-mayor, or the highest-ranking city official still alive."

"Yes, sir," Bond replied, gathering five men to help him in his quest.

"Lieutenant Mack, Lieutenant Fillion, take two men each and go through every building in town to collect any weapons that you may find. Then order everyone, be they man, woman, or child, out into the street. I want to address the entire town."

After the three officers left to carry out their assignments, the four sergeants were charged with posting guards around the hotel, and Schofield invited General Peterson to have lunch with him.

"We have but one town remaining," Schofield said over the meal the hotel provided.

"Antelope Wells," General Peterson replied. "It will be the greatest challenge. It is larger than all the other towns combined."

"And the mayor of the town, Charles McGregor, was an officer in the Black Watch," Schofield said.

"Black Watch? What is that?" General Peterson asked.

"It is a Scottish regiment in the British army. Quite a storied regiment, I might add."

"But surely, Prime Director, his experience doesn't compare to yours. You commanded the Second Division of the Fifth Corps and fought in some of the most significant battles of the war. How could McGregor possibly match that?"

"General, one of the most important lessons I learned in the war was to never underestimate your enemy."

"Yes, sir. That's true."

"Once the town of Antelope Wells falls under our control, the birth process of Tierra del Desierto will be complete. Then we will build our new nation so that we may take our position on the world stage."

"Starting a new country like this is funny, when you think about it," General Peterson said.

"Oh? And what, exactly, General Peterson, do you find funny about establishing a new country?"

"Well, sir, it's just that you and I are seceding from the United States to start a new nation. The last time someone tried this, it resulted in a war, and you and I fought to keep it from happening."

"Indeed there was a war, but then it was nearly half the country that seceded. I seriously doubt that President Arthur will be able to convince Americans to go to war to prevent half a million acres of desert from breaking away from the rest of the country. And don't forget, New Mexico isn't even a state."

"Prime Director Schofield?" Captain Bond said, stepping tentatively into the dining room.

"Yes, Captain?"

"I found him, sir. He was hiding in the basement of his house."

"You found who?"

"Why, the mayor of the town," Captain Bond said. "His name is Pete Cravens, 'n he's waitin' out front."

"Very well, Captain, show the mayor in."

A moment later a small, thin man with no more than a few strands of hair combed across a bald head was brought into the room by two of Schofield's soldiers.

"Stand there," one of the accompanying soldiers said gruffly.

The mayor, clearly frightened, stood where he was directed and slid his wire-rim glasses farther up the bridge of his nose.

"Here, here, men, this man is the mayor. We must treat him with some dignity and respect. Your Honor, I am Prime Director Ebenezer Schofield, ruler of the emerging nation of Tierra de Desierto."

"Land of the Desert? What nation is that?"

"It is what once was the Bootheel of New Mexico. This town, your town, is right in the middle of Tierra del Desierto and because two of the most important roads cross here, La Tenja is the second most important town in the new nation. You should feel honored that you are the mayor of such an important place. I will expect much of you."

"You mean, you aren't going to kill me?" Mayor Cravens asked in a voice that squeaked of fear.

"Why, no, my good man," Schofield replied with a broad smile. "Why would I do that?"

"When you and your men arrived . . . all the shooting, all the killing, I just, uh . . . thought that you were going to kill everybody."

"Yes, well, I'm sorry about that. But the birth of any new country is often painful and bloody. This show of force was necessary for it is imperative for all to understand that I and my legionnaires are recognized as the absolute and final authority. Tell me, Mayor Cravens, do you anticipate any armed resistance from your citizens to my annexation of your town?"

"No sir. To tell the truth, I don't even know how many of male citizens I have left who could even handle a gun," Mayor Cravens said.

"Well then that means I'll not be worrying about any insurrection against my authority," Schofield said. He held up a finger.

"Mr. Prime Director, the town has gathered in the street," Lieutenant Mack said.

"Very good. I'll go speak with them. It is about time the citizens of this community recognize that there is a new authority."

When Schofield stepped out in front of the hotel, he saw a pile of weapons, rifles, pistols, and shotguns lying on the porch of the hotel. He also saw what was left of the little town. A great many of the buildings had been burned to the ground, and at least a dozen blackened bodies scattered among the buildings that still stood facing the street. Smoke curled from the burned buildings, and the air was foul with the stench of not only burnt wood but burned flesh and hair.

There were nearly two hundred people standing fearfully out in the street waiting for him. The women and children outnumbered the men by a rather significant amount, and even fewer men were between the ages of eighteen and forty. At least twenty of Schofield's soldiers were standing around them, glaring at the citizens of the town as if daring any of them to make any sort of hostile move.

Hostility of any sort was the last thing on the mind of the docile gathering.

Schofield began to speak. "Ladies and gentlemen, allow me to introduce myself. I am Prime Director Ebenezer Schofield. From this point forward your fate and the fate of everyone within the confines of the annexed land will be in my hands.

"I am leaving as my regent the man you know as your mayor, Pete Cravens. I want you to understand that from this moment on anything Mayor Pete Cravens says may be construed as having come from me."

Schofield turned toward the mayor. "And, Mayor Cravens, you will not issue any orders, beyond the normal business of administering the town, without my approval. Do you understand?"

"Yes, sir," Cravens replied, trying hard to stay in the good graces of the men who had destroyed more than half of his town.

"Now, my first directive to you good people is to

rebuild your town. You have the opportunity to make it newer and better than it ever was before. Why, I've no doubt but that you could make this town the show-place of the new nation."

"What new nation?" The person who asked the question was a man who appeared to be in his late sixties or early seventies.

Schofield nodded at one of his sergeants, and the sergeant walked over to the questioner and knocked him down. There was a gasp of shock and fear from the others.

"Any further questions will be directed to your mayor," Schofield said. "Now, you are dismissed to begin rebuilding your town. Oh, and don't try to leave. I will keep men posted at every exit of the town with orders to shoot to kill anyone who attempts to escape."

Antelope Wells

Lawyer George Gilmore and banker C. D. Matthews had returned to the mayor's office to speak with Charles McGregor.

"Mayor McGregor, have you heard about what happened at Cottonwood Springs and La Tenja?" Gilmore asked.

"Aye, I have heard. 'Twas a terrible thing that happened there."

"La Tenja is the third community he has attacked. He kills almost half the population without regard as to whether they are man, woman, or child, then he occupies the town, establishing himself as absolute ruler. The same thing is going to happen here, I fear," Matthews said. "What are you going to do to stop it?"

"I've sent for someone," McGregor replied.

"That would be MacCallister?" Gilmore asked.

"Aye. Ye said yourself that ye knew the captain."

"No, sir, what I said was that I knew of him, seeing as I was practicing law in Texas when he dealt with the Kingdom Come Gang."

"Then ye have confidence in the man," McGregor said.

"He's a good man, I admit, but you may remember that we talked about contacting the army."

"Aye, I remember."

"I think it's time we asked the army to come to our aid."

"Aye, and 'tis remembering our earlier talk about this that I tell ye that I've sent two letters requesting assistance, but I've nae heard back from them."

"I have an idea, Mayor, if you are amenable to it," Gilmore said.

"My good mon, under circumstances such as these we are facing now, I'm quite willing to try almost anything," McGregor said. "What is your proposal?"

"I think you should write another letter to the US Army, requesting help. Make it even more personal, and cite what happened to the mayor of Cottonwood Springs."

"I am willing to do so, but what makes you think 'tis any more likely for this letter to be answered that my previous two?"

"Because this time, C.D. and I will personally carry the letter to the commanding officer at Fort Stanton," Gilmore replied.

A broad smile spread across McGregor's face. "Aye! Aye, that would be a great idea, I'm thinking."

Chapter Eight

Cheyenne

The closest railroad connection to Chugwater was Cheyenne, and the trip to get there took Duff and the others an entire day by horseback. It wasn't necessary to find accommodations in Cheyenne though, because the train left at eight o'clock that very night.

Once they had boarded the train, Meagan sat under the gimbal lantern, then took a book from her bag.

"Ye plan to read, do ye?" Duff asked.

"Yes, it'll be a couple of hours before the porter turns down our bunks, so I should get a good start on it." Meagan held out the book for Duff's examination. "It's one of the two books you gave me. I'm sure you'll recognize it." Then holding the book under the excellent light provided by brightly burning lantern, she began to read.

The Sword of Gideon
BY CHARLES McGREGOR

Four men waited in a grove of trees alongside the road to Jaffa. One lay napping, one was picking figs, and the other two were keeping watch on the road.

"Perhaps they aren't coming," one said.

"Nahman, have you no patience?" Gideon scolded. "I heard it myself. A Roman officer accompanied by a slave will be arriving today, carrying money that will be used to pay the soldiers."

"That's a lot of money," Phegamon said. "Why would the Romans bring in so much money without a detachment of guards?"

"They do so, because they think one officer will not attract attention. They are going to try and slip the money in without anyone knowing about it."

"Gideon," Gestas said in a harsh whisper. "They are coming!"

"How many?" Gideon asked.

"Two. A centurion and his slave."

"See? It is just as I told you," Gideon said. He drew his sword and looked at the others. "Get ready."

Meagan continued to read even after she went to bed, using the gimbal lantern beside her upper bunk to provide enough light for her to see. She took the book with her to breakfast in the dining car the next morning.

"Still have the book, I see," Duff said when he saw her.

"Oh, it is a great book!" Meagan held the book close to her chest. "And this wonderful author is actually the man we are going to see?"

"Aye, as ye can see by the name o' the author on the book, it is Charles McGregor, one and the same."

"What a great talent he has. I can hardly wait to meet him."

"Duff, you had better be careful now. That this here colonel feller we're goin' to save might wind up a-stealin' your girlfriend," Elmer teased.

"Nonsense." Duff turned his head to one side and struck a pose. "What woman could possible give up this?"

The others, including Meagan, laughed.

Midway through the second day of the trip they waited at the depot in Denver for the next train south.

"Paper. Get your paper here!" a young boy called as he strolled through the depot with a bundle of folded papers under his arm. "Paper. Get your paper here!"

"Lad, what is the paper ye are selling?"

"Why, it's the *Rocky Mountain News*, sir. The finest paper in the state, and in the whole county, too, I'm thinking."

"Sure, 'n with such an endorsement now, how could I not be for buying the paper? I'll have one."

"I'll have one as well," Meagan said.

"Yes, sir, and yes ma'am!" the boy replied. With a wide and happy smile, he exchanged paper for coin.

Elmer and Wang were absent during the transactions. They were making certain that the horses, who would be accompanying them for the entire way, were comfortable and in position to be reloaded onto the next train when they resumed their trip south.

The above-the-fold story on the front page was of the Chinese Exclusion Act. The bill passed by Congress and signed into law by President Chester A. Arthur provided an absolute ten-year moratorium on Chinese labor immigration.

After a quick read, Duff saw that it would have no effect on Wang's status. It was a story on the second page of the paper, however, that caught his attention.

Area of New Mexico Declares Independence From United States

A peculiarity in the way the border is drawn between Mexico and the United States has produced a "Bootheel" along the southern border of the territory of New Mexico. This geographic anomaly has as its northern border, the 32nd Parallel. The east, south, and west parameters of the area in question are bordered by Mexico. And though this Bootheel protrudes into Mexico itself, it is, in fact, a part of the United States.

Heretofore the ownership of this protrusion of land has not been questioned, as Mexico recognizes the area as clearly belonging to the United States. However a new presumption of ownership has been filed upon the land, not by any foreign government but from an American who has abandoned his own citizenship in this great country in order to declare the founding of a new nation.

Like the failed experiment by which eleven states attempted to secede a few years past, this new "nation" has been established by act of secession. It is being called Tierra del Desierto, or Desert Land.

According to the Declaration of Autonomy, copies of which have been widely distributed, all land within the confines of this geographic area will come under the rule of one Ebenezer Schofield, a West Point graduate who, during the late war, held the rank of major general in the Union army. After the war, he turned his back on honor and service to take part in several nefarious schemes, all of which led him to serve some time in prison.

This dishonored individual has further discredited himself by an act of treason against the country he once served. By self-appointment, the erstwhile General Schofield has established himself as the ruler of this illegal country, and has taken unto himself the rather vainglorious title of Prime Director.

It has been said that Schofield has raised a rather substantial army he calls Schofield's Legion, by which he has already occupied three of the four towns within the disputed area. However, this newspaper has been unable to validate those claims.

The *Rocky Mountain News* intends to follow future events as they pertain to the New Mexico Bootheel, and will report upon them as news comes available. In that way our readers will be well informed.

"This has to be the man that Leftenant Colonel McGregor is concerned about," Duff said, pointing out the newspaper article to Meagan.

"Oh, my!" she said after reading it. "Why did your friend have to come to you about it? Why didn't he go to the army? After all, it was the army that handled the last insurrection."

"Aye, 'tis a good question, lassie. One that will be needin' an answer."

Fort Stanton, New Mexico Territory

George Gilmore and C. D. Matthews were waiting in the outer office of the post headquarters when the post sergeant major came out of a back room.

"Colonel Dunaway will see you gentlemen now."

"Thank you," Gilmore said.

Colonel Dunaway was sitting at a large, carved desk. Behind him was the flag of the United States and a large map of the territory of New Mexico. As the two men approached, he stood and stuck his hand out. "Mr. Gilmore and Mr. Matthews, it is a pleasure to meet you." He pointed to two empty chairs. "Please, have a seat."

There was a scrape of chairs on the wide plank floors as the two men took the proffered seats.

Colonel Dunaway picked up a paper lying before him and studied it for a moment then he spoke. "If I understand this petition correctly, you want me to send army troops to Antelope Wells to put down an armed insurrection against the United States?"

"If you'll notice, Colonel, it isn't the two of us who are making the request. We are only the messengers.

This is an official petition from Charles McGregor, the mayor of our town," Gilmore answered.

"We have no military posts in the Bootheel area," Colonel Dunaway said.

"That's true, Colonel. That's why we had to come some considerable distance to Fort Stanton," Matthews said.

"You miss my point, Mr. Matthews. If we have no army posts there, that means that no army posts have been attacked. And if no army posts have been attacked, that means there is no insurrection against the United States government. What you have is a civil disturbance, and in accordance with the Posse Comitatus Act, I am not authorized to introduce any troops."

"The what act?" Gilmore asked.

"The Posse Comitatus Act," Dunaway repeated. "That, gentlemen, is a United States federal law that was signed on June 18, 1878 by President Rutherford B. Hayes. The purpose of the act—in concert with the Insurrection Act of 1807—is to limit the powers of the federal government in using its military to act as domestic law enforcement personnel in what is basically a civil problem.

"I'm sorry. I wish I could send some troops down there to help, but my hands are tied."

"Wait a minute, Colonel. Didn't we just, not too terribly long ago, fight a civil war? And the emphasis in my question is on the word *civil*," Gilmore said.

"That is true, Mr. Gilmore. But that insurrection began with an attack on a United States installation, in particular, Fort Sumter. Now, if these outlaws who purport to be engaging in a revolution against the United States were to actually attack a U.S. installation such as this very post, for example, then we would, indeed, be able to interfere.

"Until that time, however, and without specific authorization to do so from the Secretary of War, my hands are bound by the Posse Comitatus Act. I'm sorry. I wish I could be of help to you."

Chapter Nine

It was a very disappointed Gilmore and Matthews who returned to Antelope Wells to report on the failure of their mission.

They met in the city council room, giving the report to Mayor McGregor, Sheriff Campbell, as well as Hugh Poindexter, Paul Carson, and Nate Emmet. The latter three men, along with Gilmore and Matthews, made up the city council.

"I've nae heard of such a law," Campbell said. "What is the purpose of the army, if it is nae to protect the people?"

"I'm afraid, gentlemen, that we are going to be on our own," Matthews said.

"Wait. Are you saying we are going to have to fight against this madman?" Carson asked.

"It looks as if we must," Gilmore said.

"No. That's crazy!" Carson said. "In case you haven't been paying attention to things, Schofield has an army with him. He has already killed dozens of innocent people. We can't stand up to him! Why, it would be insane even to try!"

"We have no choice, Paul," Poindexter said.

"Yes, we do have a choice," Carson insisted.

"And what choice would that be?" Matthews asked.

"We could surrender to him."

"Surrender? Are you daft?" Emmet asked in an angry and disbelieving bark.

"No, I'm not. Hear me out. Almost seventy people were killed in Hachita, and even more in Cottonwood Springs and La Tenja. There is no way of knowing how many others—ranchers or people who live outside of the towns—have been killed. And what has been the result?

"I'll tell you the result," Carson said, continuing to make his point. "The result has been numerous lives lost, and in every case Schofield has wound up in control of the town. He now controls every town in the Bootheel but this one. Since there is no way we can defend ourselves against him, and since he is going to wind up in control of our town anyway, why not just surrender to him, and spare the many useless deaths that will occur if we fight him?"

"We are nae going to surrender," McGregor said resolutely.

"You aren't the king, McGregor. You are just the mayor. We have a city council, and you are bound to do what we tell you to do. I'm calling, right now, for a vote. I say that we send an emissary out to meet with this man who calls himself the Prime Director and surrender the town of Antelope Wells to him."

"All right, gentleman, the question has been called," McGregor said. "So, we'll be having the vote now. All who are in favor of sending an emissary to that brigand, Schofield, so that we may lay ourselves at his mercy, raise your hands."

Carson's hand shot into the air.

"And those who are opposed?"

Every other member of the city council voted against Paul Carson's proposal.

"The proposal has failed. Gentlemen, we will fight for our town," McGregor said.

"Who are you going to get to fight?" Carson asked.

McGregor smiled. "I've asked a friend to come help us."

"A friend?"

"Aye, here is a copy of the letter I sent him." McGregor handed the letter over to Carson.

He read it quickly, then passed it back. "So, you have invited someone who served with you when you were back in Scotland, and that is supposed to quell my concern?"

"Sergeant Major, tell Mr. Carson and the others about Captain Duff MacCallister."

Campbell smiled. "He is a one-man army, he is. We will do well to have him."

"One man," Carson said. "Mr. Gilmore and Mr. Matthews were unable to get the army to come to our aid, but we shouldn't worry because you have invited this, this Duff MacCallister, to come to Antelope Wells and save us from Schofield's Legion."

"As we have told you, Mr. Carson, Captain MacCallister is nae just any man. He is most remarkable, 'n I have absolute confidence that he is more than a match for Schofield," McGregor said.

"Aye, he will put up quite the fight," Sheriff Campbell added.

Carson shook his head and raised his finger. "Your man MacCallister will put up quite the fight, you say. Perhaps that is so, but in the end the result will be the same. Many of our citizens will be killed, and we will still be forced to surrender. You will rue the day you made this decision, gentlemen. There is no way of knowing how many men, women, and children will die in this foolish attempt to defend the town, and their deaths will be on the heads of you who voted against a reasonable solution.

"You will rue the day," he said again.

"Paul, I, too, know this man," Gilmore said. "Well, I don't actually know him, but I certainly know of him." He told Carson the story of Duff MacCallister defeating the Kingdom Come Gang. "And believe me, this gang was quite large, well-armed, and vicious enough to kill anyone with impunity. C.D. and I tried to get the army to come to our aid and were unsuccessful with our efforts. I do believe, however, that there is a reasonable hope that someone like Duff MacCallister will be able to help us."

"One man," Carson said. "You're all putting the safety of this city and everyone in it in the hands of one man. You are crazy. All of you are crazy." Then, with one final look of condemnation, Carson turned and hurried from the council room.

McGregor, Campbell, and the others watched him leave, then Gilmore spoke. "I've known Paul Carson for a long time. I've never seen him so angry."

"Ye wouldn't be for thinkin' that Mr. Carson might take it on himself to try 'n make some deal with Schofield, would ye?" Sheriff Campbell said.

"No," Gilmore said, shaking his head. "He is angry, true enough, but he is a good man, and there is no way he would sell the rest of us out."

"I wish I could agree with you, Charles," Nate Emmet said. "Oh, I agree with you that Carson is a good man, but he is also a man of principle, and if he truly believes this is our only option, he may very well try and work out some deal on his own."

"Sergeant Major," McGregor said. "Perhaps 'twould be good for you to keep an eye on Mr. Carson."

"Aye, I'll do so," the sheriff replied.

Ebenezer Schofield had returned to Cottonwood Springs, which had been designated by him as the capital city of Tierra de Desierto. At the moment he was seated at the dining table, eating from fine china. The food had been prepared and was being served by Frederica Arino, the twenty-four-year-old sultry beauty who had been confiscated along with the house.

"Señorita, you have used too much chili powder," Schofield complained. "Throw it out and start all over."

"The mayor, Señor Gilbert, always say use much chili powder," Frederica said.

"Gilbert is no longer the mayor, nor is he the master of this house. He is dead, and I am now the master. You must learn what my preferences are and respond accordingly."

"*Qué?*" the servant asked, not understanding his comment.

"Throw it out and start over," Schofield demanded, pushing the plate away.

"*Sí, señor,*" Frederica said, taking the plate and leaving quickly.

There was a quiet knock at the door.

"Prime Director?"

"Yes, come in, General Peterson."

"We have received a bit of intelligence that I think might be important."

"All right, let me see it," Schofield said, reaching for the paper that General Peterson was holding in his hand.

Dear Prime Director Schofield,

I don't know if you have ever heard of Duff MacCallister, but he is quite well-known up in Wyoming. He is a warrior of great skill and courage, and he could be a problem for you. I enclose herein, as far as I am able to reproduce, the letter that Charles McGregor sent to MacCallister. It isn't exact because I'm doing it from memory, but you'll get the idea, I'm sure.

My Dear Captain MacCallister,
Circumstances lead me to ask you for help. If you're willing to help, you'll find me in Antelope Wells, New Mexico.
I'll be easy to find because I'm the mayor of the town.

Charles McGregor

Schofield read the letters, then handed them back to Peterson. "Who sent these letters?" he asked.

"We don't know, sir. There was a third letter in which a proposal was made," General Peterson said. "Here is that letter."

Dear Prime Director Schofield,

If you are reading this letter then you have already read the other two letters, for this is the order in which I wished them to be presented to you. I am a well-placed citizen of the town on Antelope Wells. My position is such that I shall be able to provide you

*with very specific and credible information, which
you will find helpful.*

*The enclosed information is but an example of
what, over a period of time, I will be able to make
available to you. In exchange for my efforts, I would
want you, after you have consolidated all your gains
and established your new nation, to grant me certain
considerations. I would expect you to evaluate the
considerations based upon your level of satisfaction
with the information I shall provide.*

*The name I shall use in this, and all future
transactions is not my real name, but it is the way by
which I will identify myself if and when I meet you or
one of your emissaries. That name, and by which I
conclude this missive is Angus Pugh.*

Schofield lay the letter on his desk, then glanced up
at Peterson. "I must say that this sounds like quite an
intelligent bartering position. If he becomes a contin-
uous and reliable source of information that proves
helpful and reliable, I am prepared to reward him in
a way that is commensurate with the value of his con-
tributions."

"Yes, sir, I thought you might."

"Now, I would like for you to find out all you can
about this man our new ally has told us about. This
man, Duff MacCallister."

"I will, sir," Peterson promised.

Lordsburg, New Mexico Territory

It had been a long and tiring trip—started by horse
almost one thousand miles north, then by train from
Cheyenne. Having reached Lordsburg, the travelers

would once more be on horseback for the remaining ninety miles. Elmer and Wang were seeing to the off-loading of their horses while Duff and Meagan went into the train station.

Duff saw a Western Union sign, and stepped up to the counter. "Tell me, would it possible to send a telegram to the wee village of Antelope Wells?"

"Oh, indeed it is, sir. That's one of the major crossings into Mexico," the telegrapher responded.

"Good. Then I'll be for sending a telegram there if you please."

"Yes, sir. I'll be happy to do it." The telegrapher slid a tablet and a pen across the counter. "Just write your message here."

"My thanks to you," Duff said as he took the pad and began to write the message.

TO HIS HONOR THE MAYOR LEFTENANT
COLONEL CHARLES MCGREGOR STOP
I AM IN LORDSBURG AND EXPECT TO BE
IN ANTELOPE WELLS WITHIN TWO MORE
DAYS STOP
      CAPTAIN DUFF MACCALLISTER

Antelope Wells

Charles McGregor had invited Duncan Campbell to have dinner with him. "I have some news to share with you, Sergeant Major." McGregor passed a piece of paper across the table. "This is a telegram I received yesterday. As you can see, our old friend has answered my request to come to our aid. He is already in Lordsburg."

"I had nae doubt but that he would answer the call,"

Campbell said. "It will be good to see the captain again." Subconsciously, he rubbed a spot on his leg, the scar of a wound he had suffered in the Battle of Amoaful. "He could have left me on the battlefield to the mercy of the heathen Ashanti, but he braved enemy fire to come to my rescue."

"Aye, that he did. Have I done the right thing, Sergeant Major? I'm for sure and certain that Schofield will be for trying to take our wee village as he has all the others, and as ye said, there was nae doubt but that Captain MacCallister would come to our aid if I asked. But have I asked him to take part in a battle that cannae be won? Have I invited him into a trap?"

"Aye, there's nae doubt but that the blackhearted bastard will make an attempt to take our town," Campbell said. "'N Captain MacCallister is only one man. But there is nae need to remind ye, Leftenant Colonel, what a man he is."

McGregor nodded. "Aye. I sincerely believe that Duff MacCallister will be the salvation of Antelope Wells, and indeed of every other town this man Schofield has taken since he began."

"I'll have to be for meetin' him to give him a good welcome, 'n to tell him everything we know about Schofield 'n his army," Campbell said. "How long before he will get here?"

"The telegram was from Lordsburg, 'n 'tis a two-day trip from there," McGregor said.

Chapter Ten

Lordsburg

"Will we be stayin' in a hotel tonight?" Elmer asked.

"Aye, I can get us the rooms we'll need."

"Perhaps I will not be welcome," Wang suggested.

"You'll be welcome, Mr. Wang," Meagan said. "I'm quite certain that Duff will be able to make the necessary arrangements."

"I would like accommodations for the night," Duff told the hotel clerk. "Three rooms, one for the lady, one for me. My two friends will share the third room."

"If that Chinaman is one of your two friends, he'll not be sharin' a room with no one. Leastwise, not in this hotel."

"Very well, then I shall need four rooms, one for each of us."

"Mister, you aren't understanding me. It isn't that he can't share a room, it's that he can't stay here at all."

Duff assumed a very haughty British accent. "My good man, I am Sir Duff MacCallister, an envoy of

Her Majesty, the Queen. Mr. Wang is my valet. Now, if he is good enough to be a personal houseguest of President Chester Arthur, I fail to see why he may not qualify to be a paid guest in this establishment."

"Oh!" the clerk said, startled and intimidated by Duff's response. "By all means, sir, you and your personal, uh, servant—"

"He is much more than a servant, sir. He is my gentleman's gentleman." Duff leaned closer and added, "A position in my country that is regarded with much esteem."

"Yes, sir, you are all welcome in the Lordsburg House," the clerk said. "The Chinaman included. It's like you said, anyone who can be the president's guest in the White House is certainly welcome here." He turned the registration book toward Duff.

"Duff, what do you mean Wang was a guest of President Arthur?" Meagan asked as they all gathered in the upstairs hallway just outside the three rooms. "When did that happen?"

"Why, it has nae happened," Duff said. "At least, nae to my knowledge."

"But you told the clerk that he had been a guest of the president."

"Did ye nae listen, lass? I dinnae say he *had* been a guest of the President. I said he was *good* enough to be a guest of the president. And ye'll nae be denying the truth of that, will ye?"

Elmer laughed out loud. "Yes, ma'am, that's what he said, all right."

Meagan laughed as well. "Now that I think about

it, that is what you said. And I certainly agree with you, when you say that Wang is good enough to be a guest of the President of the United States. Why, I can't think of anyone who would not be graced by his presence.

"*Shifu* Duff, you, Elmer, and Missy Meagan are my friends," Wang said. "I am much humbled by your friendship."

Shortly after they went to their rooms, Duff heard a quiet knock on his door.

"Duff?"

It was Meagan's voice and he moved quickly to open the door and invite her in. "I've but one chair. Ye can sit on the chair or on the bed."

Meagan smiled provocatively. "Or we could both lie in the bed."

With an almost beatific smile, Meagan returned to her own room. Duff decided to take a walk around town. The first place he visited was the local newspaper office, where he requested any articles they may have printed about what was going on down in the Boot-heel of New Mexico.

"Oh," the newspaper publisher replied. "You would be talking about the man who calls himself Prime Director. Ebenezer Schofield, formerly a general in the United States Army. As a matter of fact I have quite a few articles, if you would care to buy the issues."

"Aye, I would glad to buy them."

"You would be surprised at just how many people want to treat the newspaper office as a lending library," the publisher said as he began gathering the requested issues. "I have to make a living the same as everyone else."

"I'm just passing through your town. Would ye mind if I sat on the bench there to read the papers?"

The publisher smiled. "Why, no, I wouldn't mind at all. To see someone reading the papers would be a good advertisement. Would you like a cup of coffee? I've some fresh made."

"Aye, 'n m' thanks to ye."

For the next several minutes Duff read the papers and sipped at his coffee. "I wonder if I might make an inquiry?"

"Sure. As publisher of the newspaper I pride myself on keeping up with events. How can I help you?"

"Why is it that the army has taken nae hand in the business south of here?"

"I see that you haven't gotten to that issue yet." The publisher looked through the papers he had given Duff, selected one, then handed it to him. "This will answer your question."

Duff read the article about the request for help from some citizens representing the town of Antelope Wells. The article went into great detail about the Posse Comitatus Act. It editorialized that the newspaper disagreed with that act and felt that the army should come to the rescue of those citizens who were being put at risk by Ebenezer Schofield.

Duff considered the implications. On the one hand, it meant that his friend Charles McGregor could count on no help whatever from the army. But there was a positive side to it. Without the army, Duff could come up with a plan of action without worrying about any interference.

* * *

When Duff stepped into the dining room later that evening, he saw that it was already crowded with diners. Sitting at one of the tables were three cowboys. They seemed to be enjoying each other's company as their conversation was loud and their laughter even louder.

He located the table occupied by Elmer and Meagan and joined them. "Where's Wang?"

"You know how particular Wang is. He went over to check on the horses to make sure they're all right."

"Aye, one of his more sterling qualities is his attention to detail."

"There he is now," Meagan said.

Looking toward the door of the dining room they saw that Wang had stepped inside and was studying the room.

Duff knew that he wasn't just looking for them, but was making himself familiar with the layout and the people in the room. His reason for such caution was instantly justified when one of the cowboys challenged him.

"Hey, Chinaman, are you sure you're in the right place? There ain't no slant-eyes allowed in here. Just whites."

Elmer got up.

"Elmer, *dinnae* be for making a scene," Duff said quietly.

"I'll be just real quiet about it," Elmer promised. He walked over to the table where the cowboys were sitting.

"What the hell do you want, old man?" asked the same man who had called out to Wang.

"I was thinkin' maybe I'd do you three boys a favor," Elmer said.

"Yeah? Well just what kind o' favor is it you got in mind? Buyin' us a drink to go with our supper, maybe?"

The other two laughed.

"No, nothin' like that. I was thinkin' more along the lines of maybe keepin' you three boys from gettin' hurt."

"What do you mean? How are we goin' to get hurt?"

"Well sir, that Chinaman that you just insulted is Mr. Wang," Elmer said. "He's my friend, and if you three are real nice, I believe I can talk him into not hurting you."

"Not hurting us?" another of the three said, then he laughed out loud. "Not hurting us, you say, and him being a Chinaman?"

All three of the men enjoyed a boisterous laugh.

"Yes, he is a Chinaman. But he isn't just any Chinaman, you see. He is what you call a Shaolin priest."

"A priest is he? Ha! I ain't never seen no Chinaman priest, but even if he is a priest, it don't make no never mind, on account of he ain't got no business bein' in here."

"He's comin' in here to pray for our souls, is he?" one of the others asked, again to the laughter of all three.

Elmer chuckled. "Truth to tell, I don't reckon Mr. Wang gives a damn about your souls. A Shaolin priest ain't that kind of a priest. He's a special kind of priest who has a special way of fightin'."

"Special way o' fightin'? Tell me ol' man, what's so special about his fightin'?"

"Well you see, it's this way. If he wanted to, he could come over here, jerk your tongue out of your mouth, and hand it to you before you would even know what happened. I've seen men like him kill a bull in full charge, just by standin' in front of the bull 'n hittin' 'im between his eyes with the edge of their hand. And you have just insulted such a man."

"Is that a fact? Well now, I didn't know a Chinaman could be insulted. I thought they was too dumb."

The conversation was interrupted by the sound of a gunshot. One of the three men called out in alarm and grabbed his hand. The pistol he had just slipped from his holster was laying on the floor

Everyone in the restaurant looked over at Duff, who was standing and holding a smoking gun in his hand.

"You shot at me. You just hit my gun, but you could have put a hole in my hand."

"Aye I could have. Ye see, m' friend was trying to have a nice chat with ye, but ye rather sneakily extracted your pistol from its holster. I'm sure ye would all admit that 'tis a bit difficult to engage in an amicable conversation when one of the participants is holding a gun. Would ye other two gentlemen be for taking your pistols out and dropping them onto the floor? I'd appreciate it very much."

"What? Why should we do that?" one of the other two men asked. "We wasn't the ones that pulled iron, it was Percy that done that."

"Ye should do it so my friend can continue his conversation with you," Duff answered. "And ye should also do it because I asked you, and because I'll put a bullet in each of your kneecaps if you don't. By the way, I should tell you that my pistol is a British Enfield revolver, which fires a .47 caliber round—large enough that it will totally destroy a kneecap. In the hands of a skilled shootist it can be quite an effective weapon. At the risk of being a labeled a braggart, I feel that I should inform you that I am quite a good marksman. Should it come to that, 'tis quite likely that you all will never walk again."

The cowboy who'd been shot at, the one named Percy said, "Dave, Neil, if you two got any sense, you'll do like he says. He's a real good shot. I mean, you seen how he shot that pistol right out of my hand."

"All right, all right. We'll do it," one of the men said as he reached for the gun in his holster.

"Would ye be a good couple of lads and stand up so that I can tell for sure you'll nae be for trying to trick me?"

Dave and Neil stood up, then dropped their guns.

"Now, Mr. Gleason, please do continue with your conversation," Duff invited.

During the conversation and the shooting, Wang had advanced no more than ten feet into the dining room and he remained there in the middle of the floor as if waiting to see how the confrontation between Elmer and the three cowboys was going to develop.

"I see you got yourself a knife there, Davey boy," Elmer said.

"He didn't say nothin' 'bout droppin' no knife. All he said was that we was supposed to drop our guns."

Elmer held his hand out. "Give it to me."

Dave hesitated for a second, then he pulled his knife from the sheath and handed it to him. "What are you goin' to do with it?"

"Are you any good with this knife? What I'm askin' you is, can you throw it?"

"Hell yeah, he can throw it," Neil said. "I once seen 'im pin a runnin' rabbit to the ground with it. That rabbit was just real good eatin' too."

Elmer handed the knife back. "Let us see how good you are. Throw it at somethin'."

"Throw it at what?"

Elmer leaned in and whispered so quietly that only Dave, Neil, and Percy could hear him.

"What?" Dave replied, shocked by Elmer's response. "Are you serious?"

"Yeah, I'm serious."

Suddenly, and without warning, Dave threw the knife at Wang.

Wang caught the knife by its handle and in almost the same motion, threw the knife back. The blade buried itself nearly an inch deep into the table right in front of where Dave was standing.

Every diner in the room had grown quiet from the beginning of the conversation, but they gasped when they saw Dave throw the knife at Wang. The gasp grew even louder when they saw Wang catch the knife and hurl it back.

"Now, what do you think, boys? Is it all right with you three if Mr. Wang joins me 'n my friends at our table for supper?"

"Uh, yeah. Yeah. Sure," Dave said. "We didn't mean nothin' by it. We was just funnin' a bit. That's all."

Duff, who had put his gun away, looked toward one of the waiters, who, like everyone else, had been staring in complete shock at the events as they unfolded.

"Waiter," Duff called out to him. He pointed to the three cowboys. "Would ye be for givin' m' new friends here a drink 'n put it on my tab?"

"What the hell? You're buyin' us a drink?" Dave asked.

"Friends do that for friends, don't they? And now that we've resolved these little differences between us, aren't we friends?"

"Yeah," Dave said with a wide smile. "We're friends." He looked over at Wang. "Why, I'm even willin' to be friends with the Chinaman."

The expression on Wang's face had not changed during the entire conversation, and it didn't change now with Dave's affirmation of friendship. He did, however, nod in recognition, then he crossed to Duff's table, the object of intense attention from everyone else in the room.

Chapter Eleven

Cottonwood Springs

It had taken General Peterson but twenty-four hours to come up with the information Schofield had asked him to gather on Duff MacCallister.

He stood in front of Schofield, rendering his report. "Duff MacCallister came to the United States from Scotland some few years ago. Since his arrival, he has become well-known enough that there is a rather significant amount of information about him in the newspaper morgue. He is a man of some considerable wealth, currently residing in Wyoming where he owns a very successful ranch just south of the town of Chugwater.

"It is neither his wealth nor his success as a rancher that has made him well-known, though. It is his unerring marksmanship and his coolness in armed engagements that has earned him a degree of fame. He has been in a dozen or more battles and has shown himself to be more than proficient. Also he has two men who are often involved in the same confrontations. I haven't been able to find out anything about them, but we must assume that they are worthy companions, for I don't believe a man such as MacCallister would be associated with men who didn't meet his standards."

"And what is MacCallister's relationship with the mayor of Antelope Wells?" Schofield asked.

"From what I have learned, he is not only McGregor's friend, but he also has a great deal of respect for him. The two men served together in the Black Watch Regiment."

"Charles McGregor." Schofield mouthed the name in such a way as to show his dislike for the man. "He is the one remaining obstacle to the successful conclusion of my goal to establish a new nation. And now you are suggesting that this man"—he picked up the letter so he could read the name—"MacCallister could strengthen McGregor's resolve."

"Yes, sir, that is exactly what I'm saying."

"After the town of Antelope Wells falls into our hands, if McGregor should survive the battle, it will be necessary to eliminate him by way of public execution. His continued presence might well inspire an uprising of the people." Schofield smiled. "We will replace him with our ally who calls himself Angus Pugh."

"How will we know who Angus Pugh is?" Peterson asked.

"I'm quite sure he will make his presence known to us. Have you any information on when to expect this man MacCallister?"

Peterson smiled. "Angus Pugh tells us that he has already reached Lordsburg."

Schofield stroked his chin as he contemplated his next move. "From there he will have to take the stagecoach, for there is no other way to get from Lordsburg to Antelope Wells. Have Lieutenant Mack take some men to Lordsburg and eliminate the problem."

"Yes, sir."

Lordsburg

While Elmer and Wang were getting the horses ready the next morning, Duff and Meagan were in the general store buying the provisions—bacon, canned beans, canned peaches, flour, coffee, and sugar—they would need for the two-day ride to Antelope Wells. Although Meagan had worn a dress while on the train, she knew a dress wouldn't be functional for a long ride in the saddle. As a result, she was wearing jeans and a denim shirt. Her attire made her the subject of many a disapproving stare, though nobody said anything about it.

Throwing their purchases in a cloth bag, they left the store and walked down to the stable, where Elmer and Wang were waiting for them with four saddled horses and two pack mules.

"There are very few water caches between here 'n there," the livery operator had told Elmer and Wang when he'd learned where they intended to go. "But the truth is they ain't always got water in 'em, 'n there are damn few cricks in the whole Bootheel."

It was the livery operator's warning that had convinced Elmer that they should buy the mules. While one carried their luggage and food supply, the other had two goatskins of water.

"What the hell! You're a woman!" the livery operator said as he saw them preparing to mount up for their trip.

"Now see there, Duff, I tole' you 'n Wang that they

was somethin' different about that one," Elmer said, pointing toward Meagan. "Turns out it's a woman, just like I was a-thinkin'."

Meagan laughed and held up her hands. "I give up. You got me. I am a woman."

"There ain't no call for a woman to be makin' this trip. It's too dangerous."

"How much danger can I be in, when I have these three brave men to protect me?" Meagan asked the liveryman. She made a clucking sound then rode away before he could respond.

"According to what the man at the hotel said, that's him," Lieutenant Mack of Schofield's Legion said as he pointed at Duff and the little cavalcade that was with him.

"I thought we was just comin' after one man," Sergeant Keaton said. "They's four of 'em."

"And there are five of us. Besides which, one of 'em is a Chinaman, 'n accordin' to the hotel clerk, one of 'em is a woman. So that's the same as sayin' that there are only two of 'em."

"How are we supposed to tell which one of 'em is the woman, when all four of 'em is dressed just alike?" Foster asked.

"It doesn't matter which one is a woman," Mack said. "I intend for us to kill them all."

"The woman, too?" Welch asked in surprise.

"Even though we are not in uniform, we are at war, and this is a military operation. Any military operation during time of war has but one objective," Mack said.

"And that is to close with, and to capture or kill the enemy. They are the enemy."

"Where at are we goin' to do it?" Keaton asked.

"With those two pack mules, they won't be moving very fast. The Notch is five miles south. We can beat them there, easy, and that'll be a really good place for us to set up an ambush. We'll be on them before they even see us."

They mounted up and turned their horses southward.

"Hey, Lieutenant, do we have to kill all of them?" Pounders asked after a while. "I mean, right away?"

"Of course we do Why do you ask?" Mack replied.

"I was just a-thinkin' 'bout the woman is all. Seems to me like if we wasn't to kill her right away, that is, at least if we was to hold off on killin' her for a little while, well we could"—Pounders paused in midsentence and flashed a wide, ribald grin, showing yellowed and misaligned teeth—"have us a little fun with her."

"Yeah, Lieutenant, what do you say?" Foster asked.

Mack studied the hungry expression of the four men under his command, then he smiled. "I'm first."

"You can be first, long as we get to watch," Pounders said.

"Why, I reckon we'll all be a-watchin', won't we?" Foster asked as they reached the Notch and reined in.

Mack laughed. "Pounders, climb up to the top of the Notch 'n keep an eye open. Let us know when you see them coming."

"All right."

"Sir," Mack said.

"What?"

"When you speak to me, you will say *sir*."

"Look, I know you're sposed to be an officer 'n all,

but this here ain't no real army. I was in the real army not too long ago, 'n I run off. Why would I want to join any other army after I left the real army?"

"How much were you making per month in the real army?" Mack asked.

"Twelve dollars," Pounders replied.

"And what are you making in Schofield's Legion?"

A broad smile spread across Pounders' face. "I'm makin' a hunnert dollars a month."

"Then if you are making that much, don't you think you could follow our rules?"

"Yeah, damn right I can . . . uh . . . sir!" Pounders replied.

"Then get up there and keep your eyes peeled."

"Yes, sir!" Pounders replied emphatically. He augmented his reply with a snappy salute, then he climbed up the side of the hill.

Duff and Megan were riding side by side. Elmer and Wang were behind them, each of them leading a mule. Traveling in relative silence, the quiet was broken only by the sound of the jangle of harness and hoof falls on the hard-packed road.

Highly attuned to all sight and sound around them, Wang remembered the words of Master Tse of the Shaolin temple of Changlin. *"It is not enough to merely observe nature. You must become nature. One who becomes nature is aware of any disruption in the natural order of things. Such a person can never be surprised by an unexpected event, for it is impossible for any event to ever be unexpected."*

Approximately five hundred yards ahead of them

and just over a relatively substantial hill on the right side of the road, the behavior of the birds was not in accord with the natural order of things.

"Master Duff," Wang called, using the respectful address.

Duff had told him many times that they were friends, and no such deferential title was required, but he'd stopped when he realized that Wang was more comfortable with it.

"Aye, Wang?"

"There are some people behind the hill that is ahead of us. I believe that they mean us harm, for they are purposely keeping their persons in concealment."

"Do you know how many?"

Wang looked again at the dispersal pattern of the birds. "I believe there may be more of them than there are of us."

"Meagan, perhaps you should—"

"I will feel safer if I am with you," Meagan said, interrupting Duff in midsentence. "Besides, now that we know they are there, we have the advantage of surprise over them, because they are unaware that we know."

"All right. You can stay with us."

"I see 'em," Pounders called down from above.

"How far away are they?" Mack asked.

Pounders carefully raised his head just enough to see without being seen. "They ain't more 'n a hunnert, maybe a hunnert 'n fifty yards now 'n they—" Pounders paused for a moment. "What the hell?" he asked in surprise.

"What is it? What's wrong?" Mack asked.

"They's one of 'em that's missin'."

"Maybe he turned back," Mack suggested.

"If he did, how come he didn't take his horse? The reason I ask is one o' the horses has an empty saddle."

"Which one of them is missing?" Mack asked.

"Looks to me like it's the Chinaman who ain't there no more."

"Yeah, well, keep an eye on 'em 'n let us know when they are about twenty-five yards or so," Mack said.

"Hey, Pounders, you sure it's the Chinaman that's missin' 'n not the woman?" Foster asked. "Don't forget, we're plannin' on havin' some fun with her."

"It's the Chinaman," Pounders called back.

Mack and the others waited in silence for several more seconds.

"Where are they now, Pounders?" Mack called up to his lookout. "Hell, they should damn near be here by now."

Mack got no reply.

"What are you doin' up there, Pounders? You got your thumb up your ass? Where are they?"

Again Mack's query was unanswered.

"Foster, get up there and see what the hell Pounders is doing," Mack ordered.

"He's prob'ly thinkin' about that woman we're about to have some fun with," Foster said with a little chuckle as he climbed up the hill.

"Well?" Mack said after a few seconds of hearing nothing from the second man he had sent up. "Foster?"

"What's goin' on, Lieutenant? What happened to 'em?" Welch asked.

"Go take a look," Mack ordered.

"No, sir. I ain't goin' to do no such thing! They's got

to be somethin' funny that's a-goin' on up there, on account of we ain't heard nothin' back from either one of 'em."

Sergeant Keaton pulled his pistol and pointed it at Welch. "You'll either do what the lieutenant says or I'll kill you right here where you stand."

Under protest, but forced by the pistol in Keaton's hand, Welch followed the same path up the hill that Pounders and Foster had followed. And like them, Welch didn't make another sound.

"They's only two of us now!" Keaton said, his voice breaking with fear. "We've got to get out of here!"

"What the hell happened to them?" Mack wondered aloud. Like Keaton, he was staring up toward the top of the hill, which from their position couldn't actually be seen.

"Oh, I expect they ran into Mr. Wang," Duff said.

"What? Where . . . ? Where did you come from?" Mack asked, startled by the unexpected appearance of someone who was supposed to be their quarry.

Duff and Elmer were standing there, and both were holding guns pointed at Mack and Keaton.

"Oh, come now, 'n haven't ye had us under observation for the last several minutes? Are ye for telling me that ye didn't see us coming up the road?"

"I doubt they was a-seein' all that much, what with Wang kind of gettin' in their way 'n all," Elmer said.

"Aye, ye have a point there. Mr. Wang!" Duff called up the side of the hill. "Would ye be for sendin' the blokes back down?"

A second after Duff called up to Wang, there was a scraping, scuffling sound, and a man came sliding down the side of the hill. Mack and Keaton saw Welch hit the ground in front of them.

"Is he dead?" Keaton asked, his voice strained by fear.

Two more came sliding down, and like Welch, they lay flat on the ground where they hit.

"Damn. All three is dead!" Keaton said, but his declaration was disproved when the three men began to move.

The last person to come down the hill was Wang himself, who slid down the hill in the sitting position. When he reached the bottom of the hill, he stood up quickly.

By then Meagan had joined Duff and Elmer.

Welch groaned, then sat up. "What happened?"

"You tell me what happened," Mack demanded, his voice laced with anger.

"I don't remember a thing."

"I don't remember nothin' neither," Pounders said. "Leastwise, I don't remember nothin' after climbin' up to the top of the hill."

"It was the Chinaman," Foster said. "When I clumb up the hill, I seen 'im standin' there over Pounders. I pointed my gun at 'im, only a-fore I knowed what was happenin', seemed to me like ever'thing turned black, 'n when I come to, I was here 'n front o' ever'one."

"What is it you're a-aimin' to do with us?" Welch asked.

"Well now, that all depends," Duff said. "Would ye be for tellin' us what it is you have in mind for us?"

"We didn't have anything in mind, except for observation," Mack replied. "You are strangers here, and we were just wondering about you. That's all."

"Aye, 'tis wondering about us ye were, when every one of ye had a long gun in yer hands."

"What are we going to do with 'em, Duff?" Elmer asked.

"I've nae yet made up my mind. Would ye be for tellin' us who sent you to spy on us?"

"We don't have to tell you a damn thing," Mack said resolutely.

"Why don't you let Wang take care of 'em?" Elmer said. "Oncet, when I was in China, I seen a Chinaman take the skin right off a feller, peeled 'im like he was peelin' an apple he did. Damndest thing I ever seen. Well sir, iffen we was ter let Wang do that to this 'n here"—Elmer pointed to Mack, who he had correctly assumed was the leader of the group—"why, you'd see just what it is I'm talkin' about. 'Course, we wouldn't be gettin' no information from him, on account of when you peel the skin off of 'em, they wind up dyin'. But whilst he would be layin' there dyin' without no skin, the others would commence a-talkin' pretty quick so as not to have that same thing happen to them."

"Wang, would ye be for tellin' me now, if ye actually can skin this man alive as Elmer says?"

"If it is your wish," Wang said, pulling his knife from its sheath and taking a step toward Mack.

"No! No!" Mack screamed out in terror. "It was the Prime Director who sent us. Schofield! Ebenezer Schofield!"

"You want me to shoot all of 'em?" Elmer asked. "I mean we may as well. If we don't we're just goin' to have to put up with 'em again."

"What?" Keaton shouted in obvious terror.

"Or maybe we should just let Wang cut 'em up.

Yeah, I think I'd like to see him do that. Why, he could carve 'em up like they was baked turkey."

"No, no!" Welch said.

"I dinnae think that will be necessary," Duff said. "If ye gentlemen would be so good as to take off your boots, we'll nae have to kill you."

The five men glared, but they didn't challenge the pistols that were pointed at them. Sitting down, they removed their boots.

"Now, remove your clothes."

"What? Look here, you can't make us do that! Why, they's a woman here!" Pounders said. "I didn't know that at first, 'cause I couldn't rightly tell by the kind of clothes she's a-wearin'. But when you look close, why, it's clear as a bell she's a woman."

"You were perfectly prepared to shoot her, were you not?"

"Yeah, but I didn't know it at first. 'N besides, shootin' her ain't the same thing as takin' off your clothes in front of 'er."

"You do have on something under those clothes, don't you?"

"Underdrawers 'n a undershirt is all."

"That's enough. Strip down."

"The hell you say. I ain't about to take off my clothes," Keaton said.

"All right. There's nae need for ye to take off your clothes."

"You're damn right there is no need," Keaton said indignantly.

"I expect the other four men will cooperate with us. Elmer, ye can go ahead 'n shoot this one," Duff said, pointing to Keaton.

"Nah, like I said a while ago, I think I'd rather let Wang cut 'im up." Elmer said with a wicked smile.

"No! No! I'll take off my clothes! I'll take off my clothes!" Keaton shouted.

A moment later all five men were standing barefoot and wearing only their underwear.

"Now get your clothes and your boots up on your horses."

The men complied, then Meagan took the reins to the five horses because Elmer and Wang were leading the mules.

"We'll leave the horses and your clothes about five miles that way," Duff said, pointing south.

"Look here, are you telling us to walk five miles out here, without boots or clothes?" Mack asked.

"Oh, I'm telling ye nae such thing. I'm just telling ye where we'll be leaving the horses. I dinnae care whether ye walk the five miles or not. Ye can stay here, as far as I'm concerned."

"I'm goin' to kill you for this, mister!" Mack shouted angrily as he pointed at Duff. "Do you hear me? I'm goin' to kill you. I'm goin' to kill you, the Chinaman, that old son of a bitch, and the woman!"

"My oh my," Meagan said. "Have you ever heard such language from a naked man before?" She laughed as she and her companions rode away, leaving the five angry men behind them.

Chapter Twelve

Five miles south of the Notch

Having reached the spot designated as the place to leave the five horses taken from Mack and his men, Duff tied off the animals.

"Will the horses be all right here?" Meagan asked. "They didn't do anything wrong. I mean we can't hold against them what their owners tried to do."

"We'll give the creatures a bit of water here, and there's plenty of graze," Duff said. "They'll be fine until the others come for them."

Duff, Meagan, Elmer, and Wang all filled their hats with water, then offered it to the five horses, all of whom drunk thirstily.

"I think we should empty their rifles 'n search the saddlebags for any more ammunition," Elmer suggested. "That'll keep 'em from runnin' us down."

"Aye, very good idea, Elmer," Duff agreed.

Some ten minutes later, with the five outlaw horses taken care of, all the rifles emptied, and spare ammunition taken, Duff and the others continued with their journey to Antelope Wells. The way south was more of a trail than a road. Heading out through the Mogollon Desert, it was filled with mesquite, creosote bushes, cholla and pear cactus, as well as a few scattered ponderosa pines.

When they made camp that night, they had traveled over sixty miles. The air was filled with the aroma of spitted rabbits roasting over the fire. Golden sparks from the fire rode the heat waves high into the sky, there to get lost among the brilliant scatter of stars.

As they waited for their meal to be cooked, Meagan used the light of the fire to read more from the book that Duff had given her.

"I thought you was finished with that book," Elmer said.

"I am, actually," Meagan said. "I'm just looking for one of the passages I wanted to read again."

"What for would you want to read it again?" Elmer asked.

"Because it is so beautifully written. Oh, here it is. Listen to this." She began to read.

Gideon was standing on a small overlook, looking down toward the Milvian Bridge, appraising the military situation. Spread out on the other side of the bridge for many rods in each direction, lay the army of Maxentius, one hundred thousand men, well armed and seasoned by battle. Dozens of colorful tents rose from the grounds across the river and flags and pennants fluttered from long poles, identifying the various legions.

A constant cloud of dust hung over the area as horses and men moved about, shifting positions and preparing for battle. Often the clarion notes of trumpets could be heard, along with the beat of drums.

Gideon had only twenty thousand men, and the contrast in the sizes of the two armies was dramatically evident now, as the two forces moved into position.

Abandoning his position, Gideon returned to the others.

"How many?" Phegamon asked.

"'Five times our number.'"

"There are too many," Nahman said.

"We have something more powerful than mere numbers," Gideon said. "We have the resolution of our purpose, the girding of honor, the approbation of our people, and the knowledge of our place in history. We will fight."

Meagan looked up, her eyes glowing golden by the light of the fire. "Oh, Duff, is that not beautiful? Is Charles McGregor not a wonderful writer?"

Duff poked at the fire for a moment before he spoke again.

"Aye, he is very good writer. He was also nearly my uncle. Or at least, my uncle-in-law."

"Yes, McGregor! I had not thought about it! Skye was his niece?" Meagan asked.

"Aye."

Meagan knew about Skye McGregor, the woman

Duff was to have married. Skye had been killed by an evil sheriff and his deputies, when she leaped out in front of Duff to prevent him from being shot.

Duff killed the sheriff and all three deputies, and it was for that reason that he had come to the United States.

Elmer and Wang also knew Duff's sad tale, and they stared quietly into the fire to allow Duff time with his own thoughts.

Meagan reached out to put her hand on Duff's. "I think there was another reason why I wanted to read this particular passage. In a way, it mirrors the situation your friend McGregor now faces. I mean an army of such superior numbers. As he contemplates what lies before him, I wonder if he is remembering what he wrote."

"Looks to me like the rabbit's about done," Elmer said after a moment of silence. It was obvious that he was trying to change the subject. "That is, if the heathen didn't ruin it when he cooked it."

"I do not wish my friend to eat bad rabbit," Wang said. "I will eat my rabbit and yours."

"No, now there ain't no need for you to be a-doin' nothin' like that," Elmer said quickly.

Duff and Meagan laughed, their laughter breaking the moment of melancholy.

"Looks to me like the *heathen* got you on that one, Elmer," Meagan said.

"Yeah, I reckon he did," Elmer replied with a submissive smile as he reached for the rabbit.

"Ladies first," Wang said.

"Who's the heathen now?" Duff teased.

* * *

It was a chagrined and dispirited group of men who returned to Cottonwood Springs to report back to Schofield.

"I trust you were successful in the job you were given," Schofield said.

"I, uh, that is we, uh, were surprised," Lieutenant Mack said.

"Surprised? I sent you out to perform a simple job," Schofield said. "Your task was to eliminate Duff MacCallister. Are you telling me that you failed to do so?"

"Yes, sir, but it wasn't nearly as simple as we thought." Mack had shed his civilian clothes and once more donned his uniform, thinking that by so doing, he would be able to salvage some degree of self-respect. "To begin with, he wasn't alone. There were three others with him, and one of them was a Chinaman who isn't like anyone I've ever seen before."

"There may well have been four of them, but there were five of you," Schofield said. "And you are an officer. Don't tell me that you are so insufficiently schooled in tactics that you were unable to use cover and concealment to set up an effective ambush."

"It's not that. It was the Chinaman, I tell you. He sneaked up on us."

"He sneaked up on you? It was his one gun against your five?"

"No, it was nothing like that. I mean, he didn't even have a gun."

"Let me see if I understand this. One unarmed Chinaman managed to disrupt the ambush that you had established with five armed men. Have I got that right?"

"I know that doesn't sound good, but that's the way it was."

Schofield reached up and jerked the shoulder boards off Mack's uniform. "You are no longer an officer," he said pointedly. "Keaton is now a private, and you will take his place as a sergeant, but I caution you, even your rank of sergeant is provisionary."

"Let me try again," Mack pleaded. "We know he is going to Antelope Wells. I can sneak in and kill him. He won't expect to see me there."

"That won't be necessary," Schofield said. "In anticipation of your possible failure I have put into position a secondary plan. Two of our number are already in Antelope Wells, poised to act in the event MacCallister got by you. And since he did get by you, the plan will automatically go into effect."

When Duff and the others first saw the irregular lumps of terrain ahead of them, they thought they were seeing only geological features. After all, the protrusions were the same color as the ground from which they had risen. But as they got closer, they realized that they were looking at buildings of adobe blocks made from the very ground upon which they were standing. They were approaching a village.

Antelope Wells was small, even when compared with the other small Western towns Duff had seen. But, because it was the first semblance of civilization he and his friends had seen in the last forty-eight hours, it was a welcome sight.

As they rode down the main street they were the object of attention from the townspeople who happened to be outside. Because of the isolation of the town, visitors were quite rare.

Just ahead of them they saw a sign that read O. D. CLAYTON LIVERY AND CORRAL and headed there to make arrangements for boarding their horses and mules.

O. D. Clayton was a big man, at least six-feet-five-inches tall and weighing well over 250 pounds. He stepped out to greet them. "Looking for a place to board your critters, are you? Well, you've come to the right place." He laughed. "Actually, you've come to the only place. How long are you going to be here?"

"We don't know," Duff said.

"Well, how about if you pay me for a week in advance, that way—"

"O.D., there's nae need for ye to be charging them anything, for 'tis the city that will be paying the toll," said a very Scottish-sounding voice.

Duff turned toward the speaker. "Sergeant Major Campbell!" With a broad smile, he extended his hand in greeting.

"Aye, 'tis me in the flesh, Captain MacCallister. 'N 'tis good to see you again after all these many years,"

The two men exchanged warm handshakes.

"Sheriff, would you sign a marker for the stay?" Clayton asked.

"Aye, Mister Clayton, 'tis glad I am to do so," Campbell said as he signed the document presented to him.

"Sheriff, is it?" Duff asked.

"Aye," Campbell replied. "Leftenant Colonel McGregor is the mayor, and 'tis high sheriff he made me." He chuckled. "Oh course, some o' the good citizens don't quite take to the title of *high sheriff*, but 'tis already a sheriff the county has, so His Honor the mayor came up with the idea of high sheriff. Come. 'Tis near time for dinner, 'n the colonel will be inviting all of ye."

"All of us?" Elmer asked.

"Sure 'n if you're talking about the Chinese gentleman with ye, he'll be the colonel's guest just as all of ye will be. 'N if there is someone who would make an objection to that fact, he'll have to settle with me."

"What do you think, Wang? The sheriff here called you a gentleman." Elmer chuckled. "There's always a first, I reckon."

"Yes, there is always a first, so you should not despair, Elmer. I am sure the time will come when you, too, will be called a gentleman," Wang replied.

Meagan laughed. "Elmer, I think Mr. Wang just scored a point with you."

"My word," Campbell said in surprise. "Ye be a woman?"

"'N would ye be for tellin' me, Sergeant Major, is it blind ye have become?" Duff asked.

"I beg your pardon, Miss, for nae taking notice of ye before now. 'Tis for sure had I looked more closely, I would have seen right away what a lovely young lass ye be."

Meagan chuckled. "Worry not, Sergeant Major, you have been redeemed by your golden tongue."

"Ah, Sergeant Major, 'tis a point ye have just proven for me, being that all we Scots have a golden tongue," Duff said.

"Duff, before we join your friends for dinner, could

we check into the hotel so that I might clean away some of the dirt 'n grime, and put on clothes that are in more keeping with a lady?"

"Come," Campbell said. "I'll make arrangements for your stay, 'n the city will be for paying your bill there as well."

"Sergeant Major, I dinnae want to cost the city so much money," Duff said. "The invitation was for me, 'tis sure I am that the colonel is nae aware that I brought my friends with me."

"Under the circumstances, Captain, Leftenant Colonel McGregor will be so glad that you're here that all will be welcome. Now, come with me 'n I'll get ye checked in to the hotel."

The five walked the block down Cactus Street to a rather substantial-looking two-story building identified by a large sign painted across the false front— DUNN HOTEL. Sheriff Campbell was carrying Meagan's carpetbag.

"Warren?" Campbell called as they stepped into the lobby. "Warren, would ye be for presenting yourself behind your desk now? 'Tis some customers I've brought you."

The desk clerk came from a room just behind the front desk. "Customers, you say?" he responded with a wide grin. The grin disappeared when he saw Wang. "Uh, Sheriff, I don't know if—"

"You don't know what?" Campbell replied, challenging Warren's obvious reaction to Wang.

"I mean . . ."

"How many rooms will ye require, Captain?" Campbell asked, ignoring the hotel clerk's protestations.

"Three."

"And a tub of hot water, if you please," Meagan added.

"The city will be paying for it," Campbell said.

"Yes, sir. Three rooms," the clerk acquiesced.

"And a tub of hot water," Meagan said again.

"Yes ma'am, and a tub of hot water."

Duff and the others were given three adjacent rooms on the second floor.

Duff's room was the first off the stairs. Meagan had the room next to his, and Elmer and Wang had the room on the other side of Meagan. All had a view of the street.

Duff didn't take a bath as Meagan did, but he did make generous use of the washbasin and pitcher of water that sat on the chest of drawers.

Chapter Thirteen

It was just under an hour after they had checked in when Sheriff Campbell, by prearrangement, met them in the lobby of the hotel. Meagan was wearing one of her finer dresses selected from her personal inventory at Meagan's Dress Emporium.

Campbell's eyes widened at the sight of her. "I cannae believe that when I seen ye at the corral I dinnae ken at once that ye be a woman. 'N 'tis more than a woman, 'tis a woman of great beauty, ye be," Campbell said.

"Why, I thank you sir, for your most gracious words," Meagan replied.

Campbell led the four down the street until they reached a restaurant called Bear Tracks. Just before they stepped inside, however, someone came up to Campbell.

"Sheriff, I was just visitin' m' friend Joe Bigby in your jail. He's done his three days. How come it is that he ain't out yet?"

"Now, Cooper, ye know that as soon as I let him out

the two of ye will just start drinkin' again, 'n next time could be that both of ye will wind up in jail."

"Nah, we're just goin' ter have a couple o' drinks is all, to celebrate him gettin' out of jail."

Campbell nodded. "Captain, if you'll go on in, you'll see the leftenant colonel. Would you be for telling him, please, that I'll be along directly."

"Aye," Duff agreed.

Having learned from Campbell that Duff had brought some more people with him, McGregor had arranged for two tables to be pulled next to each other so they could all sit together. McGregor stood so that he could receive Meagan graciously.

"The sergeant major?" he asked, not seeing the sheriff with them.

"He was called to the jail for a bit, but he said he would be here soon," Duff explained then introduced those who were with him.

McGregor made a production of holding Meagan's chair for her as she was seated.

"'Tis thanking ye I am for responding to my call for help." He smiled at Meagan. "'N the quite unexpected treat of gracing us with such a beautiful young lady."

"Oh my, Leftenant Colonel. Sure 'n the words that roll so trippingly from yer tongue are quite beguiling to the ears of this wee lass," Meagan said in a beautiful Scottish brogue.

"Och! 'N 'tis Scottish ye be?" McGregor asked, surprised by Meagan's response.

Duff laughed. "Nae, 'tis skilled in the art of mimicry she is, 'n she's but having a bit o' fun with ye, as so often she does with me."

"I do hope you forgive me, Colonel McGregor," Meagan said in her own voice.

"There is nothing to forgive, lass, for 'twas a genuine pleasure to hear the native brogue in a female voice."

As was his custom, Duff had made a thorough perusal of the room as soon as they entered, and he'd seen a man with silver hair and a perfectly trimmed beard sitting at a table in the back corner. But it wasn't his tonsorial mien that drew his attention. The man was wearing the gray and gold uniform of a Confederate general, complete with gold sash and saber. Sitting at the table with him was a very attractive young woman.

"Colonel McGregor, may I congratulate you on your book? *Gideon's Sword* was most delightful to read," Meagan said.

"What a wonderful thing for ye to say, m' dear!" McGregor said. "'Tis not often that I actually get to meet someone who has read one of m' books."

"How many have you written?" Meagan asked.

"I have had two published, and I've been meaning to start a third, but have nae been able to because of the concerns that face me now. They be the same events that have led me to call upon Captain MacCallister. 'N without my full attention, 'twould be little I could write that would be fit to publish."

"From what I have observed of your writing, I'm certain it is good."

McGregor was embarrassed by the flattery and was spared having to respond to it by the timely arrival of Sheriff Campbell.

"Sorry I'm late, sir, but I had forgotten that Bigby's three days were up. 'Twas Cooper that reminded me."

"Ye've missed nothing, for our visit is just starting." McGregor turned his attention back to Duff. "Captain, 'tis good that ye brought friends, but I think I should be for telling you what danger there be. I would nae feel right about soliciting your help without you knowing the full story."

"We're here to listen to the telling of the full story," Duff replied.

McGregor folded his hands on the table and looked at everyone before he began his narrative. "The brigand who is the cause of all our trouble is General Ebenezer J. Schofield."

"I read in the paper that he was a general, and was surprised that the rank was for real and not some affectation."

"Nae, Captain, the rank is authentic, for in truth, he was a general, a classmate of General, later to be President, Ulysses Grant," McGregor said. "And like Grant, Schofield was a Union general during the American Civil War. The affectation he has adopted is his insistence upon being called the Prime Director.

"General Schofield threw it all away when Grant became president. I don't know how much ye have followed the politics here in America, but the Grant presidency was full of corruption. Evil people like Schofield took advantage of the naïve trust of a good man like Grant. Soon they were enriching themselves in every nefarious scheme there was, General Schofield being the worst of the lot.

"Schofield was caught and sent to prison, but didn't serve very long because of his war record, 'n also because of his friendship with the president."

"'N now Schofield has added treason to his villainy, for he has raised an army to make war against his own country," Campbell said.

"Aye, the sergeant major is right." McGregor said,

continuing his story. "Schofield has an army with him. Schofield's Legion, he calls them, 'n 'tis an actual army I'm talking about. He has at least fifty uniformed men in his army, perhaps more, complete with a well-organized military command structure."

"Uniforms, ye say?" Duff asked.

"Aye, green 'n red they are, a little like those of the Bavarian Regiment."

"Yesterday we were accosted by five men. They were nae wearing uniforms, but they did tell us they were sent by this man Schofield," Duff said.

"Sergeant Major, did ye know of this?" McGregor asked.

Campbell looked surprised. "I knew nothing of it. How did anyone know they were coming?"

"A good question, for we've kept the visit quiet."

"Och, but we told General Culpepper," Campbell said.

"General Culpepper?" Duff asked.

McGregor glanced over at the man in the uniform of a Confederate general. "That is General Culpepper. Sure, Sergeant Major, 'n ye would nae be suggesting that the general would betray us?"

Campbell shook his head. "I would nae think that he would do such a thing of free will 'n evil intent. But 'tis indeed a mystery as to how Schofield learned of the captain's visit. "'N remember, the general is in his dotage."

"Dinnae forget that there be other telegraphers in the sending of messages," Duff said. "It could be any of them."

"Aye, 'tis so," McGregor agreed. "And I cannae believe that General Culpepper, even unintentionally, would be for betraying us."

"What happened to the men that ye encountered yesterday?" Campbell asked.

"Wang happened to them," Elmer said. He went on to explain how Wang had slipped up on them and managed to disarm three of them. He also told how, after all five were disarmed that they were made to undress and walk five miles, barefoot, to recover their horses and clothes.

By the time he finished his story all were laughing, McGregor and Campbell because it was new to them, while Duff, Meagan, and the others laughed with the memory of it.

"Perhaps they were nae sent to intercept them, but to collect taxes from them," Campbell suggested.

"Aye, that could be, though normally such tax-countin' teams are in uniform," McGregor agreed.

"Collect taxes? How can he do that? We aren't residents."

"In your case, he would be for calling it a visitors tax. Schofield believes that he has the right to count taxes because he has already declared this to be a sovereign state. 'Tis his claim that the taxes are to support Schofield's Legion and the army is for our protection."

"Protection, nothing," Sheriff Campbell said. "The only ones we need protection from is his army itself."

"Aye, the sergeant major is quite right."

"Have ye sent for me to help you resist the taxes?" Duff asked.

"Nae, Captain, we can resist the taxes, for we have nae paid them yet. But Schofield has already occupied every other town 'n village in all the Bootheel. 'Tis only Antelope Wells that is preventing him from conquering all the land, 'n making this a new country with himself at its head."

"Schofield is making preparations to attack the town, as he did just a few days ago in La Tenja," Campbell explained.

"Half the male citizens and many of the womenfolk 'n children were killed in that dastardly deed at La Tenja," McGregor added. "Antelope Wells is the largest and wealthiest of all the towns in the Bootheel, and so far we have managed to resist the few demonstrations he has made, but I don't believe that as yet he has brought the full thrust of his operational capabilities against us. Up until now he has been consolidating his gains, letting the other towns and villages fall into his lap, one by one. It is by that method that he intends to keep Antelope Wells in this stranglehold until we are no longer able to hold out against him."

McGregor looked at Duff and the three he brought with him. "To be honest with you, Captain, I'm beginning to have second thoughts about getting you involved. As ye are no longer in my command, I have no right to ask you to put yourself in such danger. I know now that it would take a veritable battalion to defeat him."

Duff chuckled, then took in Meagan, Elmer, and Wang with a wave of his hand. "Leftenant Colonel McGregor, meet the MacCallister Battalion."

Across the street from the Dunn Hotel, Frank Bailey and Black Jack Ketchum, the two men Schofield had sent to town as a backup, stood in the front of the Hidden Trail Saloon, watching as the entourage returned to the hotel after dinner.

"That's him," Bailey said. "That's MacCallister."

"How do you know that's him?"

"We was told that they was four of 'em, 'n that's four of 'm."

"Yeah, but how're we sposed to know which one it is?"

Bailey sighed. "Well, you know it ain't the China-man 'n it ain't the woman. That leaves only the old man and the big man. You know damn well that the old man ain't MacCallister, so the onliest one that leaves is the big un. 'N we was told that the feller we was sposed to take care of is a big man with kinda red-dish blond hair. Anyhow, even if we didn't know which one was him, why we know which room he'll be in."

"When are we goin' to do it?"

"Tonight I'll climb into his room whilst you keep watch."

"MacCallister's supposed be a hard one to kill," Ketchum said.

"There ain't nobody that's hard to kill whilst they's a-sleepin'," Bailey insisted.

Duff had no idea what had awakened him. He had gone to sleep rather quickly, the result of the long trip and having spent the previous night on the ground. But he was awake. He lay in bed for just a moment, trying to decide what had awakened him.

There it was again!

He knew the sound was real. He could hear a slight scraping sound. Immediately, he knew what it was.

Before going to bed that night, he had lifted the window a few inches just to catch a slight breeze. What he was hearing was the window being raised much higher.

Duff looked toward the window, and even though it

was dark, the moonlit window was lighter than the rest of the room. He reached over to grab his pistol, then sat up on the edge of the bed and saw a man, backlit by the brighter outside, crawling through the window.

Knowing that he could move in the darkness without being seen, he took his gun in hand and moved away from the bed. He stood to one side and watched as the intruder approached his bed. The intruder raised his hand, and in the moonlight, Duff saw the soft gleam of the blade of a knife.

"What the hell?" the intruder said in surprise when he realized that the bed was empty.

"A little late for visiting, isn't it?" Duff asked.

With a gasp of surprise, the man whirled around just in time to see Duff bringing the gun down on his head.

Duff's next thought was that Meagan might be in danger. After all, if someone broke into his room, what would stop someone from breaking into her room at the same time?

Leaving his intruder unconscious on the floor, Duff disarmed him, then stepped out into the hall, moved to Meagan's room, and knocked lightly on the door. "Meagan?"

When she didn't answer, he knocked a second time, a little harder, and he called her name a little louder.

"Just a minute," he heard.

A moment later her door opened and she stood there looking at him with a questioning expression on her face.

"Have ye an intruder in your room?" Duff asked. He knew that even if she did she would have to deny it, but he was trusting her to let him know by some facial expression.

"No, no intruder. Why would you ask such a thing?"

"Because I had one. He's still there, unconscious on the floor."

Meagan stepped away from the door. "Come on in and have a look around, if you'd like. As a matter of fact, I think *I* would like it if you would come in."

Duff went into her room, lit the lantern, then made a thorough examination of the room, but found no intruder. "I'll be for takin' my unwanted guest to the jail. Keep your window locked."

"You can count on that," Meagan replied.

Black Jack Ketchum had remained in the dark shadow between two of the buildings across the street from the hotel when Bailey left to take care of MacCallister. When Bailey didn't come back after an extended period of time, Ketchum began to believe that things hadn't gone well.

His suspicion was confirmed a few minutes later when he saw MacCallister exit the hotel, carrying someone over his shoulder. Because it was dark, Ketchum couldn't see well enough in the dark to confirm that it was Bailey, but he knew it had to be.

What he didn't know was whether Bailey was dead or alive.

Chapter Fourteen

"What do you want for breakfast?" Sheriff Campbell asked. "Bacon 'n eggs, or eggs 'n bacon?" He laughed at his little joke. "Now, me, I'd prefer a bit o' haggis myself."

Bailey sat up on the cot in the jail cell and experienced a bit of dizziness. Lifting his hand to his head, winced in pain as he felt a bump. "What happened? Am I in jail? How did I get here?"

"How did ye get here? Captain MacCallister brought ye here himself. 'Twas slung across his shoulder you were, 'n sleepin' like a baby. Well, ye weren't exactly sleeping. 'Twas more like you had been knocked out."

"Knocked out? How?"

"The captain says you came into his room in the wee hours of the night, bent, no doubt, in harming him in some way. But you dinnae get the job done, did ye?"

"Yeah, I remember now. I was goin' to kill 'im but . . . son of a bitch! He was behind me! How did he get behind me?"

* * *

When Duff and Meagan went to breakfast, they were greeted by Susie York, owner of the restaurant.

"Oh, you two were here last night, at the mayor's table," the attractive middle-aged woman said. "I remember you."

"Yes, we were," Meagan replied with a friendly smile.

"I've just turned out a fresh batch of biscuits. They are wonderful with butter and jelly."

"And would ye be for having eggs, with a bit o' cheese scrambled with them?" Duff asked.

Susie laughed. "Why, if you don't sound just like Mayor McGregor."

"They're both Scotsmen," Meagan said.

"So is our sheriff. Did all of you know each other over in Scotland?"

"Aye, that we did." Duff noticed that the gentleman he had seen the night before, the one wearing the uniform of a Confederate general, was again at the table in the corner. And, as she was the night before, the young woman was with him.

"I see that the same young lady is with the general this morning."

"Yes, that is his daughter, Lucy. She has given up everything to look after her pa. Why, any other woman would have been married by now, but she's almost thirty, bless her heart, and still not married."

Elmer and Wang came in then.

"You four good folks have a seat, and I'll get breakfast out to you," Susie said.

Shortly after they sat down, the young woman who had been sitting with the general came over to their table. "Captain MacCallister?"

Surprised to hear the woman address him by name, Duff looked up at her. "Aye?"

"I'm Lucy Culpepper. I hate to impose on you, sir, but my father has expressed a wish to speak with you."

"Aye, I would be glad to speak to him." Duff glanced at the others around the table. "If ye would excuse me for a wee time?"

Meagan's nod affirmed for all at the table, and Duff followed Lucy to where her father sat, waiting for them.

"General Culpepper, I'm Duff MacCallister." The Scotsman extended his hand.

To his surprise, instead of taking his hand, the general saluted, and he held the salute until Duff returned it.

"Please, Captain, have a seat," Culpepper said.

"After the lady," Duff replied, noticing that Lucy was still standing.

"As befitting an officer and a gentleman," General Culpepper replied as first Lucy, and then Duff sat down.

"It is my understanding that you have served with Colonel McGregor before," the general said.

"Aye, sir, I have."

"I have been most pleased with the colonel ever since he came under my command. And I'm glad to see that he has added a staff officer in whom he has full trust and confidence."

Duff was a little surprised by Culpepper referring to McGregor as being in his command, but he didn't let the expression on his face give it away. He did notice the expression on Lucy's face though. She seemed grateful that Duff had displayed no reaction to the general's remark.

"'Tis pleased I am to join the colonel again," Duff said.

"Tell me, Captain, as you came through the perimeter, were you able to reconnoiter the Yankee troop dispositions?"

"Yankee troop dispositions?" Duff looked over at Lucy and though she said nothing, the expression on her face pleaded with him to go along with the general's delusions.

"General Schofield, sir," Culpepper said, by way of explanation.

"Oh, uh, not entirely, General. But we did encounter one of Schofield's patrols as we were on our way here."

"And what was the outcome of that encounter, if I may enquire?"

"Aye, ye may ask. 'Tis happy I am to say that we disarmed then, 'n sent them on their way empty-handed." He smiled as he thought of them, not only weaponless, but without shoes or uniforms. However, he offered no further elaboration.

"Good, very good," Culpepper said with an approving nod. "Captain, I am convinced that you will be a welcome addition to my command. You are dismissed, sir."

Duff stood, then, because he realized that the general was expecting it of him, he saluted.

General Culpepper returned it sharply.

After breakfast, Duff visited Mayor McGregor in his office.

"Sergeant Major Campbell told me about your visitor last night," McGregor said.

"Is he someone you know?" Duff asked.

McGregor shook his head. "I cannae say that I do know him, but he told the sergeant major his name was Frank Bailey. 'Tis a suspicion of the sergeant major that Bailey may be with Schofield, though he says Bailey denies it. Perhaps 'twas only his intent to rob ye."

"Aye, that may be so, though he clearly meant to kill me first."

McGregor chuckled. "Ye be a hard man to kill, Duff MacCallister. Sure 'n I learned that a long time ago."

"I've managed to avoid getting killed so far," Duff replied with a broad smile.

"So ye have, lad, so ye have."

"Colonel, tell me what ye know about the man who calls himself General Culpepper."

"Oh, he doesn't just call himself a general," McGregor replied. "For 'tis a general he truly is. He graduated from West Point, and he served in the Mexican War, then resigned his commission with the US Army to accept the appointment as a general in the Confederate army.

"Let me tell ye an interesting story about the Battle of Petersburg. 'Twas quite late in the war, in 1864, I think it was. Lee had already tried to invade the North, but as all know, he was turned back at Gettysburg. After that, the Union army seemed invincible until they encountered stubborn resistance in Virginia. They were halted outside the city of Petersburg.

"'Twas there that Grant ordered one of his generals to attack the northeastern end of the Southern lines and the general in command of the attacking force did so with a strength of sixteen thousand men. But his attack was met with so much resistance that 'twas for certain he was, that the force in front of him must have been much larger than his own army.

"The truth of it was that his sixteen thousand men were facing a defensive force of less than twenty-five hundred men, and most of them were not part of the regular army, but were members of the Home Guard. That meant that their ranks were filled with old men and young boys.

"Had that Union army general pressed his attack, 'tis nae doubt the city would almost certainly have fallen, 'n perhaps the war would have been rather significantly shortened. But he withdrew from the field, leaving the city in the hands of the Confederates.

"During the night General Lee was able to bring up reinforcements so that when General Grant attacked Petersburg the next morning, he found a well-fortified string of Confederate lines manned by more than fifty thousand soldiers. There was naught General Grant could do but withdraw from the field and leave the Confederate army in possession of the city."

"Aye, I've read of that battle," Duff said.

"And did ye read the name of the Confederate general who led that twenty-five hundred old men and boys in their brilliant defense of the city?"

Duff smiled. "Are ye for telling me that it was General Culpepper?"

"Aye, 'twas the same. But, here's another bit of interesting information for you. The name of the Union general who, with sixteen thousand men was beaten back by General Culpepper and his twenty-five hundred men was—"

"Wait," Duff said. "The Union general was Ebenezer Schofield?"

"Aye, lad, 'twas the same."

"That is interesting," Duff said. "But what happened? Why is he—?"

"In his dotage?" McGregor said, finishing the question. He shook his head. "I've asked Lucy that same question, and she says that he was never the same after he came back from the war. He had sacrificed everything, given up his career in the US Army to fight for the South. Also the land that had once belonged to his family was taken by taxes. And when Lucy's mother died, her father got worse."

"So, ye and Miss Culpepper are well acquainted, are ye?"

"True that is, m' friend, and 'twere it my choice we would be much better acquainted. I've never met a finer young woman, and 'tis totally dedicated to taking care of her father, she is."

"Aye, for the brief time I was visiting with the general, I saw the tenderness with which she cares for him."

"It isn't always tender she is," McGregor said with a quick smile. "Let someone say something unkind about her father, or his condition, and Lucy, wee lass that she is, will be on them like a duck on a june bug."

"Duck on a june bug?" Duff asked with a little chuckle.

"Aye, 'tis an American idiom I've picked up. From Lucy herself, in fact."

"Frank Bailey is in jail." Black Jack Ketchum was in the Desert Star Saloon at Cottonwood Springs, reporting to Schofield, who was sitting at the table that had been reserved specifically for him. "I was waitin' outside whilst he clumb up to the winder of MacCallister's room, only somehow it was MacCallister who got him, 'stead o' him gettin' MacCallister. I was listenin' to some o' the things folks was sayin' 'bout MacCallister. Turns out he's 'most famous on account of some of the things he's done."

"I'm quite aware of Duff MacCallister's many storied accomplishments," Schofield said. "That's why I issued orders for him to be taken out of the equation.

"We must have Antelope Wells," Schofield insisted. "The fate of our new nation depends upon the capture and subjugation of Antelope Wells. In fact, I intend to leave only an occupying force here in Cottonwood Springs, and make Antelope Wells the capital city of Tierra de Desierto."

"It's going to be a lot harder to take than this place or Hachita or La Tenja was. How are we going to do it?" one of men nearby asked.

"May I suggest that you leave tactics and strategy to me, First Sergeant Cobb?" Schofield said. "I not only matriculated from the finest military school in the entire world, I have also led mighty armies in desperate struggle."

"Yes, sir. Well, I didn't mean nothin' by it. I was just wonderin', is all."

"Hey," Welch said. "Did you say they was a Chinaman with this feller?"

"Yes, there were three people who come into town with 'im," Ketchum said. "An old man, a Chinaman, 'n I thought the other 'n was a man too, on account of the way she was dressed. But damn if it didn't turn out that she was a woman."

"Yeah, that's them, all right. Them's the same son-of-a-bitches that me 'n the others run acrost when we tried to ambush 'em. We was told about MacCallister, but there didn't nobody say nothin' 'bout that Chinaman. 'N I tell you true, that Chinaman ain't like nobody I've never knowed before. He's somebody you got to look out for."

"It is becoming increasingly clear to me that this man, Mr. MacCallister, and those with him, are going to have to be eliminated before we can attain our ultimate goal," Schofield said.

"Let me do it," the former lieutenant, now sergeant, said. Although Mack had been listening to the report of Black Jack Ketchum, it was the first time he had spoken.

"Are you sure you want to try this? You have already encountered MacCallister and his entourage once, so you know them to be rather formidable adversaries."

"Know them to be what?" Ketchum asked.

"They will be hard to kill," Sergeant Mack explained. He turned his attention back to Schofield. "I know they will be hard to kill. I've already encountered them once. But I would like another chance, and this time, I am forewarned. And it is as they say: forewarned is forearmed.

"As I explained in my initial report, it was actually the Chinaman who caused the problem the last time. We were totally unaware of his unique skill, therefore the three men I sent up onto the ridge were taken unawares, and they were overcome. But this time we won't be fooled by him, or by anyone else.

So if you are wanting MacCallister and that Chinaman son-of-a-bitch killed, Keaton, Welch, Foster, Pounders, and I will do it for you."

"Yeah, 'n that old man that's with 'em too," Keaton added.

"Very well, you may do so. And if you are successful, Sergeant Mack, you will be Lieutenant Mack again, and Private Keaton will once more be Sergeant Keaton. Also, there will be a one-thousand-dollar bonus for the lot of you."

Keaton smiled, then looked over at Mack. "How 'bout that? We not only get to kill the son of a bitch that fooled us, but me 'n you'll be gettin' our rank again, 'n we'll all be gettin' a thousand dollars, too."

"That isn't a thousand dollars apiece. That is one thousand dollars for the five of you to split," Schofield said.

"Still, two hunnert dollars is a lot o' money," Keaton said. "I'm already thinking about how I might spend it."

"You would be better served to think about how you are going to kill MacCallister," Schofield said.

"Prime Director, is it true that you have offered a thousand dollars to Mack and the others, if they kill MacCallister?" General Peterson asked.

"Yes."

"That's a great deal of money, isn't it?"

"Are you questioning me, General?"

"No, sir, I meant no challenge. I was only satisfying a curiosity, is all," Peterson said.

"General, you, of all people, are aware of the

significance of Antelope Wells. It is vitally important to my plans that we take control of that town. MacCallister is like a rock in my shoe. He must be eliminated for the walk to be comfortable."

"Yes, sir," Peterson replied.

Chapter Fifteen

Antelope Springs

Duff, Meagan, Elmer, and Wang were having a late dinner at Bear Tracks Restaurant when Lucy Culpepper came in alone. Seeing them, she smiled and stepped over to their table.

The three men stood.

"Oh, heavens, please sit down," Lucy said, making a motion with her hands. "I was just going to stop by and say hello."

"Where's the general tonight?" Duff asked. "Will he be joining you soon?"

"He said he was tired and wanted to stay home and read. So, I thought I would give him some time alone."

"Well then, since the general isn't with you, won't you join us?" Meagan invited.

"Yes, please do," Duff said. "Mayor McGregor is going to join us shortly."

Lucy smiled. "Thanks, I would love to. That is, if you don't think it would be an imposition. I know that you and the mayor probably have some private matters to discuss."

"From the conversation I had with the general, in your presence, I doubt there's anything secret about why we are here."

Wang held the chair for Lucy to be seated.

"Are you a native of Antelope Wells, Miss Culpepper?" Meagan asked.

"Please, call me Lucy. I am so often with my father, sometimes I miss the sound of my name being spoken by a feminine voice."

"Why, I would be glad to call you Lucy. And you must call me Meagan."

"Thank you. And to answer your question, Meagan, no, we are from Mississippi originally. But after the war, and after Mama died, Papa had no wish to cooperate with the—" she paused and chuckled. "Excuse my language, but the 'Damn Yankees.' So we started to Mexico, where Papa planned to offer his services to the Mexican government. Seems like they are always having to put down a revolution. But, when we got this far he had second thoughts.

"He said, and I quote, 'I have already violated the oath of fealty I took upon the Plains at West Point when I left the US Army to accept a commission from the Confederacy. I have no intention of doing so again.' So, here is where we stopped."

"Here is the mayor," Elmer said.

As McGregor came to the table he saw Lucy and smiled broadly. "Lu . . . uh, Miss Culpepper. 'Tis nice to see ye dining with m' friends."

"I know that you have a meeting planned. I hope my being here isn't an imposition."

"Och, 'tis nae of the sort. 'Tis always glad to see ye, I am. And your father? Is he in good health?"

"Yes, he's fine, thank you." Lucy provided him with

the same explanation of her father's absence that she had told Duff and the others.

Over dinner, Duff and McGregor discussed the defense of the town. Neither Elmer nor Wang added to the discussion, but they did listen intently.

Meagan and Lucy carried on their own conversation, speaking quietly enough so as to not interfere with the discussion of the men, but bonding in an almost immediate friendship.

At dinner's end McGregor begged the pardon of the others, explaining that he had to take care of some city business. Meagan invited Lucy to extend their visit by joining her in the hotel lobby.

"You ladies have yourself a nice visit," Duff said. "I think I'll have a drink down at the saloon. One can learn a great deal by keeping his ears open."

"Duff, seein' as they was somebody that tried to kill you last night, I think it might be better if me 'n Wang maybe stayed back at the hotel 'n kept a eye on the two womenfolk."

"Aye, if ye don't mind, I think that would be a good idea," Duff agreed.

"Go with *Shifu* Duff, Elmer," Wang said. "I will stay and watch over Miss Meagan and Miss Lucy."

"You sure you don't mind?" Elmer asked. "I would like to wet my whistle a bit."

"I see no need for either of you to stay behind," Meagan said. "Lucy and I will be having our visit in the hotel lobby in full view of everyone. I don't think anyone would be foolish enough to attempt anything under those conditions."

"I would feel better if Wang stayed with you," Duff said.

"Maybe she don't want the heathen to be near 'em," Elmer suggested with a big smile.

"Elmer! What an awful thing for you to say!" Meagan said, though her own smile showed that she was fully aware that Elmer was teasing. "Wang, of course you are welcome to stay."

Wang nodded, but maintained the same inscrutable expression that was his hallmark.

As this discussion was going on, Mack and the others who had come down from the north with him materialized out of the darkness, then rode on into town. Mack had visited Antelope Wells before without being noticed because he had never come to town in uniform. As during all previous visits, he and the others were dressed in mufti.

The ambient light was so restrained they could be seen only as shadows within shadows. The clopping sounds their horses made echoed loudly back from the building fronts, and as they continued on into town, they passed in and out of the little golden patches of light that were cast from the windows onto the boardwalk and sometimes out into the street.

They tied their horses off in front of the Hidden Trail Saloon, then stepped inside.

Two dozen lanterns were attached to a couple of wagon wheels that hung suspended from the ceiling. In addition to the overhead lanterns, there were an equal number of lanterns in wall sconces so that the resultant illumination was enough to read by, anywhere in the room.

The arrival of five men significantly increased the number of people who were already in the saloon, so they did arouse some interest from the others. All five stepped up to the bar.

"Yes, sir," the bartender said, moving down in front of them. "What can I get for you gentlemen?"

"Whiskey," Mack said, and the other four matched his order.

"You gentlemen coming to settle down in Antelope?" the bartender asked, unable to restrain his curiosity any longer. He poured the five drinks.

"No."

"The reason I ask, is I was just wondering if . . ."

"Why are you standin' here, beatin' your gums? Don't you have somethin' else you could be doin' to keep busy?" Mack asked.

"Yes, of course." Piqued by the uncivil response, the bartender moved to the far end of the bar to give them space.

"Damn. I was pretty sure MacCallister would be here. I mean where else is there to go in this town?" Mack asked.

"We may as well just wait here for 'im," Foster suggested. "You're right. There ain't no place else for nobody to go."

"Where do you reckon the sheriff is?" Keaton asked. "I ain't seen hide nor hair of 'im since we come in. He normally spends a lot o' time in here, don't he?"

"Hell, he's got Bailey in jail. Could be that he's over there babysittin' with 'im," Welch said.

Pounders laughed. "Yeah, I wouldn't doubt it none at all, knowin' Frank."

"Mack," Keaton said in a harsh whisper. "There he is! MacCallister just come in."

"Yeah," Mack said in a low growl. "That's him all right."

"They's two of 'em," Foster said.

"Yeah, that old man is with him."

"Hell, an old man like that? How much of a problem can he be?" Keaton asked.

"Hello, Captain MacCallister, Mr. Gleason," the bartender said as Duff stepped up to the bar. "Where's the Chinaman? I certainly hope he realizes he is welcome in the Hidden Trail."

"Aye, he is aware that he is welcome in your fine establishment, but he decided to remain in the hotel this evening," Duff replied.

"Well, as long as he knows that he's quite welcome here. Now, gents, what will it be?"

"I'll have a beer," Elmer said.

"And you sir?" the bartender asked Duff.

"Would ye be for having any scotch?"

"Do you really have to ask such a thing? With the mayor and sheriff both being Scotsman like yourself, how could I not have any? Would Glenlivet be to your taste?"

"Aye, 'tis as fine a drink as can be made. I'll have a wee dram if ye please. 'N I should have known that the leftenant colonel and the sergeant major would have demanded such." He chuckled as he realized that he was still thinking of them by the military ranks they once held.

Both men were civilians now, and both had honorable civilian titles. McGregor was a mayor, and Campbell was a sheriff. Duff would have to keep that in mind when thinking of them, and certainly when speaking to or about them.

Mack had watched MacCallister and Gleason take their drinks over to an empty table. "We got the sons of bitches now." Slowly and unobserved, Mack pulled his gun from his holster.

"How we goin' to do this?" Foster asked. "Are we goin' to just commence a-shootin'?"

"Yeah, but first the rest of you sort of scoot down so's that we're spread out all along the bar." Mack said.

After the five men moved down to the other end of the bar, Mack held his pistol pressed up against the side of his leg so it wouldn't be seen.

"Duff," Elmer said. "They's somethin' funny 'bout the way them five men at the bar just spread out like they done— Tarnation! You know who them men are?"

"Aye, I recognize them. I suggest ye draw your gun and be ready. If there is shooting, you start from this end, I'll start from the other end."

"Now!" one of the men at the bar shouted, and all five brought their pistols to bear.

Duff and Elmer had their own guns drawn, and suddenly the room was shattered with the roar of several pistols being engaged simultaneously. The other patrons in the saloon yelled and dived or scrambled for cover. White gun smoke billowed out from the guns, coalescing in a cloud that filled the center of the room. For a moment, the cloud obscured everything.

When the cloud of gun smoke rolled away, the five men who had been standing at the bar were on the floor. Duff and Elmer made a quick, but thorough perusal of the rest of the room, checking to see if anyone else was laying for them. Their pistols were cocked and they were ready to fire again if they encountered another adversary, but no additional shots were necessary.

Seeing no other threats, Duff and Elmer holstered their pistols. Slowly the other patrons began to reappear from under tables, behind the bar, and from under the staircase.

At that moment Sheriff Campbell pushed in through the batwing doors. "Here, what happened here?"

Everyone started talking at once. In the cacophony, it was impossible to understand anyone.

Campbell held his hands up, palm out, then addressed the bartender. "Barkeep, would ye be for tellin' me now what happened?"

"These men here," the bartender said, pointing to the men lying on the floor, "commenced shootin' at Cap'n MacCallister 'n Mr. Gleason." He pointed to Duff and Elmer. "'N I'll be damn if them two didn't put all five of 'em down."

"These men shot first?" Campbell asked.

"Yes," the bartender replied.

Half a dozen more patrons of the saloon shouted their confirmation.

"I ain't never seen nothin' like it," one of the other patrons said. "It was like a battlefield with all the shootin' 'n such, 'n so much smoke that they didn't nobody know for sure what was goin' on. But when all the smoke cleared, well, it was them two still a-standin', 'n them five that started it lyin' dead on the floor."

Campbell looked over at Duff. "Sounds to me like 'twas a pretty close call ye had, Captain."

"Will there be need for an inquest, Sergeant Major?" Duff asked.

"I see nae need for such a thing. 'Tis clear from all who saw the shooting that 'twas clearly justified. 'Tis wondering I am, though, why these men would come here just to shoot you."

"They are the same men who tried to ambush us on our way here," Duff said.

"Aye, then 'tis sure I am that they were . . . *soldiers* . . . in Schofield's Legion." Campbell set the word *soldiers* apart from the rest of the sentence, showing his scorn for the concept.

McGregor came into the saloon then, and took a quick glance at the men lying on the floor. "Some of Schofield's men, are they, Sergeant Major?"

"Aye, 'tis sure I am that they are."

McGregor chuckled. "Well, if he keeps sending his men in a few at a time, we'll have nae problem in dealing with them. Barkeep, would ye be for providing one round of drinks for everyone in the house, on me?"

"Hurrah for the mayor!" someone shouted as everyone rushed to the bar, stepping over and around the bodies as if they weren't there.

Chapter Sixteen

Cottonwood Springs

"He killed all five of them, did he?" Schofield asked after he heard the report given him by Captain Bond the next morning.

General Peterson was standing beside Schofield's desk as Bond rendered his report.

"Yes, sir. Well, according to Sergeant Martell, who I sent in just to keep an eye on Mack and the others, there were two of them, MacCallister and Gleason. Gleason is one of the two men who came to Antelope Wells with him. But, Martell said that Mack and the others already had their guns out and it was they who initiated the shooting."

"Well, Mack had already shown his incompetence, so I'm not really surprised," Scofield said, showing no more agitation in his response than he would have, had he been told it was raining. He held his cup out for Frederica to refill it. "*Gracias*, my dear," he said as the dark brown liquid poured from a silver pot.

"*De nada*," the beautiful young woman replied.

"You said MacCallister was going to be a hard man to kill, and you were right," Bond continued. "Now, thanks to him, we've lost five men."

"I'm sure you realize, Captain Bond, that Mack and the four men who were with him were expendable," Schofield replied. "They had rendered themselves so when they failed on their first attempt. I didn't really expect them to succeed, but I wanted an accurate gauge of what we're dealing with in our encounters with MacCallister."

"I can tell you right now, we don't have anyone who is capable of going up against him, one-on-one," Bond said.

"Nor do I intend to attempt such a thing. From now on, MacCallister and the people he brought with him, will be dealt with tactically."

"Yes, sir, and that's another thing. Do we actually know anything about the others?" Bond asked. "I mean other than the fact that one is an old man, and the other 'n is a Chinaman."

"Lieutenant Mack said that it was the Chinamen who neutralized three of them during the attempted ambush," Lieutenant Miles said.

"Have you forgotten that Mack was no longer an officer?" Schofield asked.

"Uh, yes, sir. I meant Sergeant Mack."

Schofield turned to Peterson. "General, please tell the others what we have learned about those who came with MacCallister."

General Peterson set his coffee cup down and patted a napkin against his lips before he spoke. "The older man, Elmer Gleason, fought as a guerilla with William Quantrill, Wild Bill Anderson, and others during the war. He has been a longtime associate of Duff MacCallister, and has proven himself quite capable in circumstances that may require armed confrontation.

"The Chinaman, apparently, is exceptionally skilled in some sort of Chinese fighting that is extremely effective and very different from anything with which we might be familiar."

"What about the woman that's with him?" Lieutenant Miles asked. "Is she some sort of really good shot or something?"

Peterson shook his head. "As far as we know, she is only here because of some relationship that exists between her and MacCallister."

"Thank you, General," Schofield said. "Gentlemen, from this point on, we will not think of any of these people as individuals, but only as a military unit. And in developing our strategy for the final attack on Antelope Wells, we will take that into consideration."

"When are we going to attack them?" Bond asked.

"Have patience, my good man," Schofield replied. "General Peterson and I have been developing the tactics we will use when we engage the enemy."

"What about the other things we're doing?" Bond said. "Are we goin' to keep doin' them? Or are we goin' to stop everything and just concentrate on capturing Antelope Wells."

"By *other things*, I take it that you mean our tax collections and the occasional forced confiscation of money from reluctant contributors to our cause?"

"Yes, sir. Especially the, uh, forced confiscation."

"You do agree, do you not, Captain Bond, that we must maintain our source of operation funds?"

"Oh, yes, sir. I quite agree."

"Good. That being the case, we will continue all ongoing revenue enhancement operations," Schofield said, definitively.

Antelope Wells

Duff, McGregor, and Campbell were gathered in McGregor's office.

"I've been talkin' to the prisoner, Frank Bailey," Campbell told the others. "'Twould seem that Schofield plans to send some of his men out to rob the Lordsburg stagecoach on its next trip down."

"Aye, 'twouldn't be the first time the blaggard has done such a thing," McGregor said.

"I've a plan," Campbell said.

"And what is the plan?"

"As ye know, Colonel, I've formed a sheriff's posse. 'Tis thinkin' I am that I may take four of them 'n ambush Schofield's men before they can rob the stagecoach."

"How would ye be for knowing where they will be?"

"I'm goin' to allow Bailey to escape. He'll not know that I'm allowing it, 'n he'll think what a clever fellow he is for havin' outwitted me. But my four lads 'n I will be waiting just outside of town 'n when he starts out to join up with the others, we'll follow him."

"I'll go with ye," Duff offered.

Campbell held up his hand. "'Tis thankin' ye I am, Captain. But I'm certain that Schofield plans to attack Antelope Wells as he did Cottonwood Springs and La Tenja. And 'twould be better, I believe, for ye to be organizing the defense of the town."

"Aye, the sergeant major is right," McGregor said. "The stopping of the villains from holding up the

Lordsburg stage is a good thing, but 'tis even more important to defend the town. As long as Antelope Wells holds out, whatever nefarious plans Schofield may have will be thwarted. I would feel better if ye stayed here 'n organized the men of the town into an army."

"Very good, Leftenant Colonel. That shall be my task," Duff said.

Somewhere between Lordsburg and Antelope Wells

Beans Marshall was driving the stagecoach and Hogjaw Magee was riding shotgun. Three passengers were inside the coach—two drummers and a very attractive young woman who had identified herself to the others as Ethel Marie Joyce. She had been a saloon girl in Lordsburg, but an overly aggressive boss, who also happened to be married, caused her to look for employment elsewhere. She thought back to that day just a week ago.

"Come on. You mean because I got little grabby?" Lambert said. "Hell, woman, that's what you get paid for. It's your job to entertain the customers."

"That's just it," Ethel Marie replied. "You're my boss, not a customer. And you are married."

"What does me bein' married have anything to do with it? Good Lord, woman, you wasn't thinkin' that I might marry you, was you? I was just wanting a bit of fun, is all."

"No, I wasn't thinking you might want to marry me. I was thinking of Mrs. Lambert, and what a nice lady she is. And I want no part of you cheating on her."

"You give yourself too much credit," Lambert answered, *twisting his mouth into a patronizing sneer. "Anyway, you don't really want to go down into the Bootheel. There's rumors of bad things going on down there."*

"Yes, I've heard those rumors," Ethel Marie replied. *"But what is going on here is also bad. And here, it isn't just a rumor."*

"All right. Have it your own way," Lambert said, gesturing in such a way as if he were washing his hands of her.

Riding in the stagecoach and seeing the dust being whipped up by the wheels, she was beginning to have second thoughts. She wasn't having second thoughts about quitting her job with Lambert—there was no way she intended to keep working for him—but she was having second thoughts about going south. She would have been better off catching a train and going back to Memphis.

"Here comes the stagecoach," one of the possemen said to Sheriff Campbell. "What do you think we should do? Think we should ride along beside it and escort them?"

"Aye, that might nae be a bad idea," Campbell said. "If they see us, perhaps they will nae attack the coach."

"Too late, Sheriff, there they are!" shouted one of the other men and he started toward the group of uniformed men who were headed toward the coach.

"Nae, wait! You'll be for givin' us away. We need to—"

Even before Campbell could finish his warning,

Schofield's soldiers saw the approaching posse and turned to meet them.

Six of Schofield's men moved quickly into a battle-front formation against the four men of Campbell's posse. He saw at once the disparity between six well-trained soldiers and four eager but disorganized men.

The battle was brief and fierce, and within a moment, all four of the men of the posse were down.

Sheriff Campbell had no choice but to retreat. He galloped away for about half a mile, then he turned and rode back, staying out of sight in the trees. He watched as Schofield's men hurried out to meet the oncoming stagecoach.

"What the hell?" Beans said. "Hogjaw, what is that in front of us?"

"I don't know," Hogjaw replied. "Look to me like they're wearin' some sort of uniform."

"Don't look like no uniform I've ever seen before. Mexicans, maybe?"

"Could be, I spose, but what are Mexicans a-doin' up here?"

"I don't know. You don't reckon we've gone to war with Mexico 'n don't know nothin' about it, do you?"

"I don't have no idee," Hogjaw said.

The six uniformed men spread out across the road in front of the coach.

One of them, a man with sergeant stripes on his sleeves rode forward a few feet then raised his hand. "Stop the coach right there, driver," he called out.

"Oh, good. You're Americans," Beans said. "Me 'n Hogjaw here was a-feared you might be Mexicans or some such." He chuckled. "We was a-feared that we might be in some kind of war that we didn't know nothin' about."

"We ain't Mexicans, 'n we ain't Americans neither. And there is a war."

"What kind of war? 'N if you ain't Mexicans 'n you ain't Americans, then who the hell are you fellers?" Beans asked.

"It's a war of liberation, and we are soldiers of Tierra de Desierto. We have stopped the coach to collect a transport and visitor's tax."

"I ain't never heard of no such tax," Beans said.

"You have now. Private Nelson, Private Hamby, turn out the passengers."

"Yes, Sergeant Cobb," Nelson replied as he and Private Hamby moved to the stagecoach to carry out Sergeant Cobb's orders.

Nelson reached down to jerk open the coach door. "You folks climb down from there," he called.

"See here, my good man, I happen to represent the Jacob Bromwell Company of kitchen appliances," one of the drummers said haughtily. "They are the largest kitchen appliance company in American, and they will not be pleased with you treating one of their representatives in such a fashion."

"Turn out your pockets," Nelson said.

"I suggest that we do what he said, Lennie," the other drummer said. "Look over there." He pointed to two men who were lying still on the ground.

"Oh, my Lord! Are they dead?" Lennie asked, shocked by what he was seeing.

"That they are, sonny," Private Nelson said. "Now, turn out your pockets like I told you."

Quickly Lennie and Bert, the other drummer, emptied their pockets.

Nelson looked at Ethel Marie and smiled. "Well now, little lady, I'm goin' to give you a choice. You can either open up that there handbag you're a-carryin', or you can give me a kiss. Your choice."

"Hold on there, Nelson, iffen she takes that deal, she's got to kiss me, too," Hamby said.

"Clearly, that is no choice," Ethel Marie said with a disdainful smile. "I would rather you take everything I have." She pulled the drawstring open on her purse and handed it to Nelson.

"One dollar?" Nelson said, looking into the purse. "One dollar is all you got?"

"I am a poor woman," Ethel Marie said.

"Yeah? Well, you shoulda give me 'n Hamby a kiss is what you shoulda done." He took the dollar. "Now you're even poorer 'n you was, on account of now, you ain't got nothin' a'tall."

"Soldiers, recover!" Sergeant Cobb called, and Nelson and Hamby hurried back to join the others.

Sheriff Campbell remained in the tree line until Sergeant Cobb and his men had completely withdrawn. He rode toward the stagecoach just as the passengers were reboarding. Hogjaw raised his shotgun.

"Hold on there, Hogjaw. That's Sheriff Campbell," Beans said, holding his hand out to prevent Hogjaw from shooting.

"You're right. That is the sheriff," Hogjaw said. "Sheriff, where was you just a while ago when we needed you?"

"I was here. I brought some lads with me to try and stop this, but there were too many of Schofield's men, 'n they ambushed us." Campbell stroked his chin and shook his head. "Sad to say that all were killed."

"Damn!" Beans said. "How many were with you?"

"Only four. 'N I'll be for askin' ye to help me get these brave lads back home. Their horses ran away, 'n I'll not be leavin' them out here for any critters as may come around."

"Yeah, all right. We'll toss 'em up on top o' the coach."

Beans, Hogjaw, and Sheriff Campbell dragged all four men up to the coach, then Hogjaw climbed up on top of the coach as Beans and Campbell started to pick up the first body.

"Just what do you think you're doing?" That indignant question came from Lennie, one of the two drummer passengers.

"It should be clear to ye," Sheriff Campbell replied. "For 'tis obvious that we are loading these bodies on top o' the stage so as to take them back home."

"I paid good money for passage on this stagecoach, and I'll not be sharing a ride with dead bodies."

"Ain't no need for you to be sharin' a ride with these dead men, mister," Beans said. "It's only about five more miles to Antelope Wells. You can prob'ly walk it in no more 'n a hour, or maybe an hour 'n a half at the most."

"What? Why, I'll do no such thing!" Lennie said, his irritation growing.

Unlike Lennie and Bert, Ethel Marie had not stepped down from the coach when the sheriff arrived. While she was alone inside, she reached down between the seat and the side and recovered a wad of money bound by a red ribbon. She had hidden the more than two hundred dollars the moment she realized that the stagecoach was being robbed.

Once the bodies were loaded, and with Sheriff Campbell riding as escort, the coach resumed its trip to Antelope Wells.

"I shall most assuredly register a complaint with the headquarters of the Lordsburg Stage Coach Line," Lennie said in a self-righteous grumble.

"What good will that do?" Bert asked.

"Those robbers took forty dollars from me. I intend to petition the stage line to return the money."

"Don't know as they'll do it," Bert said. "But I reckon I might try the same thing."

Ethel Marie thought of the two hundred dollars she had saved, and smiled.

The remainder of the trip back to Antelope Wells was uneventful.

Chapter Seventeen

"'Twas nothing I could do about it," Campbell told Duff and McGregor that evening when he reported on the results of his encounter with the uniformed men of Schofield's Legion who robbed the stagecoach. "The blaggards were waiting on us, 'n we rode into an ambush. They knew we were coming."

"How is it that they knew?" Duff asked.

Campbell shook his head. "I'm not sure I know the answer to that, Captain, but 'tis thinking I am, that somehow Bailey got word o' what we had planned, 'n he told the others."

"Four killed," McGregor said.

"Aye, four, 'n good men they were, too," Campbell said. "We've nae that many to defend the town as it is, 'n to lose four of them weakens us even more."

"And poor Mr. Dunnigan had a wife 'n two wee ones," McGregor added.

"Leftenant Colonel, 'tis thinking I am, that 'twould be a good idea to have an army of our own," Duff suggested.

"Aye, 'tis a great idea," McGregor agreed.

"M' friends Elmer, Wang, and I will train them."

"I'll be glad to help you, Captain," Campbell offered.

"Nae, let the captain do it, Sergeant Major. Ye would be of more help by continuing on as sheriff."

"I agree. We will be needing civil authority now, more than ever," Duff said. "'Twould make the training easier if I know that you're still in charge of the law."

"Aye, then that is what I'll do," Campbell agreed.

That evening four men were sharing a table in the Hidden Trail Saloon.

"Four of 'em," Anton Drexler said. "The sheriff took four men with 'im to set a trap for some of Schofield's men, onliest thing is, it was Schofield that actual set the trap, 'n how it wound up is, we had four men kilt."

"What about that feller McGregor sent for?" Morley was a former soldier and shotgun guard for the Desert Stagecoach Company. Now he was a wagon mechanic.

"That would be MacCallister. Only he didn't go with 'em, it was just Sheriff Campbell, Peabody, Slater, Logan, and Dunaway. 'N all of 'em but Campbell got killed," Anton Drexler said.

Of the conversationalists, Morley and Ed Truax worked in the freight wagon yard. Jay Collins worked in the feed and seed store.

"Why do you reckon he sent for MacCallister, if MacCallister didn't even go along with the sheriff to help 'em out?" Truax asked.

"Well, hell, I can tell you that," Morley said. "Ain't you heard? This here MacCallister feller is a-plannin' on raisin' up an army here in Antelope Wells. McGregor's thinkin' is that if this feller MacCallister can raise up an army, why, it'll help us stand up agin Schofield."

"Yeah, well, Paul Carson sure don't think we can stand up agin 'em. Carson says what we ought to do is just surrender to 'em," Drexler said.

"Wait a minute. Are you tellin' me we should just walk out to the edge of town holdin' up a white flag whenever Schofield rides in 'n tellin' 'em we give up?" Truax asked.

"That's what Carson says. He says they ain't nobody goin' to be able to stand up agin Schofield 'n his army," Drexler said.

"That's the whole idea, ain't it?" Morley asked. "I mean ain't that why we're goin' to get us our own army, so's we can stand up to 'im?"

"Hell, Schofield's Legion is a real army. He's got hisself men with uniforms 'n officers 'n all that," Truax said.

"Instead of just surrenderin' to 'im, like Carson wants, or tryin' to fight agin 'im the way the mayor wants, seems to me like maybe it might be that the best thing we could do would be to just join up with 'em," Drexler said.

"Wait a minute. Are you sayin' we should join up with the army that's comin' to attack us?" Truax asked.

"Well yeah, but I ain't talkin' 'bout joinin' up with 'im 'n fightin' agin our own," Drexler said. "What I'm talkin' about is joinin' up with 'im, so's maybe I could talk to 'im some. 'Cause I don't know if you've heard anything or not 'bout them other towns he's done attacked, but more 'n half the men was kilt in ever'one of 'em. Could be that joinin' up with 'em might be 'bout the only way we have of savin' the town."

"It ain't the only way for me," Collins insisted. "'Cause I don't want nothin' to do with Schofield, or none of his army, neither."

"Hell, they don't nobody that actual wants that, but the way I'm lookin' at it, we may not have no choice in it," Drexler said. "I'm thinkin' that maybe Carson is more 'n likely right. Seems to me like Schofield's Legion is goin' to be takin' over this town whether we like it or not."

"Yeah, well, I don't plan to stand by 'n let Schofield just ride in 'n take over," Morley said. "I fought agin' the Injuns when I was in the army before, 'n there ain't nobody that's a better fighter than an Injun. I reckon I can fight again. I aim to join up with the army that this MacCallister feller is raisin' up."

Word had gone out all over town for every male citizen between the ages of fifteen and sixty to gather in the street at two o'clock that afternoon. Forty-eight men answered the call, though there were a few who looked younger than fifteen, and an equal number of those who looked to be older than sixty.

Duff culled them out right away, then he ordered those who remained, the number now cut to thirty-six, to form into three rows of twelve men each.

Once more Duff walked by inspecting the men, stopping often and touching someone on the shoulder. "Step out, please," he said to each of the men he had touched so that he had two groups. Those he had touched were gathered in a disorganized group to one side, leaving twenty-four who were still standing in formation. He had used no specific procedure in making his selections. He had just relied upon some sort of gut instinct to help him separate the two groups. He turned to the ones he had touched out—the ones that he thought would not make very good fighters.

"All ye lads in this group can go back to your work or families," he said. "I'll not be needing ye."

Most were pleased to have been eliminated, though one or two felt they had been slighted by the procedure. Once they were gone, Duff turned to address those who remained.

"Captain MacCallister?" One of the men who had been touched out questioned Duff before he could begin his talk.

"Aye?" Duff replied, turning toward him.

"I've no wish to bear arms against my fellow man, but I would be remiss if I didn't offer my services in some other capacity."

"And would ye be for telling me what capacity that might be, sir?"

"I am Reverend Ken Cooley, pastor of the Antelope Wells Christian Tabernacle Church." He took in the formation with a wave of his hand. "Many of these men are valued members of my congregation, and I would like to be chaplain for your army, if you would have me, sir."

Duff smiled and extended his hand. "Chaplain Cooley, 'tis indeed an honor to have ye join us. Would ye be for rejoining the formation, please?"

Duff turned to the men who had remained after the thinning out. "I'm thanking you for answering the call of duty, for 'tis from your group that we will build an army that will stand off Schofield. Who among ye has been in the army?"

A few of the men raised their hands.

"Were any of ye officers?"

No hands were raised.

"Noncommissioned officers?" Duff asked

"I was a sergeant with General Nelson Miles up on the Yellowstone," one of the men said."

"What's your name?" Duff asked.

"Morley. Chris Morley."

"Now, ye be Sergeant Morley once again," Duff said. "And ye can help in the training of the others."

"Look here," one of the others asked. "Are we goin' to have to learn to march 'n salute, 'n do all such things?"

"There'll be nae need for salutin', as we'll be fighting. But we will learn how to drill. Drilling together instills discipline, order, and the ability to act together," Duff replied.

"What's drill?"

The men who had served with the army laughed. "Don't worry about it, Sonny," one of the veterans called out to him. "I figure you'll be learnin' about it soon enough."

The other veterans joined the first in laughter.

"There will be other things ye need to learn. How many among you own a rifle?"

Fourteen hands were raised.

"Are there any among you who has less than fifty rounds?"

"Fifty what?" someone asked.

"Bullets," Sergeant Morley said. "Does ever'one have at least fifty bullets?"

"Oh, yeah. I got near on to two hunnert bullets. Forty-four forties, they are."

An inventory showed that there were fourteen rifles and four hundred rounds.

"Cap'n." Sergeant Morley pointed to one of the soldiers. "Hawkins there was a bugler."

"A bugler?"

"Yes, sir. I know we won't be havin' no need for the soundin' of 'Charge,' or 'Reveille,' or 'Taps,' or nothin' like that. But iffen you was to need us to all come a-runnin' when you wanted, why ole' Hawkins there could get it did."

"What is the call you would use to get everyone gathered?" Duff asked.

Hawkins smiled. "Assembly."

"Do you have a bugle?"

"Yes, sir, I do."

"Go get it, and return as quickly as you can."

"Sergeant Morley, 'tis unfamiliar I am with the American bugle calls." He smiled. "I'm more familiar with the sound o' the pipes. But there would be a couple that I would want the men to learn. To call them together in a formation so I can talk to them, 'n another one that would tell the men to prepare for battle."

"Yes, sir," Morley said. "Them two calls would be 'Assembly,' 'n 'To Arms.'"

"I'm goin' to leave you in charge of the men now, while I see if I can round up a few more rifles 'n a lot more ammunition. I want enough ammunition that we can have some of the lads practice shooting without fear of runnin' out of bullets. While I'm looking around, I'd like ye to teach the men these two bugle calls, 'n also put them through a few drills."

"Yes, sir!" Morley replied, boasting a proud smile.

"I checked with Alfred Sikes. The lad has seven Winchesters, four Henrys, and one thousand rounds of ammunition," McGregor reported a short while after having received the request from Duff to see what he could find in the way of additional weapons and ammunition.

"That's good. And does the city have sufficient funds to make the purchase of rifles and ammunition so that our army will be fully armed?"

"Aye, we can do that. 'Twill strain the budget, that's for sure, but 'tis better to have a free town that's in debt, than to have a town that is held in the grips of a tyrant."

"Aye, for such are my thoughts as well," Duff agreed.

For the next two days the town of Antelope Wells was converted into an army training post. The sound of bugle calls was heard and soon after the first bugle call of the day, men began marching up and down the street in formation, their parade witnessed by the citizens of the town.

Shortly thereafter the sound of gunfire permeated the town and at its beginning some of the townspeople were frightened, fearing perhaps that they were about to experience the same fate as the other towns in the Bootheel, those that had already fallen to Schofield, and at the cost of many lives. They soon learned, however, that they were listening to the sounds of an army in training.

The Antelope Wells Standard, the local newspaper, published a story on the front page above the fold, extolling the determination to defend the town, and the courage of the young men who had joined the Home Guard in order to do so.

Home Guard to the Defense

BY CLINT H. DENHAM

*Listen, my children, and you shall hear
Of the midnight ride of Paul Revere,
On the eighteenth of April, in Seventy-Five:
Hardly a man is still alive
Who remembers that famous day and year.*

So, my dear readers, begins the poem of one of the most thrilling times in the history of our Republic. It is a poem which holds reverent the memory, not just of the silversmith who spread the alarm, but of those who answered the call, from shop, field, and farm.

And now we, the citizens of Antelope Wells, have found within our own population men of courage who are prepared to defend our fair community from the brutal savagery of a despot's evil intent. Captain Duff MacCallister, late of the Black Watch, the same famed regiment in which our esteemed mayor and sheriff once served, has put together, and is in command of, the Antelope Wells Home Guard.

Already we have seen clerks and mechanics, blacksmiths and stable hands, cooks and bartenders step out from their daily toil to join with their friends and neighbors in creating a fighting force that stands ready to defend hearth and home.

Take heed, Ebenezer Schofield, you of infamy and ill repute, you who would turn your back on the nation that once nourished you, know now that your evil ambition will not be satisfied here. We stand shoulder to shoulder as have our fathers, grandfathers, and great-grandfathers before us to say with one, resolute voice, "Here, it will end!"

Chapter Eighteen

General Peterson entered headquarters in Cottonwood Springs. "Prime Director, perhaps you should read this article, sir." He showed Schofield a copy of the *Antelope Wells Standard*. "Apparently they have organized themselves into a defensive army."

Schofield read the article, then lay it aside.

"They have little hope of putting together any kind of a cohesive defense force," Peterson said with a mocking laugh. "Clerks? Liverymen?"

"General Peterson, have you forgotten the lesson that General Grant learned at Petersburg?" Schofield asked. By that question he shifted the blame of the failure in that battle from himself to Grant.

"Uh, no sir, I haven't forgotten. I well remember that battle."

"Then you understand how a group of determined men, though they may not be trained in the art of warfare, can, with the advantage of position and the leverage of confidence, be quite a formidable foe."

"Yes, sir," Peterson said. "I am well aware of the benefit of such a situation."

"How far along are they in their training?" Schofield asked.

"A few days," Peterson said. "Less than a week."

"I assume they have at least posted a guard," Schofield said.

"Yes, sir, they have."

"And just how efficient is our contact within the enemy's lines? Does he know the guard's duty station?"

Peterson smiled. "You're talking about Angus Pugh? Yes, sir, thanks to him, we know exactly where the guard is posted."

"Good, we'll hit them early tomorrow morning. But the first thing we are going to have to do is take care of the sentry."

Dooley Jackson was on the roof of the McCoy and Tanner building at the extreme north end of Antelope Wells. From there, looking north, he could see at least a mile, which meant that from the first time he saw them, he would have plenty of time to warn the others. The disc of the sun had not yet appeared, but bars of orange color were just beginning to spread above the eastern horizon, announcing the arriving dawn.

Dooley had come on guard a little over two hours ago and was due to be relieved within another hour. Already he could smell the coffee and the cooking bacon of the early risers, and realized that he was getting hungry.

He kept his gaze on the plains to the north, but there was nothing there.

He almost wished that he could see something. If he gave the warning, why, he'd be a hero to the town.

Jackson heard someone coming up behind him, and because it was still a little too early for him to be relieved, he turned apprehensively toward the sound. "Oh. It's you," he said with a smile. "Seems like you could have at least brought me a cup of coffee."

Half an hour later twelve men wearing the uniforms of Schofield's Legion came galloping into the town without warning. The men were led by a shouting soldier who wore what appeared to be the shoulder boards of an officer.

Duff had, but a moment before, gone into the sheriff's office, and was talking with Sheriff Campbell about the training exercise he wanted to conduct. Though the sheriff himself was not a part of the Home Guard, Duff, in recognition of his position, liked to keep him informed as to his schedule.

When they heard the shooting and the shouting, Duff hurried to the window and saw the attackers galloping up the street, firing wildly.

"Sergeant Major, I've nae a rifle with me. Hand me a rifle!" Duff shouted, reaching his arm back. When Campbell didn't reply, Duff looked around, but Campbell wasn't there. He had gone out the back door.

The rifles were locked in the racks and without Campbell, Duff had no access to them, so he did the next best thing. He stepped out onto the front porch and began shooting at the riders with his pistol.

As he popped away at them, he heard someone else shooting close by, and looking to his right he saw that the sheriff, too, was shooting at them. And, like Duff,

Sheriff Campbell was using a pistol. Elmer was across the street from the sheriff's office, also firing at the attackers. Hawkins, the bugler, was blowing "To Arms," which was an appropriate call under the circumstances.

One innocent citizen had been caught out in the open—the young boy who delivered the papers every morning. At the moment he was standing right in the middle of the street, frozen in fear as he watched the horses galloping toward him.

Suddenly Duff saw Wang dash out into the street, grab the boy, and push him down to the ground. Then Wang got down and used his own body to cover the boy. As the horses dashed over them, Wang and the boy were obscured and there was a moment when Duff could see nothing but horse flesh and flashing legs.

After the horses passed, Duff was sure he would see two battered bodies lying dead in the road. But what he did see was Wang stand up, pull the boy to his feet, then both dash to the other side.

Duff wasn't the only one to see them, for a rider at the rear of the galloping horses turned in his saddle and held his pistol out, taking aim at the two who had escaped being run over. Duff shot first, and the Schofield man fell from the horse, then lay still on the ground.

By the time the raiders reached the far end of town, two of their number lay in the street behind then. Rather than make a second run through the gauntlet, they left town on the opposite end from which they had entered,

Out in the street one of the two started to get up, but there was the sound of a shot, and he went back down. The shot had come from Duff's right, and looking that way, Duff saw Campbell holding a smoking gun.

"'Twould have been better to keep him alive so we could talk to him," Duff suggested.

"He was about to shoot," Campbell said, pointing.

Duff saw that the raider was, indeed holding a pistol. "Aye, perhaps ye made the right move."

"'Tis wondering I am, why Jackson dinnae give us the warning," Campbell said. "I know him well, and he is a man to be trusted."

"That's a good question," Duff said. "Why dinnae he give us a warning?"

As Duff and Campbell started down to the north end of town, Wang and the young paperboy came out of the apothecary where they had taken shelter.

"Wang, what were ye trying to do, get ye and the boy killed? Surely, mon, ye dinnae think ye could be for shielding the boy with your own body?"

"If a galloping horse sees a man on the ground, he will turn and not run over him," Wang said.

"And you knew that for a fact?"

Wang smiled. "It is something I believed to be true. And, as fortune smiled, I was right."

"'Tis good to be a man of convictions," Campbell said with a smile.

"'N would ye be for tellin' me your name, lad?" Duff asked the boy.

"It's Ernie, sir," the boy replied. "Ernie Wallace. I deliver the morning newspapers for Mr. Denham," he added, proudly.

"Well, Ernie, the next time you see a lot of horses galloping down the street, 'twould be best if you'd run out of the way. Mr. Wang may not be there for you next time."

"Are you a Chinaman?" Ernie asked, turning to Wang.

"Yes," Wang replied.

"I've heard of Chinamen, but I ain't never saw one before." Ernie reached up to touch Wang, just below his eyes, fascinated by the epicanthic fold that made his eyes look different. "I would like to shake your hand for saving my life. Do Chinamen shake hands?"

For answer, Wang extended his hand and, with a big smile, Ernie took it.

"We had three killed," McGregor said, joining Duff and the others who were standing in the middle of the street. "Mr. Rafferty was about to open up his store and was shot down on his front porch. Also, sad to say, that Mrs. Finney and her little girl Ellie May were killed. Mr. Finney was still getting dressed 'n says they must have just come out to see what was goin' on."

"How'd they get in here without us a-knowin' about it?" Elmer asked. "I thought the whole idea was for us to be able to see 'em comin' in long enough ahead of time so's that Hawkins could blow a warnin' on his horn."

"That is a good question, Elmer. Why didn't Mr. Jackson provide us with a warning? He was well enough positioned to have a good view of the way the raiders came into town, 'n I've nae idea as to why he dinnae warn us."

"I don't like to say it, but I've got me an idee as to why he didn't," Elmer said.

Duff nodded. "Aye. I have the same idea."

A few minutes later Duff, Elmer, Wang, Campbell and McGregor were all standing on the flat roof of the McCoy and Tanner building.

"Och," Campbell said. "'Tis as we feared."

The scene that had elicited the comment from Campbell was quite gruesome. Dooley Jackson's throat had been cut, and he was lying in a large pool of blood.

Duff checked the rifle Jackson had been holding, and it had not been fired. "He wasn't shot. 'Tis wondering, I am, how 'tis that someone could get close enough to use a knife without Jackson trying to defend himself," Duff question.

"Aye, 'tis a wonderment," Campbell agreed.

Cottonwood Springs

"We killed four," Sergeant Mack said. "But we lost Boyle and Cleaver."

"You only killed four?" Lieutenant Fillion asked.

"That's all right, Lieutenant. This was a reconnaissance operation only. Tell me, were you able to determine their defensive positions?" Schofield asked.

Bond smiled. "Yes, sir, I was. They have not built any fortifications. They had only one guard posted, and the resistance we encountered was sporadic and undisciplined. A well-planned, coordinated attack of the kind in which you excel, Prime Director, cannot help but be met with great success."

"Very good job, Captain," Schofield replied. "Good report."

"Thank you, sir," Bond said, beaming from the praise.

"When are we going to attack them, Prime Director?" General Peterson asked.

"Soon. I want to attack before they are able to get themselves too well organized, but I don't want to be too quick about it, either. Antelope Wells is not only the most important of all the towns we have attacked so far, it is also the last town we will have to take. I believe we will succeed, for now we have them cut off from the rest of the Bootheel in a stranglehold." Schofield demonstrated by holding his hands out before him, then squeezing them shut, as if choking someone by the neck.

"Soon a new nation will take its place among the nations of the world," he added.

"One hundred years from now our descendants will look back upon these times and celebrate the birth of our nation," General Peterson said proudly.

"General, we cannot afford to fail in this campaign. Keep our men in readiness, while I work out the plan of attack."

"Yes, sir," General Peterson replied.

From the *Antelope Wells Standard:*

Dastardly Attack Beaten Back
BY CLINT H. DENHAM

On the third instant, a group of uniformed villains proclaiming themselves as Schofield's Legion launched a cowardly dawn attack upon our town. They were able to use the element of surprise against us, because their entry was unannounced. Dooley Jackson, who had been posted to a most excellent lookout position on top of the McCoy and Tanner building, was unable to give the alarm.

It wasn't because of a failure of duty that there was no alarm given. Failure to give the alarm was the result of person or persons using stealth to gain access to Mr. Jackson's sentinel position, where they killed him.

Without prior warning being given, a

relatively small band of Schofield's Legion swept into town, not for some sustained campaign of battle, but rather for a nuisance raid which resulted in the death of four of our citizens. Also killed, in addition to Dooley Jackson, were Dan Rafferty, proprietor of Rafferty's store, and Mrs. Emma Finney and her young daughter, Ellie Mae.

Captain MacCallister has declared that from this day forward, a rather substantial force of our Home Guard will be in fortified positions, ready to do battle. With the unprovoked attack of Schofield's Legion, the tocsins of war have been sounded, and we, the citizens of Antelope Wells, stand ready to defend home and hearth.

Chapter Nineteen

A few days after the initial attack from Schofield's Legion, Lucy approached the table where Duff, Meagan, and McGregor were having their dinner. Both Duff and McGregor stood.

"I know this may be an imposition on you, but my father has expressed a desire to join you for dinner tonight," Lucy said. "Do you suppose that would be possible?"

"'Twould not only be possible, 'twould be a pleasure," Mayor McGregor said.

A moment later General Culpepper, in full Confederate uniform, complete with a golden sash wrapped around his middle, joined them at the table. "Thank you, ma'am and gentlemen, for the invitation to join you."

"'Tis our pleasure," Duff replied.

"If you don't mind, gentlemen, and if the ladies will show us some forbearance, I would like to discuss some tactics with you."

"Tactics?" McGregor replied.

"Yes, particularly with regard to the reconnaissance scout that General Schofield launched yesterday."

"Reconnaissance? 'Tis your belief that the wee fracas we had yesterday was but a reconnaissance?" McGregor asked.

"Oh, indeed," General Culpepper replied.

"'N would ye be for tellin' us why you think such a thing?" Duff asked.

"Consider this, Captain. Had it been an attack, he would have used more men, and he would have deployed them in enfilade to assault any fixed positions. He clearly didn't do that, which means this was not intended to be an attack." Culpepper smiled. "But we have no fortifications for him to discover, do we?"

"That's my fault," Duff said. "I wanted a little more training for the men before I actually assigned defensive positions."

"Ah, but that is a good thing," General Culpepper said. "Now we can establish a defense perimeter without Schofield knowing where our positions are."

"Aye, good point," McGregor said.

"Here is something I noticed about Schofield during our previous encounters. He is a leader who depends more upon numbers than tactics. He has quite a large force with him now, and he is well aware that our numbers are limited. He will do all that he can to take advantage of the disparity in strength." Culpepper smiled. "And *we* can take advantage of that. What we lack in numbers, we will compensate for in the disciplined implementation of tactical planning."

"Tell me, General, would ye be for having any suggestions as to how best we should apply these tactics?" Duff asked.

Culpepper nodded. "I do indeed, gentlemen, but such things would be better discussed at another time and another place. We've two young ladies with us, and I've no wish to bore them with such a subject. May I suggest that, for now we become more pleasant company for the ladies and enjoy our meal?"

By prearrangement, Culpepper met Duff, Elmer, and Wang in the lobby of the Dunn Hotel the next morning.

"I've drawn a map with my recommendations," Culpepper said, showing a paper to Duff.

The map was beautifully drawn with the buildings along Cactus Street drawn to exact scale. On the east side of the street the northernmost building was the McCoy and Tanner building, then Fahlkoff's Book and Stationery. Next came Buckner and Ragsdale Clothing, White's Drugstore, Hidden Trail Saloon, The *Antelope Wells Standard* newspaper office, McGill Feed and Seed, the Desert Stagecoach office, and the O. D. Clayton Livery barn. On the west side of the street, the first building going up from the south end was the Western Union office, then Antelope Wells Christian Tabernacle Church. Antelope Wells Public School, the Bank of Antelope Wells, Potashnick Wagon Freight, Sikes Hardware, Chip's Shoe Alley, Bear Tracks Restaurant, Norton and Heckemeyer Law office, the Stallcup Building, Golden Spur Saloon, and the Dunn Hotel.

"It will take some work, but if we put all of my suggestions into play I believe we can make our town impregnable," Culpepper said. "Or at least, as impregnable as is possible."

Duff studied the map, looking at the suggestions Culpepper made. He chuckled. "You are right, sir. It will take some work to do all that ye suggest."

"And?" Culpepper asked.

"And it will make the town nearly impregnable," Duff added with an agreeable nod.

For the next few days the men of the town worked feverishly to build up the fortifications before another attack. For the construction of the fortifications, even those who had been turned away from service in the Home Guard were called upon. The space between every building was fortified by double walls built five feet high and with eighteen inches of space between the walls. The women worked as well, carrying buckets of dirt from the excavations to the fortifications, where they poured dirt into the space between.

As each of the fortifications were completed, a rifle was fired into it to test whether or not the walls would actually provide protection to anyone who was behind them. Every fortification passed the test.

Cottonwood Springs

"Sergeant Yancey," Schofield said to one of his NCOs. "I have a mission for you to perform. Are you ready to serve our cause?"

"Yes, sir."

"I want you to leave before dawn tomorrow morning and ride into Antelope Wells, drawing as little attention to yourself as possible. I would like an accurate assessment as to the number of armed men they can muster. Also determine anything they may be doing in order to prepare a defense against us."

"I thought we already had us someone in town that was sposed to be doin' stuff like that," Yancey said.

"We do, but he isn't able to keep us as informed as we need to be. If you would rather not do this, I can get someone else, perhaps someone who is better suited to wear your stripes."

"No, no, sir. There ain't no need for you to be a-thinkin' that way. I'll be glad do it," Sergeant Yancey said. "It's just that I thought you already had someone in town a-doin' that, 'n I didn't want to get in the way, is all."

"Don't worry, Sergeant Yancey, you won't be working at cross-purposes. Quite the contrary. I want you to make contact with him so that we can coordinate our efforts. Also, he may have additional information for us that he has not been able to get out. Your presence in town can facilitate that for him."

"Yes, sir, but that's goin' to be kind of a problem, though."

"Oh? And what would that problem be?"

"I don't know who this feller is that I'm sposed to be seein'."

"It isn't necessary that you know who it is," Schofield said. "Not even I know he is. As I'm sure you can understand, our man in Antelope Wells is taking a great risk working for us, and the fewer who know his name, the more efficiently will he be able to operate."

"Yes, sir, maybe that's right 'n all, but how is it that I'm goin' to be able to contact him, if I don't know who it is?"

"I will tell you how to identify yourself, and he will contact you."

"How will I know that the one that contacts me is really the right one?"

"We have devised a password to use in order to validate any contacts we may have," Schofield said. "The passwords are *Hill Climber. Hill* is the challenge; the correct countersign will be *Climber.* Do you have that?"

"*Hill Climber.* Yes, sir, I got it."

"I shall want you to ride into town as soon after sunrise tomorrow as is practicable."

"I'll most likely have to leave in the middle of the night in order to get there just after sunrise tomorrow mornin'," Yancey said.

"I'm quite sure you will, Sergeant."

Just after dawn on the third day of constructing the fortifications Elmer climbed up onto the roof of the Dunn Hotel in Antelope Wells to visit with Buddy Cox, who was on guard duty.

"Who's there?" Cox challenged as Elmer stepped out onto the roof.

"It's me, Mr. Cox. Elmer Gleason." He held out his hand.

"Sorry," Cox said. "I guess that after what happened to Dooley Jackson, I'm just a little jumpy, is all."

"It's good that you're jumpy," Elmer said. "Ever'one should be jumpy."

"Yeah, it's too bad that Dooley wasn't. He was a good man. Sorry to see him get kilt that way. I mean, lettin' someone sneak up on 'im 'n all."

"Maybe there warn't nobody that snuck up on 'im," Elmer suggested.

"What do you mean? I heard he warn't shot, 'n if he warn't shot, then that means somebody snuck up on 'im. He was cut with a knife, 'n there ain't no way you could get close enough to someone to cut 'em with a knife, unless you was to sneak up on 'em."

"You sure 'bout that? You heard me a-comin', didn't

you? I was walkin' real quiet, 'n I didn't have near as far to come acrossed this roof to get to you as whoever the feller was that kilt Dooley had to go."

"Well, how else would someone a-got to Jackson like they done if they didn't sneak up on 'im?"

"What if they just walked up on 'im in plain sight?"

"Why, they couldn't nobody a-done that lessen—" Cox stopped in mid-sentence. "Damn! If it was somebody that Dooley knowed 'n trusted, why whoever it was coulda just come right on up to 'im, couldn't he? 'N Dooley wouldn'ta thought nothin' about it."

Elmer nodded. "That's what I'm thinkin'."

"Then that means that most likely there would be someone that's right here in town that's a traitor, don't it?"

"Yeah, that's exactly what it means."

"I wonder who it is," Cox asked.

"I don't know. It could be anybody. The point is, ever'one of us is goin' to have to be real careful."

"Yeah," Cox agreed.

Elmer saw a single rider approaching town. "Here comes someone," he said, nodding toward the rider. "You got any idea who that might be?" Elmer asked.

Cox stared at the rider, then shook his head. "I ain't never seen 'im before. But bein' as he's comin' in all by his ownself, 'n he ain't wearin' one o' them fancy uniforms like them fellers was a-wearin' when they all come in the other day, then I don't see no need for us to put out no warning."

"How often do you get strangers riding into town?" Elmer asked.

"Well, a-fore all this business started with this here Schofield feller, we used to get quite a few folks that was comin' in near 'bout ever' day. Mostly it was folks that was just goin' over into Mexico on a visit for a few days or somethin'. But the truth is, we ain't been a-gettin' 'em all that much here lately. Do you think maybe I ought to tell the sheriff about this here feller that just come a' ridin' into town?"

"No, there ain't no need for you to do that," Elmer said. "I'll keep an eye on 'im today, 'n if I get suspicious of 'im, I'll talk to Duff about 'im."

Yancey wasn't wearing the uniform of Schofield's Legion, but he did have a piece of red cloth tied to his horse's bridle. That had been decreed by Schofield as part of the methodology by which he could be identified by their local contact. In carrying out the rest of the identification procedure he rode very slowly down the entire length of Cactus Street. He stopped in front of the Hidden Trail Saloon, started toward the door, stopped before he went inside, then returned to his horse and rode it to Golden Spur Saloon. There he did the same thing—dismounted, started toward the entrance of the saloon, then returned to his horse and rode down to the livery, dismounted and led his horse into the livery barn.

These seemingly indecisive moves were by design. They, along with the red cloth tied to the bridle, were the means Schofield had described by which Yancey was to make contact with the mysterious resident of Antelope Wells. The man called himself Angus Pugh, and whatever his real name was, he was the one who was betraying his fellow citizens.

After turning his horse over to the stable hand, Yancey walked to the back of the livery and looked out across the corral. He was looking into Mexico, and he really didn't have to look far. The Mexican border was less than one hundred yards beyond the far side of the corral.

"Hill," a voice said from behind him.

"What?" Yancey started to turn around to face the man who had spoken to him.

"Don't turn around," the voice said. The man repeated the word *hill*.

"Oh, yeah. Uh, climber," Yancey replied.

"Hold your hand out behind you," the voice ordered.

Yancey did so, and felt a piece of paper being put into his hand

"What is this?" Yancey looked at what he had been given, but saw that it was in a sealed envelope marked for the Prime Director. Yancey was very curious as to what might be in the envelope, but he knew better than to open it. "You got anything you want me to tell 'im?"

There was no response to his question.

"Hello, Pugh? You still there? Can I turn around now?"

There was still no answer, so despite the mysterious visitor's admonition against it, Yancey turned around. And just as he thought, nobody was there. He might think that he had been visited by a ghost, had it not been for the envelope he was holding. The envelope was quite real.

Yancey slid the envelope into his shirt pocket, then, leaving his horse at the livery walked down the street a bit until he reached the Hidden Trail Saloon. He was greeted by a provocatively dressed and heavily made-up, though pretty, young woman.

"Hi, cowboy. My name is Ethel Marie. What's yours?"

"The name is Yancey." He looked around the nearly empty saloon. "Where is everyone?"

"Why, everyone is out getting ready for Schofield," Ethel Marie answered.

"Getting ready, how?"

"Ethel Marie, there's nae need for ye to be answering such questions from a stranger," said one of the few customers of the saloon. He was wearing a star pinned to his vest.

"Are you the sheriff?" Yancey asked.

"Aye, Sheriff Campbell. Ye told the lass that your name is Yancey. 'N would ye be for tellin' me, Mr. Yancey, what would be your business in Antelope Wells?"

"I ain't got no particular business to take care of here, but I don't see how it's none of your business for you to be a-knowin' what my business was, iffen I had any business bein' here in the first place."

"Aye, Mr. Yancey, I can see how 'tis that ye might be thinkin' such a thing." Campbell pointed to the star on his vest. "But seeing as I am the sheriff of Antelope Wells, the safety of all the citizens of this town are my responsibility, and that makes your business my business. Now I'll be asking ye again, would ye be for telling me why you are here?"

"It's like I told you, I ain't got no particular business other 'n I just come in to have a look around is all."

"Ye would be best served if ye would just leave town. Now is nae a good time for to be visiting," Campbell said.

"Sheriff, are you running me out of town?"

Campbell shook his head. "I'll nae be running you out of town, Mr. Yancey, for I cannae think of a reason to do so. But in case ye have nae heard, there is a vandal by the name of Schofield who has it in mind to attack our town with an army, 'n all who are here would be in danger. Ye not being a citizen of our town would be foolish to stay 'n put yourself in such a position when ye've nae need to."

"Yeah, well I tell you what, Sheriff, you just take care of your business of lookin' out for the town, 'n I'll look out for me." Yancey smiled at Ethel Marie. "Barkeep, I'll have a whiskey, 'n I'll be buyin' a drink for this purty thing here, iffen she'll take the time to drink it with me."

"I'd be glad to, honey." Ethel Marie looked around the saloon, which had but three other customers at the moment—Sheriff Campbell and two men who were much too old to be sharing the labor of the other men of the town.

"It's not like anyone else is bidding for my time," she added.

Chapter Twenty

The women who were not engaged in the actual physical labor of constructing the walls prepared meals, then served them from long tables made from planks stretched across sawhorses in the middle of the street.

Lucy and Meagan were among the women who were preparing the meals, and at the moment Duff and Meagan were sitting on the edge of the porch in front of Sikes Hardware, each with a plate balanced on their laps. Across the street from them, they could see Lucy and McGregor sitting in front of the Norton and Heckemeyer Law Office, doing the same thing.

"Miss Culpepper and the leftenant colonel seem to be getting along well," Duff said.

Meagan laughed.

"What is it? Why do ye laugh?"

"Have you no eyes, Duff MacCallister?" Meagan said. "Can't you see that they are in love?"

"What? 'N would you be for telling me why you would say such a thing?"

"It is as obvious as the nose on your face," Meagan

said. "Why, I saw it the first time Lucy came to our table, the way she and Mayor McGregor looked at each other. She won't do anything about it, though, because she has a sense of obligation to her father."

Elmer stepped over to talk with Duff and Meagan. "Duff, did you see that feller that went into the Hidden Trail Saloon just a minute or two ago?"

"Nae, I dinnae notice."

"Well, I was up on the roof o' the hotel just a-fore dawn this mornin', visitin' with Buddy Cox when I seen him come ridin' in. Cox said he warn't from here. I been pretty much keepin' an eye on 'im all day, 'n he ain't done one lick o' work to help anyone out. But he sure has been curious 'bout what all it is that we're a-doin'. I can tell you that much."

"Spying on us, do you think?" Duff asked.

"I'd bet a kiss from a pretty girl that he is."

"Ye may be right."

"If you don't mind, I think maybe I'll step inter the saloon 'n see if I can find out who he is, 'n what he's doin' here."

"I think that might be a good idea," Duff replied.

Elmer stepped up to the bar a few minutes later and ordered a whiskey.

"Hello, Mr. Gleason," Ethel Marie greeted.

"Why, hello, Miss Ethel Marie," Elmer replied with a friendly smile

She started toward him.

"Just a minute. Hold on there, woman!" Yancey called out to her. "What are you doin' walkin' away from me like that?"

"Why, I'm doing exactly what I'm supposed to be

doing, honey," Ethel Marie replied. "I'm greeting the customers."

"Yeah? Well he don't need no greetin'. I mean look at 'em, an old man like that? Why would you be a-wastin' your time on someone like him anyhow? *I'm* a customer, and besides which, *I'm* the one that bought you a drink," Yancey insisted. "That means you ain't got no right to be a-spending any of your time with anyone else."

"Now, look here, Mr. Yancey. You may have bought me a drink, but you didn't buy *me*," Ethel Marie said.

"Yeah? Well, that's where you're wrong, on account of when you buy a drink for a saloon whore, then that's the same as if you was to buy the whore her ownself."

Ethel Marie got a hurt expression on her face. "I'm not a whore. I'm a hostess."

Elmer gave the bartender a dime. "Mr. Usher, would you please give that loudmouthed feller the cost o' Miss Ethel Marie's drink back to him, so he don't feel cheated none with her walkin' away."

"Who the hell are you, old man, to be a-buttin' inter my business?" Yancey asked, angrily.

"I was just seein' to it that you got your money back so that you wouldn't be so upset, is all."

"Woman, if you don't come back down here, I aim to kill that old man," Yancey said.

"What? No!" Ethel Marie shouted. "You have no call to do anything like that!"

Elmer stepped away from the bar and into the middle of the floor. By that move he managed to separate himself from Ethel Marie. "I may be an old man, sonny, but even I know you can't kill someone while your gun is still in the holster."

"You're right," Yancey said, and then with a wide, confident smile on his face, his hand darted down to his pistol. As he brought his pistol up to bear, the confident smile was replaced by an expression of shock as he realized that the old man had drawn his own gun faster. There was no time for the shock to change to fear, before both guns roared.

The bullet from Elmer's gun plunged into Yancey's chest. The bullet from Yancey's gun went wide of its mark and slammed into the front wall of the saloon, right next to the door frame.

Ethel Marie, Sheriff Campbell, Usher the bartender, and the other two saloon customers stood by, shocked by how suddenly an otherwise minor difference of opinion had developed into a deadly shoot-out, for Elmer's bullet had gone right to the heart. Mo Yancey, a deserter from the US Cavalry, and now a sergeant in Schofield's Legion, was dead before he hit the floor.

"Duff!" Meagan called out in sudden alarm at hearing the gunshot. "That came from the saloon that Elmer's in!"

Standing quickly, Duff drew his own pistol and ran down the boardwalk to the saloon. When he pushed through the batwing doors he saw Elmer standing, holding a smoking gun down by his side, looking at a man who was lying on the floor. Sheriff Campbell was bending over the prostrate form.

"Elmer! Are ye all right?" Duff called out in concern.

"Yeah, I'm fine," Elmer said. "He ain't doin' so good, though." He pointed to the man on the floor.

"Elmer!" Meagan said, coming into the saloon a moment behind Duff.

"He's all right, lass," Duff assured her.

Meagan hurried over to Elmer to give him an embrace.

"Ha!" one of the two older customers said. "I reckon that feller on the floor there figured that him bein' a lot younger, he could beat you on the draw. Mr. Gleason, I'm proud of you for stickin' up for us old folks, ever'where."

Elmer chuckled. "Well now, Mr. Bledsoe, I ain't nowhere nigh as old as you are, so don't get to thinkin' me too old, now."

"Maybe not, but you're old enough that me 'n Dale here can be proud of you," Bledsoe said.

"Hey, did you see this feller's face right after he drawed his gun?" Dale asked. "I can tell you just what it was, that he was a-thinkin'."

"What was that, Mr. Kelly?" the bartender asked.

"He was a-thinkin', 'oh damn, have I ever made a mistake here.'"

The others in the saloon laughed.

Sheriff Campbell pulled a letter from the dead man's shirt pocket. Opening the envelope he examined the paper inside, then let out a low whistle. "Och, I wonder what this might be?"

"What have ye found, Sergeant Major?" Duff asked.

Campbell held the paper out toward Duff. "'Tis a map. A map of all the fortifications we've been putting in. Everything all neatly marked."

Duff examined the map then nodded. "Aye, 'tis a right thorough job, too."

"I would say that the blaggard has had a busy

morning," Campbell said. "There are no secrets left, for he has it all marked, 'n even the sentinel postings."

Elmer shook his head. "No, sir, he didn't do that this morning."

"Why do you say that?" Duff asked.

"Well, sir, for one thing, I seen 'im when he come inter town this mornin', 'n I've been keepin' an eye on 'em all the time. I ain't seen 'im makin' no notes or drawin' no pictures neither."

"Someone gave him this map," Duff said, looking at it.

"How do you know that for sure?" Meagan asked.

"Take a good look at it," Duff said, showing it to the others. "The fortifications here, here, and here are marked."

"Aye," Campbell said. "'Tis as I said."

"I see, Duff," Elmer said after he looked at the map, then showed it to the others. "'N here's another reason someone give 'im the note. These here places that Duff's talkin' about, that's marked all good 'n proper here? Some of 'em ain't even been put in yet."

"Damn! That really does mean we have a spy right here in town, don't it?" Usher said.

"We're going to have to find him before he does too much damage," Duff said.

"Captain MacCallister, ye have too much to do to be trainin' our lads to defend the town, 'n finish up with the forts 'n all," Campbell said. "I'm the sheriff, 'n seems to me I should be takin' care o' lookin' out for any spies as may be among our midst. Ye just leave that to me, 'n 'tis this promise I'll give ye. I will find the spy, 'n we'll deal with him by whatever way it takes."

Duff nodded. "My thanks to you, Sergeant Major. You're right. I've many more things to do to get ready for Schofield. And 'tis good to be for knowing that I'll nae have to worry about a spy among us."

"I wonder who the son of a bitch is," Usher said, then he saw Meagan and Ethel Marie. "Ladies, I ask that you forgive me my language."

Ethel Marie laughed. "That's all right, Mr. Usher. If there is a spy in town, he really is a son of a bitch."

The others laughed.

Chapter Twenty-one

"I've examined all the fortifications, Captain MacCallister," General Culpepper said over dinner that evening. "I must say that your men are doing a very good job in putting them into place."

"Thank you, General," Duff said.

"How will you deploy your forces?"

"'Tis my thinking that I'll have the heaviest concentration of men at the north end of Cactus Street," Duff said. "That way it will make it hard for Schofield's men to even get into town."

General Culpepper nodded. "Yes, heavy defense at the point of attack could stop them, and that is certainly one way to do it, and since this is your command, the decision is yours. But that tactic, while preventing them from entering the town, would probably turn them away with minimal casualties. If you would allow me to make a suggestion?"

"Aye, by all means, do make a suggestion," Duff said.

"In all of Schofield's previous campaigns in his quest to take over the Bootheel, he has met with only sporadic resistance. As a result they have grown complacent to the degree that they are overconfident. Suppose the north end of town, which we all agree is the most likely point of contact, was lightly defended? Meeting little resistance at the initial point of contact would draw them in, then when they are totally committed, we'll hit them with everything we have. That way we can inflict the greatest number of casualties, maybe even to the point that Schofield will be dissuaded from any further attempts."

Duff smiled. "Aye, now that is a great idea, General."

"Thank you, my boy, thank you." Culpepper yawned. "And now, if you good people would excuse me, I think I'll go my room and go to bed. I'm an old man but"— he looked at the other four at the table, Duff and Meagan, and McGregor and Lucy—"I'm not too old to see when my presence at this table is superfluous. Enjoy your dinner."

"Captain MacCallister, from the bottom of my heart, I want to thank you," Lucy said after the general left. "My father has been more animated in the time since you arrived than I have ever seen him. You have given him purpose and self-pride."

"Aye, that may be, lass," Duff replied, "but your father's observations and suggestions have been most helpful. 'Tis thankful I am that we have a man with your father's skill in the military arts to help us prepare for Schofield and his army of miscreants."

The next morning the members of the Home Guard, as well as those who weren't part of the Home Guard but who had worked on the fortifications, were all standing in the middle of Cactus Street, having been summoned to the meeting by Duff. General Culpepper was there as well, standing alongside Duff. Elmer and Wang were also present, but they were standing somewhat back from the gathering.

"Gentlemen. 'Tis pleased I am to tell ye that the general and I have inspected all your work 'n can find nothing else that needs to be done," Duff said. "Your work here . . . that is, the labor . . . is done."

The assembled crowd, which also included a few women, cheered at the news.

"Now, with the work done, I'll be for letting ye all go about your business. We'll have four guards posted at all times, one on the McCoy and Tanner building and one on the roof of the Dunn Hotel. To the south we'll have guards posted on top of the Western Union office and across the street at the livery stable. Sergeant Morley will work out the schedule. If there's some reason that ye cannae stand guard, let me know 'n we'll see if we can come up with a solution."

"Why are we goin' to have somebody at the south end?" someone asked. "It ain't the Mexicans that's goin' to attack."

"And would ye be for tellin' me ye think Schofield would nae cross the border?"

"Oh, yeah. Well, I reckon he could do that."

"Bugler?" Duff called.

"Yes, sir?" Hawkins replied.

"Would ye blow 'To Arms' for us?"

Hawkins raised the instrument to his lips and blew the bugle call as requested.

"Now, gentleman, that stirring piece of music so beautifully performed by Maestro Hawkins"—Duff took in the bugler with a wave of his hand—"will be the summons for ye to take up your positions to repel an attack. So wherever you are, 'n whatever ye may be doing, the very minute ye hear the bugle call, stop doing whatever it is that ye may be doing, and proceed at once to your duty station."

"To our what?"

"Your duty station, the place which you will assigned to man during any attack on the town."

"Yes, sir, but now, here's the thing, Cap'n. We ain't none of us been given one o' them duty stations."

"Sergeant Morley, post!" Duff called.

Chris Morley stepped out from the rest of the men.

"Sergeant Morley, as soon as this meeting ends, I would like for you to assign the men to the fortifications as we discussed."

"Yes, sir!" Morley replied, proud of the responsibility. He saluted Duff, and Duff returned it with a smile.

"Are we all finished here, now?" The man who called out was Darrel Wright, one of the older men. He had been turned away from the Home Guard because of his age.

Duff had seen him working during the construction of the fortifications, and he had more than carried his own weight, so much so that Duff wondered if he had made a mistake in not including Wright as a member of the Home Guard.

"Those of ye who are not part of the Home Guard may leave now, but the Home Guard must remain so Sergeant Morley can assign you to your position of defense in the event of an attack."

"What do you mean 'in the event of?'" one of the men asked. "We're goin' to be attacked for sure 'n certain, ain't we?"

"I would say that the answer to that is aye, we will be attacked. 'N because of that ye can see the need for bein' told where you must be when the fighting starts.

Also, there is the need to work out the guard station assignments and times. Sergeant Morley, ye have the command."

"Yes, sir!" Morley said, saluting again.

After leaving the Home Guard in Sergeant Morley's hands, Duff walked down to the mayor's office to report that all construction was completed, and the men were being assigned their duty stations. The conversation turned to the incident in the saloon the day before when Elmer shot and killed Yancey.

"I think 'twas a surprise to everyone when they saw how rapidly Mr. Gleason could draw 'n engage his weapon," McGregor said.

"Ye mean because of Elmer's age?" Duff asked.

"Aye. One tends to think of gunfighters as being young men with good hands and quick reflexes."

"Ye should nae let Elmer's age discompose ye. He is most skilled with a gun, as he has demonstrated many times."

"Aye, for the facts cannae be argued. 'N 'twas a good thing that that Sergeant Major Campbell went through the man's pockets, for who would have known that Schofield's man had a map of all the new fortifications?"

"Aye, if that information had been taken to Schofield, we would have lost the element of surprise, 'n that will be our strongest weapon when the attack comes."

"'Twas smart of you, Captain, to see that the map that Sheriff Campbell found on the brigand was not of his observation, but was given him by someone in our own midst," McGregor said.

"It wasn't hard to figure it out," Duff said. "Especially after Elmer said that he had kept an eye on the man from the moment he had come into town, and he had not had time to draw up the map. In addition to which he had fortifications marked on his map that we had nae yet constructed."

"'Tis not a good thing to learn that we have a traitor among us," McGregor said. "But the sergeant major is a good man, 'n 'tis comforting to know that finding the guilty one is in his hands."

At that same moment, Ed Truax was in Sheriff Campbell's office.

"Is it true that you found a map on that feller that Gleason kilt yesterday?"

"Aye, 'tis true."

"'N on that map, what's wrote and drawed on it tells about all the work we've been doin in gettin' ready for Schofield, does he decide to come?" Truax asked.

"Aye, that's true as well," Campbell replied.

"Folks is sayin' that it more 'n likely come from someone here in town, that we got us a spy," Truax said.

Campbell nodded. "I'm afraid they may be right."

Truax sighed and shook his head. "Damn. I was hopin' it warn't him."

"'Twasn't who? Who would ye be speakin' of?"

"I hate to say it. I mean seein' as I ain't got no proof nor nothin'. But I got me an idea as to who the spy might be. It's him that works with me. Anton Drexler."

"'N would ye be for tellin' me lad, why ye think it would be Drexler?"

"Well sir, me 'n Drexler 'n Collins 'n 'Morley was talkin' 'bout things a few days ago, 'n Drexler up 'n said that he was goin' to join up with Schofield."

"What?" Campbell replied in a shocked voice. "Drexler said he was goin' to join Schofield's army?"

"No, sir. That is, that ain't quite exactly what it was that he said. But it's what he did say that's got me to thinkin'. What I done is, I ask 'im outright, 'Are you sayin' we should join up with the army that's comin' to attack us?' 'N what he said is, 'No, but they's other ways of joinin' up with Schofield besides joinin' up with the Legion 'n actual fightin' with 'em.'

"Then he talked about how many was kilt in them other towns that Schofield attacked, 'n said it could be that joinin' up with 'im might be 'bout the only way we have of savin' all the lives of the people in Antelope Wells.

"So what I'm thinkin' is, I mean Drexler sayin' he was goin' to join up with Schofield, but he warn't goin' to actual join the army, well sir, it just seems to me like he's most likely the one that drawed up the map for 'em. Could be that he figured that's what he would do 'stead of actual joinin' up with 'em."

Campbell stroked his chin as he listened to the explanation of why Truax suspected Drexler.

"I'm tellin' you 'bout this 'cause I thought you should know," Truax concluded.

"'Tis thanking you I am for that information, Mr. Truax. But the truth is, I don't know if I can arrest 'im with no more evidence than just something that he said. I'll talk with the mayor about it. In the meantime, I'd like for ye to be tellin' some of the others what ye just told me. That way, even if the mayor says I cannae arrest the blaggard, we can at least all keep our eyes on him so that he cannae do such a thing again."

Truax nodded. "Yeah. Yeah, that's a good idea. I'll spread the word around so that ever'body else will know what it is that he's done."

* * *

A few minutes later, Truax was in the Golden Spur Saloon. Unlike the last few days when the saloons had been relatively empty because of the necessity of building up the fortifications, today the saloon was quite crowded. Nearly everyone there had toiled long hours in putting together the defensive redoubts, some of whom were a part of the Home Guard, and would actually man the defensive positions. However, the largest majority of the saloon patrons at the moment was composed of men who had worked on the defenses, but had not been chosen to become a Home Guardsman.

"A map it was," one of the saloon patrons said. "Can you believe that? I mean he actually had a map that showed where ever'thing was, 'n it even had where the guards would be posted."

"Really? You mean Schofield knows where ever'thing is?" another asked.

"No, he don't know where nothin' is," Truax said. "Leastwise, he don't know nothin' yet, on account of Elmer Gleason kilt him a-fore it was that he could take the map to him."

"Oh, well, then there ain't no need to be a-worryin' about it, is there? I mean, seein' as Schofield ain't actual seen the map that feller drawed up yet."

"Yes, there is a reason to worry," Truax said.

"Why do you say that?"

"On account of this Yancey feller that got kilt ain't actual the one that drawed up the map. Someone else done it, 'n when Yancey come into town what he done was, he met up with whoever it was that actual did draw up the map. 'N that feller is the one what give the map to him."

"You mean there was two of 'em that come into town? I ain't seen no other strangers. Any of you seen a stranger in town? I mean, other 'n that Yancey feller that Gleason kilt."

There were half a dozen negative responses to the question.

"There ain't no need to be a-lookin' for nobody else from Schofield's army that come into town 'cause Yancey is the only one that did," Truax said. "The one that drawed up the map 'n give to Yancey was Anton Drexler."

"Hell, I know Drexler. He's one of us. Why would he do somethin' like that?" someone said.

"Yeah, well I know 'im too," one of the others said. "'N if you was to ask me about 'im, I'd say this is just like somethin' that sneaky devil would do."

Truax then told the others about the conversation he'd had with Drexler.

"You mean he actual said that he would join up with Schofield?" another asked.

By now everyone in the saloon had been drawn toward Truax as he told the story.

"Was they anybody else with you when he told that story?"

"Yeah. Collins 'n Morley was both with me, so if you don't believe me, you could ask one of them."

"Hell, if Morley was with you, that's good enough for me. Morley is a good man, 'n now he's our sergeant," said one of the members of the Home Guard.

"Listen. How come you ain't told that story to the sheriff?" another asked.

Truax shook his head in frustration. "I have told 'im about it, but he said he didn't think there was nothin' he could do about it. He told me that I should tell ever'one else about it, so's we could all keep a eye on Drexler."

"Keep a eye on 'im. Hell! I say we should string the traitor up!" one of the group said in frustration.

"Yes! Somebody get a rope!" another yelled. "We can hang him from the livery stanchion!"

What had been a convivial group of men, resting from their labors over a drink and the shared experience of hard work, quickly took on the appearance and conduct of a mob.

"Let's hang the traitor!" still another shouted.

The saloon was nearly emptied of its patrons as there was an angry and determined rush toward the front door.

Chapter Twenty-two

Cottonwood Springs

"Yancey isn't back?" Schofield asked.

"No, Prime Director," Peterson said. "I'm beginning to think that he has been compromised in some way."

"I don't like it," Schofield said. "Without intelligence as to the layout of the enemy positions, an army is blind."

"Prime Director, we had no problems with the other towns we took—Hachita, La Tenja, Cottonwood Springs. Why are you so concerned about Antelope Wells?" Captain Bond asked.

"This man MacCallister wasn't in the other towns," Schofield replied. "And he has already proven himself to be a most formidable adversary. I don't believe that we will be able to take Antelope Wells as easily as we took the other towns. I hoped that Sergeant Yancey would be able to supply me with the information I need to plan the attack, but it is now obvious that he has failed us."

"Yes, sir, I'm afraid you may be correct," General Peterson said.

"We must have some information about the town," Schofield insisted, hitting the palm of his hand with his fist.

"Perhaps I can go in, Prime Director," Captain Bond offered.

"No. I've no doubt but that we have lost Sergeant Yancey. My officers are too valuable to the success of the mission to take the chance of losing them. And unfortunately, Yancey has made it all too evident that my noncommissioned officers are inadequate to the task."

"Perhaps I can take the spyglass," Bond said. "If I am far enough away to avoid any personal danger, but close enough to be able to use the spyglass to see what is going on, I might be able to gather some useful information."

"Yes," Schofield said enthusiastically. "Yes, you may well be able to do so. Very good, Captain, proceed at once."

Elmer and Wang were standing at the bar of the Hidden Trail Saloon when Truax and two other locals of Antelope Wells—men who had been with him at the Golden Spur—came in.

"Hello, Ed," one of the men at the far end of the bar. "Come have a drink with us. We're celebratin' gettin' all the work done for the fortin' up, 'n all."

"Yeah," Truax said. "That's good, but we got somethin' else to do first."

"Oh? What's that?"

"You know that the feller that was kilt in here yesterday had him a map of all our forts 'n such."

"Yeah, I heard that."

"Yes, sir. Well, did you also hear that he got the map from someone right here in town?"

"What? No, I didn't hear that."

"That's right. We got us a traitor right here in town. Turns out that one of our own has turned agin us."

"Damn! Who do you reckon that was?"

"We don't have to reckon. We know who it was," Truax said. "It was Anton Drexler."

"Drexler? Are you sure? Hell, I've known Drexler for a long time. I never woulda figured him for doin' such a thing. What makes you think it was him?"

Truax told the patrons of Hidden Trail the same story he had told the men at the Golden Spur, as to how he, Collins, and Morley had heard Drexler say that he intended to join Schofield. "There ain't no doubt in my mind but what it was Drexler who drawed up that map 'n give it Yancey," he concluded.

"Have you told the sheriff about it?" someone asked.

"Yeah, I told 'im."

"What did he say? Is he goin' to put Drexler in jail?"

"He said he ain't goin' to do nothin' 'bout it, on account of he don't have no real evidence."

"So does that mean we're just goin' to let Drexler walk around town free as a bird 'n ready to spy on us again?"

Truax smiled. "No, it don't mean that a'tall. The reason I come over is to tell you that we're goin' to hang 'im. Some of the others has already gone to get 'im. If you want to be a part of this, meet us at the livery. We're goin' to string the traitor up from the hayloft stanchion."

"Hell, I ain't goin' to miss this. Let's go!" someone shouted, and with his shout the saloon emptied.

"Wang, do you know where Duff is?" Elmer asked.

"He is taking his meal with Missy Meagan and the mayor," Wang said.

"We need to let him know what's going on."

The two men left the Hidden Trail Saloon and crossed the street to Bear Tracks Restaurant.

"They're plannin' on lynchin' Drexler," Elmer told Duff as soon as he and Wang approached the table.

"What?" McGregor asked. "'N would ye be for telling me why they would be doin' such a thing? Why, I know Mr. Drexler. He was one of the first men I met when I settled here. He's never been anything but a fine, upstanding citizen."

"They're sayin' he's the one that give the note to this Yancey feller to give to Schofield," Elmer said.

McGregor shook his head. "I don't believe Drexler would do such a thing."

"You may be right, Mayor. He might not have been the one what done it, but right now it don't make no difference whether he done or not, 'cause the whole town is a-gatherin' down at the livery barn to watch 'im hang."

"I'd better tell the sheriff," McGregor said.

"Aye, that you'd better do," Duff agreed. "I'll see if I can stop them."

"Oh, Duff, this is a mob you're talking about!" Meagan said. "Not even all three of you can stand up against a mob. Hadn't you better wait for the sheriff?"

"If we wait for the sheriff, lass, it'll be too late. Drexler will be dead. The men in that mob think they're doin' the right thing. Perhaps all we have to do is convince them that they're making a mistake."

"Be careful, please," Meagan said, putting her hand on Duff's arm.

As McGregor left to find the sheriff, Duff, Elmer,

and Wang hurried down to O. D. Clayton's Livery and Stable. There, they saw at least thirty men gathered near the front opening. Drexler was sitting on a horse in front of the barn with a hangman's noose looped around his neck. His hands were tied behind his back.

"I didn't do it!" Drexler said. "Please, fellers, you got to believe me. I didn't do what you said!"

"You said you was goin' to join 'em, Drexler. You condemned yourself!" Truax said. "Give that horse a slap," he said to a man standing by the horse.

"Git!" the man shouted, slapping the horse on the rump.

What happened next caught the men by surprise, for few saw the knife thrown by Wang to cut the rope. All they saw was that no sooner was Drexler pulled from the horse's saddle, than the rope parted and Drexler, still very much alive, fell to the ground.

"What the—? What happened?" someone shouted.

"Get 'im up again," Truax ordered.

As a couple of men started toward Drexler, they were stopped by the sound of a pistol shot.

"Leave him be!" Duff shouted.

When the others looked toward Duff they saw that he was holding a smoking pistol.

"Elmer, would ye be for helping Mr. Drexler to his feet 'n untying his hands?"

"Wait a minute, Cap'n MacCallister! What are you doing?" Truax asked. "Maybe it is that you don't know what happened here, but Drexler tried to get word to Schofield about all the work we'd done. If Schofield knows that, why he can plan for it."

"I didn't do it, I tell you," Drexler shouted.

"Yeah, well I heard you say that you was goin' to be a-joinin' up with Schofield," Truax said. "Are you goin' to lie 'n say you didn't? On account of Collins 'n Morley also heard you say that."

"Hold on there, Truax, don't you go usin' my name in this," Morley said.

It was clear to Duff that Morley had not been a part of the would-be lynch mob, for he was just arriving then.

"'Cause I didn't take it that he was goin' to actual join up with 'em, 'n if he says he didn't give that feller the map, well, I'm sayin' that I believe him."

"I didn't give nobody no map about nothin'!" Drexler said as Elmer was untying his hands.

"Gentlemen, I want ye to think about what you're doing here," Duff said. "If ye hang this man, be he innocent or guilty, it's a thing that will stick with ye for the rest of your life.

"Gibson, I know that ye have a fine wife 'n two wee ones. Can ye face them for the rest of your life 'n know that ye took part in hangin' a man? Especially if the man is innocent?"

"I . . . I have to confess, I wasn't feelin' all that good about what we was doin'."

Duff looked at the bugler. "Hawkins, you were with them?"

"I ain't no more," Hawkins said.

"Lads, we have a war to fight," Duff said. "That means we have to be together. Now whether Drexler gave the map to Yancey or not—"

"It warn't me!" Drexler shouted again.

"The point is, something like this would come in among you and fester like an untreated sore."

"Yeah, maybe the Cap'n is right," one of the others said. "I mean even if Drexler did do this, we ain't got no right to take the law inter our own hands. This is somethin' for the sheriff to take care of."

"He done said he warn't goin' to do it," Truax said.

"Aye, I did say that." Campbell was arriving then with McGregor. "But I dinnae expect a lynching. Mr. Drexler, come with me. I'll be putting ye in jail now."

"What for?" Drexler demanded. "I'll tell you like I told ever'one else. I didn't give no map to nobody!"

"'Tis safer ye will be in jail than out of jail, for who knows but what someone might decide he'll be for taking care of you all by himself?"

"The sheriff might be right, Mr. Drexler," Duff said. "Ye may be safer in jail than out."

"It's for sure that if Schofield attacks, you won't be shot while you're in jail," Morley said. "That'll be about the safest place in town."

"We'll get this all straightened out, lad. 'Tis promising ye I am about that," McGregor said.

Drexler nodded. "All right. All right, Sheriff, I'll go with you. I didn't do what they're sayin', but I'll go with you."

When Captain Bond returned to Cottonwood Springs, he gave the telescope back to Schofield.

"Did you see anything of interest?" Schofield asked.

"I did, but I don't know if it relates to us in any way. I saw a lynching. Or at least, a near lynching."

"What do you mean by a near lynching?"

Bond described what he had seen from the time the rope was put around a man's neck, until the would-be lynch victim fell from the horse to the ground. "I don't know if they had done it merely to frighten him for

some reason, or if the rope broke . . . but I don't see
how the rope could have broken."

"Did they put him back on the horse and try again?"

"No."

"Then it is obvious that they were trying to extract
some information from him," Schofield said. "Was it
Yancey? It could be that they have taken him prisoner
and they used the threat of a hanging to encourage
him to tell all about us, our strength, our troop dispositions, and such."

"No, sir, I don't know who it was, but I do know that
it wasn't Yancey."

"Prime Director, do you think it might have been
our spy?" General Peterson asked.

"It might have been."

"Well if it was, and they didn't kill him, that means
he might have given them some information about us."

"I sincerely doubt that," Schofield said. "He has
no information about us that would be of any use to
MacCallister. On the other hand, Yancey could be of
some considerable value to them if he is still alive."

"Do you think we should send somebody in to find
out if he is still alive?"

"No. I think the best thing we can do now is attack.
Not merely a demonstration as before, but a full-scale
attack just like the ones we conducted against the
other towns."

"Yes, sir!" Peterson said with a broad smile.

"Assemble the men, General. I will address them."

Half an hour later the men of Schofield's Legion,
in full uniform, were standing in a military formation
in the middle of Malone Street. Schofield, also in uniform, came out the house he had confiscated in order
to address them. Several of the townspeople drawn by

curiosity and barely contained fear had gathered nearby to watch.

"Officers and men of Schofield's Legion," Schofield began in a stentorian voice. "We shall leave immediately for Antelope Wells. At some distance from the town we shall bivouac for the night, then shortly after dawn tomorrow morning, I will put you in motion to offer battle to the defenders of Antelope Wells. With the resolution and disciplined valor becoming fighting men such as yourselves, we cannot help but ride to a decisive victory and thereby complete the total subjugation of this land which shall become a new nation—a nation in which you shall in your lifetime realize great monetary gains, and in the years to come, occupy positions of honor to the future citizens of Tierra de Desierto.

"You are expected to show yourselves worthy of your valor, whose noble devotion in this cause has never been exceeded in any time. With such incentives to brave deeds and with the trust you have shown in me as your Prime Director, I and General Peterson, as well as your officers and noncommissioned officers, will lead you confidently into the battle with the absolute assuredness of success."

The men gave a throaty hurrah at the conclusion of Schofield's speech.

Chapter Twenty-three

The men of Schofield's Legion had made their bivouac about two miles north of Antelope Wells and were beginning to stir. Unlike a cattle drive where one cook fed the entire company, the Legion, as had the armies of the North and South during the recent war, had several "eating clubs"—gatherings of no more than five or six men who built their own cooking fires and prepared their own meals. That morning nearly a dozen fires were spread out across the camping ground and the aromas of bacon and coffee permeated the area.

Lieutenant Fillion had stepped away from the main encampment and was relieving himself when he saw a rider approaching from the south. A single rider might not have attracted his attention except for the fact that the rider was carrying a white flag.

"What the hell?" he said quietly.

Fillion returned to the fire that represented his eating group. "Harper, Logan, arm yourselves. I've got a detail for you."

"What you got, Lieutenant?" Harper asked.

Fillion pointed south. "A rider bearing a white flag is coming this way. Go get him and bring him here."

Fillion watched as his two men accosted the rider, then started back with him. Harper walked in front, leading the horse by the reins he had taken from the rider. Logan was walking alongside the rider.

"Dismount," Fillion ordered the rider when the three men reached him.

"Are you Schofield?" the rider asked.

"No. Who are you?"

"My name is Carson. Paul Carson. And I demand to be taken to see Schofield."

"Mister, you aren't in position to be demanding anything," Fillion said. "You may have noticed that you are in the midst of an armed camp while you are unarmed."

"Yes, and you may have noticed that I have come under a white flag of truce," Carson replied. "And international convention demands that a flag of truce be accorded peaceful access to negotiation."

"Whooee, he sure does talk purty, don't he, Lieutenant?" Logan said.

Fillion stared at Carson for a long moment, then nodded. "All right, Mr. Carson. Come with me."

"You're going to take me to Schofield?"

"Come with me," Fillion replied without directly answering Carson's question.

Schofield and Peterson were standing in front of Schofield's tent when Fillion approached them. Fillion had his pistol pointed at Carson, who was still carrying a stick to which he had attached a white flag.

"Who do we have here, Lieutenant?" Schofield asked.

"Prime Director, this man just came riding into our camp carrying that white flag that you see there. He says his name is Carson, and he's been demanding to speak with you."

"Are you Schofield?" Carson asked.

"Mister Carson, you will do well to speak only when spoken to," Peterson said. "And when you do address the Prime Director, you will address him as such, not by his name."

"Well, which one of you—"

"I'm Schofield. What can I do for you, Mr. Carson?"

"You can accept our surrender," Carson said.

It was Schofield's time to be confused, and it showed on his face. "You want to surrender?"

"Yes, sir, we do," Carson replied. "We are well aware of what has happened in all the other towns you have attacked. *Pillaged* would be a better word for it. And from what we have observed, you have killed more than half of the men in every town."

"Are you the mayor of Antelope Wells?"

"No sir, I am not. I am, however, a member of the city council."

"Tell me, Councilman Carson. Have you brought an instrument of surrender negotiated by your mayor?"

"No, I haven't."

"Then by what authority do you offer to surrender your town?"

"By the authority of reason," Carson said. "I don't want to see wanton killing going on in my town."

"Reason is a platitude, not an authorization. I cannot accept the surrender from you, Mr. Carson. I can accept it only from someone who is authorized to tender an instrument of capitulation. And since you are unable to do that, the attack will take place as scheduled."

"If you will not accept my surrender, then please

understand that I have no choice but to return and warn the others of how imminent an attack is," Carson said.

"I'm afraid I can't let you return," Schofield said. "You must remain here until after the attack."

"What? No, you can't do that. I came under a white flag. You must let me return. You have no right to hold me!"

"Lieutenant Fillion, appoint two men to . . ."

Suddenly Carson broke into a run, heading back in the direction of Antelope Wells. Schofield, unhurriedly, picked up a rifle, jacked a round into the chamber, raised the rifle to his shoulder and aimed at the fleeing Paul Carson.

The loud pop of the rifle garnered the sudden attention of all in the camp, most of whom were unaware that there had even been a visitor. Those who saw the running man also saw him throw both arms into the air, drag his foot a short way, then pitch forward to fall facedown.

One of the men nearest the man who had been shot ran toward him, looked down at him for a moment, then turned to call back. "He's dead!"

Schofield merely nodded. "General Peterson, prepare the men to advance upon our objective."

"Yes, sir," General Peterson replied.

Back in Antelope Wells, Duff had a lifelong habit of rising early. He was standing at the window watching the early morning display of color in the eastern sky. The window was open and he could smell coffee and bacon from the hotel kitchen. The smells were enticing, and he wondered if he would dare wake the others and tell them he was ready for breakfast.

He didn't have to contemplate the idea very long, because a light knock on his door was followed by a call from Meagan.

"Duff? Duff, are you awake? Do you want . . . oh!"

Her startled response was a result of the fact that even before she was able to complete her question Duff jerked the door open.

"Aye, lass, I'm awake and as hungry as a bear."

Meagan smiled. "Good, then we can wake up Elmer and Wang and go to breakfast."

The door to Elmer's room jerked open. "There ain't no need to wake us up, seein' as there can't nobody sleep with all the caterwaulin' that's goin on out here," he teased.

Less than ten minutes later the four of them were in the hotel dining room, waiting on their breakfast to be served.

"Do you think Drexler was tellin' the truth when he said that he warn't the one that give Yancey the map?" Elmer asked.

"I dinnae know," Duff replied. "I want to believe him. He did seem awfully sincere."

"Yeah, but here's the thing," Elmer said. "If it warn't Drexler that give that map to him, who was it? On account of I seen when Yancey come into town, 'n I seen 'im most off the mornin', 'n I sure didn't see 'im drawin' that map."

"It almost makes a person wish that Drexler is the one who gave him the map," Meagan said.

"Why do you say that?" Elmer asked.

"I know what she means," Duff said. "If it was Drexler, we would nae have to be worrying about it anymore, since Drexler is in jail and out of the way. And if it was nae Drexler, then we still have a spy in our midst, and still have someone to worry about."

"Yeah, I see. 'N that means it could be anyone, don't it?" Elmer asked.

"Aye."

"Duff, you don't reckon it would be General Culpepper, do you? I mean, ain't he the one who drawed up the plans in the first place?"

"He is indeed the architect of the plans," Duff agreed. "But 'tis totally convinced I am that he is nae the spy we seek."

"I don't think he is, either," Meagan said. "Elmer, how could you possibly accuse that sweet old man?"

"Well now, I ain't exactly accusin' 'im," Elmer said. "I just pointed out that he's the one that drawed out the plan in the first place. That don't mean he's the one that drawed the map, though."

"Elmer is quite right to trust no one and be suspicious of everyone," Duff said.

"Well, that is a good tactic I suppose," Meagan smiled sweetly at Duff. "But I certainly hope you aren't suspicious of me," she teased.

Before Duff could answer, Wang spoke. "The mayor comes."

Looking toward the entry into the hotel dining room, and following Wang's gaze, Duff saw McGregor. Without being told, Wang took a chair from a nearby empty table and moved it over to their table.

"Paul Carson is gone," McGregor said as he sat down. "Hugh Poindexter was standing guard this morning and saw him leave."

"Who is Paul Carson?" Duff asked.

"Oh, that's right, ye have nae yet met him. Mr. Carson is a member of the city council, 'n he has made it plain enough that he does nae agree with the defending of the city. That's why he dinnae join with the other men in forming the Home Guard or in building the defenses."

"Well if he don't want to defend the city, what does he want to do?" Elmer asked. "Surrender?"

McGregor nodded. "Aye, that is exactly what he wants to do, for he has made that proposal, most avidly, and on more than one occasion."

"Why in the world would he want to surrender?" Elmer asked. "You think maybe he believes if he surrenders that Schofield will cut some special deal for him?"

"He says that surrendering the town to Schofield will save many of our citizens' lives. 'N I think 'tis his sincere belief that that is so."

"Do ye think his leaving town might have something to do with that?" Duff asked.

"Aye, that is my thought. 'Tis no pleasure for me to be saying this about a man who is on my own city council, and who I considered a friend, but 'tis thinking I am that he has gone to find Schofield and try to surrender to him."

"Why, he can't surrender the town by himself, can he?" Elmer asked

McGregor shook his head. "He has nae authority to do so. But, and this is what I fear, he can tell Schofield about the fortifications we have built."

"Then there will be no surprise," Wang said.

"Tell me, Leftenant Colonel, do ye think Mr. Carson may have been the one to provide the map to Yancey?" Duff asked.

McGregor let out a surrendering sigh. "Aye, Duff, I believe he may well have been the one."

"If that is so, then there is a bright side to this, Duff," Meagan said.

"Aye. If Carson is the spy, we've nae further worry with the matter."

"I had better go the sergeant major," McGregor said. "He will need to know about this."

When McGregor stepped into the jail a few minutes later he saw Drexler and Campbell having breakfast together. Although Drexler was inside the cell and Campbell outside, they had drawn their chairs up against the bars so they could carry on a conversation as they ate.

"Ye can let Drexler out of jail, Sheriff," McGregor said.

"Mayor, I appreciate that"—Drexler smiled—"but can I be a guest of the city at least long enough to finish my breakfast?"

"Aye, but there's nae need for ye to stay in the cell. Come on out 'n eat in more comfort."

"What's happened, Mayor? Why are we letting him out?"

"We know now that Paul Carson is the spy," McGregor said. "Poindexter saw him riding out of town this morning, 'n there can be nae need for it, save to go meet with Schofield."

"Why would Mr. Carson want to do such a thing? I know him. He's a good man," Drexler said.

"It's something he said at a city council meeting," McGregor said. "He wanted to surrender to Schofield. He thought if we would do that, there would be nae killing."

After McGregor left the hotel dining room, Duff, Elmer, and Wang talked about the disposition of their forces in order to meet any attack from Schofield.

When breakfast was finished, Meagan, who had remained quiet throughout the discussion, spoke. "Duff, if you don't mind, I'm going to take some coffee up to the men who are standing guard on the roof of the hotel."

"Aye, 'twould be good of ye to do so. I know they'll appreciate it."

Meagan ordered a pot of coffee and two cups, then as Duff and the others left the dining room, she took the three flights of stairs up to a door that opened out onto the roof.

"I'm tellin' you, Clay, I seen 'im do it!" one of the two men was saying. "Coolie spread all them cards out on the table 'n asked Pollard to take one of 'em, then he put his hand on Pollard's forehead, 'n the next thing you know, why, he told Pollard whatever card it was he took. He was readin' his mind."

"Come on, Deekus. That's just a card trick. You know damn well he wasn't actually readin' Pollard's mind." Clay laughed. "For one thing, Pollard ain't smart enough to have a mind to read in the first place."

The two men laughed.

"Gentlemen?" Meagan called.

Startled, Clay and Deekus turned toward the sound of her voice.

She held up the coffeepot.

"I thought maybe you gentlemen would like some coffee."

"Yes, ma'am, we truly would! Miss, you are an angel, 'n that's for sure," Deekus said.

The two men held out their cups for Meagan to pour their coffee.

She did so, then looking beyond them saw a large

group of mounted men approaching. "Is that something we should be worried about?"

Seeing the expression on Meagan's face, the guards turned to look at what she was calling their attention to.

"This is it, Deekus! They're comin' to attack. Get word to Cap'n MacCallister 'n Hawkins so he can blow the warnin'."

"Thanks for the coffee, Miss. Sorry I ain't got no time to drink it," Deekus said, tossing the coffee over the side.

"Miss, you'd better get back down into the hotel 'n stay away from the winders," Clay said.

By the time Meagan was safely back in the hotel, she was already hearing Hawkins playing "To Arms" on the bugle.

Chapter Twenty-four

"What was that?" Captain Bond asked. "General, did you hear that? It sounded like a bugle call."

"It was a bugle call," Schofield said, answering for Peterson. "It was 'To Arms.' It would appear that they have discovered our approach, and if they are able to have a bugler play 'To Arms,' we must also assume that they are well organized and prepared to meet our attack."

"Are we still going to attack?" Captain Bond asked.

"Of course we are going to attack," Schofield said. "General, form the Legion into two battalions in columns of four. You will ride at the head of the attack," Schofield ordered.

Peterson hesitated for just a moment. He knew that leading the attack would put him in the most exposed, and consequently, the most dangerous position.

"Do you question that order, General?" Schofield asked.

"No, sir! I feel it an honor to be able to lead our men on this, the most important of all our campaigns."

Schofield smiled. "Gentlemen, though we haven't

had to use him in any previous campaign, I am happy to report that we have our own trumpeter. Trumpeter Kendig, front and center."

A rather smallish man hurried to respond to Schofield's call.

"As soon as the attack phalanx is formed, you will take your position just behind General Peterson. Upon his command, you will blow 'Charge,' and you will continue to do so until the first shot is fired."

"Yes, sir," Kendig replied.

In Antelope Wells, the bugler was still blowing "To Arms."

"Mr. Hawkins, ye may discontinue the bugling." Duff smiled. "I think all the lads are in place now."

Hawkins lowered the bugle. "Yes, sir."

At that moment Drexler came running across the street carrying a rifle.

"What the hell are you doing here?" Truax asked. "I thought you was in jail."

"The mayor knows I ain't no spy, 'n he told the sheriff to let me go. I know I didn't train none with the Home Guard, but I can damn well shoot."

"That's true, Ed. I oncet seen 'im shoot a coyote from near five hunnert yards away," Collins said.

"And if some sonofabitch is plannin' on attackin' our town, I want to do somethin' about it," Drexler said.

"Uh, look, Anton," Truax said. "I mean, 'bout us almost hangin' you 'n all. Uh, well, we thought you was a spy. 'N truth is, you'd more 'n likely do the same thing if you thought someone else was spyin'. Anyhow, what I'm sayin' is, I'm sorry we purt nigh hung you, 'n I'm glad we didn't. Are you goin' to hold any hard feelin's agin us?"

Drexler put his hand to his neck. "It didn't seem like nothin' a friend would do." He smiled. "But long as you don't try 'n do it again, well, I reckon I'm fine with it."

Truax grinned back at Drexler. "Then climb over here with us 'n let's shoot us a few o' them when they come into town."

"Let's shoot a lot of 'em," Drexler replied as he took his position within the fortification.

Elmer had taken a position at the north end of town, from which direction the attack would come. Wang went to the south end of town, and Duff took up a position in the middle of the town behind the barricade that sealed off the passageway between Chip's Shoe Alley and Sikes Hardware.

As they waited in place, they heard a bugle.

"Is that Hawkins?" Truax asked. "What's he playin' the bugle for?"

"That ain't Hawkins," Morley said. "That there bugle is blowin' 'Charge.' I've heard it blowed before."

The call was repeated several times, sounding louder as it came closer.

Peterson led the army into town, surprised that the resistance was much lighter than he had expected. He felt a sense of elation as the army galloped down the street, the thunder of the hoofbeats echoing back from the buildings, joining with the roar of gunfire. Why, it was no harder than had been the attacks on

Hachita, La Tenja, or Cottonwood Springs. The town would fall within minutes, and the war would be won!

Suddenly the roar of gunfire grew much louder, and Peterson heard cries of pain and surprise as some of his soldiers were shot from their saddles. He realized then that he had led his men into a trap. The defenses of the town had been set up to allow an ambush to be sprung upon them when they reached the center of town.

"Retreat! Retreat!" he shouted, and just as he had led his men into town, he led them in retreat. And whereas the attack had been made in a controlled formation, the retreat was a disjointed rout as the formation broke, and the men galloped away as fast as they could.

"Cease fire! Cease fire!" Duff ordered as he saw the last of the attackers clear the north edge of town. Six of the attackers had been left behind and were lying in the street. Four of them were perfectly still, but two of them were still moving.

"Sergeant Morley, would ye be for checking on our lads and see if anyone is hurt. If so, get Dr. Urban to have a look at them."

"Yes, sir," Morley said.

Duff, with his pistol drawn, stepped out into the street to check on the attackers who were down. Four of them were dead, but two were still alive. Neither of the two survivors were very badly hurt.

"Ah, Sergeant Major," Duff said as he saw Sheriff Campbell coming toward him, picking his way gingerly around the bodies. "Here are a couple of lads for ye jail."

"Aye, jail for these two," Campbell replied, then he

glanced to the four dead. "'N I'll get Mr. Nunlee to take care of the others. Have we any dead or wounded?"

"There were nae dead or wounded where I was," Duff replied. "I've asked Morley to check on the others."

Even as Duff was talking to Sheriff Campbell, Morley came up to join them. The big smile on his face answered the question before it could be asked.

"Nobody killed, 'n not even nobody was wounded neither," Morley reported happily. "Looks to me like we gave Schofield a pretty good whuppin'!"

"Aye, the lads acquitted themselves very well," Duff said. "Sergeant Morley, prepare the men for a second attack."

"Yes, sir," Morley said. "All right, you men, a lot of shootin' was goin' on, so what you need to do is reload your weapons so that when they come back again, we'll be ready for 'em."

"You think they'll for sure be comin' back, Morley?" Truax asked. "I mean it seems to me like we give 'em such a whuppin' that it won't be nothin' they'll be a-thinkin' about doin' again no time soon."

"They'll be back," Morley said assuredly.

"I shall say another prayer, gentlemen," Chaplain Cooley said.

"You really think prayin' is goin' to do us any good, Preach?" one of the men asked.

"Why, most assuredly, sir," Chaplain Cooley replied. "How do you think we repulsed them the first time, if not by prayer?"

When Peterson returned to Cottonwood Springs with the dispirited army, the expression on Schofield's face was one of anger and disbelief. "What happened? Why have you returned?"

"It was a trap, Prime Director," Peterson said.

"What do you mean, it was a trap?"

"They were waiting for us. They have built fortifications between every building, fortifications that our bullets won't penetrate, and behind every one of them are several men armed with everything from pistols to rifles to shotguns. It was like riding into a hornet's nest."

"Captain Bond?" Schofield called.

"Yes, sir?"

"Dismiss the men, have them cool their horses, then await further orders."

"Yes, sir."

As Captain Bond relayed the orders to the dispirited and somewhat disoriented soldiers of the Legion, Schofield turned his attention back to his general. "You say the entire town was fortified?"

"Yes, sir, it wasn't anything like any of the other towns we've attacked."

"Yancey must have seen that, and somehow, he was discovered," Schofield said. "It could be that I have underestimated Mr. MacCallister."

"We aren't going to give up on the town, are we?" Peterson asked.

"Of course not. Why would you even ask such a thing?"

"The reason I asked is, I think now that we know what they have, we could attack again and with proper preparation, be successful," Peterson said.

"General, the fortifications will be no less impregnable because you know they are there," Schofield said.

"No, sir, you're right. We won't be able to prevail against them with a frontal attack."

"Frontal attack?" Schofield smiled. "You have an idea, do you, General Peterson?"

"Yes, sir, I do."

Peterson knelt down. Picking up a stick, he began sketching in the dirt. Within a minute he had drawn a map of the town, showing where the fortifications were.

"Before, we went in this way," he said, indicating the north end of the street. "The resistance was light until we got here." He put his stick right in the middle of town. "Here, the shooting was intense. It was also effective because we were exposed and they were protected by the walls they had built. But," he moved the stick behind the row of buildings, "if we come in between the buildings from this end, there are no fortifications to protect them, only these walls." He indicated the barricades that faced the street. "And those same walls that protected them from a frontal attack will now trap them and prevent their escape."

"Excellent suggestion, General. Draw up the attack plan, let me examine it, and I will approve the operation."

In Antelope Springs, three tables had been pulled together in the Bear Tracks Restaurant, necessary in order to accommodate more people—Duff, Meagan, Elmer, McGregor, Lucy, General Culpepper, Sergeant Morley, and Ethel Marie. The young woman who'd arrived on the coach that had recently been robbed had moved quickly into the fabric of the town. Although she had initially gone to work at the Hidden Trail Saloon, she had been looking for an investment opportunity, and within the last few days, she had used the money she had managed to hide from the robbers to buy a partnership in a hairdressing shop. Her partnership was with Morley's sister, and that proximity with Morley had led to a blossoming relationship between the two.

"Yes, sir, we sent 'em skedadlin' away with their tails tucked betwixt their legs," Morley said with a happy chuckle. "I tell you, Cap'n MacCallister, that was one jim-dandy idee you had 'bout puttin' them walls up 'tween all the buildin's like we done. Why we suckered them in like drawin' a beaver into a trap. There they was, right out in the open, 'n we was safe behind all them walls we built."

"Aye, the fortifications were a very good thing, but that was none of my doing." Duff held his hand out toward General Culpepper. "'Twas the general who came up with the idea. And 'twas nae just the fortifications, either, for the plan of battle, the way we drew them in, was also his idea."

"Ladies and gentlemen," McGregor held up his glass of wine as he spoke. "May I propose a toast to General Culpepper 'n his military acumen?"

"His what?" Elmer asked.

"Never mind, Elmer. Just drink the toast," Meagan said with a smile.

"Yes, ma'am. They don't nobody have to tell me two times to take a drink." Elmer held his glass out with the others.

"To the general," McGregor said.

"To the general," Duff repeated, and everyone drank the toast.

General Culpepper beamed under the praise. "Gentlemen, I know that my wearing this uniform of a lost cause, and my insistence that I am still a general may be indicative of deteriorating mental acuity. And in my more lucid moments, I am quite aware that I may be an embarrassment to myself and to my daughter, as well as a great burden to her, and an oddity to others. But, at this moment, I feel that I am surrounded not only by friends, but by men of military accomplishment. And I salute you."

He completed his rather lengthy response by holding his glass out toward all present, then taking a drink from his own glass.

"Papa," Lucy said. "You are neither a burden nor an embarrassment to me. I am very proud of you."

Culpepper smiled. "And, as it was your young man proposed the toast, then I choose to believe that he supports your feelings toward me."

"I do, sir." McGregor reached for Lucy's hand and raised it to his lips to kiss it. "For how can I think any other way of the man that I hope someday will be my father-in-law?"

Over in the jail, Sheriff Campbell stepped up to the bars of the cell that held the two prisoners. They had given their names as Jake Hunter and Abe Libby, and both had been examined and treated by Dr. Urban.

Campbell was holding two plates. "Would ye be wanting yer lunch now?"

"How long are we goin' to stay here?" Hunter asked.

Campbell chuckled. "Anxious to get out, are ye?"

"Yeah. I mean you really got no right to hold us here," Hunter said as he and Libby took the plates that were passed through a gap in the bars that had been designed for such a purpose.

"And would ye be for tellin' me why 'tis thinking you are that two men such as yourselves, as might come ridin' into town with guns blazing away, don't belong in jail?"

"We didn't kill nobody," Libby said.

Campbell chuckled. "Aye, 'tis true. You killed no one."

"Which means you ain't got nothin' on us but disturbin' the peace," Libby said.

"Yeah!" Hunter added quickly with a laugh. "All you got agin us is disturbin' the peace."

"And attempted murder," Campbell added. He walked back over to his desk where his own lunch lay, and picking up the plate, he came over to sit down just outside the cell.

"Tell me about Schofield," Campbell said.

"What do you want to know about him?"

"Is he a man of honor? When he gives his word on a thing, can he be trusted?"

"Why are you askin' that?"

"If Schofield said that he would do a thing, like not attack a town, could he be believed?"

Hunter chuckled. "Sheriff, me 'n Libby, we ain't nothin' but privates 'n Schofield—"

"The Prime Director," Libby corrected.

"Yeah, we can't forget that. He likes to be called the Prime Director," Hunter said. "Anyhow, like I was sayin', the Prime Director, he don't have nothin' much to do with us privates. So I can't really answer your question whether or not Schofield is a man that keeps his word, on account of me 'n him ain't never actual talked about nothin'."

"Some, there are in town, are thinking that because the attack was beaten back that Schofield may leave us alone 'n not make another attack," Campbell said.

"Ha!" Libby said. "Even without me 'n Hunter never actual havin' talked none to the Prime Director, I can tell you right now that he ain't goin' to leave this town alone. He'll attack it again, 'n by now he knows all about how you've built up them walls betwixt the buildin's 'n all, so it ain't goin' to be no surprise to him next time. I 'spect this here town will belong to him by nightfall, 'n me 'n Hunter will be let outta jail then."

"We'll see," Campbell said, holding his hand out to retrieve the two empty plates from his prisoners.

Chapter Twenty-five

Wang was sitting behind the barricade between Chip's Shoe Alley and Sikes Hardware. Five other men were there, too, and they were still talking about the battle that had taken place early morning.

"If you ask me this here war, that is, if you are a-wantin' to call it a war, is over," one of the men said. "Yes, sir, it's over 'n we won it. Why, them men come ridin' in this mornin' a-wearin' them purty uniforms, struttin' along like they was some rooster in a yard full o' hens, but they turned tail 'n run like a bunch o' scairt rabbits once we commenced shootin' at 'em."

"You got that right, Red," one of the others said. "I don't reckon none o' them will be comin' back, 'cause they've had enough of us."

"Yeah, we sure as hell showed them," a third said.

"Wonder what's goin' to happen to them two men that got put in jail after this mornin'?" asked a man named Blackwell, but who was known as Bull.

"Ain't no tellin' what's goin' to happen to 'em. I mean, seein' as the territorial prison is in Santa Fe, 'n we ain't

got no way to get 'em there no more, on account of
Schofield is controllin' the road between here 'n the
railroad at Lordsburg," Darby said.

Wang had been listening to the conversation but
not participating as he sat there drinking his tea. Then
he heard it. Not one other person in the group, nor
anyone else in town, would have heard it, because they
didn't know what to listen for. But to Wang, it was as
jarring to his ear as an out-of-tune violin would be to
the conductor of the performance of a Beethoven
concerto.

Again he remembered the words of Master Tse of
the Shaolin temple of Changlin.

*"There is a natural rhythm to things; a music of the wind,
the shifting sand, the rippling water, the creep of crawling
things, the flutter of wings, the calls of creatures, and even the
voices of humans in daily commerce. All these sounds are to
nature, as the flute, the bamboo pipes, the lute, and the seven-
string qin are to the symphony orchestra. Listen to all the elements with the musical ear, and if you hear a discordant note,
you will know that danger is near."*

Wang put down his cup of tea, stood, and cocked
his head to one side.

"Hey, what's the Chinaman up to?" Bull asked.

"Seems like he's heard somethin'," Red said.

"Hey, Chinaman, what is it you're a-hearin'?"
Darby asked.

Without responding to any of the questions, Wang

climbed up the side of the wall leading to the top of the hardware store.

"Damn, did you see that? How the hell did he do that? Why, he clumb up that wall like he was a lizard or somethin'."

Red's voice floated up to Wang as he climbed. He ran across the roof of Sikes Hardware and leaped across the gap to Bear Tracks Café, then to the Norton and Heckemeyer Law office, the Golden Spur Saloon, and finally to the Dunn Hotel.

"Where the hell did you come from?" the guard asked.

"They are coming again," Wang said.

The guard, whose name was Emerson, looked around. "No they ain't. There ain't nobody on the road."

Wang looked closely then he saw a horse passing by a narrow opening between two hills of a ridgeline that was just to the west of the road. That horse was followed by another, and then by another. Looking to the east, Wang saw the same thing. Two columns of riders were approaching the town, not on the road as the first attack had been, but secretively, using the ridgelines to provide cover.

Wang didn't point them out to Emerson. The appearances had been sporadic and now that the two columns had passed by the narrow openings, they were no longer in view. Also, a swift study of the paralleling ridgelines showed that there would be no more opportunities to see the approaching riders.

He climbed down and hurried into Bear Tracks. A quick perusal found the table where Duff and the others were seated.

"Wang!" Duff said, looking up with a smile. "Good, you've come to join us."

"They are coming back," Wang said.

"Schofield's men are coming back?" Morley asked.

"Yes."

"How come we didn't get warned?"

"The guards have not seen them."

"Then, can we be certain they are coming?" McGregor asked. "We did beat them rather thoroughly."

"Leftenant Colonel, if Wang says they are coming back, then 'tis for certain they are," Duff said. "The lad has a history of knowing such things in a way that we can nae understand."

Elmer had already stood, and Duff and Morley did as well.

"'Twould be wise to stay off the street until this be finished," Duff said to the others as they left.

"We need to get the men back where they belong," Elmer said. "Like as not they're near 'bout all celebratin' somewhere."

"I'll find Hawkins," Morley said.

"No," Wang said, holding out his hand. "Do not blow the horn. Our enemy does not know that we have seen them."

Duff nodded. "Wang is right. If they don't know that we have seen them, the advantage is ours."

"But if we wait until they all suddenly appear at the end of the street, it will be too late."

"I think they will not come down the street," Wang said. "I think they will come up behind the buildings."

"Aye, that is what they plan," Duff said, striking his fist in the palm of his hand. "Elmer, Sergeant Morley, round up some o' the lads. Be quick, but quiet about it. Bring them to center fort at the hardware store."

Five minutes later Elmer and Morley had rounded up ten men, and they were gathered in front of Sikes Hardware.

"We believe they will be coming up through the alley on both sides of the street," Duff said. "There is nae doubt but that they plan to move up through the space between the buildings and trap us against the fortifications. But," he added with a smile, "we'll nae be on that side. We'll be on the street side."

Wang, who had climbed to the top of Sikes Hardware, dropped back down onto the street. "Some are coming up the road now."

Just as he finished his report, Deekus came running up, out of breath. "They're . . . comin' again. Only . . . ."

"Only what?" Morley asked.

"There ain't near as many of 'em this time. This mornin' there was near fifty of 'em, 'n this time I don't see no more 'n fifteen or twenty."

"Sergeant Morley, have Hawkins blow 'To Arms,'" Duff ordered.

"I thought we wasn't goin' to do that," Elmer said.

"We'll do it now, because they'll be expecting it," Duff said. "'Tis my thought that what they plan is to make a demonstration only, to draw our fire and attention on them, believing them to be the attacking force. That would leave the other two columns free to come up behind us. Sergeant Morley and Deekus, as soon as the troops answer the call, put them all at the head of the street to welcome the feint with maximum firepower. That will keep them from entering the town to back up their clandestine elements, and it will also prevent them from seeing how we plan to meet them."

"Uh, Cap'n, I don't really know what it is that you just said," Deekus replied with a puzzled expression on his face."

"Don't you be worryin' none about it, Deekus, I know exactly what he was talkin' about, 'n it's somethin' real smart, too," Morley said. "You just go find Hawkins 'n tell him to blow his horn. I'll be down there tellin' the men where to go when they show up."

Wang climbed back up onto the top of the hardware store, but he kept himself low so he could observe the two columns, one on the west of the town and the other on the east side.

General Peterson was at the head of the men coming up the road, following the same approach as had the unsuccessful attack earlier in the morning. He heard the sounds of the defenders' bugler playing "To Arms," and he smiled.

"Gentlemen, our deceptive maneuver appears to be working. They have spotted us and are getting into position to face us." He laughed. "They have no idea that the real threat will be behind them."

When they got to within two hundred yards of the north end of town Peterson called for his trumpeter.

"Men, come on line and, at the trumpet call, advance at a gallop," Peterson said. "Trumpeter Kendig! Blow 'Charge,' if you would!" Peterson ordered.

As the first notes of the stirring call wafted across the distance, Peterson advanced his reduced force toward the north end of town, and the defenders got into position to meet the attack.

General Peterson expected a light resistance at the point of engagement, just as he had experienced earlier. The significant damage had not occurred until the attack was totally involved, having been drawn in to the middle of town where the heaviest concentration of defenders had brought maximum fire to bear. His current plan was to advance beyond the perimeter defenses and get the men in the center of town to commit themselves. That would leave them vulnerable to attack from behind and once the shooting began the defenders would be engaged from both sides.

As Peterson's group approached the end of the street, the defensive fire was much more intense than it had been in the morning. In fact, it was so intense that Peterson realized almost immediately that his men, exposed as they were, and with a combatant strength that was even less than the defenders, could not advance any farther. He saw some of his men going down from the heavy fire, and realized that MacCallister had changed his tactics and intended to prevent him from even gaining access to the city.

"Retreat!" he ordered. "Retreat!"

If he had as many men with him as he'd had earlier, he would have continued the attack, and no doubt would have carried the objective. As the attacking troops rode away though, he smiled anyway. He knew that MacCallister and those with him were not aware that his attack had been a diversion only. The real attack would be coming from behind the defenders and even as he rode away, he could hear the opening shots.

* * *

With Captain Bond in command of the column on the east side of Cactus Street and Lieutenant Fillion in command of the western column, the two officers waited in the alley and ordered their men to gallop up the between the first two buildings. The idea was to catch the defenders behind their cover, which would make them sitting ducks to the charge.

Almost instantly, there was a drastic failure in the plans. The defenders weren't behind the wall. They were on the street side! And they were expecting Schofield's men!

With the opening volley, Bond and Fillion realized that the defenders also had men on the roofs, shooting down on an attacker as he rode up the narrow gap between the adjacent buildings. The attacking men of Schofield's Legion had ridden into a trap! The two attacking columns had no choice but to withdraw.

"Come back, come back!" Bond shouted to his men. To his absolute horror he saw that of the ten men he had committed to the attack only six were still in the saddle. Four horses, with their saddles empty, left the death trap that had been created by attacking up a narrow chute with no room to maneuver, and no way to avoid heavy fire from a fortified position.

On the other side of Cactus Street Lieutenant Fillion had fared even worse. Only five of his ten-man attack team made it out of the killing ground.

"What are we goin' to do now?" one of Lieutenant Fillion's men shouted in absolute terror.

"We're going to get out of here!" Without any further

orders, Fillion broke into a gallop, putting as much distance as quickly as he could between himself and the town.

Because he had given no orders, there was a momentary bit of confusion before the rest of his men realized they were retreating. Riding at a gallop as they crossed the border into Mexico, Fillion saw Bond leading his own troops in retreat.

When all had regathered at the Schofield's Legion bivouac an hour or so later, a count of their remaining manpower disclosed the grim picture of the cost of the day's operations.

They had lost six men that morning. Although two of the casualties were in jail in town, Schofield didn't know that, and had to assume that all six had been killed. Peterson's demonstration against the north end of town had cost six men, and the two strike columns commanded by Bond and Fillion had cost another nine men. They were down twenty-one men from their operating strength of the morning, and had lost twenty-six men since the operation in the Bootheel had begun.

"What are we going to do now, Prime Director?" General Peterson asked.

"We are going to get some artillery," Schofield said resolutely.

Chapter Twenty-six

From the *Antelope Wells Standard*:

A Heartening Beginning
BY CLINT H. DENHAM

For the last six weeks a man who calls himself Prime Director Schofield has rolled through the towns of the New Mexico Bootheel like Conquest, War, Famine, and Death, better known, perhaps, as the Four Horses of the Apocalypse.

The juggernaut, in the guise of Schofield's Legion, managed to capture, with little effective resistance put forth by the residents, the towns of Hachita, La Tenja, and Cottonwood Springs. And even though resistance among those towns was low, casualties among the innocent citizens of the affected towns were high.

Not so in Antelope Wells! So far, the despot has failed in his attacks against us, and his failed attacks have cost him twenty-eight men. Twenty-six have been killed and two have been captured.

We owe the success of our battles with Schofield to the effective marshaling and handling of men, heretofore untrained in military tactics, into an effective fighting force. And for that, we must thank Captain Duff MacCallister and the two men he brought with him, Elmer Gleason and Wang Chow.

But, dear readers, Captain MacCallister will be the very first to tell you that the tactics and strategy by which we have so soundly defeated Schofield's first attempts against us are the result of military brilliance of one of our own permanent residents. I am talking about General Lucien Culpepper. It was General Culpepper who designed the strategy of our fortifications, and it was he who developed the tactics with which these fortifications were used in the battles thus far.

Despite our earlier victories, Mayor McGregor wants the citizens of the town to know that this war is not over. "Ebenezer Schofield is a discredited general, one who was dishonorably discharged from the US Army and served time in a federal prison," the mayor said. "He has nothing to lose by continuing to pursue his nefarious scheme, and he is evil enough to care not how many

innocents may die in attaining his goal.
I ask all the residents of Antelope Wells to
remain in a constant state of readiness
so that we may repel as many more attacks
as Schofield may launch against us."

The residents of Antelope Wells who had fought
behind the barricades were being honored as heroes
by the citizens of the town. The ranks of the defending Home Guard swelled as others pleaded to be
included.

"You know what we need, don't you?" Collins asked
the others as they drank in the Golden Spur Saloon.
"We need uniforms."

"Uniforms? You mean like them things that
Schofield's men are wearing?"

"No, we need our own uniforms so's that ever'one
in town will know that we're defendin' 'em."

The idea gained popularity, and Morley took it
to Duff.

Duff spoke of it over the dinner table at Bear Tracks
that evening.

"Don't be thinking lightly of such an idea," General
Culpepper replied. "During the war we learned that
the men who wore uniforms had a sense of unity and
pride that served them very well in battle. Of course, I
don't know where or how we can get uniforms for our
men, but I wish we could."

"I'll make them," Meagan offered.

"Oh, do you think you could do that?" Lucy asked.

"I'm a seamstress. I own a dress shop back in Chugwater," Meagan said.

"That sounds wonderful! Will you allow me to help?"

"Of course I will. And if we can get a few more of the ladies involved, we can turn out these uniforms in no time."

"What a great idea," McGregor said. "Nothing gives a group of lads a sense of esprit de corps as much as a sharp uniform."

In addition to Meagan and Lucy, three other ladies—Ethel Marie Joyce, Lydia Morley, and Cynthia Hughes—from the town joined in the uniform project. Lydia was Sergeant Morley's sister, and Cynthia was a friend of Lydia's. The only cloth they could find in sufficient quantity to actually make thirty uniforms was the tan-colored canvas that Sikes Hardware had on hand to be used for wagon covers and tents.

"This will do nicely," Meagan insisted.

While Meagan and the others busied themselves sewing uniforms, Prime Director Schofield and General Peterson were not licking their wounds. The two men had traveled across the border into Mexico to meet with Pedro Bustamante.

Bustamante had been a colonel in the Mexican army but he broke his command away from the federal army to form a revolutionary brigade, which he called *Brigada de la liberdade* or "Freedom Brigade."

At the moment the three men were meeting in the *Sombra de Montaña* Cantina.

"We should be allies, you and I, Colonel Bustamante," Schofield insisted. "You wish to carve your own nation from Northern Chihuahua, and I from Southern

New Mexico. We can enter into an alliance that will serve us both."

Bustamante downed a jigger of tequila and sprinkled salt upon a lime and squeezed some of the juice into his mouth before he responded. "How can I benefit from such an alliance?"

"My nation would separate your nation from the United States, and your nation would separate my own country from Mexico. Would it not be good to have a friendly nation as your neighbor?"

"*Sí.*"

"And as friendly neighbors, we can also do things for each other, can we not?

"If I ask you to do something for me, you will do it?"

"Yes, if I can. What do you wish me to do for you?" Schofield asked.

"It would help very much if in the town of Puxico, the Rurales would all be killed," Bustamante said.

"You want them all killed?"

"*Sí.*"

"How many of the local police are there?" Schofield asked.

"There are twelve, señor. And there are five federales. They, too, must be killed."

"That's only seventeen men, and I know you have at least one hundred men. Why is it that you cannot kill them yourselves?"

"I am known, señor," Bustamante said, stabbing his thumb into his chest. "I am a famous man in my country. If I killed the Rurales and Federales, I would not be able to win the support of the people. But if some evil *norteamericanos* killed them, I could offer my services to defend the people against that happening again."

Schofield smiled. "All right. I will be the evil North American who will come and kill all the police for you."

"For that I will give you ten thousand dollars in American money."

"I don't want money," Schofield said.

Bustamante looked confused. "Then, I do not understand, señor. If you do not want money, what do you want?"

"I want artillery pieces," Schofield replied. "I want three twelve-pounder Napoleons, and three ten-pounder Parrott guns."

Bustamante nodded. "Very good, señor. If you kill the Rurales and the Federales in Puxico for me, I will give you the guns you want."

Antelope Wells

Lydia and Ethel Marie had temporarily closed the hairdressing salon so they could use the building as a place to do their sewing. Meagan designed the uniform, modeling the cut of the uniform after the US Army uniform. The shirt was worn tucked into the trousers, and the trouser legs were tucked into the top of the boots. Because the textile fabric they used was of a dull brownish-yellow hue, the uniforms were about the color of the desert sand.

The collar tabs of the uniform were black, with the rank designated by small, vertical bars made from a gold fabric.

"Do you think this uniform will fit your brother?" Meagan asked Morley's sister.

"Yes," Lydia replied. "I think it would fit him nicely.

Do you want me to ask him to come here so that he may try on the uniform?"

"No, I will ask Duff to bring him here," Meagan replied.

Half an hour later the four women were waiting anxiously for Duff and Chris Morley to come to the salon.

"Is something wrong, sis?" Morley asked.

Lydia, Ethel Marie, Cynthia and Meagan were all standing side by side, doing so in such a way that they were blocking Morley's view of the table behind them.

"No," Lydia said, the smile on her face broadening. "Nothing is wrong. Why do you ask?"

"Cap'n MacCallister said you wanted to see me."

The four women stepped aside so that Morley could see the uniform lying on the table.

"Would you try it on, please?" Meagan asked.

"Yes, ma'am, I would be glad to," Morley said, picking up the uniform. A few minutes later he returned from the back room wearing the uniform.

"Well now, and if ye nae be a fine-looking soldier in khaki," Duff said, having arrived while Morley was changing.

"Khaki?" Morley asked.

"Aye, for that is the color of your uniform," Duff said. "'Tis often the color I wore when I was in Her Majesty's army. 'Tis a fine color indeed."

Morley put his finger on the black tab on his collar. "And these little stripes here would be because I'm a sergeant."

"Ye are nae a sergeant, lad, for a sergeant's stripes will go on the arm."

"Oh, I thought I was a . . . uh, well, never mind," Morley said in a somewhat dispirited voice.

"Those are captain's bars," Duff said. "For 'tis a captain ye be."

"What?" Morley literally shouted the word. "Are you telling me I'm an officer?"

"Aye lad, that's what I'm telling you. Now, I'll be for needing ye to find me a couple of lieutenants and a couple of sergeants. When the uniforms are all done, we'll have a fine army indeed."

By mutual agreement, Morley did not wear his uniform until one week later, by which time every uniform was completed. Darby and Drexler were the new lieutenants, Truax and Collins the new sergeants. When the Home Guard turned out in their new uniforms for the very first time, they did so before the entire town. The townspeople cheered when Captain Morley marched them to the south end of Cactus Street, then to the north end, and then back to "Fort MacCallister" as the men were calling the fortified area between Chip's Shoe Alley and Sikes Hardware.

Morley dismissed all his men except for a token force, cautioning them to be ready to respond should they hear the bugle call "To Arms."

"It has been two weeks since the last time Schofield made an appearance," Meagan said over dinner that evening. "I've heard some of the men talking, and they are convinced that we turned him back from his last attempt so decisively he won't try it again."

"He has to try it again," General Culpepper said.

"Why do you think that, Papa?" Lucy asked.

"Consider the situation, Daughter. Schofield has made it plain by the declaration he issued that it is his intention to rule all of the Bootheel. He has already taken every other town in the Bootheel, and just when victory seemed in his grasp, he happened upon Antelope Wells." General Culpepper smiled. "But he was totally unprepared for what he encountered here. He didn't expect Captain MacCallister to come to town and wield our citizens, clerks, liverymen, mechanics, and merchants to come together as an army that, thus far, has been invincible.

"Which means," Culpepper held up a finger, "he can't just give it all up and walk away now. Captain MacCallister's military acumen and our young men's bravery stands between this tyrant and his evil ambition. He will come again."

"The general is right. He will come again." Duff had a serious expression on his face as he studied the others around the table. Then he smiled broadly. "But when he comes, we'll be ready for him."

Chapter Twenty-seven

Puxico, Chihuahua, Mexico

Schofield made the decision that his incursion into northern Mexico, specifically the state of Chihuahua, would be less conspicuous if they did so without wearing uniforms. And so it was that he undertook his end of the bargain that he had made with Pedro Bustamante.

Seeing twenty men arriving at one time was a very rare experience for the citizens of Puxico. And to see that all twenty men were *norteamericanos* made the arrival even more peculiar.

"*Mira. Cabalgan como soldados,*" said one of the citizens of the town.

"*Sí*, they do ride as soldiers, but they do not wear uniforms."

"What do they want?"

Captain Bond was leading the men, and when they reached the Oficina de la Rurales, he stopped and had his men form into a semicircle facing the police office.

The local chief of police came out to stand in front of the office. Ten of his policemen came with him.

"Señor, why have you come to Puxico with so many men?" the chief asked. "And why do you threaten my office in such a challenging way?"

"A thousand pardons, *Señor Capitán de la policía*," Bond said, mixing English with Spanish. "But we are looking for the Rancho de Juan Mendoza. I want to buy horses and I have brought many men with me so that I may drive the horses back to my ranch in Los Estados Unidos."

"Ah, *sí, sí*," the chief of police responded, relieved that there didn't appear to be any immediate threat from the large number of Americans. The chief and several of the other police began to point in the direction of the horse ranch.

Bond gave the signal. "Now!" he shouted, and he, and all the men with him, began to fire.

The street echoed with gunfire as twenty guns blazed away. Other Rurales and Federales in town hurried down to protect their friends but they were too few and too late. Within moments every policeman in the town of Puxico, whether federal or local, lay dead or dying. A few of the citizens of the town were killed as well.

Bond regrouped his men and they rode out of town exactly as they had ridden in.

Not one citizen of the town made any effort to stop them.

Two days later Schofield met Bustamante at the border. Schofield had brought his entire legion with him and, unlike when they had raided Puxico, his men were all in uniform. He wanted to make an impression on Bustamante, knowing that seeing mounted and uniformed men would go a long way toward establishing the validity of his claim to have founded a new nation.

"You did well, señor," Bustamante said. "I have put many of my soldiers in Puxico and the citizens of the town are *muy agradecida* that we will protect them from *bandidos norteamericanos*. Here are the *piezas de artillería* that we bargained for."

Schofield smiled as he sat in the saddle and looked over his newly acquired artillery pieces, three Napoleons and three Parrott rifles. The guns, which were caisson mounted, had come complete with an ample supply of ball and powder in the case of the smooth-bore Napoleons, and conical shell and powder in the case of the rifled-barrel Parrott.

"Look at them, Julian," Schofield said to General Peterson. "How is it that instruments of death such as these can, at the same time, be so beautiful?"

"They are beautiful," General Peterson replied.

"You know what artillerymen say, don't you, Julian?"

"No, sir. What is it they say?"

"They say that artillery lends dignity to what would otherwise be but a common brawl."

General Peterson had heard that before, and he knew that was the quote Schofield was going to use, but he laughed as if hearing it for the first time.

"The guns are yours, señor," Bustamante said. "But each caisson requires a team of two horses, and that you must furnish yourself."

"Yes, I understand. I brought sufficient animals to move the guns back to my headquarters."

Schofield watched as the teams were switched out, then felt a sense of self-pride as his army started north, stretching for some length along the road, the column of riders interspersed with caissons of gleaming pieces of artillery, as well as the ammunition limbers which were attached to, and trailed behind each of the heavy guns.

"Now," Schofield said, "with artillery I can plan the infiltration and ultimate capture of Antelope Wells. And Mr. MacCallister and his Home Guard, or whatever MacCallister wants to call those men he has assembled to defend the city, will feel the brunt of a full-scale military operation. Antelope Wells will become known in history as the crowning event in my war to liberate the New Mexico Bootheel and found a new nation."

"A military ball?" Duff asked, replying to a comment made by Meagan during lunch.

"Yes, it was Lucy's idea actually. And Duff, you have to admit that the entire town has been under a lot of stress lately. The men have had to man the barricades and fight the battles, and the women have had to stay at home with their children, worrying about their men. A dance would go a long way toward alleviating all the stress." Meagan smiled. "And it would give you, Elmer, Wang, and all the others the opportunity to wear your uniforms for a reason other than to make war in them."

Duff laughed. "Are ye forgetting, lass, that neither Elmer, Wang, nor I have a uniform."

"Oh, but that's where you are wrong," Meagan said. "For the three of you have the grandest uniforms of all. You are a general, and Elmer and Wang are colonels."

"What? And would ye be for telling me, lass, how came we by such ranks?"

"General Culpepper suggested it to Mayor McGregor, and he made the appointments himself."

"And 'tis your idea that the men of the Home Guard will like such a thing as a military ball?"

"Duff, the ladies will like it," Meagan insisted. "Enough said?"

"Enough said," Duff agreed with a capitulating smile.

Three nights later, the ballroom of the Dunn Hotel was brightly lit and filled with music provided by a band made up of local performers. Out on the floor, men in their new uniforms weaved through the squares with their ladies dressed in butterfly-bright gowns.

Like the men in his command, Duff was also in uniform, but his uniform, as Meagan had indicated, was much grander than the khaki uniforms of the troops. Duff's uniform was similar in cut to that worn by General Culpepper, complete with tunic and shoulder epaulets. Duff's rank was indicated by a large wreathed star. The uniform was completed by a golden sash that angled down from one shoulder and circled his waist. The biggest difference was in the color of the uniform, for while General Culpepper's uniform was light gray, Duff's uniform was a much darker, charcoal gray.

The uniforms worn by Elmer and Wang differed only in the rank insignia they wore. In the case of each of them, three unwreathed stars denoted the rank of colonel.

"Choose your partners for the Virginny Reel!" the caller shouted.

"Duff?" Meagan said, holding out her arm with a smile.

Morley was with Ethel Marie, and McGregor was with Lucy.

Five hundred yards north of town Schofield had brought his guns up under cover of darkness. With the barrels gleaming dimly in the moonlight, all six of the artillery pieces were brought on line with their muzzles pointing toward the town.

"Load your weapons!" General Peterson called.

Bags of powder, then the rounds were loaded through the muzzles, cannonballs for the Napoleons, and conical shells to take advantage of the rifled barrels for the Parrotts. All six guns would be firing explosive shells designed to inflict the maximum casualties.

"Stand by," Peterson ordered.

All six gunners took their positions.

"Fire!" Peterson shouted.

There was a loud roll of thunder as the six guns roared. The Parrotts fired shells with point-detonating, impact fuses, but the Napoleons fired cannonball bombs, and the path of those missiles could be followed by the trail of sparks spewing from the fuses that had been lit by the propellant charge.

Shortly after the initial barrage, the men of Schofield's Legion were rewarded by the sight and sound of the deadly missiles exploding in the town.

* * *

To the revelers enjoying the dance in the Dunn Hotel, the explosions of the incoming rounds sounded like thunder from a very close lightning strike.

"What was that?" someone shouted, putting into words the question on the lips of nearly everyone present.

"Thunder?" another asked.

"It was nae thunder," Duff said. "'Tis nae telling how the blaggard came by them, but that was the sound o' cannons we heard. We are under an artillery attack."

The sentence was no sooner from Duff's mouth than Lester McGill, owner of McGill Feed and Seed company, came running in. "We're being bombarded by cannon fire!"

Immediately following McGill's report came the sound of more bursting bombs.

"Are there any cellars in town?" Duff asked McGregor.

"Aye, 'tis one in this building, another at the bank, and a root cellar behind Mr. Abernathy's house," McGregor replied.

"Captain Morley, take as many men as ye need and get all the citizens of the town into bombproofs!" Duff ordered.

"Yes, sir!" Morley replied.

"Sheriff Campbell, we can start with the people here now," McGregor said. "Would ye be for getting everyone in this room, and every hotel guest into the cellar?"

"Aye!" Campbell replied, the level of his voice raised in excitement and nervousness over what was happening. "Ladies 'n gents, to the cellar now, if ye please!"

Campbell's order was followed by the loud explosions

of still more bursting bombs, and that was followed by frightened screams.

Morley divided the men of the Home Guard into teams, then sent them out through the town to every house and building, looking for occupants to lead to shelter in the few cellars within the city.

As that was going on, Duff, Elmer, and Wang left the hotel ballroom and went out into the street. They heard a rushing noise, similar to the sound an unattached railroad car made when it was rolling down the track, then the thunderous roar of more exploding shells. Pieces of shrapnel whistled as it flew from the point of impact, sending deadly and invisible shards of metal through the night sky.

Three buildings were afire, they being the Stallcup Building, McCoy and Tanner, and Chip's Shoe Alley.

"We've got to get these fires put out," Elmer shouted. "On account of if we don't get 'em put out they're likely to set some o' the other buildin's afire."

"We'll nae get anyone to brave the cannon fire to get the job done," Duff said. "We'll have to do it our—" Duff stopped in midsentence. "Where's Wang?"

"I'll be damn!" Elmer said. "There he is, up on top of the Stallcup Building."

Duff looked in the direction Elmer had pointed and he saw Wang running across the roof of the burning Stallcup Building, carrying two buckets. Setting one of the buckets down, he poured water from the other onto the fire.

"Come on, Duff. We have to help him," Elmer said. "We can pass the buckets up to him."

"We can do better than that," Duff replied, starting toward the fire station garage.

A short while later, Duff and some of the volunteer firemen were rushing toward the burning building, pushing and pulling a pumper, complete with a large tank of water. Within moments the hose had been passed to Wang, who was standing on the roof waiting to have pressurized water available to use to extinguish the burning flames.

A few more bombs burst in the city.

The men who brought the pumper began laboring over the device and soon Wang was able to direct a very strong stream of water all the way across the roof to the flames on the far side.

"General Peterson!" Schofield shouted. "Secure the pieces and prepare to withdraw!" he ordered. "I don't wish to risk the cannon. I want to be out of here before dawn." He smiled. "I think we have left them our calling cards, and no doubt given MacCallister something to think about."

"Yes, sir!" Peterson agreed.

Over the next several minutes the barrels of the gun were swabbed, which cooled and cleaned them. Then the teams were attached and the caissons were drawn back to Cottonwood Springs. Behind them, several columns of smoke twisted up from the effects of the shelling of Antelope Wells.

"Well, what do you think, Prime Director?" Peterson said as they rode away. "With artillery, people will sit up and take notice of us now. We aren't some half-assed group of outlaws. We are an army with artillery, by damn!"

From the *Antelope Wells Standard:*

Terrible Cannonading
BY CLINT H. DENHAM

Last night a military ball was held by our town to honor and thank those brave men who have, thus far, so valiantly defended our city. They are not only an army worthy of feting; they are also an army that is now splendidly attired in uniforms designed by Miss Meagan Parker, a visitor to our city. Under Miss Parker's direction, the uniforms were cut and sewn by volunteer ladies from our own fair city, those ladies being Miss Lucy Culpepper, Miss Ethel Marie Joyce, Miss Lydia Morley, and Miss Cynthia Hughes.

Were the story to stop here, being only a report of the music, dance, festivities, and fellowship extended to our brave defenders, it would be complete and satisfying on its own. Unfortunately it doesn't stop here, for it was during this celebration that an abominable act occurred that defies all understanding of one who would consider himself possessed of human qualities. Last night during the very celebration mentioned, our town was subjected to a cruel attack by cannon fire.

This morning the blackened remains of four private homes and the charred walls of three badly damaged businesses give evidence, if such were needed, as to the unmitigated evil of Ebenezer Schofield and the perfidious men who follow him.

Using the cover of a night as black as his heart, Schofield began a systematic shelling of the innocent people of our town, to include women and children. Indeed one such child, Emma Lou Rittenhouse, was injured when she was hit by a piece of shrapnel from an exploding shell. Dr. Urban has assured the anxious parents that the little girl will recover without fear of a disfiguring scar, but it is only the result of a Benevolent and Divine Providence that this is so.

Duff MacCallister, recently appointed general in command of our group of intrepid Home Guard, has said that we will bring all our strength and effort to bear in order to defeat Schofield once and for all.

Chapter Twenty-eight

Cottonwood Springs

Schofield called Peterson in to show him a map he had drawn of the town of Antelope Wells. "This is my plan. I will put three guns here, to the west of the city, and three guns here, to the north. We now know where their fortifications are, and I believe that by a concentrated artillery barrage from the west, we can reduce those positions to rubble. In the meantime, the guns that we will establish here in the north will be used to fire at the businesses and homes."

"You mean to shoot at nonmilitary targets, Prime Director?" Peterson asked.

"Yes. I realize that on the surface it might seem gratuitously cruel, but consider this, General. We have already learned that the casualties from our last artillery attack were practically nonexistent because the citizens of the town were able to find bombproofs. I don't anticipate that the results of this bombardment will produce any greater casualties. But," Schofield added, holding up a finger to make a point, "what it will do is create fear and confusion. And once we have eliminated the fortifications, we will be able to take advantage of the disorientation, not only of the civilians, but of the Home Guard personnel who will be concerned about their families. And, that being the case, we will be able to launch an attack that will meet with little resistance.

"As a result of all that, I've no doubt but that the town of Antelope Wells will fall into our hands before nightfall."

"How are we going to administer the town, Prime Director? The other three towns fell so quickly and without organized resistance, that it was easy to establish our will over them. I don't know if we will be able to find someone so subservient in a town that has so effectively defended itself against us."

"Ah, but don't forget. We have a secret weapon in Antelope Wells. We have a partner, so to speak, in Angus Pugh."

"But wasn't the one who approached us with the flag of truce Angus Pugh?"

"I thought so at first, but I no longer believe that to be the case. If Mr. Carson had been Angus Pugh, I believe he would have identified himself as such, and offered a response to the password challenge. The fact that he did not do so, tells me that he was but a coward who made a foolish attempt to surrender the town when, clearly, he had no authority."

"We still don't actually know who Angus Pugh is, do we?" Peterson asked.

"There is no need for us to know who he is, at least not at this point. We do have an authenticator, don't forget. We have but to challenge anyone who may lay claim to being our asset, and if he provides the appropriate response, we will know that we have found our Angus Pugh."

"Yes, very good, sir. This will be an excellent way of utilizing Angus Pugh to our maximum advantage."

"And what think you of our plan of attack?" Schofield asked. "By that I mean in establishing two different bases from which to conduct our artillery barrage."

"I believe it to be positively brilliant, sir. And you are right, the town of Antelope Wells will fall into our hands tonight like an overripe plum so easily plucked from a tree."

"I leave it to you, General, to deploy the troops for battle."

In Antelope Wells, Duff and General Culpepper were walking along Cactus Street surveying the damage from the artillery attack and discussing what might be the correct tactical response.

"I don't know where or how Schofield came up with his artillery," General Culpepper said. "But I'm quite certain that the acquisition of those guns has given him a new sense of superiority."

"Aye, and the fact that he had nae compunctions about using cannon fire against innocent women and children tells me he will employ them in any way he thinks most advantageous to him," Duff said.

"I don't believe that he will use them in the same way again, though," Culpepper said. "The last time he used them he did nothing but fire indiscriminately into the town. He could have but one purpose for such an action, and that would be to instill fear in our citizens and intimidate our defenders. His next use of artillery will be more planned, and, I am sure, will be followed by an attack against our positions."

"By planned you mean?"

"Aimed at specific targets," Culpepper replied.

As they were strolling south, they met Mayor McGregor and Sheriff Campbell coming north.

"Thanks to the sheriff, 'tis happy I am to say that every citizen now has a safe place to go when the cannonading starts again," McGregor said.

"Aye," Campbell said. "We have located every place that can be used as a bombproof and assigned them to the people. When the first cannonball falls within the town, all know where to go to stay safe."

"'Tis a good thing to keep the people safe, but there is nae a way to protect the homes and businesses unless we can stop the cannonading," Duff said.

"I agree with you, but I've nae idea how we can do that," McGregor replied.

"Nor do I," Duff admitted. "But 'tis something I will be thinking about."

At headquarters, Schofield put Captain Bond in command of the field pieces that would flank the town from the west side. Unlike the three guns at the north, which were to be used to terrorize the town, Bond's guns were to be used against specific targets. The shells fired by the Parrott guns were smaller and had less of a bursting range than did the Napoleon cannonballs. The bigger rounds were good for the job of terrorizing, but because the Parrotts fired shells through rifled barrels, they were considerably more accurate than the smooth-bore Napoleons. It was for that reason that Bond had been given the three Parrott guns and the six men who made up the two-man crew for each of the three guns.

A low-lying ridgeline about five hundred yards west of Antelope Wells would be perfect for the operation. The guns could be put into position, elevated for the proper range and flight path of the shell, and fired, all without coming under observation.

"Prepare your guns," Bond said, having reached the ridge.

The three Parrott rifled guns were disconnected from the team that had drawn them, then moved into position. As the firing crews were readying their weapons, Bond crawled to the top of the ridge. Lying on his stomach, he observed the target through his binoculars.

He knew, from his previous armed attacks against the town, where the fortifications were, and located the one between Chip's Shoe Alley and Sikes Hardware.

"Line your guns up along my arm," he instructed the gun crews. Holding his arm at about a thirty-five-degree angle, he pointed toward the fortification he had just located.

"Load your weapons, then stand by and await my command to fire."

By arrangement with General Peterson, Captain Bond was to withhold fire until he heard the explosions of the first rounds the general would be firing into the town. But before Peterson could do that, he needed to know that Bond was in position.

Bond scooted back up to the top of the ridge, lined up the mirror with the sun, and began sending repeated flashes.

* * *

Wang saw the flashes of light and instantly realized that the flashes were not the result of some natural phenomenon. Shortly after he saw the flashes he heard something that sounded like a distant thunder. He had heard the same sound last night and knew what to expect next.

A few seconds after the distant boom, came the whooshing sound of cannonballs in the air. Looking up, he saw three black dots silhouetted against the bright blue sky. The dots grew larger as they came closer, and he saw that each of them was leaving a little trail of smoke.

One of the cannonballs landed short of the town. The other two came on into town and burst with loud explosions in the middle of Cactus Street. Shards of metal from the casing of the ball whistled out in a three-hundred-sixty-degree cone from the point of impact, though no one was injured and there was no damage done.

"Cannon fire!" someone shouted. "Everybody head for your bombproofs! Cannon fire!"

For the next few seconds the town was alive with the residents filling the boardwalks and crowding out into the street as they ran toward their designated shelters. Mothers held the hands of their children. A few mothers hurried along with babes in arms.

It wasn't just people dashing for shelter, as more than a dozen dogs were running as well, barking loudly, and keeping pace with their owners.

Wang heard three more distant thumps coming from somewhere west of town. The shells from those three guns arrived much more quickly after the sound of cannon fire than did the original three, and he knew those second guns were much closer. Based on the flashes of sunlight he had observed a moment earlier, he knew exactly where the guns were.

"I am going to go look for the guns that are there," Wang told Duff, pointing west.

"Aye, 'twould be a good idea for us to know about them," Duff agreed. He didn't tell his friend to be careful, because he knew that Wang would exercise as much caution as he could, while still accomplishing the task he had set out for himself.

The guns north of town fired a second barrage. One of the cannonballs hit just below the roof of the McCoy and Tanner building, but the guards on top of the building were not wounded. The other two balls fell into the street, and like the previous bursting bombs, injured no one.

The second barrage from the guns west of town was a little more effective. Two of the rounds fell into the open gap between Chip's Shoe Alley and Sikes Hardware, but the third actually hit on top of the fortification and knocked out a significant portion of the wall.

"I can't see the fortification from here, so I don't know if we are hitting it or not," Bond called down to the three gun crews. "But we're certainly dropping them in between the two correct buildings, so I think you should just continue to fire as before."

Bond wriggled back up to the top of the ridge so he could continue to observe the target.

Wang, who had not been noticed by Bond, had made a wide circle of the ridge and was coming up from behind the three gun crews where he saw the horses, ground tethered. Moving through the horses, he got a closer look at the men who were manning the field guns and was pleased to see that not a one of them was armed.

Behind the three guns sat the limbers, with their ammo chests open. Because the men were busy loading, aiming, firing, then swabbing the gun barrels, it was very easy for Wang to approach the first limber without being seen. Once there, he was able to hide behind the little ammunition wagon for a moment until the men, all of whom were wearing uniforms of Schofield's Legion, were distracted. When they weren't paying attention, he stepped quickly up to the first crew, killing both of them with chops on the back of their necks. Afterward, he moved again behind the limber.

"Hey, Miller, how come you haven't sponged the barrel yet? You want to set off the next charge before—" The loader for number two gun stopped in midsentence. "What happened to 'em? They're both down on the ground."

"What?" the gunner asked.

"Miller 'n Simpson. They're both lyin' on the ground."

"You think maybe they was shot from town?"

"I don't know."

The gunner and loader for gun number two hurried over to check on Miller and Simpson.

As they examined the two men, Wang took advantage of their lack of attention to step up to them. He was on them before either of them saw him.

"What the hell, who are—"

Two quick jabs to the ends of their noses sent bone shards into their brains, killing both of them instantly.

Suddenly there was a gunshot, and Wang felt the air pressure of a bullet passing very close to his ear.

"Hey, Cap'n, what are you shootin' at?" one of the remaining two men shouted.

"Get him!" Captain Bond shouted as he pointed. "Kill that Chinaman!"`

Bond shot again, and the men who had been manning gun number three hurried back to the limber that had been serving their cannon, where each of them grabbed a Winchester rifle.

The advantage in this confrontation had switched quickly from Wang to Captain Bond and the remaining two men of his detail. Having lost the advantage of surprise, Wang glanced around to determine the most expeditious way to escape the situation and quickly decided the best way would be to run straight for the horses, believing the Legion men wouldn't want to take a chance that they might shoot one of their own animals.

"Don't shoot until he's clear of the teams," Captain Bond called. "We'll chase him through to the other side."

Bond had caught up with his men, and they pushed their way through the herd. The animals were still agitated from Wang's passage but a moment earlier, and they wheezed, whickered, and stamped around.

"There he is!" Bond said when they emerged from the horses a few seconds later.

They saw Wang just standing there, making absolutely no effort to flee.

"Kill him!" Bond said. "He isn't even armed."

"No, he ain't armed," Elmer said. "But me 'n Duff is both armed."

As Elmer spoke, he and Duff stepped out from behind a knee that ran at right angles to the ridge. It wasn't a very large knee, but it was large enough to have successfully concealed the two of them as Bond and his men had chased after Wang.

"What the hell! Shoot 'em, shoot 'em!" Bond yelled and, forgetting all about Wang, the three men turned their weapons on their new targets.

The little valley rang with the roar of half a dozen or more gunshots. When the smoke cleared Bond and his two men were down, while Duff and Elmer, holding still-smoking guns, and Wang, who had not moved since being confronted by Bond, were still standing. Not one of the seven men who had brought the Parrott guns to Crowley's Ridge was still alive.

Chapter Twenty-nine

"What the hell, Drexler! Look at that! Damn if Schofield ain't bringin' them cannons in big as life. Three of 'em. Shoot 'em! Shoot 'em!" Truax shouted as he raised his rifle to his shoulder.

"No, wait!" Drexler called, holding his hand out to stop the shooter. "That's MacCallister!"

"Yeah," Truax said, lowering his own rifle. "'N Gleason 'n the Chinaman is both with 'im. What the hell do you think it is that they're a-doin'?"

Drexler laughed. "It looks to me like they're bringin' us some cannons. Three of 'em."

"Damn it if don't!" Truax laughed.

And not only Truax but all the others who were gathered there joined in the laughter.

When Duff, Elmer, and Wang arrived with the three Parrott rifles, they were greeted enthusiastically by as many as a dozen of the Home Guardsmen.

"How in the world did you come by them three guns?" Morley asked.

"They was sittin' out there 'n there warn't nobody a-usin' 'em, so we just took 'em," Elmer said.

"How is it that you shoot them things?" Truax asked.

"Are you serious?" Morley asked. "You don't even know how one of them is shot?"

"I ain't never been in the army before, 'n I ain't never seed none of 'em what was bein' shot at the time I was lookin' at it."

"Captain Morley," Duff asked, using Morley's newly appointed rank. "Would ye be for thinkin' that ye could show a few of the men how to use these guns?"

"Yes, sir, I can show 'em;" Morley replied. "We goin' to turn the tables on Schofield, 'n shoot back at him?"

Duff smiled. "Aye, 'tis my intention to do so."

"When are we going to attack, General?" Lieutenant Fillion asked.

Peterson held up his hand. "Our attack is supposed to be coordinated with the concentrated artillery fire upon their fortifications, but we've heard nothing from Captain Bond for a while."

"Maybe he is waiting to hear from us," Fillion suggested.

"We have sent him heliograph signals, but have gotten no response, and I hesitate to attack until our efforts can be well coordinated."

"I wonder why Captain Bond quit firing," Fillion asked.

"First Sergeant Cobb?" Peterson called.

"Yes sir?" Cobb replied.

"Take the fastest horse and ride around Crowley Ridge to where Captain Bond has established his base of operations. Tell him I am most displeased with his failure to carry out my orders. I wish to attack at the soonest opportunity, so he is to continue firing."

"Yes, sir," Cobb replied.

Selecting a fast horse, First Sergeant Cobb left the encampment to carry out General Peterson's orders. Cobb didn't like Bond, and he smiled as he contemplated being able to tell Bond that the general was displeased with him. He intended to make Bond well aware of how displeased Peterson was.

It took him no more than fifteen minutes to reach the area where Bond was supposed to be, but he didn't see any of the guns. He understood why they hadn't heard any firing, recently. It was obvious that the guns had been moved.

Sergeant Cobb's smile grew larger. He was well aware that any movement would have been made without the approval of General Peterson. That, Cobb knew, would make Peterson even angrier, and that would give Cobb more ammunition in expressing the general's displeasure.

"Bond, you're in for it now," Cobb said under his breath. "Yes, sir, when I get through with you, you'll . . ." He grew quiet in midsentence and stopped riding. Standing in his stirrups, he examined the ground before him. Seven lumps were lying on the ground, which he knew to be the seven men who had begun shelling the town. There was no need for a closer examination to determine that the seven men were dead.

But where were the three Parrott guns?

"How do you plan to use the artillery you just acquired?" General Culpepper asked.

The question was asked over lunch in the Bear

Tracks Restaurant. Mayor McGregor was there, as were Meagan and Lucy.

"'Tis my intention to move the guns to the north end of town and use them in defense of Schofield's next attack," Duff replied.

"Might I make a suggestion?" General Culpepper asked.

"Aye, I would welcome any suggestion ye might have."

Culpepper had a piece of paper and a pencil before him. "The five men you and Mr. Gleason killed in the Hidden Trail Saloon were Schofield's men," he said as he put down the number five. "Mr. Gleason killed a man who was discovered to have a map of our fortifications on his person." Culpepper added a one. "During their reconnoiter, they lost two men. During their first full-scale attack they lost six men. Only four were killed but two were captured, so the effective loss is six. Nine of Schofield's men that we know of were killed in their second attack, and it is quite possible that more were lost north of town that we know nothing about. You, Mr. Gleason, and Mr. Wang killed seven more when you captured the guns."

Culpepper added up his figures. "That is a total of thirty-six men who have been removed from Schofield's active roster, and even if we take the most inflated estimate of his strength, this means his effective fighting force has been cut in half." He smiled. "I believe the time has come to go on the attack."

Duff's return smile was even broader. "General, that is an excellent idea!"

* * *

The Home Guard had increased in size. Having accepted many of those he had previously eliminated, Duff had an army of forty men standing in front of the hardware store, gathered there to hear him share his plans.

"Gentlemen, we'll nae be waiting for Schofield to come to us anymore. From here on we'll be the attacking army."

"Hear! Hear!" Morley shouted in appreciation, and the others cheered their approval.

"Have any of ye experience with cannons such as these we have acquired?"

Darrel Wright, who had initially been turned away from serving in the Home Guard for being too old, raised his hand.

"Ye have experience with cannon such as these?" Duff asked.

"They ain't cannons," Wright said. "Cannons is smooth bore. These here is Parrott rifles, on account of they have rifled bores."

"'Tis thanking ye I am for the information," Duff said. "Tell me, Mr. Wright, would ye be for knowing how to operate such weapons?"

"I was a sergeant in General Henry Hunt's Artillery at Gettysburg," Wright said.

"I remember General Hunt," Culpepper said. "One of the most capable Yankee generals of the entire war, and one who employed his artillery brilliantly. If this gentleman was with Hunt, he will indeed be an asset to our little army."

"Mr. Wright, ye are now Lieutenant Wright, in

command of our artillery. Please find the men ye will need and train them to operate the guns."

"Yes, sir!" Wright said with a broad proud smile. He selected the men for the three guns, and began instructing them on how to load, aim, and fire the weapons.

Not counting Elmer and Wang, that left Duff with thirty-three men, and he organized them for the attack. They would advance on foot in three ranks of eleven.

Within the hour all was ready, and the three newly acquired guns of the Home Guard artillery fired their first barrage.

The question as to what had happened to the three missing guns was answered when the first rounds fell within the confines of the encampment Peterson had set up a mile north of Antelope Wells.

"They're shooting our own cannons at us!" one of Peterson's men shouted.

"Artillery, return fire!" Peterson ordered.

The Napoleons had already been loaded in preparation for the planned attack, so men responded immediately to Peterson's order. The roar of the three guns rolled out over the encampment.

"They're coming! They're coming!" The shouts came from a mounted legionnaire who came galloping up from the south. He had been sent out earlier with instructions to keep an eye on the town so Peterson would know what his men would be riding into when he launched the attack.

"They're coming! They're coming!" the rider repeated as he reached the encampment.

"Lambert, what are you shouting about?" Peterson asked.

Before Lambert could answer the question, three more rounds came crashing into Peterson's encampment, the bursting shells sending out whistling shards of jagged metal.

"Damn!" someone called. "That shell kilt Dolan!"

"Who is coming?" Peterson asked when he could be heard again.

"The men from town," Lambert replied. "They must be at least forty of 'em. 'N guess what? They got uniforms! I mean, it's a regular army that's comin' after us. This ain't nothin' like what we run into before. These people ain't just stayin' there a-waitin' for us. They're comin' after us!"

Peterson looked out over his troops. He had begun the operation with not quite thirty men, but Bond and the six men he had taken with him had been killed. Dolan was killed just a moment ago, and two of his men had been wounded. That left him with less than twenty effective men.

"How many did you say there were?" Peterson asked.

"A lot more 'n we got," Lambert answered.

"Are they mounted?"

"No, sir, they ain't."

Peterson nodded. "Good, that will give us time to withdraw before they get here."

"General, we ain't a-runnin' from 'em, are we?" First Sergeant Cobb asked in surprise.

"I did not say *run*, nor did I say *retreat*," Peterson said sharply. "I said we are going to *withdraw*. That, First Sergeant, is a tactical maneuver."

"Yes, sir."

"General, if we're goin' to skedaddle, then we got to get our teams hooked up to these caissons and limbers," the gunnery sergeant said.

"Are you charged and loaded now?" Peterson asked.

"Yes, sir, we are."

"Fire one more barrage, then make haste to withdraw."

The gunnery sergeant nodded, then turned to the three gun crews. "Fire!" he shouted, and once more the encampment area was filled with a deafening roar.

As Duff and his men advanced at a swift walk, they heard the boom of cannon fire and expected the balls to fall within their ranks. Instead, the cannonballs flew way over their heads.

"You got to wonder what it is that they are a-shootin' at," Elmer said. "'Cause it sure ain't us, seein' as them rounds passed so far over us that I wouldn't be surprised if they didn't land somewhere in Mexico."

"It looks as if they are shooting at the town," Duff said.

"What are they a-shootin' at the town for?" Elmer asked. "You'd think they'd be shootin' at us, seein' as we're the ones that's comin' after 'em."

"Maybe they don't know we're coming," Duff suggested.

Less than a minute after Duff's comment, Wang came toward them from the north. He'd been sent in advance of the column more than half an hour before and was returning at a rapid trot. "They are gone."

"You mean we ain't fixin' to attack the right place?" Elmer asked, confused by Wang's three word report.

"No, I mean they were there, but now they are not. They are gone."

"Are they changing positions to attack us from a different direction?" Duff asked, knowing that was exactly what he would do if he were in command.

Wang shook his head. "No, I saw them. They were riding their horses that way, very fast." He pointed to the north. "I think they do not want to fight."

Elmer laughed. "I don't think they want to fight, either. I think they are a bunch of cowards."

"Could you tell how many of them there were?" Duff asked.

"It was difficult to count because I was so far away from them," Wang said. "But I believe the number to be not more than twenty."

Duff smiled. "General Culpepper was right. We do outnumber then now."

Chapter Thirty

Duff, Mayor McGregor, Sheriff Campbell, and General Culpepper were having a strategy meeting in McGregor's office. George Gilmore and C. D. Matthews were there as well.

"Looks to me like we've won," Matthews said. "I don't think they'll be looking to attack us again." He chuckled. "I'd say that about now they know they've bitten off more than they can chew."

"You aren't saying we should disband the Home Guard, are you, C.D.?" Gilmore asked.

"No, no. Now that we've got them trained and ready, I think we should keep them. As well as the cannons that Mr. MacCallister and his friends brought us."

"'Tis not enough, I'm thinking," McGregor said.

"Mayor, what do you mean that it's not enough?" Gilmore asked. "I'm pretty sure that Schofield isn't going to make the mistake of attacking us again. When you think about it, we not only saved the town, we have struck him quite a severe blow. His ill-considered attacks turned out to be quite costly insofar as the number of casualties he suffered."

"But would ye be considering this, Mr. Gilmore? 'Tis nae way we can really be free until the entire Bootheel is free. We've friends and neighbors in other towns who are suffering under this despot's draconian rule," McGregor said.

"Mayor, they could have defended themselves when Schofield struck their town, just as we defended our town," Gilmore insisted. "I don't feel that it is up to us to do their job for them."

"But to be fair, Mr. Gilmore, when Schofield attacked the other towns they were caught by surprise. 'Twas what happened to them that gave us a warning of what could happen if we dinnae prepare for them," McGregor said.

"If we don't strike Schofield while we have him on the defense, he will just rebuild his army and attack us again," General Culpepper said. "We were able to beat him off because we had the element of surprise on our side. Now he knows that any attack against us would meet with stiff resistance, and he will plan accordingly."

"Aye," Duff agreed. "And there is another thing to be considered. As long as Schofield controls the rest of this area you call the Bootheel, you are cut off here. Consider that you are in the bottom of a sack. Schofield has but to close the mouth of the sack. We will nae be able to come in or out, we will nae be able to get more supplies, not only ammunition, but food as well."

"What you are saying is, he really will have us in a stranglehold," Matthews said.

"What you are calling a stranglehold, stopping all from leaving or entering, is a classic military maneuver known as a siege," General Culpepper said.

"You've convinced me, General," Gilmore said. "I say we should find Schofield and attack him before he is able to lick his wounds."

"Aye," Sheriff Campbell said, speaking for the first time. "But where is the brigand hiding?"

"We will know the answer to that by tomorrow," Duff said.

"How are we going to know by tomorrow?" Matthews asked.

Duff smiled. "Ye might say that we have a secret weapon."

"Why are you puttin' that mud on your face?" Truax asked, as he watched Wang prepare himself for a scouting mission that night. "I mean if you're tryin' to make your face darker, that mud ain't much darker 'n your face already is, you bein' a Chinaman 'n all."

"All skin has natural oils that will shine in the moonlight," Wang said as he continued to dab the mud on his cheeks. "This is not to make my skin darker. This is to keep the oil from shining."

"I'll be damned," Drexler said. "How is it that you know stuff like that?"

"He learned that, 'n a whole lot more in that fightin' school he went to," Elmer said.

"Fightin' school? What kind of fightin' school?" Truax asked.

"It was a temple," Wang replied, then without further response he started running and soon, disappeared into the night.

"Damn," Truax said. "He run off without a gun."

"He don't never use a gun, 'cause he don't never need one," Elmer said.

At that moment, unknown to Elmer or any of the others who had been present when Wang ran off into the darkness, Jake Hunter and Abe Libby were at the Clayton Livery.

"Them's our horses down there," Hunter said.

"Yeah, I told you he'd more 'n likely keep our'n separate from the others."

"Hey, who do you think that was that throwed the cell key in through the back winder like he done?" Hunter asked.

"I don't know," Libby said. "When I clumb up on the bed to try 'n get a look to see who it was, he was already gone."

Hunter laughed. "I'll bet that foreign-talkin' sheriff is goin' to be some surprised when he comes back 'n sees us gone."

"Yeah, well, we ain't a-goin' to be gone if we don't get them horses saddled 'n get out of here afore anyone sees us."

By alternating his running and walking, Wang reached the town of Cottonwood Springs shortly before midnight. Most of the houses and buildings were dark, but one of the buildings, a saloon, was brightly lit. Even from where he stood, Wang could see that it was quite busy. Moving down the alley, he reached the saloon, climbed up the back of the building, and let himself in through a dark window.

As he stepped inside he could hear the rhythmic breathing of a woman who lay sleeping alone in the bed. He had stepped into the bedroom of one of the working girls of the saloon, who, fortunately, was not entertaining a man in her bed at the moment.

Walking very quietly so as not to awaken her, Wang crept over to the door, then let himself out into the hall. He followed the hall until it reached a balcony that overlooked the main floor of the saloon. Stepping out onto the balcony, he kept in the shadows and moved all the way down to one side where he could remain hidden. Unseen, he could observe and listen to what was being said below.

Most, but not all of the customers were wearing the uniform of Schofield's Legion.

"If you ask me, we shoulda just kept on shootin' them cannon at the town while we had the chancet. Why, when we had all six of 'em, we coulda blowed up ever house 'n buildin' in town," one man was saying.

"Hell, Muley, what good would that a-done? If we'da blowed up the whole town 'n kilt ever'one in it, then the town wouldn't be worth nothin'.'"

"Yeah, 'n they wouldn'ta been able to run us away neither, would they?"

"Hey, look!" someone said. "There's Libby 'n Hunter!"

Looking toward the front door of the saloon, Wang saw the two men who had just come in. The last time he had seen them, they had been prisoners in the Antelope Wells jail.

"We thought you two was dead!" someone said.

"Yeah, how'd you get here?" First Sergeant Cobb asked. "I seen both of you get shot off your horses."

"Yeah, we was shot, but we wasn't bad hurt," Hunter said.

"Well, where've you been? How come you just now gettin' here?"

"We're just now a-gettin' here on account of after we was shot, we was took to jail," Libby said.

"Then if you was in jail, how'd you get out?"

"Did you know we got us a friend in Antelope Wells?" Libby asked.

"Yes, I heard we had someone in the town," Lieutenant Fillion said. "Nobody knows who it is, though, not even the Prime Director."

"Yeah, well the way we figure it, he's the one that let us out of jail," Libby said.

"You've met him then? Who is it?"

Libby shook his head. "We don't know. We didn't see 'im. He just throwed some keys in from the back alley is all he done."

"Don't forget the note," Hunter said.

"What note?" Fillion asked.

"The note that got throwed in with the keys," Libby said.

"What does the note say?" a new voice asked.

"Prime Director!" Libby said, glancing toward Schofield and General Peterson, both of whom had just come in.

"You were speaking of a note as I stepped in," Schofield said. "Who did it come from, and what did it say?"

"It's like I told the others, Prime Director," Libby said. "We didn't neither one of us see who it was that throwed the keys in to us, but whoever it was, also throwed in the note. 'N I don't know what it says, 'cause seein' as it's addressed to you, neither me nor Hunter read it."

"Hell, that don't mean nothin'," one of the others said. "Hunter can't read nohow."

The others laughed then grew quiet as Schofield read the note, doing so aloud.

"'MacCallister and the Home Guard he has assembled are making plans to free the Bootheel. To that end, they intend to attack you in Cottonwood Springs and destroy the legion.' It is signed, Angus Pugh." Schofield looked up with a grin on his face. "Mr. Pugh has just provided us with some very valuable intelligence. Gentlemen, they are planning on attacking us."

"Oh, damn! They done give us one whuppin'," one of the men said. "I ain't lookin' forward to them comin' here 'n givin' us another 'n."

Schofield shook his head. "Worry not about that. Forewarned is forearmed. The fact that we know they are coming has already taken away any advantage of surprise they might have. The surprise will be on our side. Come, gentlemen, we must prepare for our visitors."

It was just after dawn when Duff was awakened by a tap on his door. He reached for the pistol by his bed. "Yes?" he called.

"It is Wang," said the quiet voice from the other side.

Ten minutes later the two men were drinking coffee in the hotel dining room.

"The name is Pugh, Angus Pugh," Wang said.

"What? Who is Angus Pugh?"

"The man who lives among us but is a spy for the enemy is called Angus Pugh."

"How do you know this?"

"I heard them say the name."

Duff was quiet for a long moment before he spoke again. "So they know that we plan to attack them, do they?"

"Yes."

"All right. We'll just have to deal with it."

"I shall require paper and pencil," Wang said.

Duff went into the hotel lobby and got a sheet of paper and a pencil from the desk clerk. Returning to the hotel dining room, he gave the two items to Wang. Wang was working on the paper when McGregor and Campbell arrived a few minutes later.

"Good, 'tis an early breakfast ye have come to," McGregor said. "We've a bit of bad news."

"Our prisoners have escaped," Campbell said.

"Aye, this I know. 'Twas someone from the alley who tossed in the keys to provide the means for Hunter and Libby to escape," Duff replied.

"Och, then that explains why the keys were lying on the floor and the door to the cell was open when I went in this morning," Campbell said.

"Tell me, Captain, how is it that ye know of such a thing?" McGregor asked.

"Wang heard Schofield and his men talking about it last night."

"What? Wang heard Schofield talking?" Sheriff Campbell asked. "But how is this possible?"

"Wang was in a saloon in Cottonwood Springs. The person who freed the prisoners is the one among us who is the traitor. He freed the prisoners, and he sent a note telling Schofield that 'tis our intention to attack him today."

"Och, then that means he will be ready for ye. Best ye not attack, for I fear that with foreknowledge

Schofield will establish a position that is impregnable," Sheriff Campbell said.

"Nae so, my dear Sergeant Major. We have an advantage over Mr. Schofield now." Duff smiled and lifted a finger.

"Aye," McGregor agreed, joining in the smile. "The brigand doesn't know that we know that he knows."

"My goodness, that's a lot of *knows*," Meagan said as she and Elmer approached the table then.

"The more *knows* there are, the more knowledge there is," Duff said cryptically.

"What?"

Duff brought her up to date on the situation, including the fact that someone had helped Hunter and Libby escape the night before.

"Wang, what are you working on so hard?" Meagan asked, seeing the Chinaman concentrating so hard on the paper that he had failed to even notice her arrival.

"This is a map of Cottonwood Springs."

"Aye, 'tis a good idea," McGregor said. "For with the map, I think we can see where best to make the attack."

"Aye," Campbell added enthusiastically. "Let's draw up a plan for the attack now."

"I intend to do so," Duff said. "But the general has been so helpful that I would nae like to draw up plans without him."

"Captain MacCallister, 'tis wondering I am why ye lack the confidence to do something without confirming every move with the general. Remember 'twas I who invited ye here to help defend the town," McGregor said. "I would nae want ye to forget that the sergeant major and I are not without experience in matters military."

"Believe me, Leftenant Colonel, 'tis well aware I am of the martial acumen of both ye and the sergeant major. But I was thinking of General Culpepper's unique situation in that he knows Schofield and has fought against him before."

The expression of irritation that had so quickly discomposed McGregor's face just as quickly left to be replaced by an easy smile. "Aye, of course that would be the case. And I agree 'twould be wise for ye to make plans with the general."

During breakfast Chris Morley came in to the hotel dining room, then crossed over to the table where Duff and the others were sitting. Morley saluted, and Duff returned the salute.

"Captain, uh, I mean General, do you have any particular time when you want me to have Hawkins to blow *Assembly* on his bugle?"

"Are most of the men at home with their families now?"

"Yes, sir."

"Then let's give them at least another hour. With what is in front of them, the more time they can spend with their families, the better it will be."

"Yes, sir," Morley said, saluting once more before leaving.

McGregor and Campbell left soon after Morley departed, leaving Duff and the others to linger at the table for another cup of coffee.

Duff stared into his coffee for a long moment, as if steeling himself to ask a question of Meagan. Finally, he said, "Meagan, have ye ever heard the name Angus Pugh?"

She smiled. "Angus Pugh? Yes, of course I have."

"And would ye be for telling me lass, where 'tis that ye have heard the name?"

"Why, Duff, you know as well as I do where I heard the name. Angus Pugh is the villain in the book I'm reading now, *Pirates at Ebb Tide*." Having brought the book with her, she held it up to show him. "Here, I'll read a bit to you.

> The moon, waxing crescent, was little more than a silver sliver in the midnight sky, sometimes emerging, sometimes slipping behind high, fleecy clouds. The USS *Intrepid*, a fairly small, two-masted, gaff-rigged, square tops'l ketch, slipped through the night. The whisper of wind spilling from the sails and the quiet ripple of water along its sleek hull made the only sound.
>
> At the bow of the ship, Lucas McKenzie kept a sharp eye for hidden reefs. Six months earlier a French Naval Ship, Victoire Ailée had run aground on such a reef. Now that formidable vessel, which boasted twenty-three eighteen-pound guns and sixteen carronades capable of shooting thirty-two-pound cannonballs, was flying the black flag of the pirate Angus Pugh.

Meagan looked up from the book. "Angus Pugh, the pirate."

"Angus Pugh is the name of our traitor," Duff said.

"Why, Duff, you know that Angus Pugh isn't a real person. He is but a character in a book that Charles McGregor wrote."

"Aye," Duff said with a saturnine nod of his head. "I

well know who wrote the book, and where the name comes from."

"Prime Director?" Libby said, approaching Schofield at headquarters when nobody else was around.

"Yes, what is it?"

"This here Pugh feller, the one that throwed in keys and the note?"

"Yes, what about him?"

"They was actual two notes, the one you read before, 'n the one was in this envelope."

"Why are you just now giving it to me?"

"On account of what it says on the outside of the envelope," Libby replied, handing the missive over to Schofield.

Private message for Schofield only

Schofield took the envelope, then looked pointedly at Libby. For a moment Libby didn't understand why Schofield was staring at him so intently, then he realized that he was being told to go away.

"I'll, uh, leave you to read your letter," Libby said.

Schofield waited until Libby was gone, then he opened the envelope and took out the letter.

Schofield,

MacCallister plans an attack on your positions at Cottonwood Springs. It is my belief that he now has enough well-armed men to successfully dislodge you. Should you see that happening, I would suggest that you abandon the field of battle, leaving your men behind to cover your withdrawal. You can always recruit more men, but without you, the revolution will fail.

*Just north of the San Simon Ridge is an
abandoned cabin at the base of the Pyramid
Mountains. There is water nearby. I have stocked
the cabin with bacon, beans, flour, and coffee.
Should it be necessary for you to escape, I will meet
you there, and we will discuss our future options.
I will, of course, identify myself with the challenge
and password we have established.*

Angus Pugh

Chapter Thirty-one

"He will, in all likelihood, put his guns here." In the dining room of the hotel, General Culpepper pointed out a position on the map Wang had drawn. "This will give them a field of fire toward advancing troops, and, because the guns are set up in a densely populated area, it will be difficult to return fire without endangering innocent civilians."

"Aye," Duff said with a nod of his head. "He is just evil enough to do that very thing."

Culpepper examined the map a bit longer. "Here and here"—he pointed to two more places—"are natural choke points because the streets lead you here." Culpepper smiled. "He will be attempting to use our own tactics against us, because we will have an easy go of it until you reach here. Then he can quite easily establish an ambuscade that will prevent you from going any farther forward, or even from withdrawing, without being subjected to extremely heavy fire. And, as Schofield will have no particular concern as to what might happen to innocents who may be caught in the crossfire, I have no doubt but that he will employ his cannons here." He pointed again. "And since they are smooth bores, he will undoubtedly have some scrap metal cut up for the shot. At close range one gun can be devastating."

"Aye, I've seen cannon deployed in such a way before. Seems to me like the most important thing we can do is take care of the guns before we start our attack."

"Have you any idea as to how you might do that?" General Culpepper asked.

"Nae, but I'll be giving it some thought," Duff said.

Schofield and Peterson were eating apple pie that Frederica had baked for them when Fillion came into what had been Mayor Gilbert's house in Cottonwood Springs.

"Prime Director, General," Fillion said. "They're here"

"Where are they?" Schofield asked as he lifted a bite to his mouth.

"They are no more than five hundred yards south of town," Fillion said. "They're in easy range for the cannons, and they are making no effort whatever to advance any farther or to go to cover. I think we should take them under cannon fire."

"No," Schofield said. "That is exactly what they want us to do. If we use our guns on them, we'll not only give away their position, we would not be able to use our grapeshot loads, for they would lack the range we would need. It is best to wait."

"You mean we're just goin' to let them stay out there?"

"Yes, Lieutenant, we are just going to let them stay out there," Peterson said. "Can't you see what they are doing? They are trying to lure us out after them, or at the very least draw cannon fire from us. That would compromise our position. The Prime Director is right. We'll just wait them out."

"Of course I am right, General," Schofield said in a voice that showed his irritation. "And in the future, it will not be necessary for you to validate anything that I might say. The simple fact that it is I, saying it, is validation enough."

"Yes, Prime Director," Peterson replied.

"Captain Morley, you know what to do," Duff said from the steps of the Dunn Hotel.

"Yes, sir."

"You may begin."

"Bugler!" Morley called. "Begin the sequence of calls."

Hawkins blew "First Call," then "Reveille," "Assembly," then "Guard Mount," "First Sergeant's Call," then "Dismounted Drill," then "To Arms" and "Tattoo." Then he played them all over again. With every bugle call the assembled troops fell out, moved from one position to another, then reassembled in a new formation in a new location, doing so with shouts and hoorahs.

"What the hell are they doing?" First Sergeant Cobb asked from south of town.

"It looks like they are trying to coax us into attacking them," Fillion said. "They are wanting to draw us out."

"That is correct," Schofield agreed. "Pass the word for everyone to remain in position. We will not fall for their trick."

"Yes, sir, Prime Director," Fillion replied. Then he shouted to the others. "Hold your position, men! We are well defended here and will make them come to us. When they do attack, kill as many as you can."

With Schofield and his men occupied by the diversionary maneuvers being conducted by Morley and the rest of the Antelope Wells Home Guard, Duff, Elmer, and Wang circled the town unseen, then snuck in from the north, which was the opposite end from where Schofield and the legionnaires waited for what they were certain was an impending attack.

Schofield's three heavy guns were set up in the middle of the main street, purposely placed there so any artillery fire directed toward them would endanger the town itself. The gun crews stood by their guns, looking to the south end of town, awaiting the order to fire. Because of that, none of them noticed Duff, Elmer, and Wang as they approached.

A few of the citizens of the town did notice, however, and when Duff held his finger to his lips to ask that they remain quiet, they nodded in the affirmative. They watched silently as Duff, Elmer, and Wang stepped right up behind the six men.

"Would ye be for telling me, lads, what ye might be looking at?" Duff asked in a conversational tone of voice.

"What?" one of the men said. As he turned, Duff took him down with a smashing blow to the chin.

The other cannoneer took a right to the jaw.

As Duff was dealing with the two men at the gun nearest him, Elmer and Wang were taking care of the other four. Elmer used the butt of his pistol, Wang used the side of his hand. Within seconds all six men were on the ground.

"Have ye a jail in town?" Duff asked one of the onlookers.

"Yeah, damn right we got one. 'N some of our people's in there now that ought not to be."

"Let them out and put these men in," Duff ordered, removing the pistols from the unconscious cannoneers and passing them out to some of the citizens of the town.

"Yes, sir!" the man replied with a smile.

"We must work quickly, lads," Duff said as he pulled a narrow, barbed, steep spike from his pocket. Elmer and Wang had similar instruments and, within seconds the touch holes of the cannons, by which the powder was ignited, were sealed shut, rendering the cannons impossible to fire.

No more than fifteen minutes later Duff, Elmer, and Wang had rejoined the Home Guard.

"Captain Morley, the enemy guns are spiked," Duff said. "We can begin to move forward now."

"Yes, sir!" Morley replied. "We'll move forward by wings. Right wing advance one hundred yards, then go to ground and hold."

With a challenging roar that came deep from their throats, ten men from the extreme right side of the position got up and, covered by the gunfire of the other two thirds, rushed forward for one hundred yards, then fell into the prone position.

"Second element advance!" Morley called, and ten men from the middle started forward, their advance covered by fire from the other two elements. In less than one minute, the entire Home Guard had moved one hundred yards closer to the town.

* * *

"All right. This is what we have been waiting for. They are within range now!" Schofield shouted. "Bring up the artillery loaded with grape!"

"The cannons can't be used, Prime Director," Lieutenant Fillion said a moment later.

"What do you mean, they can't be used?" Schofield asked, spittle flying from his lips as he shouted the question in rage.

"The guns have been spiked."

"Spiked? Who the hell spiked them?"

"I don't know. The men we left behind to man the guns? They're gone."

"We have been betrayed!"

A bullet flew by Schofield's ear, passing by so closely that it made a loud pop. Looking back, he saw that the attacking Home Guards had moved still closer.

"General Peterson and Lieutenant Fillion, come with me," Schofield ordered.

Peterson left the line.

To First Sergeant Cobb, Schofield said, "General Peterson, Lieutenant Fillion, and I are going to have an officers' conference to decide how best to respond to this situation. You will be in command until I return. Do all you can to stop any farther advance until we come back with a plan of operation."

"Yes, sir," Cobb replied. "Uh, Prime Director, you better come up with something quick. I don't know how much longer we can hold 'em off."

"You let me worry about that, First Sergeant," Schofield said. "You are bordering on insubordination."

"Yes, sir. Sorry, sir," Cobb said contritely.

"Gentlemen," Schofield said to Peterson and Fillion. "Come with me. We had better hurry."

Schofield trotted back into town, away from the forward line of resistance, followed by Peterson and Fillion. Schofield led them into the livery barn.

"Colonel Fillion, saddle our three horses," Schofield ordered as they stepped into the barn.

"I beg your pardon, sir. Did you say *Colonel* Fillion?"

"I did. The battle here is lost, but the war for an independent nation isn't lost. I intend to build another army, and I will build it around my two most loyal officers, General Peterson and Colonel Fillion. In order to do so, we must abandon the field now, so we can start anew. Saddle the horses."

"Yes, sir!" Fillion said, enthusiastically.

"Prime Director, when you say abandon the field, you mean abandon the men?"

"I do mean that, General. Do you have an objection?"

Peterson smiled. "No, sir, I have no objections. I just hope they can hold them off long enough for us to make a clean getaway."

A moment later Fillion brought the three saddled horses over.

"Gentlemen," Schofield said as he swung into the saddle. "Let's ride!" He dug his spurs into the horse's flanks deeply enough to bring blood. The horse sprang forward at a gallop.

Peterson and Fillion, surprised by Schofield's sudden exit, moved quickly so as not to be left behind.

"What the hell?" one of the men in the defensive line shouted. "Cobb, look!" He pointed at the three galloping horses.

"What is this? What's going on here?" Cobb asked, shocked by the sight.

"I'll tell you what's goin' on. They're leavin' us here to fight 'n die for 'em."

"No, they ain't," Cobb said.

"What do you mean, they ain't? You see 'em runnin' away same as I do."

"I seen 'em run away, all right, but we ain't goin' to fight 'n die for 'em. Who's got a white shirt?"

"A white shirt? What do you want a white shirt for?"

"I want to use it as a white flag. We're surrenderin'."

"Duff, lookie there. They're wavin' a white flag," Elmer said.

"Aye, so 'twould appear," Duff said. "Captain Morley, come with me. We'll see what this is about. Elmer, if this be a trick . . ."

"You don't need to worry none about that, Duff. If it is a trick, there won't a damn one of 'em live to see the sun set tonight."

Duff and Morley started toward the town as two men in uniform came toward them. One of them was carrying the white flag, and the other had sergeant's stripes. They held no weapons.

"This here ain't no parley," said the one with sergeant's stripes. "I'm First Sergeant Cobb, 'n this here is a surrender. We're givin' up, all of us."

"Schofield sent a sergeant out to surrender?" Morley asked.

Cobb shook his head. "No, Schofield don't know nothin' about it."

"Excuse me, Sergeant, but if Schofield knows

nothing about it, how are we to accept this surrender as binding for your entire army?" Duff asked.

"On account of I'm in charge of the whole army," Cobb replied. "Schofield 'n the other two that was with 'im has run away 'n left us here."

Duff turned back toward Elmer and the troops of the Antelope Wells' Home Guard. "Elmer! Bring the lads up."

A minute later every man of the Home Guard had advanced and stood in a long rank, facing the defenders.

"Now, First Sergeant Cobb, if ye would please, tell your men to lay down their arms and advance toward us with their hands raised high into the air," Duff ordered."

Meekly, the remaining troops of what had once been the formidable army of Schofield's Legion put down their weapons and advanced as ordered.

From the *Antelope Wells Standard:*

VICTORY
BY CLINT H. DENHAM

Were we a nation at war, bells would toll across the nation. When the insurrection of the Southern States was put down, the great cities of the North rejoiced, and in time, so too did the errant sisters of the South take heart in once more being reunited as one nation. When the despot Napoleon was defeated and all Europe freed from his megalomaniacal ambition, the capitals of the Old World shouted hallelujah for their deliverance.

So too it is with Antelope Wells and the other municipalities of the Bootheel of New Mexico. Once again the citizens of Hachita, Le Tenja, and Cottonwood Springs may breathe the air of freedom. And though we of Antelope Wells never lost our freedom, we were faced with the fear of war and the attendant loss of life and destruction of property.

We were spared all of that by the bravery of our Home Guard, and the brilliant leadership of Duff MacCallister and our own General Lucien Bogardus Culpepper.

Let there be dancing in the streets! Schofield has been defeated, and the war has been won!

Chapter Thirty-two

Although the message from Angus Pugh had indicated that the cabin would be abandoned, it looked quite substantial, standing just at the base of Pyramid Mountain.

"Prime Director, that cabin doesn't look abandoned to me," Fillion said.

"It doesn't look that way to me, either," Peterson added. "You don't think it's a trick, do you? Luring us into an ambush?"

"I see no horses in the lean-to stable," Schofield said. "They could be hidden in one of these draws. Might I suggest that you stay back, while Lieutenant Fillion and I check it out?"

"*Colonel* Fillion," Fillion said.

"Colonel Fillion," Peterson corrected. "You go around the left side, taking a close look at everything you can see, and I'll do the same thing on the right side. We'll meet behind the cabin and approach it from the rear."

"Yes, sir."

Schofield dismounted and found a rock outcropping that was at just the right height for sitting.

He sat there and watched as Peterson and Fillion conducted their scout, moving carefully to either side of the cabin.

How had this happened? He was so close to establishing his personal fiefdom. Now he had been reduced to only two men, and they were scouting a cabin in the middle of nowhere. Had Angus Pugh set him up for an ambush? Who was Angus Pugh, anyway? And what did he mean when he'd said that *we* would discuss *our* future options?

Obviously he intended to cut himself in as a full partner.

"Mr. Pugh, whoever you are, I appreciate the help, and I will use you in whatever capacity I can," Schofield said aloud. "But disabuse yourself of any idea that you and I will ever be equal partners."

"Come ahead!" Peterson called from the front door of the cabin. "It's all clear!"

As invited by the *Antelope Wells Standard*, the town of Antelope Wells held a victory celebration that involved just about every citizen of the town. Tables set up along Cactus Street were filled with fried chicken, roast beef, pork chops, an assortment of vegetables, as well as pies and cakes. The children, happy to be outside without fear, darted in and out among the tables. There was laughter among the adults, too, as the tension had been lifted from their shoulders.

"I'll tell you the truth, Mayor," C. D. Matthews said. "When you said you were going to ask someone you had known back in Scotland to come down and give us a hand, I thought you had gone plumb loco. But Mr. MacCallister did a bang-up job. Why, he not only

protected Antelope Wells, he wound up freeing the
entire Bootheel. You know what you should do? You
should send a letter off to the governor asking him to
recognize MacCallister in some way. After all, you are
both writers, at least for the newspapers. Why I bet he
would listen to you."

"C.D. 'tis pleased I am to say that I have already
done that. And I know that 'tis a welcome relief for
him, for how can a governor not be concerned when
someone tries to carve off a big piece of the territory?"

"I wonder, though, if we may not be celebrating
too soon?" General Culpepper asked.

"Why do ye say that, General?" Sheriff Campbell
asked.

"I say that because the rapscallion who was the
cause of it all is still free to work his evil. Yes, we have
seventeen of his men spread out in jails from Hachita
to La Tenja, to Cottonwood Springs to here, but the
deranged man who started it all is still free."

Sheriff Campbell laughed. "I would nae worry
about Schofield, General. I think he has learned his
lesson when it came to dealing with us. If he still has it
in mind to be for building his own country, he'll nae
be trying it here, anymore."

"Perhaps you're right, Sergeant Major," Duff said.
"But the general is correct when he says that the evil
brigand is still out there, and even if he does nae try it
here again, he may well try it somewhere else."

"Aye, perhaps that is so," Campbell said. "But I
cannae help but feel glad that he'll nae be our problem again."

As the celebration continued, Morley and Ethel Marie
came up to see Duff. Both were wearing big smiles.

"General MacCallister?"

"Here, now, Mr. Morley. The war's over, and I am nae longer a general." Duff laughed. "And if truth be told, I never really considered myself to hold such a rank in the first place. Not like General Culpepper, who earned his rank by education and his leadership during war."

"Yes, sir, well, I figured you was a general, 'n so did all the boys. But the reason I'm comin' up to you like this is . . . well—" He stopped in midsentence and looked at Ethel Marie.

"Oh, for heaven's sake, Chris. If you won't ask him, I will. Mr. MacCallister, what Chris is trying to say is, we're going to get married tomorrow. And seeing as my father lives many miles from here, and I have no folks that live anywhere close by, I would consider it a huge favor if you would give away the bride in the ceremony."

"Aye, lass, I would consider that to be a high honor, and would be proud to be a surrogate for your father."

The public victory celebration continued through the rest of the day. A quieter one, attended by Duff, Meagan, Elmer, Wang, General Culpepper, Lucy, and Mayor McGregor, was held that night at Bear Tracks Restaurant.

"Leftenant Colonel, I would be asking ye a question." Duff had a noticeable change in his demeanor from what had been celebratory to one of some disquiet.

"Aye, Captain. Is there something that ye find concerning?" McGregor asked, having picked up the subtle change in his facial expression.

"Ye recall that Wang sneaked into Cottonwood

Springs and heard Schofield read a note that warned of our attack?"

"Aye, that I recall."

"I think ye should hear the note," Duff said. "Wang, would ye be for telling us what ye heard?"

Wang repeated the note, speaking the words in a monotone voice indicative of having memorized them. "MacCallister and the Home Guard he has assembled are making plans to free the Bootheel. To that end, they intend to attack you in Cottonwood Springs and destroy the legion. The note was signed Angus Pugh."

"Angus Pugh?" McGregor said. "Wait a minute. Are you certain that the person who wrote the note signed it as Angus Pugh?"

"Yes," Wang replied.

"But I don't understand. That is impossible. There is nae such person as Angus Pugh."

"Mayor, I have just finished reading *Pirates at Ebb Tide*," Meagan said. "It is a wonderful book."

"Then ye know that Angus Pugh is but a character in a novel. He is nae a real person."

"Aye," Duff said, answering for Meagan.

"Captain MacCallister! Surely, sir, ye were nae suspecting me of being the traitor?"

"I must confess, Leftenant Colonel, that upon hearing the name of the brigand who has betrayed us was Angus Pugh, and knowing that ye created the name in one of your books, I was given pause. But I also knew that ye were nae the treasonous one."

McGregor sat for a moment in silent contemplation before he responded. "How do ye know?"

"Because I know you, and I know ye are not the kind of person who would betray your principles."

"I thank ye for your confidence," McGregor said.

"But we are left with an obvious conclusion," Meagan said. "The traitor is someone who has stolen the name from your novel. Have you any idea how many have read your book?"

McGregor gave a self-deprecating chuckle. "Och, my dear, I wish I could say everyone in town read it. But I'm afraid—'twas very few who did."

"If we can find out who read it, then we'll find our traitor from among that group," Duff said.

"That should be fairly easy to do," Meagan suggested. "How would someone get the book?"

"They can buy the book at Fahlkoff's Book and Stationery Store. Of course, they can check it out from the library."

"Library? I was nae aware that the town had a library," Duff said.

"'Tis a small one, maintained by the school," McGregor replied.

"Well then, it will be easy to check with the library to see how many have taken the book."

"I know that at least five have been sold because I have autographed that many. Och, and they be friends all. I would nae like to think that our traitor would be one of them."

"I wonder, Charles, if I might make a suggestion," General Culpepper said.

"About finding the traitor?"

"No, not about that. For the moment the traitor is unimportant because Schofield is no longer an immediate threat. Forgive me for the abrupt change of subject."

"Believe me, General, I welcome a change of subject,

for talkin' of a traitor using a name from m' own novel is quite disconcerting. What would your suggestion be?"

"My suggestion has to do with preventing Schofield or anyone else from being able to mount another significant campaign against us. That is, if you are open to such a recommendation from me."

McGregor chuckled. "Duff MacCallister gives you much credit for helping to save our town, and so do I. What have ye in mind?"

"I think it would be a good idea if others would follow our example here, and organize Home Guard companies in every town in the Bootheel. Then you should contact your friend, the governor, and ask him to recognize the Home Guard companies as a regiment of the Territorial Militia, with Mr. Morley as its colonel."

"Sure now, General, 'n that is an excellent suggestion," McGregor said. "Why, if all in the Bootheel were so organized, that brigand Schofield would nae be able to repeat his devilment even if he did raise another army. Nae, nor would anyone else who might try and follow in his footsteps. But 'twould be better if you were to be the colonel."

"Why should the general take a demotion?" Duff asked. "Ye could have Morley as the regimental colonel, and ask Governor Ross to appoint General Culpepper to the rank of general in the militia. That way he could continue giving advice and help."

"Would ye be for accepting such an appointment, General?" McGregor asked.

"Yes, I would be honored to once again serve my country and my state—or in this situation, the territory in which I reside—in some official capacity."

"Then it shall be done," McGregor said. "We will form the Bootheel Regiment of the New Mexico Territorial Militia."

"And, Mayor, could I also make a suggestion as to a name for the regiment?" General Culpepper asked.

"Aye, would ye be for calling it the Culpepper Regiment? Such a suggestion would be welcome," McGregor replied.

"No, sir. What I would propose is that we call it the Bootheel Black Watch Regiment in honor of, and with respect for, the service you gentlemen rendered to that noble organization."

"Captain MacCallister, what say ye to this?" McGregor said.

"Leftenant Colonel, I can think of no higher accolade," Duff replied.

"Then why is ever'one jabberin' about it?" Elmer picked up his glass. "Ain't this somethin' we ought to be drinkin' to?"

"Aye, Elmer, 'tis a good suggestion," Duff said as he lifted his own glass. "To the Bootheel Black Watch Regiment."

"And to that noble band of warriors from which we have taken the name," General Culpepper added as the glasses were clinked together.

Chapter Thirty-three

The next morning the Antelope Wells Christian Tabernacle Church was filled with citizens of the town, all of whom were guests for the marriage of Chris Morley and Ethel Marie Joyce. The Reverend Ken Cooley would be officiating at the service. Morley had chosen Anton Drexler as his best man; Ethel Marie had chosen Lucy Culpepper as her maid of honor. The organist began playing the wedding march and everyone looked back toward the front door of the church to see the bride coming up the aisle, holding on to Duff's arm.

When Duff and Ethel Marie reached the front of the church, Cooley began the service.

"Dearly beloved, we are gathered together in the sight of God to witness and bless the joining together of Chris Morley and Ethel Marie Joyce in marriage. Chris and Ethel Marie come to give themselves to one another in this holy covenant.

"I ask you now, in the presence of God and these people, to declare your intention to enter into union with one another. Ethel Marie, will you have Chris to be your husband, to live together in holy marriage? Will you love him, comfort him, honor and keep him, in sickness and in heath, and forsaking all others, be faithful to him as long as you both shall live?"

Ethel Marie looked directly at Chris with a broad smile. "I will."

"Chris, will you have Ethel Marie to be your wife, to live together in holy marriage? Will you love her, comfort her, honor and keep her, in sickness and in health, and forsaking all others, be faithful to her as long as you both shall live?"

"I will," Chris said, returning Ethel Marie's smile.

"Who offers their blessing to this marriage?" Cooley asked.

"On behalf of her mother and father, I do," Duff said.

Sitting in the back row of the church, General Culpepper was observing the wedding ceremony and beaming at what a beautiful maid of honor his daughter Lucy was. He felt a twinge of regret that she had felt it necessary to give up so much of her life to look after him. Since she was close to thirty years old, he was beginning to fear that she would never marry . . . although he realized there was a possibility she could marry Charles McGregor. He knew that they had feelings for each other, and he decided that he was going to encourage those feelings.

Those thoughts were passing through his mind as the words of the marriage ceremony droned on.

"Psst, General!" The words were spoken in a loud whisper.

Curious, as well as a little irritated, General Culpepper

turned toward the door to see who might be calling out to him.

"General!"

It was Sheriff Campbell. For a moment General Culpepper considered waving him away, but the sheriff had a serious expression on his face as if there was a problem.

Was Schofield coming back? That certainly didn't seem probable. Still, the sheriff's summons did seen insistent.

"Please come with me," Campbell asked.

Quietly and as unobtrusively as possible, General Culpepper left the church. Not until he was outside with the door closed behind him did he ask about what problem was serious enough for him to be called away from the wedding that was in progress.

"What is it, Sheriff? What is wrong?"

"'Tis needing ye I am for a wee bit of a problem," Campbell said without being any more specific.

"Well now, I seen somethin' this mornin' that I didn't never think I'd be a-seein'," Elmer said.

The words were spoken at the wedding reception which was being held at the ballroom of the Dunn Hotel.

"What was that, Elmer?" Meagan asked.

"I seen Duff comin' up the aisle in a church, escortin' a woman whilst there was a weddin' goin' on."

Meagan nodded. "Yes, I can see how that might be a bit surprising to some people."

"Onliest thing is, it was the wrong weddin' 'n the wrong woman. Shoulda been you that he was a-bringin' up the aisle."

"Oh, my." Meagan laughed. "You don't see yourself as Cupid, do you?"

"Well, if you mean do I see myself as that little naked feller with wings 'n a bow 'n arrow, no ma'am, I don't see myself that way a'tall. I was just kinda pointin' out what things should actual be, is all."

"I think it would be best to just let things work out on their own, don't you, Elmer?" Meagan asked, rather pointedly.

"Yes, ma'am. I reckon I'll go get me a piece o' that cake now."

On his way to the refreshment table, Elmer saw Wang standing off by himself. Believing that his friend might be feeling a bit left out, he disdained the slice of cake and walked over to talk to him. "You had any of the cake yet, Wang? I know you can't eat it with chopsticks, but it's pretty good anyway," he said, trying to make a joke.

"I do not wish cake." Wang seemed to be carefully looking around the room, and though most of the time the Chinaman's facial expression was inscrutable, Elmer knew him well enough to perceive that his friend was concerned about something.

"You seem worried. What are you worried about?"

"I do not see General Culpepper nor his daughter," Wang said. "They should be here."

"You're right," Elmer said, as he also began to peruse the room. "You'd think they would both be here, wouldn't you? I mean, especially seein' as she was in the weddin' 'n all."

"I feel something bad has happened," Wang said.

"Well, I ain't goin' to say never mind. I've knowed you too long now, 'n it seems like anytime you ever get one o' them feelin's like that, why you're most always right. Tell you what, I'll go palaver some with Duff 'n McGregor. Could be they might know somethin' about it."

Elmer had taken no more than a few steps when he heard a loud, almost hysterical shout. Looking toward the sound, he saw that Lucy Culpepper had just stepped into the ballroom.

"My father is gone!" she shouted. There was a look of complete terror on her face. "I've looked everywhere, and I can't find him!"

Meagan and Ethel Marie rushed to offer the distraught young woman what comfort they could.

"Where's the sheriff?" someone asked. "The sheriff needs to look into this."

"General, if ye dinnae quit stallin', I'm goin' to be for shooting ye dead 'n that's a fact," Campbell said.

He and General Culpepper were both mounted and riding alongside the San Simon ridgeline, about three miles northwest of the town of Antelope Wells.

"You won't shoot me, Mr. Campbell," Culpepper said. "If you wanted me dead, you would have shot me long before now. No, sir, you need me alive for some reason, though I confess that I have no idea why you would need that."

"'Tis right ye be, General, I do need ye alive. But I have nae need to keep ye from bein' shot up a little. 'N if ye don't start movin' a wee faster, I'll start carvin' up on ye a bit."

"I never would have believed that you would be the traitor among us."

"I prefer to look at myself as more of an opportunist than a traitor."

"Why, Sheriff Campbell? Why did you betray all of us? And your friend Mayor McGregor. How could you betray him?"

"He was the easiest of all to betray," Campbell said. "'Come with me to America,' he said. 'In America everyone is equal.' So we came to America and here, as before, I am his lackey. He is still the leftenant colonel, and I am still the sergeant. Well, it will nae be that way anymore. When Schofield and I start our own country, I will be the landowner. I will be the upper class."

"Sheriff, I know Schofield. I have known him for a long time. He was a general and a confidant of the president of the United States. If you think he is going to share any of his power or position with a sergeant, you are going to be greatly disappointed."

"Och, but what power does he have now?" Campbell asked. "I will answer the question for ye. He has nae power now, and he will have nae power until I give it to him. And I will only do so if he agrees to share that power."

"And I am to be the way you give him that power?"

"Aye. We shall use ye for ransom. If McGregor wants to see ye alive again, he will turn over the city to us. We shall have control of Antelope Wells and every other wee village within the confines of the Bootheel with nae need of firing another shot."

"Sheriff, do you really think the citizens of Antelope Wells will allow McGregor to enter into such a bargain? They will not trade their freedom for my life. Nor would I expect McGregor to do so."

"Have ye been blind all this time, General? Do ye nae know how McGregor feels about your daughter?"

"I have long suspected that they had feelings for one another."

"Aye, but did ye nae know that I had those same feelings for the lass?"

"You?"

"Aye, me. But McGregor poisoned the girl toward me, reminding her that I came from, and always would be from, a lower class. He said to me that to keep peace between us, I was nae to have anything to do with Lucy. Well, this will show him."

"Are you insane, Campbell? Do you really believe you can win my daughter's love by taking her father prisoner?"

Campbell's laughter was low, and had about it, a touch of insanity.

"I have nae need for your daughter's love, General. I need only her obedience."

It took another two hours before they saw the cabin at the base of the mountain. Horses could be seen in the adjacent stable.

"We'll stop here," Campbell said.

"Wait a minute. I know this place," General Culpepper said. "This is Abe Goddard's place, isn't it?"

"Aye, 'twas his place before his wife died 'n he went back to Denver. He gave it to me to put up for a sheriff's auction. 'Tis a shame it only sold for fifty dollars. I kept ten dollars for the sheriff's fee."

"Fifty dollars? Why this place is worth ten times that amount of money," General Culpepper said.

"Aye, 'tis worth that. And if the auction had nae been held at midnight, perhaps someone other than I would have come," Campbell said with a little laugh. "Here, ride in front of me and hold this white flag up over your head." He took a white cloth from his saddlebag and handed it to Culpepper.

"And why would I want to be holding up a white flag?"

"So Schofield won't shoot you." Campbell chuckled. "And ye are for riding in front, so that Schofield will nae shoot me."

"Why would he shoot you? Aren't the two of you allies?"

"We've never met, and he doesn't know who I am," Campbell replied.

"Prime Director, there are two riders coming toward us," Fillion said from the window of the cabin. "Damn! I recognize one of them! It's the sheriff from Antelope Wells!"

"The sheriff? Are you sure?" Schofield asked.

"Yes, sir, I'm damn sure. How the hell did he find us so quick?"

Patterson picked up his rifle. "They're in easy range. Do you want me to shoot them?"

"They are carrying a white flag," Schofield replied.

"Yes, sir, but it might be because they are wanting to ask us to surrender," Fillion suggested. "I mean, why else would the sheriff be here?"

"Fillion, you step out front with me. Peterson, you stay inside and keep your long gun on them. If they have come to parley for our surrender, I will hold my arm out, and that will be your signal to kill them both."

"Yes, sir," Peterson replied.

Schofield and Fillion stepped out front, and Schofield waved the two men on in. He waited until they were close enough to talk to and within easy range of Peterson's rifle.

"That's far enough, Sheriff," Schofield called.

"Do ye know who I am?" Campbell asked.

"Yes, I know. You are the sheriff of Antelope Wells. What do you want?"

"Aye, 'tis the sheriff I am. But ye also know me as Angus Pugh."

"Angus Pugh?"

"Aye."

"I don't believe you. You're the sheriff. How do I know you haven't arrested Angus Pugh and you are using that name to get to me?"

"Would ye be for challenging me, Prime Director?" Campbell asked.

"You're damn right I'm challenging you."

"Nae. I mean for ye to challenge me with the password."

"Oh. All right. *Hill*," Schofield said.

Campbell smiled. "*Climber.*"

Schofield was silent for a moment, then he nodded. "All right. I'll take you for who you say you are. Who is—" He paused in midsentence. "I know you! You are Lucien Culpepper!"

"We meet again, Ebenezer," General Culpepper replied.

"What the hell is Culpepper doing here?"

"This man, Prime Director, is the key to our taking control of Antelope Wells," Campbell replied.

"Oh? And how is that?"

"Ye've nae idea how General Culpepper is loved by the people of the town. They will make any bargain to get him back safely."

Chapter Thirty-four

"Where is the sergeant major?" Duff asked, meaning the sheriff.

He, Elmer, and Wang were meeting with Mayor McGregor to decide what to do about finding General Culpepper.

"'Tis a mystery to me. 'Tis not like Campbell to be gone at a crisis time like this," McGregor said.

"Why don't we just get started lookin' for the general without worryin' none 'bout where the sheriff is?" Elmer asked.

"Aye, that is what we should do," Duff replied.

"Duff, now 'tis concerned I am about the sheriff as well. While ye and your friends look for the general, I'll try and find the sheriff."

"May I suggest that we meet in your office in one hour?" Duff proposed. "Unless we find the general sooner."

"Aye, 'tis a good idea," McGregor agreed.

They searched the entire town. Because General Culpepper was of advanced years, Duff feared the worst and was prepared to find the general collapsed somewhere, perhaps of failure of the heart or some other malady. But a thorough search turned up nothing.

"This ain't makin' no sense at all," Elmer complained. "We've got half the town lookin' for 'im, 'n seems to me if the general was still here, someone woulda found 'im by now."

"Aye, that is a reasonable assumption," Duff said.

"Don't you think we should be a-goin' to the mayor's office?" Elmer asked. "We said we was supposed to meet there in an hour."

"'Tis not quite an hour yet," Duff replied. "I want to go back to the hotel and check in with Meagan and Lucy."

By the time they returned to the Dunn Hotel the reception ballroom was nearly empty. Only the women of the town and a few of the older men remained.

Seeing Duff and the others come in, Morley hurried to them. "Did you find him?" asked anxiously.

"Nae," Duff replied, shaking his head. "'Tis a shame this has happened to break up the celebration."

Morley gave a dismissive wave of his hand. "No, now there ain't no need to be worryin' none about that. Me 'n Ethel Marie's goin' to be married for a long time, 'n this party's nice 'cause it was give by our friends, but the most important thing is findin' the general."

"And the sheriff," Elmer added.

"The sheriff is missing too?" Morley asked, surprised by the announcement.

"Aye."

"Maybe he's out lookin' for the general."

"Yeah, that's what we been thinkin' too, only we ain't run into 'im whilst we been a-lookin'," Elmer said.

"Colonel Morley, are Meagan and Lucy in there?" Duff asked, indicating the ballroom.

"No, sir, I seen 'em both go upstairs some while ago."

"Elmer, you and Wang stay down here in case we get some news. I'm going to go upstairs and talk with Miss Culpepper. I sure wish I could take her some good news."

"The news ain't all bad," Wang said. "We didn't find the general dead."

Duff nodded. "Aye, there is that." He hurried upstairs, then knocked lightly on Meagan's door. "Meagan?"

The door opened quickly. "Any news?" she asked hopefully.

"Nae. How is Miss Culpepper?"

"Very upset. Come on in." Meagan moved aside.

As Duff stepped into the room he saw Lucy lying on the bed. She wasn't crying at the moment, though it was obvious that she had been. He walked over to her, and she sat up.

"I heard you tell Meagan there was no news," she said as she dabbed at red-rimmed eyes with a handkerchief that was already wet with her tears.

"When is the last time you saw your father?"

"It was during the wedding. He sat in the back row." Despite her tears, she managed to smile. "He always sat in the back row in church. But, when the ceremony ended, I looked back there and he was gone. I didn't worry about it too much. I figured he had just left early. But I couldn't find him at home, and when I looked everywhere that I thought he might be, I didn't find him anywhere. That's when I went to the reception and . . . oh! I have ruined the most important day in Ethel Marie's life! I must apologize to her!"

"There is nae apology needed, lass. 'Tis well aware she is about your concern."

Duff spent a few more minutes with Lucy but she was unable to add anything else that might solve the mystery of her father's absence. Taking his leave of them, he, Elmer, and Wang walked to the mayor's office.

When they stepped into the office McGregor was sitting in his chair with a dispirited expression on his face. There was a piece of paper on his desk.

"Leftenant Colonel, what is it?" Duff asked anxiously. "Have you learned something?"

"Aye, I have learned something. Ye asked about Angus Pugh, and who would know to use it?" McGregor pointed to the piece of paper. "This is a letter from the brigand who used the name. 'Tis a shock and a mortification that it would be him, of all people. Him that I trusted and loved like a brother." He closed his eyes and pinched the bridge of his nose as Duff reached for the letter.

Charles—

Aye 'tis Charles I am saying, not Leftenant Colonel and not Mayor. All these years I have had to salute you, and kowtow to you because you outranked me. But now I have the upper hand, for I have taken General Culpepper as my prisoner and I am holding him in a place known only to me.

If you haven't figured it out by now, Charles, I am the elusive Angus Pugh that we have searched for, and 'tis thanking you I am for providing me with

*the name behind which I could hide. For some time
now I have been working with Ebenezer Schofield to
establish a new nation in which I shall have power
and prestige.*

*Schofield was defeated on the battlefield, but I have
come up with a way to snatch victory from defeat. It
is my intention to put the general's life to forfeit,
redeemable only by the total surrender of Antelope
Wells. It is I who have the upper hand now. You will
be contacted again when final plans are made for
the transfer.*

Duncan Campbell

"Never would I have expected such a thing from the sergeant major," Duff said, handing the letter over for Elmer to read. "I have always considered us to be friends."

"'Tis an evil thing to say, but 'twould have been better if you had let him die at Amoaful," McGregor said.

"Have ye any idea where this secret place may be?" Duff asked.

McGregor shook his head. "I have nae idea at all."

"I know where it is," Lucy said after reading the letter.

"What? Are ye sure? How is it that ye would know such a thing?" McGregor asked.

"I should have said I know *what* it is, rather than saying that I know where it is," Lucy corrected.

"Lucy, forgive me, lass, but that makes nae sense. What do ye mean that ye know what it is?"

"Sheriff Campbell has, uh, tried to pay court to me

on occasion, and once he attempted to make himself more appealing by telling me of his secret place."

"But he dinnae tell ye where this place might be?" Duff asked.

"No. He just said that he had bought it very cheaply and was trying to decide whether to keep it or sell it for profit."

McGregor shook his head. "I know of nae property that the sergeant major has bought. I fear he was just trying to impress ye."

"It should be fairly easy to find out whether or not Sheriff Campbell has purchased any property," Meagan said. "Aren't the deeds of purchase kept on file somewhere?"

"Aye but there hasn't been a transfer of property since—" McGregor stopped in midsentence and snapped his fingers. "Auction! There was a sheriff's auction a few months ago. Campbell said that nobody showed up for it. 'Tis thinking now, I am, that he maybe bought the property himself."

Fifteen minutes later McGregor held the document in his hand. "'Twas the Goddard place that was auctioned, and here is the filing of the deed." He showed it to Duff.

"Purchaser, Duncan Campbell," Duff read aloud.

"Do you know where this place is at?" Elmer asked.

"Indeed I do," McGregor replied. "I'll mobilize the Home Guard again."

Duff held out his hand. "Nae, if Campbell or Schofield sees an army coming toward them, I fear they will kill the general. Elmer, Wang, and I will take care of it."

* * *

It was easy to see how the Pyramid Mountain range got its name, for the tallest peak, easily visible, looked exactly like the pyramids of Egypt. Duff, Elmer, and Wang had left their horses almost half a mile back and come the rest of the way on foot until they were within one hundred yards of the little cabin. Due to the topography of the area, they were certain they had not been discovered.

From that distance they could see someone in front of the cabin, holding a rifle in the crook of his arm.

"The way they got that feller standin' out there like that means they ain't takin' no chances on nobody a-sneakin' up on 'em, are they?" Elmer asked.

Duff looked past Elmer. "Wang, can ye take care of him for us?"

Wang nodded, but didn't answer. He drew back into the arroyo behind them then crouched over and began to trot.

Duff and Elmer waited for nearly half an hour with no sign of Wang.

"Wang ain't goin' to be able to do it," Elmer said. "I bet he's done figured that out too, 'n has prob'ly give up on tryin'. Maybe we should wait 'til it gets dark then—"

"There he is," Duff said, interrupting Elmer.

"I'll be damned. Just how in hell did he get up there?"

Wang was on top of the cabin, and having just come over the peak of the pitched roof, was sliding down the front side of it while in the sitting position. When he reached the edge of the roof, he jumped down behind the armed guard and quickly dropped him to the ground.

"All right. He got the guard. Let's go," Elmer said.

Wang held out his arm with the palm of his hand facing toward Duff and Elmer as if signaling them to stay in place.

"Wait," Duff said.

"What's he plannin' on doin' with that?" Elmer asked. "I ain't never seen him use no gun before."

"I don't know, but he has something in mind."

With rifle in hand, Wang ran around one side of the cabin, then disappeared. A moment later, Duff and Elmer heard gunfire coming from behind the cabin.

"That's it! He's created a diversion!" Duff said. "Come on. Quickly!"

With pistols in hand, Duff and Elmer sprinted to the front of the cabin. Duff tried the doorknob and finding it unlocked, opened the door.

Three armed men were looking out the back, trying to determine the cause and location of the shooting.

"Fillion, you were outside," said one of the armed men. "What was that shooting?"

"I expect that was my friend, Wang," Duff said in a conversational voice.

"What?" Schofield shouted, spinning around. "Shoot them, shoot them!" he shouted, pulling the trigger even as he called out the order.

The cabin was filled with the deafening roar of gunfire. Smoke from the shots that were fired billowed out so thickly that for a couple of seconds it was difficult to see anything. When the smoke cleared, Schofield and Peterson lay unmoving on the floor. Sheriff Campbell, the third armed outlaw, was still upright and unhurt. He was standing behind Culpepper, holding his gun to the general's head.

"What happened to ye, Sergeant Major?" Duff asked. "I met many a sergeant major while I was in Her Majesty's service, and ye were the best I ever knew."

"'Tis thanking ye I am for the compliment, Captain MacCallister. But I wanted more, and now I'm about to get it."

"And why would ye be for saying that, Sergeant Major? All your friends are dead."

"That just means more for me," Campbell said. "And I can get new friends."

"I thought the leftenant colonel was your friend. I thought I was."

"Then 'twas wrong ye were thinking. Do ye play chess, Captain MacCallister?"

"And why would ye be asking me if I play chess?"

Campbell cocked the pistol that he was holding against General Culpepper's head. The sound of the hammer coming back sounded deadly in the small, single room of the cabin. "Because, Captain"—a grin that could almost be described as demonic spread across Campbell's face—"'twould seem that I have ye in check."

The British Enfield revolver that Duff carried was in his hand, and as his right arm was hanging loose by his side, the pistol was beside his leg, pointing down. Locking Campbell's gaze to his own, he slowly and unobtrusively rotated his hand so the muzzle was no longer pointing down, but was being aimed by kinesthesis.

"Checkmate," Duff said quietly.

"What?" Campbell asked, confused by the unexpected response.

Duff pulled the trigger, and the bullet transited

from its entry in the forehead, to its explosive exit from the top of Campbell's head, spewing blood and brain matter.

Eight months later

It had been five months since Duff and Meagan had returned from their three-month tour to Scotland when Duff stepped in through the front door of Meagan's Dress Emporium.

"'N would ye be for tellin' me, Mr. MacCallister what think ye of your tartan being made into my skirt and scarf?" Meagan asked in her perfect brogue mimicry. She held out the finished item fashioned from a plaid cloth of red, green, and blue.

"'Tis lovelier than the sky of Scotland," Duff replied.

Meagan held the material to her face and flashed a beautiful smile. "Oh, Duff, thank you for taking me to Scotland with you. It was such a wonderful trip, and Scotland is so beautiful, it's no wonder that you love it so."

"I love it, lass, because 'twas the place of my birth. But there's no place I love more, now, than right here."

"Oh, how glad I am to hear that." Meagan noticed then, that Duff was carrying a package. "What have you there?"

"I heard from Charles McGregor today," he said.

"Oh, has Lucy had her baby?"

"Not yet, but the newlyweds are both happy and healthy. Charles sent four books to me. This one is for you." He took the book from the package and handed it to Meagan.

She examined the cover.

WE WILL BE FREE

by
CHARLES MCGREGOR

"Oh, it's his new book!" Meagan said excitedly.

"Open the cover."

"He autographed it? Wonderful!"

"Yes, he did autograph it," Duff said.

Meagan opened the book and looked at the autograph on the frontispiece.

> *To Meagan Parker—*
> *A lady of courage, grace, and beauty*
> *And if I may be whimsical*
> *The good taste to enjoy books*
> *By Charles McGregor*

"Oh, how wonderful!" Meagan said.

"There's more."

"More?"

"Turn the page."

She did, then gasped.

> This book is gratefully dedicated to:
> DUFF MACCALLISTER, MEAGAN PARKER,
> ELMER GLEASON, and WANG CHOW,
> My Great Friends
> and
> *A sheòid* (my heroes)

TURN THE PAGE FOR AN EXCITING PREVIEW

Johnstone Country. Keeping the West wild.

*U.S. Marshal Will Tanner is one hell of a manhunter.
But this time, he's chasing six men across three states
with one gun and no backup. This isn't justice.
This is a suicide mission . . .*

DIG YOUR OWN GRAVE

It starts with a prison break in Missouri.
When notorious bank robber Ansel McCoy
busts out, he teams up with five other outlaws.
Then he and his gang rob a bank in Kansas.
When they cross state lines into Oklahoma Indian
Territory, U.S. Marshal Will Tanner steps in.
Other marshals from Kansas and Missouri have
already lost the trail, which means Tanner has to
go it alone. Deep in the wilderness. Outnumbered
and outgunned. One good man against
six blood-crazed killers. Even if he manages to
survive the elements and find McCoy's hideout,
it's not just the end of his search. It's his funeral . . .

DIG YOUR OWN GRAVE
A Will Tanner Western

by National Bestselling Authors
William W. Johnstone
and J. A. Johnstone

Chapter One

Looks like Tom Spotted Horse was right, he thought. He dismounted and dropped Buster's reins to the ground, then preceded on foot to get a better look at the camp by the water's edge. The Chickasaw policeman had told him Ike Skinner had passed through Tishomingo, headed toward Blue River. Will wasn't surprised. He figured Ike was on his way to Texas after a series of train station robberies south along the MKT. So when Dan Stone had sent him to arrest Ike, he had headed down the line to Atoka in hopes of cutting him off before he reached that town. Unfortunately, he was too late by half a day to intercept him in Atoka, but he had an idea that Ike might cut over to Tishomingo. He was sweet on a Chickasaw woman named Lyla Birdsong, who lived there, and that was where Will had arrested him before. Ike was never a man to use good judgment and it looked like the two years he had spent in prison did little to teach him any common sense.

Will had also been too late to catch him at Lyla Birdsong's father's cabin in Tishomingo, but he hadn't been hard to track from there. Ike had not waited long to camp for the night, which didn't surprise Will, since he hadn't seen Lyla in two years. *He should have waited at least until he crossed the Red and celebrated their reunion in Texas,* Will thought. He almost felt sorry for him. Ike was not a cruel criminal by any standard. He just wasn't smart enough to make a living from anything but stealing. *Better get my mind back on business,* Will reminded himself, and made his way carefully through the stand of oaks on the banks of the river. Close enough to see the two people seated by the fire clearly now, he took a moment to verify what he had suspected. The other person with Ike was, indeed, Lyla Birdsong. He had hesitated because Lyla had apparently grown some in the two years since Ike was away, not so much up, but out. Will had seen her before on only one brief occasion, and she was a husky woman then. Looking at her now, she looked to be more woman than Ike could handle. He could only assume that she had come with Ike willingly, so he wouldn't have to be charged with abduction on top of the armed robbery charges.

Will moved a few yards closer before suddenly stepping out from behind a tree and calling out a warning. "Don't make a move, Ike, and we'll make this as easy as possible!" As he expected, the warning was wasted as Ike, startled, tried to scramble to his feet. Ready for just such a possibility, Will had his Winchester in position to fire. He placed a shot that kicked up dirt at Ike's feet and stopped him from running. Then he quickly cranked another round into the chamber and placed a second shot in the dirt on the other side of Ike when he started to run in the opposite direction. "I ain't gonna waste any more ammunition in the dirt," Will threatened. "The next one's gonna stop you for good." The warning served its purpose. Ike hesitated a moment, but gave up on the idea of running for cover.

"Will Tanner," Ike moaned plaintively, "I shoulda known it would be you." He stood by the fire, feeling helpless as Will approached, his rifle cocked and still trained on him. "Dadgum it, how'd you find me so quick?"

"You're a creature of habit, Ike," Will replied. "You need to change your old ways, if you're plannin' to be an armed robber the rest of your life. Now, with your left hand, unbuckle that gun belt and let it drop." While Ike dutifully complied, Will kept an eye on the Chickasaw woman, who had so far shown no reaction to his intrusion. Sitting calmly, her stoic expression registering no sign of alarm, she prompted Will to be extra cautious, lest she might suddenly explode.

"Whaddaya botherin' me for, Tanner?" Ike implored. "I ain't done nothin' to get the law on my tail."

"You held up the train depot in McAlester and again in Atoka," Will answered. "Both stationmasters identified you as the bandit."

"How can they be sure it was me?" Ike blurted. "I was wearin' a bandanna on my face." A pregnant moment of silence followed immediately after he said it. "Uh . . ." he stumbled, an expression of utter frustration cramping his whiskered face. "I mean, he was most likely wearin' a mask, weren't he?"

"Yeah, he was wearin' a red bandanna, like the one you're wearin' around your neck," Will said. "Now, you've rode with me before, so you know I don't give you any trouble as long as you don't cause me any." He turned to the somber woman still sitting there, watching impassively. "How 'bout you, Miss Birdsong? There weren't any reports that Ike had anybody with him when he held up the railroad offices. I'm guessin' Ike just picked you up last night. Is that right?" She looked up to meet his gaze, but did not answer his question. "I'm gonna take that as a *yes*," Will said, "so you're free to go on back home." He watched her carefully while she considered what he had just said. "Ike's gonna be gone for a long spell," he added.

"I go," she spoke finally, and got to her feet. It would have been hard to miss the reluctance in her tone. Will could easily understand why. Lyla had an ugly scar on her nose that testified to having been marked with a knife for entertaining too many men. Almost certainly, she saw Ike Skinner as her only chance to escape her father's cabin, for no men of her tribe would have anything to do with her. No doubt her father would be disappointed to see her return home just as much as she would be.

When she started toward her horse, Ike pleaded, "Lyla, honey, don't leave me. I came to get you as soon as I got outta prison. We was gonna make it down in Texas."

"You not go to Texas," Lyla said. "You go to jail. I not go to jail with you. I go home."

"I reckon this just ain't your day, Ike," Will said. "She wouldn't have stayed with you for very long, anyway." He pointed to a small tree close by. "You know how this works." Ike knew it was useless to balk, so he walked over and put his arms around the tree. Will clamped his wrists together with his handcuffs, then went to help Lyla saddle her horse and get her things together. When she had packed up her few belongings and ridden away, he saddled Ike's horse, then went to retrieve Buster. In a short time, he rode up from the river, leading Ike and his packhorse behind him. Ike didn't have a packhorse. Will suspected that was Ike's packhorse that Lyla was now riding. The makeshift Indian saddle had led him to believe that to be the case. Her father might not have gotten rid of her, but at least he gained a horse.

Will figured three and a half to four days to make the trip to Fort Smith, barring any interruptions along the way, and he didn't expect much trouble from Ike. When he was working in this part of the Nations, and headed home, he usually camped overnight at Jim Little Eagle's cabin on Muddy Boggy Creek near Atoka. He decided there was enough daylight left to make it to Jim's before dark, and the horses were already rested. Jim, the Choctaw policeman, was a good friend of Will's, and his wife, Mary Light Walker, was always a gracious hostess. With that in mind, he started out with thoughts of maybe a couple of biscuits from Mary's oven for him and his prisoner.

They rode for only about thirty minutes before striking a trail that ran between Atoka and the Arbuckle Mountains, a trail that Will had ridden many times before. Following the familiar trail, they approached a low line of hills and a stream that ran through a shallow pass between them. Will usually paused there to let the horses drink, and that was his intention on this day. Sensing the water ahead, Buster quickened his pace in anticipation of a drink. Will leaned forward on the big buckskin's neck to give him a playful pat, instantly hearing the snap of a rifle slug passing directly over his back. It was followed almost at the same time by the report of the rifle that fired it.

Acting on instinct, he didn't wait to hear the next shot. Hugging Buster's neck, he shifted to the side as much as possible while giving the buckskin his heels. There was no time to worry about Ike following behind him. His reins were tied to a lead rope behind Will's saddle. His first thought was to find cover, so he drove Buster into the trees beside the stream as a second shot whined through the leaves of the trees. He pulled up only when he felt he had put enough trees between himself and the shooter, who he figured was on the other side of the stream.

That was mighty damn careless of me, he thought as he told Ike to dismount. He had a pretty good idea who the shooter was. "Hug that tree!" he ordered.

"You tryin' to get us both kilt?" Ike complained. "You can't leave me locked to a damn tree with somebody tryin' to shoot us!"

"Hurry up and get down off that horse," Will demanded. "I don't wanna have to shoot you outta that saddle." He waited just a moment to make sure Ike did as he ordered. "I don't think you've got much to worry about. I'm pretty sure I'm the target." Once he was satisfied that Ike was secured to a tall pine tree, he made his way back toward the bank of the stream, where he could scan the other side. There had been no more shots fired after the first two, so all he could do was try to guess where the sniper was hiding. As he shifted his eyes back and forth along the stream, he decided that the best place for the shooter to hide was a narrow ravine that led up the slope. He figured the sniper, having missed the kill shot, might be inclined to depart, so he decided to try to keep that from happening. "You just sit tight," he said to Ike when he came back into the trees and started trotting downstream.

"Where the hell are you goin'?" Ike blurted.

"Just sit tight," Will repeated without turning his head. "I'll be back to get you."

In a matter of seconds, he was lost from Ike's sight, and when he decided he was far enough downstream not to be seen, he crossed over the stream and climbed up the hill on the other side. With his Winchester in hand, he hurried along the top of the hill, back toward the ravine he had spotted. He paused briefly when he suddenly heard a wailing from the trees he had just left across the stream. "Lyla, honey!" Ike's mournful voice called out. "Is that you? Be careful, he's comin' to get you!"

"I shoulda stuffed a rag in his mouth," Will mumbled, and started running along the crest of the hill, thinking he'd have to hurry to catch her before she ran. Then he spotted Lyla's horse still tied behind the hill. More careful now, he slowed down as he approached the top of the ravine, expecting to meet her climbing up out of it. There was no sign of her, however, so with his rifle at the ready, he started making his way down the narrow ravine. He had not gone halfway down when he saw her. She had not run at all, but had remained sitting behind a low shoulder of the ravine, her old Spencer carbine still aimed at the trees across from her.

Taking pains to be as quiet as possible, he inched down the ravine until he was no more than thirty feet from the unsuspecting woman. "Make a move and you're dead," he suddenly announced, causing her to freeze for a few moments, afraid to turn around. "Lyla, forget about it," Will warned when she hesitated, as if trying to decide to act or not. "I'll cut you down before you have a chance to turn around. Now, drop that rifle and raise your hands in the air." She hesitated a few moments more, painfully reluctant to admit defeat, then she finally realized she had no chance and did as he instructed. "Doggone it, Lyla, I let you go before, because you hadn't committed any crime. Now you've gone and tried to shoot me, and all to free that worthless saddle tramp, Ike Skinner. So I'm gonna have to arrest you, and I reckon I oughta warn you, white, Indian, man, or woman, it doesn't matter to me. If you don't do like I tell you, or try to run away, I won't hesitate to shoot you. You understand?" She did not reply, as was her custom, so he asked her again, this time a little more forcefully.

"I understand," she said. "I no run."

"Good," he said. "Now we'll go get your horse. Start climbin' up outta this ravine." He followed her up, carrying her old Spencer as well as his Winchester. Once out of the ravine, they went down the back side of the hill and got her horse. She went along without protest, knowing she had been arrested for trying to kill a U.S. Deputy Marshal and would most likely go to jail for it. She had failed in her attempt to free Ike Skinner, but she had managed to complicate the deputy's job of transporting his prisoner. He didn't want to bother with Lyla, even if she did take a shot at him. *I'll decide what to do with her after I get to Atoka*, he told himself.

Upon approaching the spot where he had left Ike and the horses, Will stopped short and dropped the carbine to free both hands to fire his rifle. He was looking at the tree where he had handcuffed Ike, but Ike was gone. Then he noticed a few broken limbs and branches at the base of the tree. They prompted him to look up to discover Ike about fifteen feet up the trunk, clinging to a limb that was obviously too big to break off. Will was frankly amazed. Ike had climbed up the trunk like a telegraph lineman until reaching the limb that stopped him. As insane as it was, Will had to ask, "What the hell were you tryin' to do? Did you think you could climb right up over the top of the tree?"

Ike didn't answer at once. He had to rethink his failed attempt to escape. Still clinging to the limb fifteen feet up the trunk, he finally replied, "I weren't sure it would work, but I figured I'd give it a try."

Will shook his head and shrugged. "Well, shinny back down. I brought you some company, and I'm plannin' to ride awhile before we stop for the night, so hurry up." He figured he had enough time to make it to Jim Little Eagle's cabin before darkness really set in. He was sure he could count on Jim for some help with his prisoners. Since he had brought only one set of handcuffs with him, he had to tie Lyla's hands with his rope. So he busied himself with getting her in the saddle to the accompaniment of little yelps of pain behind him as Ike descended the rough trunk of the pine. Having arrested the simple man before, Will was inclined not to be surprised by any harebrained plan Ike came up with. Lyla, on the other hand, could not be taken lightly. She had already proven to be more dangerous.

The Chickasaw woman's attempt to shoot a lawman in order to free her lover was a notable boost to the slow-witted outlaw's confidence. "I knew you'd try to get me back, darlin'," he said when they were both in the saddle. "I'm sorry we wound up in this fix after you waited so long for me."

The stoic woman replied with nothing more than a grunt. It was Will's opinion that Lyla's decision to take a shot at him was not an act of devotion toward Ike.

It was more an attempt to avoid growing old in her father's cabin. In view of her past indiscretions and unfortunate physical appearance, she was desperate to go with any male who would have her. In spite of what she had done, he felt sorry for her.

The sun was already about to drop below the far hills west of Atoka when Will and his prisoners entered the clearing on Muddy Boggy Creek where Jim Little Eagle had built his cabin. Will called out and identified himself before approaching the cabin. A moment later, Jim, carrying a lantern and his rifle, walked out of the barn. "That you, Will? I wondered who was coming to call this late in the day. Who's that with you?"

Will rode on in and reined Buster to a halt beside the Choctaw policeman. "I've got a couple of prisoners I'm transportin' to jail. Sorry to be ridin' in on you so late, but if you don't mind, I'll camp here on the creek tonight."

Jim walked back, holding his lantern up to get a better look at the prisoners. When he got to Lyla, he held the lantern up a little longer. Walking back beside Will's horse, he commented, "One of them is a woman. One of our people?"

"Chickasaw," Will replied. "I was thinkin' about turnin' her over to you, her being an Indian. Figured it was more under your jurisdiction. I'll take Ike back to Fort Smith for trial."

"What did she do?" Jim asked, and took a second look at the sullen woman.

"Not much, really," Will said. "Took a shot at me and that's really the only reason I arrested her." He went on then to tell Jim the whole story.

Jim turned his gaze back on Ike then. "So this is the man that stuck a .44 in Sam Barnet's face and rode off with twenty-two dollars."

"That's the man," Will replied. "Twenty-two dollars, huh? Is that all he got?"

They both looked at Ike then, and Jim said, "Yeah, Sam just gave him the little bit in the cash drawer. He said the safe was sitting there with the door open and about twenty-five hundred dollars in it, but your man was in a hurry to run." Ike hung his head, embarrassed upon hearing of his folly. Back to the other issue, Jim said he could put Lyla in jail, since there was no one presently occupying the small building that passed for the Atoka jail. She would be held there until the council could meet to decide her sentence. "Are you charging her with attempted murder?" Jim asked Will.

Lowering his voice to keep Ike and Lyla from hearing, Will said, "I really don't wanna charge her with anything. I'd just like you to keep her till I can get away from here in the mornin' and not worry about her maybe taking another shot at me. Keep her a day, then turn her loose and tell her to go on home."

Jim nodded slowly. "I can do that." He smiled and said, "You're getting a little softhearted. Maybe you've been in this business too long." That reminded him of another subject. "Ed Pine was over here a week ago. He said you were going to get married. Any truth to that?"

"That's a fact," Will answered. "I finally got up the nerve to ask her and damned if she didn't say she would."

"Good for you," Jim said, beaming at Will's sudden blush. "Mary will want to know this. She said you'd never get married. You're gone all the time. Not many women like that." When Will shrugged, Jim went on, "Maybe you can hang up your guns and settle down on that ranch you own in Texas."

"Maybe. At least I'm thinkin' about it. I ain't even sure she'd like it there in Texas."

"When's the wedding?" Jim asked.

"To tell you the truth, I don't know. She and her mama are makin' a lotta fuss about planning a big weddin'. Her mama wants to have it around Christmas. I don't care, myself. I'd just as soon jump a broom and be done with it."

"Christmas?" Jim responded. "That's almost five months away."

"Yeah," Will acknowledged with a chuckle. "I think her mama's hopin' Sophie will change her mind before Christmas." He shrugged and said, "I'd best get my prisoners camped and comfortable. I'll bed 'em down in that same spot I used before."

"Who are you talking to out here?" The voice came from the cabin, followed a few seconds later by the appearance of Mary Light Walker. Seeing Will, she answered her own question. "I thought it must be you, Will, so I mixed up some more biscuits. I just put them in the oven. They oughta be ready by the time you set up your camp."

"Howdy, Mary," Will greeted her. "I apologize for showin' up so late in the evenin'. I didn't expect to bother you with fixin' any food for me and my prisoners."

"You never were a good liar, Will Tanner," Mary replied. "Go ahead and take care of your prisoners. Hurry up, or those biscuits will be cold." As her husband had done, she took a second look at Lyla, but made no comment.

"We can lock the woman up in the smokehouse," Jim volunteered. Will had hoped he would. It would not be the first time they had used the smokehouse this way, and it would make it a lot easier on Will. It was a great deal more trouble to take care of a female prisoner, and even greater trouble to have to tend to a male and female. As they had done before, a blanket and a pallet were placed in the smokehouse for Lyla's comfort, as well as a bucket for her convenience. After she was locked inside the smokehouse, Will made his camp by the creek, secured Ike to a tree, and took care of the horses. Even though Will insisted he would take care of feeding his prisoners, Mary fixed extra ham and biscuits for them. She was happy to do it because, during the time she and Jim had known Will, they had always been the recipients of his generous sharing of any spoils confiscated as a result of arrests and captures.

After everyone had finished supper, Will said good night to his friends and returned to his camp and his prisoner. "I'm damn glad you showed up again," Ike greeted him when he returned. "I gotta get rid of that coffee I drank, and I can't do nothin' with my hands locked around this tree." After that was taken care of, Will sat him down at the tree again, locked his hands, and tied his feet around the tree as well.

When Jim Little Eagle got up the next morning, Will had already gone. He checked on his prisoner in the smokehouse and decided the Chickasaw woman had passed the night peacefully, for she was fast asleep.

She was awake when he returned with Mary and her breakfast. "What will you do with me?" Lyla asked.

"Will said he wouldn't make any charges if you promise to go back home and behave yourself," Jim told her. She promptly agreed to do so, but Jim kept her in the smokehouse until afternoon before releasing her.

Chapter Two

As he had figured, it took three days to ride from Atoka to Fort Smith, and Will rode straight to the courthouse with his prisoner. Ron Horner, the night jailer, met him at the jail under the courthouse. "Whatcha got there, Will?" Ron greeted him.

"Got another guest for your hotel," Will answered. "This is Mr. Ike Skinner. He's stayed here before. I hope he ain't too late for supper."

"He's just in time," Ron said. "They're just gettin' ready to serve it. I'll go ahead and check him in. What's he in for?"

"Robbery," Will answered. "He won't cause you any trouble. He ain't mean, he just makes some bad decisions." He stood there until Ron led Ike inside and closed the door behind him. He shook his head and sighed. He couldn't help feeling a measure of compassion for the simple soul who was Ike Skinner. *He's probably better off locked up*, he thought. Then he rode down to Vern Tuttle's stable to leave the horses, and he left his saddle and packsaddle there as well.

After a short conversation with Vern, he took his rifle and saddlebags and headed back to the courthouse to see if he could catch his boss before he went home for supper.

"You're just the man I want to see right now," U.S. Marshal Daniel Stone declared when Will walked into his office. "When did you get in?"

"About a half hour ago," Will said. "I brought Ike Skinner in."

"Good," Stone said, then quickly changed the subject, obviously not interested in details of the arrest of Ike. "I might need to send you out again right away, but I won't be sure till I hear something more from the marshal's office in Missouri. How soon can you be ready to ride? I know you just got in and you'd probably like to catch a few days in town."

"Well, I'd like to rest my horse," Will said. "In the mornin', I reckon."

Stone couldn't help but laugh. "That long, huh? Tell you what, come back tomorrow morning and maybe I'll know if we're gonna be called on to help the Missouri office out."

There were a lot of thoughts running through Will's mind as he walked toward Bennett House, as Ruth liked to call her boardinghouse. Most of these thoughts circled around Ruth's daughter, Sophie, and the fact that he never seemed to be in town for any length of time. He had not been around for any of the wedding plans, a fact that made him just as happy, but it seemed to irritate Sophie more and more. He had always thought that planning a wedding was usually the bride's job, with little or no help from the groom. He figured he was like most men, preferring to just have a preacher tie the knot and be done with it.

Walking past the Morning Glory Saloon, he paused and looked at his watch. They would most likely be finished with supper at the boardinghouse by now and probably cleaning up the dishes. If he went home now, he was sure Sophie would insist that he should eat, and he didn't want to cause her the trouble of fixing anything. He hesitated a moment longer, then decided to get something in the Morning Glory.

"Well, howdy, Will," Gus Johnson greeted him from behind the bar. "I see you're back in town."

"You don't miss a trick, do ya, Gus?" Will japed. "You think Mammy might have anything left for supper?"

"She usually does when she knows it's you that's wantin' it," a voice declared over his shoulder.

Recognizing the husky tone of Lucy Tyler, Will turned to say hello. "How you doin', Lucy?"

"I've been better," the prostitute replied. "Ain't seen you in a while. You been outta town, or have you just given up associatin' with the common folk?"

"I've been outta town," he answered.

"Will's wantin' some supper," Gus said, and winked at Lucy. "I'll go see." He walked over to the kitchen door and stood just outside it. "Hey, Mammy, somebody's wantin' some supper. Is it too late to get a plate?" He turned back toward Will and Lucy, a wide grin plastered across his face, and waited for the expected response.

"Hell, yes, it's too damn late!" the scrawny little woman screamed back. "I'm already cleanin' up my kitchen." Gus remained by the door and waited, still grinning. After a long moment, another screech came from the kitchen. "Who is it wantin' to eat?"

"Will Tanner," Gus answered, trying to keep from chuckling. "I'll tell him it's too late." He walked back to the bar.

In a moment, Mammy appeared in the doorway and craned her skinny neck toward them to make sure it was Will. When she saw him, she stuck her lower lip out and blew a thin strand of gray hair from in front of her eyes. "I've still got some soup beans and a chunk of ham. There's a couple of biscuits to go with it. It'll keep you from starvin', I reckon."

"Yes, ma'am," Will said. "I surely would appreciate it."

When Mammy went back inside, Gus shook his head and marveled, "Ain't nobody else in this town Mammy would do that for. Beats all I've ever seen."

"Maybe that's the reason you don't ever wanna go upstairs with me," Lucy joked. "Maybe it ain't that little gal at the boardin'house who's got you buffaloed. Maybe all this time it was Mammy."

"Could be, at that," Will pretended to admit. "Most likely I remind her of her son, if she ever had one." He hesitated to continue with what he started to admit, but decided they would know sooner or later. "You might as well know, I'm supposed to get married around Christmastime."

They were both surprised, Lucy more so than Gus. "Well, I'll be damned . . ." she drew out. "That little gal at the boardin'house, right?" She didn't wait for Will to answer. "I knew that was bound to happen. Did you ask her, or was it her idea?"

"Of course I asked her," Will replied. "At least, I

think I did." When confronted with the question, he wasn't sure now.

Lucy continued to stare at him in shocked surprise, finding it hard to believe. She somehow never expected Will Tanner to get married. He seemed to have been bred a loner. Finally, she congratulated him and wished him a long and happy marriage. Then she returned to her teasing. "Christmas, huh? Well, I reckon me and Gus are gonna be invited to the wedding."

"Right now, I ain't sure *I'm* on the invitation list," Will said. The japing was cut short when Mammy came from the kitchen and placed a plate of food on one of the tables. Already sorry he had confessed to his impending trip to the altar, he quickly retreated to eat his supper. It failed to save him further embarrassment, however, for Lucy followed him to the table.

When she saw him place his saddlebags on a chair and prop his rifle against the wall before sitting down, it occurred to her that he was on his way home. It prompted her to ask to be sure. "Are you on your way home?" He nodded. "And you stopped here first?"

"I didn't wanna put her to any trouble," he explained.

"Well, she ain't likely to be very happy if she finds out you stopped at a saloon before you came home to her. I swear, Will, I'm tellin' you as a friend, you'd better eat that food quick and get your ass home. You gonna be in town for a while now?"

"I don't know for sure till I see my boss again in the mornin'," he answered, choking his food down as fast as he could chew it.

Gus laughed when he heard Will's answer, and Lucy

remarked, "Damn! You might be one helluva lawman, but you don't know the first thing about women."

"Well, it ain't like I've got a choice," Will said in his defense.

He paused at the gate in front of the rambling two-story house Ruth Bennett's late husband had built shortly before he died of consumption some twenty years ago. Two of Ruth's longtime borders were sitting on the porch, enjoying their usual after-supper smoke. "How do, Will?" Leonard Dickens greeted him. "Glad to see you got back all right again."

"You were gone for a good while," Ron Sample said. "You'd best hurry inside before the women clean up the kitchen."

"No hurry," Will replied. "I figured I was a little late, so I grabbed a bite at the Mornin' Glory on my way back."

"Just as well," Leonard said. "Margaret fixed her special chicken and dumplin's. I swear, that woman sure ruined a good chicken. She's a pretty good cook with most things, but she don't know a real dumplin' from a lump of clabber dough. My late wife made the best dumplin's I ever et."

Will opened the front door when Ron took his cue from Leonard and began a testimonial on his late grandmother's dumplings. Will found Sophie standing in the parlor, talking to her mother. "Will!" Sophie exclaimed, and moved quickly to greet him. He dropped his saddlebags and rifle when she stepped into his arms, ignoring his embarrassment when her mother witnessed her embrace. When she stepped back, she held him by his shoulders at arm's length as if to examine a wayward child. "No new wounds," she declared. "Thank goodness for that. You must be starving. I wish you could have gotten here when we had supper on the table, but I'll fix you something."

He took a moment to say hello to Ruth before telling Sophie it wasn't necessary. "I knew I was too late for supper, so I got somethin' at the Morning Glory on my way home."

"You stopped at a saloon before you came home?" Sophie responded. He realized then that it would have been best left unsaid. He should have listened to Lucy Tyler's comment. "Gone as long as you were, I would have thought you'd want to come to see me before anything else," Sophie started, then reconsidered. "But never mind, at least you're finally home. For a good while, I hope, because we've got a lot to discuss, a lot of planning for our wedding." She glanced at her mother, and Ruth nodded to confirm it.

That was not particularly good news to him, but he supposed he was going to have to get involved with the wedding plans, so he tried to put on a good face for his bride-to-be. "Let me take a few minutes to clean up a little bit, and we'll talk about it," he said.

"Well, I must say you look a little better," Sophie commented when Will walked into the kitchen to join her. "You were a little scruffy-looking when you came in the door. I wasn't sure that was you under all those whiskers and dirt."

He smiled and rubbed his clean-shaven chin thoughtfully before responding. "I reckon I did, at that, but a man doesn't get a chance to take a bath when he's transportin' a prisoner across Indian Territory."

He pulled a chair back and sat down at the table, prompting her to get up and go quickly to get a cup of coffee for him.

"If you had come straight home to supper, instead of stopping at that broken-down saloon, you could have had a piece of apple pie with this coffee," she chided, "but it's all gone now."

"I know," he interrupted, "but I told you I didn't want to cause you any extra work." He had already been scolded for his stop in the saloon before coming home—he didn't need more chiding.

She was about to continue, but Ron Sample came into the kitchen at that moment. "Excuse me for interruptin', Will, but Jimmy Bradley's out there on the porch lookin' for you—says it's important."

Surprised, Will asked, "Did he say what it's about?" Jimmy was Clyde Bradley's son. Clyde was the owner of the Morning Glory Saloon, and Jimmy liked to hang around the saloon doing odd jobs for Gus Johnson. Will had just seen Jimmy sweeping the floor behind the bar when he had stopped in earlier.

"No, he didn't," Ron answered, "just said it was important."

Will looked apologetically at Sophie, who returned the look with one of exasperation. He shrugged as if helpless. "I'll go see what he wants. I'll be right back." He pushed his chair back and followed Ron to the front porch. Sophie sighed and put his saucer on top of his cup to keep the coffee from cooling too fast.

"Jimmy," Will said when he found him waiting by the bottom porch step. "What is it, boy? You lookin' for me?"

"Yes, sir," Jimmy replied, speaking almost in a whisper.

"Gus sent me to get you. There's some trouble at the Morning Glory."

"What kinda trouble?" Will asked. Ron and Leonard Dickens, their conversation having stopped, leaned forward, straining to hear Jimmy's message.

"That feller, Maurice, he was there when you came by this evenin'." When this drew a blank expression from Will, Jimmy continued, "He was settin' at a table with Lucy when you came in."

"All right," Will replied. "What about him?"

"He's raisin' hell in the saloon, throwin' glasses at the wall and breakin' chairs and I don't know what all," Jimmy reported, his eyes getting wider by the moment. "He pulled his pistol and shot a hole in the front window."

"Gus sent you here?" Will asked. "Didn't he tell you to go to the sheriff's office?" He was somewhat puzzled. Gus would normally send for the sheriff and one of the sheriff's deputies would handle a roughneck drunk.

"He said to go get you," Jimmy maintained firmly. "Maurice dragged Lucy upstairs and said he was gonna kill her. He hit her, hard, busted her lip pretty bad, said he was gonna beat her to death. Now he's holed up in her room with her and says he'll shoot anybody who tries to come in."

Will didn't have to be told why Gus sent for him, then. This type of trouble in the city of Fort Smith was supposed to be handled by the Fort Smith sheriff's office. Sometimes, however, the sheriff, as well as his deputies, was satisfied to let the saloons take care of their altercations themselves. And this time, the life of Lucy Tyler was involved. Gus knew that Lucy was a friend of Will's and Will would come to her aid.

"Tell Gus I'm on my way," he said to Jimmy, and went back to the kitchen to tell Sophie.

Reading the look of concern on his face, Sophie asked at once, "What's wrong?"

"There's been some trouble I've gotta take care of," Will answered.

"Right now?" she asked. "Where?"

"In town," he answered. "I hope I won't be long, but it's important. I'll see you when I get back." With no desire to give her any details, he turned then and hurried out the door.

"Will?" she called after him, at first baffled by his behavior. Seconds later, exasperated by the infuriating habit he had of darting in and out of her life, she spat, "Your damn coffee! It's getting cold!" Resisting the urge to throw the cup against the wall, she stood there until she heard his footsteps as he bounded down the back stairs. She ran to the kitchen window in time to see him run past outside. Seriously concerned now, she hurried out to the front porch, where Ron Sample and Leonard Dickens were still sitting. "What was that all about? Where's he going?" she demanded.

"Gone to the Mornin' Glory," Leonard replied. "There's a feller up there gone crazy drunk, threatenin' to shoot the place up. They sent for Will."

"The saloon?" Sophie exclaimed. "He's going to the saloon to arrest a drunk? That's not Will's job! That's not the job of a U.S. Deputy Marshal."

"I expect that's right," Ron said, "but this is different. This feller has got Lucy Tyler locked up in the room with him, and he says he's gonna kill her."

Sophie was struck speechless. She knew who Lucy Tyler was, a common whore who preyed on the drunken drifters that frequented the Morning Glory Saloon.

Gradually at first, but steadily picking up speed, the anger deep inside her began forcing its way to the surface of her emotions until she could no longer contain it. "Damn him!" she cursed. "He just left that hellhole of a saloon and now he's running back to save a whore!" She looked around at the two men in the rocking chairs, staring at her, and realized she had lost her temper, so she spun on her heel and went back in the house.

Ron looked at Leonard, his eyebrows raised, and shrugged. "I don't think she took that too well," he remarked.

"Didn't seem to," Leonard agreed.

Will covered the short distance to the Morning Glory at a trot. In his haste to respond, his rifle was the only weapon he'd taken. As he trotted, he checked to make sure the magazine was fully loaded. He stopped before the two swinging doors that Clyde Bradley had installed at the beginning of summer and peered over them before stepping inside. The barroom was empty of customers, all having fled when the shooting started. Only Gus Johnson remained and he stood behind the bar, his shotgun on the bar by his hand. Will didn't see Lucy or her captor, so he pushed on through the doors. Gus turned when he heard Will come in and came at once to meet him. "I'm sorry as I can be to bother you, Will, but that crazy fool is gonna kill Lucy. I'da sent Jimmy to fetch the sheriff, but he mighta sent one of those two deputies workin' for him, or he might notta sent nobody. I knew you'd come when you heard it was Lucy."

"Where are they?" Will asked. "Up in Lucy's room?"

"Yeah, he's got her up there and the door locked," Gus replied.

"Which room is it?" Will asked.

"I forgot, you ain't ever been up to Lucy's room with her." Remembering then, he said, "That was what she was always complainin' to you about." He paused for a brief moment until he saw Will's look of impatience. "Top of the stairs, first room on the right," he blurted. When Will started toward the stairs, Gus caught his arm to stop him. "There's somethin' else, Will. He said he's gonna kill her, but he said after he done for her, he was gonna kill you." That was a surprise and Will had to ask why. "Lucy was settin' at the table with Maurice when you came in," Gus said. "When she saw you, she left him settin' there and went to say hello to you, so Maurice thinks he's got to kill you to make sure she don't run to you again."

"Why the hell didn't somebody explain it to him?" Will replied. "Lucy and I are just friends. Somebody coulda told him that."

"You ever try explainin' somethin' like that to a damn drunk?" Gus responded. "Especially when he thinks he's in love and you're standin' between him and his lady."

"I reckon you're right," Will said. "You don't think this fellow's just another loudmouth drunk with his whiskey doin' the talkin'?"

"I don't know for sure." Gus shook his head slowly as he thought about him. "He fetched Lucy a pretty stout fist in the mouth when she told him to go to hell. Then he pulls his handgun and starts shootin' the place up—ran all my customers out and shot a hole in the front window. I tell you, it's a wonder there ain't nobody got shot."

"And now he's locked himself up in Lucy's room," Will declared with a tired sigh. "I'll go upstairs and see if I can talk to him." He started up the steps, not certain what he could do to defuse the situation. If this Maurice fellow refused to open the door, he'd likely have to kick it in, and then he'd have to worry about what would happen to Lucy, once he did. Maurice might be the kind to take it out on Lucy, in the form of a bullet in the head.

When he reached the top of the stairs, he paused a moment to listen for any sounds coming from inside the room. All he could hear was a constant series of guttural mumbling, typical of a rambling drunk running his mouth. He decided that Maurice was in the bragging phase of his drunk, probably telling Lucy what a big man he was. This might be a good time to give him a chance to prove it to her, so he rapped sharply on the bedroom door. "All right, Maurice!" Will bellowed. "Let's see if you've got the guts to back up your big talk!" The rambling voice stopped and Will challenged again. "That's what I thought, all talk!" In a few seconds, he heard a piece of furniture crash when it hit the floor, and the shuffling of unsteady boots on the other side of the door.

Will heard the bolt slide open on the door and it opened to reveal the unsteady form of Maurice Cowart, a six-gun in hand. He stood there for a fraction of a second, snarling his drunken defiance, before Will planted his fist on the bridge of his nose. Maurice went down like a felled tree, his head slamming against the edge of the bedside table he had knocked over on his way to the door. He was out cold, stopped so suddenly that he had not had the time to pull the trigger in reaction to the blow from Will's fist.

Will kicked the pistol that dropped from Maurice's hand across the floor before looking at Lucy, huddled in the corner of the room. Her mouth and nose were swollen and her clothes were torn from her captor's abusive attempts to conquer her. She didn't get up at once, just gazed at him until slowly, huge tears welled in her eyes. After a moment, she spoke when he walked over and extended his hand to help her up. "I'm glad he didn't get to see me cry," she said, defiantly. Then she looked up at Will. "I thought he was gonna kill me." She put her arms around him and gave him a tight squeeze, like a mother hugs her child. "Thanks, Will, thanks for coming."

He didn't know what to say, so he held her by the shoulders while he took a look at her damaged face. "We might better get Doc Peters to take a look at those bruises," he said. "First, I reckon I'd better take care of ol' Maurice, here, before he takes a notion to wake up."

"I don't know," Lucy said, already beginning to regain some of her confidence. "He went down pretty hard, and he cracked his head on my good side table. I was hopin' he was gonna talk himself to sleep before you came, 'cause he drank almost all of a quart of whiskey."

"I'll haul him outta here," Will said. He grabbed Maurice's boots and dragged him out the door into the hallway. "I swear, he weighs a ton." He dragged him to the top of the stairs and then down several steps before he managed to take his arms and, using the angle of the steps, pulled the limp body over to settle on his shoulder. Gus ran up the steps to help him turn around and steady him as he carried his burden downstairs. "I reckon that's his horse at the rail," Will said. "It was the only one there when I came in."

"Stop just a second," Gus said. "Lemme look in his pockets to see if he's got any money to pay for some of the damage he did."

"Well, hurry up," Will said. "He ain't gettin' any lighter.

He carried the unconscious man outside, and with Gus's help, plopped him across his saddle, just as Deputy Johnny Sikes walked up. Sikes watched silently until the body was resting on the horse. "Will," he said, and nodded. "A feller came in the office and said he thought there was some trouble down here."

"There was," Gus answered. "There ain't now."

"His name's Maurice Cowart," Will said, and told Sikes what had happened, what Maurice had done to Lucy, and the damage he had done to the saloon. "So I reckon you might wanna put him in your jail for a while till he sobers up. Then you might wanna warn him not to come near the Mornin' Glory or Lucy Tyler again."

"I expect so," Johnny replied. "I'll take care of him, and much obliged."

Gus stood with Will for a few moments, watching Johnny untie Maurice's reins from the rail and lead the horse back up the street toward the jail. Then they went back inside to help Lucy. "I'll walk you down to Doc Peters's to let him take a look at you," Will offered when he saw Mammy cleaning the blood from Lucy's face.

"No need for that," Lucy said. "Mammy's took care of me before. This ain't the first time I've been punched by a loudmouth drunk, besides, Doc Peters has already gone home by now."

"Suit yourself," Will said. "You're in pretty good hands with Mammy, especially if she's half as good a doctor as she is a cook," he added, primarily to please Mammy. The only acknowledgment he received from the scrawny little woman was a snort of indifference. "I reckon I'll say good evenin', then." He nodded to Gus, then looked at Lucy again when she called his name.

"Thank you again, Will," she said. "When you come back, I'll owe you a drink, or supper. And anything else you might want," she added wistfully.

"'Preciate it, Lucy, but you don't owe me anything. I'm just glad I could help a friend."

He found Sophie waiting for him in the parlor when he returned and he knew without asking that he was in trouble. The frown she greeted him with seemed to be permanently etched on her face. "Trouble at the Mornin' Glory," he offered weakly. "I don't know why Gus didn't call the sheriff instead of me." She said nothing, but continued to stare at him with eyes as cold as ice. "Fellow named Maurice," he continued bravely, "shot a hole in the window and mighta killed somebody, if he wasn't stopped. Had to put him in jail—got back as soon as I could."

When he paused, finished with his explanation, she continued to stare icily at him for a long moment before asking, "Is Lucy Tyler all right?"

"What? Oh . . . yeah, she's all right, got roughed up a little, but she's all right." He had hoped Lucy's name wouldn't come up, but evidently Ron or Leonard had told Sophie what they had overheard on the porch. He would have preferred that she not know that he had been summoned primarily because Lucy was in danger, but now that he was facing her cold accusation, he decided it was time to stop acting like he was guilty of something. "Look, Sophie, Lucy Tyler's a friend of mine, that's all. I ain't one of her customers, I never have been. I've also got other friends that are on the wrong side of the law." Oscar Moon came to mind. "But they ain't got nothin' to do with you and me, and I sure as hell ain't had nothin' to do with any woman but you. The sooner you accept that, the sooner you'll keep thoughts like that outta your pretty head."

She continued to look him hard in the eye, until she had to smile. It was the first time he had shown any side of himself other than an innocent confusion in her presence. "All right," she said, "I accept it." She took his hand then and led him to the sofa. "I just hope you're going to be home for a while this time."

"I hope so, too," he said. "I reckon I'll find out when I report in to Dan in the mornin'." She raised an eyebrow at the remark, but gave him a big smile. The rest of his evening was spent listening to the plans she had for their wedding. When they finally said good night, he was finding it hard to believe it was going to happen to him. He could only imagine the look on Miss Jean Hightower's face when she heard the news. Will could imagine it would seem to her like her son was taking a wife. As for Shorty and the boys at the J-Bar-J in Texas, they wouldn't believe it until he showed up with Sophie on a lead rope.